# POWER
# SHIFT

# POWER SHIFT

## REGGIE RIVERS

SCA Publishing, Ltd.
10 Inverness Drive East, Suite 210
Englewood, Colorado 80112

# Reggie Rivers

To order additional copies of Power Shift, call SCA Publishing, Ltd. at 303-790-2020. Please have the ISBN listed below handy when you call.

Library of Congress Cataloging-in-Publication Data

Rivers, Reggie
  Power shift / by Reggie Rivers.
    p. c.m.
  ISBN 0-9704542-0-1 (alk. paper)
  1. Football players–Fiction. 2. Journalists–Fiction. I Title.
  PS3568.I833 P69 2000
  813'.54–dc21

                    00-11241

PUBLISHER'S NOTE
This is a work of fiction. Names, characters, places, and incidents either are the product of the author's imagination or are used fictitiously, and any resemblance to actual persons, living or dead, business establishments, events, or locales is entirely coincidental.

Printed in Canada
1 3 5 4 2

## ACKNOWLEDGEMENTS

I owe thanks to many people for helping me complete this book. My brother Mike, for his feedback and encouragement. Dan Caplis for his legal advice. Ric Nepomuceno for shooting the cover photo, designing the cover and laying out the book. Ray Crockett for the use of his body and his Ferrari on the cover. Aileen Martinez for her editing help and plot suggestions. David Spilver for helping me develop the story. Sharon and Steve Cooper for supporting me through the process. Cindy Koder for believing in me, and to my other family and friends for your love. Anything that I've done well in this book is a credit to the guidance my family and friends have given me. Any mistakes I've made are mine alone.

# ONE

"THERE'S A SEMANTIC DIFFERENCE between jail and prison, but from the inside of a cell they look remarkably similar," Richard said.

He had that far-away look again as though he was in a library, brandishing a pipe. In Martin's estimation, Richard Mobley was a wealthy, arrogant guy who looked down his narrow nose at his neighbors, but he was wearing county blues like the rest of them. "Other inmates, inveterate recidivists with misguided pride, brag of their stints in tougher institutions. 'Dis ain't prison,' they say in the vernacular of the uneducated, 'dis here daycare.'"

"What do you say?" Martin wondered. He was on the floor in the tiny room studying the pattern of cracks in the concrete ceiling.

Richard sighed, "About what?"

"You think this is daycare?"

Richard shrugged. "I have no real basis for comparison. I've never been to prison."

"But you might go up this time, huh? Third time's the charm and all." Martin figured, doctor or not, a guy racking up three DWIs in a year can't be too smart. "You ever operate on people when you were drunk?"

"I'm not a medical doctor. I'm a scientist." Haughty now. Offended.

"Oh." That was good news.

Mobley was 52 years old and well on his way to a full head of gray hair. He used to teach biology at Trinity University, but that job went the same way as his wife and kids after the drinking got worse and the DWI's racked up. "From what I understand, never having experienced it myself, mind you, the difference between jail and prison is dimensional. Not physical dimension—though prisons certainly have more sophisticated security systems than this facility—but in emotional currency. Jail lacks real substance. Prison, on the other hand, has tremendous depth. Cells crowded with regret. Faces stained by fear. Anger boiling in deep psychic wells.

Violence roiling beneath the surface. Assault, rape, murder. Prison harbors inmates with make-shift weapons and poor social skills."

"There are no soft sounds in prison," Richard continued. "Tough shoes waging continuous battle against the concrete floor. Hard voices barking orders, yelling good-natured obscenities, laughing raucously. Metal clanging against metal. Groans of fatigue. Screams of impatience."

Martin looked off, bored. The cell was precisely 12'3½" x 9'2¼". His mattress was sour; a rancid blend of sweat, mucus and fear. He'd been there nearly a month; Richard had joined him two weeks ago. The doctor had been hauled in after a cop watched him stumble out of a bar and get behind the wheel. Mobley was pulled over and arrested before he drove a hundred yards.

"Why didn't you call a cab?" Martin said when he first heard the story.

"Why should I waste money on a taxi when I own a vehicle?" Richard shot back.

"Yeah, but you already had two DWIs and you knew a third one would land you in prison. You could do the math on that couldn't you?"

Richard shook his head: "Martin, you don't understand the complex issues at play here. I am the victim of unjust prosecution. Arresting me for driving a vehicle while under the influence of a drug—in this case alcohol—is a clear violation of my constitutional rights. They're prosecuting me not for a crime that I *have* committed, but for a crime that I *might* commit. There is no need for a law of this sort. If, by getting behind the wheel after having a few drinks, I truly have impaired my performance, then they merely need wait for me to make a moving violation to arrest me. If my inebriated condition causes me to drive faster than the posted limit, then arrest me for speeding. If I'm weaving, then arrest me for driving erratically. If I crash into something, then arrest me for failure to control my vehicle. But as long as I'm obeying all of the traffic laws, how can they arrest me simply for being intoxicated? They've adopted an unreasonable position, and I plan to appeal this all the way to the Supreme Court if necessary. Seriously Martin, what's next? Are we going to prosecute people who have too much caffeine in their systems? What about women who drive at that time of the month when their hormones are raging? What about people who are behind the wheel drowsy because they have a full stomach from lunch or dinner? How far do we take this ridiculous notion? The government should punish my actions, not my diet. Our police forces engaged in unreasonable search and seizure, violating my Fifth Amendment right to privacy by requiring me to give them a sample of my breath and my blood. Mark my words, Martin. I will prevail in this battle. This will be a landmark decision."

Martin shook his head. *It had been me, I'd have taken a cab.*

The floor was suffused with striped sunlight. Not the entire floor; just a small square in the center of the room. Martin liked to lie there, his head a neat fit into that small block of warmth, hands crossed neatly on his chest, legs extended to the toilet. In those quiet moments, he watched birds soar in the distance, twisting and turning in the breeze. Thin shadows marked Martin's face in evenly spaced intervals; even his view was incarcerated.

Martin's trial was scheduled to begin the following day. The good news was the prosecutor wasn't seeking the death penalty; the bad news was the charge: Felony murder. It was a mandatory life sentence with no possibility of parole; a seamless blanket of incarceration until the day he died. No hopes. No dreams. Nothing but walls and bars and angry men.

"The toughest aspect of jail or prison is the absolute dearth of decisions," Richard said. The man would not stop talking. "All the little things that so many of us take for granted on the outside. Deciding what time to get up in the morning, what to wear, what to eat for breakfast, what route to take to work, where to eat lunch, what to eat for lunch and with whom. What route to take home from work, how much television to watch, what time to go to bed. Life is full of decisions, few of them truly meaningful until they're taken away. But once you're imprisoned you lose everything. You follow the regiment of the county or the state. Just shut down your mind and follow orders."

Martin was learning to cope with the regimentation of incarceration. During his month behind bars he'd learned that Richard was right. Don't resist. Don't think creatively. Don't hope that things will get better. Don't dream of making decisions. Just mindlessly follow directions. Jail is an exercise in continually lowered expectations.

The judge denied bail, which was a shock considering Martin's fame. Everyone figured he'd be released on his own recognizance, but the prosecutor fought against bail arguing that the charge was felony murder, and that flight was less of a concern than suicide. Severe depression set in after Martin's arrest. He didn't eat for nearly a week. Sleeping all day, lying awake all night, seriously thinking about ending his life. The prosecutor believed in the death penalty, but not if it was self-imposed.

After that hearing, Martin spent 10 days in a mental institution talking with a psychiatrist who eventually said Martin was fit for transfer to jail. Martin's attorney argued quite cogently that the psychiatrist's release demonstrated that his client was ready for bail. The prosecutor disagreed. Even if Martin wasn't a threat to himself, the prosecutor believed the charge against him was too serious to warrant bail. Martin's mother screamed in anguish when the judge denied bail the second time. Martin sat quietly. No movement. No reaction. The newspapers described his demeanor as stoic, which was inaccurate: He just had low expectations.

While Richard droned on about the subtle disparities between jail and prison, Martin watched the news on a small television. They kept replaying the video from the day of his arrest; he was walking with his head down, hands cuffed behind his back, eyes wet with shame. As the video rolled, a reporter talked about the bodies the police discovered in his garage. Two bodies. Still warm. Martin was there when the police arrived. Leaning against his Suburban, arms crossed defensively. They asked him questions, easy ones at first, progressively harder as time passed, but he didn't respond. His mind was cloudy and his tongue was thick. He couldn't speak.

On the television screen, an officer pushed Martin's head down helping him into a police car. It was Martin's first visit to the back door of San Antonio's police headquarters. He'd been through the front door once as the keynote speaker for a Police Activity League fund raiser.

Richard said a few days ago: "Martin, the charges against you are very serious, and there will be a certain segment of the population that will believe you committed the murders no matter what the jury says. Are you concerned at all that you will become more infamous than you are famous?"

Martin shrugged. "What's the difference?"

"Oh my, Martin!" Richard exclaimed. "There's a world of difference between the two. Fame is being known and loved for something good. Infamy is being known and largely hated for something bad. Abraham Lincoln is famous; Charles Manson is infamous. John F. Kennedy was famous; Fidel Castro is infamous. Michael Jordan is famous; Dennis Rodman is infamous. You see the difference?"

Martin didn't respond. *Is that where I'm headed? Is that all that's left for me?*

The booking officers were polite when they processed him as an prisoner. Treated him as if he was a guest checking into a five-star hotel. "Mr. McNeil, we'll need to get your fingerprints now. Mr. McNeil, we'll be taking your picture over here. Face forward, please. Thank you. Now turn to the side. Thank you."

Martin was delivered to his cell by an entourage of guards. Nearly a dozen of them, crowding him with the eagerness of small children, all trying to talk at once.

"Who's guarding the jail while you guys are walking me down?" Martin said, trying to sound light-hearted and relaxed.

"Everyone wanted to meet you. Get your autograph," said one of the younger guards. "This will be your cell, Mr. McNeil," pointing to his right. "You mind signing a few things for our kids?" Each of the guards was holding a trading card, a football or a T-shirt. Martin grabbed the proffered marker and started writing his name.

"You're not going to put anyone big and hairy in the cell with me are you?" Martin said, hearing real fear in his voice despite his best efforts. He was scared to death. He was about to be locked inside a jail cell. He was about to have his freedom taken from him for the first time in his life. In movies, the accused stroll casually into their cells, confidently proclaiming their innocence and invoking the names of their attorneys who will negotiate their release within a matter of hours. Actors have a knack for making jail look like a pleasant vacation from real life, but Martin held no such illusions. There was real panic bubbling just below the surface. He wanted to beg, to ask the guards to make an exception, to let him stay with them in the office. He'd promise to be quiet. He wouldn't be a nuisance to anyone. But Martin didn't ask the guard for anything. He kept his head down and continued to sign the objects that were handed to him.

"No," the guards promised. "You'll have your own cell as long as we're not too crowded in here. If we do have to put someone in with you, it'll be a white-collar criminal. Nobody violent. We'll make sure you don't have any problems in here. Anybody bothers you we'll take care of it."

Martin shrugged as though it really didn't matter. He wanted them to believe that he'd asked the question out of curiosity not fear, but they knew he was scared. They'd seen that look on the faces of many first-time offenders. The average law-abiding citizen was simply not prepared for the shock of jail. The door slammed behind Martin; his breath gushed out in a panic.

The first few days were tough, but Martin got through them. After about a week, his sadness turned the corner and became a mixture of anger and frustration. He was mad at himself for getting into this fix, but he was settling in, learning to handle it.

Unfortunately, Martin's mother wasn't making the adjustment. She was struggling, weeping every day; heaving sobs during her visits at the jail and judging by the condition of her eyes and face, she cried through most nights too. Big plaintive tears rolling down her cheeks, marking tracks in her makeup. She was inconsolable. Already lost one son, afraid of losing the other. Martin watched her surreptitiously from the corner of his eye. He felt terrible for doing this to her. He wanted to say something to make her feel better, but there were no words. His shame was so overwhelming that he couldn't meet her gaze. His cellmate's semantics aside, Martin's mother had taught him the difference: He was in jail; she was in prison.

"Richard," Martin said, wanting to be sure that the guards hadn't made a mistake when they saddled him with the motor-mouth doctor, "is DWI a white-collar crime?"

Mobley paused his lecture just long enough to say, "Driving while intoxicated is not a crime, Martin. When will you understand that simple fact?"

That was that.

Martin turned the television to Channel 12. His face appeared in a box over the anchor's shoulder; sturdy, bald head, skin the color of vanilla coffee. It was a familiar face, and until now, he'd been a hero. He was adored, emulated, even worshiped. He could no longer pretend to be that person. Not when he was on television with a row of incriminating white numbers under his chin. It was the mug shot from his arrest. He didn't look like a hero.

The story on the television continued. Video of Martin running down a field, leaping into the air, catching a football, sprinting into the end zone, spiking the ball. He watched the television with a sense of awe. He remembered that play, that game, that life. It seemed distant. Cut to his arrest. Hands behind his back, smile gone, face emblazoned with guilt.

"The trial of San Antonio Stallions wide receiver Martin McNeil will start tomorrow. McNeil is charged with felony murder in a bizarre case that led to the deaths of two men. . ."

Two bodies in his garage and another victim a few days earlier—but the media didn't know about that one yet. It sounded like a psychotic rampage. His mother couldn't understand it.

His attorney Joseph Steadman was confident that the jury would acquit him. Where that confidence came from was a mystery to Martin. Seven women, five men deciding the case. Three dead bodies and one prime suspect. It seemed pretty cut and dry. Martin figured the trial would go as far awry as the rest of his life had during the past few weeks. He and the professor might be spending a lot more time together. Richard for committing the "non-crime" of driving while intoxicated; Martin for participating in the "definite crime" of murder.

"Martin," Richard said, "if you don't mind an indelicate question." He paused long enough to see his cellmate raise his eyebrows. "Given everything that has happened to you the past six weeks, do you hate your brother?"

It was a fair question.

"No," Martin said softly. "No matter what he's done, I'll always love Brandon." That brought a rush of silent tears.

Brandon was dead.

# TWO

As CHILDREN, BRANDON AND Martin McNeil were never friends. Born two years apart, they grew up in a middle-class neighborhood on the west edge of Houston.

The boys were like opposite sides of the same coin, always together, but never seeing the world from the same vantage point. Brandon was a child with a breathtaking capacity for deviltry. At birth, he left the womb sideways, tangled in his umbilical cord, tearing at his mother's insides, nearly killing her during 22 hours of labor. He came out screaming and spitting in the operating room, developing a body temperature of 104 degrees. In the neonatal unit, he resisted the nurses. Swiping his tiny impotent arms at them, closing his toothless mouth around their fingers, kicking his feet. When he finally went home after two weeks in the hospital, he slept no more than an hour at a time, screaming continuously, driving his parents to the brink of madness.

When Brandon started to crawl, it wasn't the aimless exploration of the typical toddler. He moved with purpose toward the nearest exit. Demonstrating keen intelligence, he'd hide near closed doors waiting for someone to come through from the other side to enable his escape. As his mobility improved so did his jaunts. Always moving away from his parents, away from home. Instinctively knowing that his disappearance was the quickest way to arouse panic in those who cared for him. Once, when he was 17-months old, he got out of the house and walked nearly a mile before a woman gardening in her front yard spotted him, picked him up despite his resistance and called the police. No one was quite sure what to do with the ornery child. They couldn't identify him, and he'd twice nearly succeeded in escaping from the officers watching him. Finally, the boy was matched to a frantic 911 call from a baby sitter saying that a toddler was missing from her care. A police car sped to the house, practically throwing young Brandon through the front door when it opened. They were glad to be rid of him.

About a month after Brandon's second birthday, Martin was born. He was a curiously happy child with a ready smile and a quick laugh. He rarely cried even with the discomfort of a soiled diaper or hunger pains.

Brandon would often visit his new brother late at night, watching the baby sleep, then playing with his toes or tickling his ears, trying to disturb him. Trying to make the infant cross and irritable. Make him cry so Mom or Dad would have to get up to check on him. Then they'd be tired and cranky, and that would make Brandon happy. But Martin spoiled his plans. The infant never jolted awake with a scream building in his lungs. Instead his eyelids would flutter open softly, his gaze falling on Brandon's face staring malevolently between the slats of the crib. The baby's eyes would shine brightly in recognition and a smile would crease his chubby face.

Martin adored his older brother.

AS THE BOYS GREW older, the admiration Martin held for his Brandon developed with a passion that only younger siblings will ever understand. Brandon was the first to experience everything in life. First to go to the playground by himself; first to spend the night with a friend; first to have a girlfriend; first to get a driver's license, and first to move out of the house. Every new frontier in Brandon's life brought new longing for Martin. His older brother's experiences made Martin's own seem childish and insignificant by comparison. Envious admiration spilled out of Martin, a deference that he showed his brother in everyday interaction.

The advantage Martin had over Brandon was his incredible ability. From a early age it was clear that Martin was a natural athlete. He excelled at every sport he tried. He was a good student, a quick learner, and a hard working, congenial child. Brandon didn't have his younger brother's ability and not nearly Martin's work ethic. Brandon struggled with his class work and was nearly held back in first grade not because he wasn't capable, but because he simply didn't care. He was constantly in trouble with his parents and teachers. He was as lazy as his younger brother was dedicated. They were perfect icons for the nature side of the debate against nurture: Siblings, born of the same parents, exposed to the same home environment yet developing markedly different personalities.

DESPITE BRANDON'S RESISTANCE, MARTIN tried to forge a friendship with his brother. He dreamed of the day that he and his big brother would play together, build forts in the back yard, trade scary stories in bed late at night and guard secrets together.

But Brandon wasn't interested in Martin as a sibling, and certainly not as a friend. He was annoyed with the little brat always hanging around all the time. *Get your stupid ass away from me!* He would scream at Martin the moment they were out of range of the house. Martin would stop walking and watch his big brother march away. The bubbling hatred that boiled inside his brother only made Martin love him more, as though his love could douse the fire that threatened to consume Brandon.

Yet, in spite of Brandon's apparent indifference to his younger brother, there was a bond between them, and that bond was strong enough to save Martin's life.

IT WAS A PALE yellow Texas afternoon at the Cantarka River when Martin was 12 and Brandon 14. The two boys went to the river with a group of eight other preteens. The Cantarka River was just a mile from the McNeil's house and was a favorite summer-time swimming hole. The river was running high after days of heavy rain, but the boys were undaunted. They planned to swim across the swollen creek to a regal pecan tree that leaned out over the water bearing a rope on one sturdy branch. They'd take turns swinging out, letting go of the rope, whooping and hollering as they fell seven or eight feet into the middle of the river.

Trouble hit halfway across. Martin never a great swimmer, couldn't handle the pace of the river. The current was just too strong. The boys were wearing shoes because there were sharp rocks on the river bed. Martin's high tops filled with water, pulling his feet down. He didn't panic at first because he'd crossed the river many times before. He knew it was only six feet at its deepest point, so when he was tired, he'd sometimes take a break from swimming, sink down, let his feet hit bottom then propel himself back to the surface. With his shoes soggy with water, Martin sank toward the bottom expecting to feel the river bed. It wasn't there. The river was running five feet higher than normal. Panic struck. Martin tried to reverse his direction, but his shoes were lead weights. His arms churned for the surface. Finally, his head broke through, and he sucked in a hungry breath. He looked around and saw that the current had carried him downstream from the other boys. He paddled furiously for the shore. His heart pounding, his shoes still tugging. He managed a feeble "help" before he went under the second time. He tried to swim underwater toward the bank. Still trying to get back to the surface, but trying to get close to the bank as well. His arms pulling furiously; his lungs were burning. Finally, he reached the surface again took a deep breath. Water rushed into his lungs, and he realized that he wasn't on the surface. He was still underwater. He was drowning. The world went black.

The next thing Martin remembered was lying on the bank coughing up water, and then vomiting as his body tried to expel all of the river that had invaded. He felt terrible, but it was the most wonderful terrible he had ever experienced. He was alive. When he finally opened his eyes, the terror began anew. Brandon was lying on his back, not moving, not breathing. There was a man leaning over him, dripping wet, performing CPR. Martin started to cry. Silent tears leaking down his cheeks, as he watched this stranger alternately pump his brother's chest and them force air into his lungs.

"Somebody go call 911!" the man screamed.

Several of the boys raced off to find a phone. Martin sat very still, staring, no longer feeling the spasms that racked his midsection. "God, please don't let Brandon die. Please don't let him die." He said it over and over again, his face screwed up in pain. The man pumped and blew, but Brandon didn't respond.

Then, finally, a small breath. A cough of water erupted from Brandon's mouth. Followed by another, and another. Martin let out a weary whoop and covered his mouth with his hands. He was crying in earnest now, tears of joy. A low sound emanated from the back of his throat. The man sat back on his haunches and let out a relieved sigh as Brandon continued to cough and hack his way back to life.

Brandon spent the next three days in the hospital undergoing tests to determine whether he had suffered permanent brain damage. His heart had stopped for nearly three minutes that day on the river bank.

From the other boys, Martin learned that Brandon was already on the opposite bank when his little brother started having trouble. When Martin yelled for help, Brandon jumped back into the river and swam toward him. Martin never resurfaced, but Brandon kept going down and coming up, trying to find him. At last, he reappeared, dragging Martin with him, pushing his brother toward the bank; two other boys pulled the younger boy ashore. The attention of all the boys was riveted on Martin. They didn't immediately notice as Brandon, who was so fatigued that he could barely move his arms, sank beneath the surface. That's when a man named Scott Barber dove into the water. Barber lived half a mile away and had seen the boys walk past his house on their way to the river. He guessed that they were planning to swing from the tree rope, and he knew that was a mistake with the river running so high. He threw on a pair of tennis shoes, ran out of the house and hustled down to the bank to try to stop the boys from going into the river. He arrived just in time to see Brandon go down.

Barber leaped into the water, and swam with powerful strokes toward Brandon. He found him, pulled the boy to shore, and immediately started CPR.

Martin sat in his brother's hospital room for as long as his parents and the medical staff would allow every day. Brandon had saved his life and nearly died in the process. Martin's love for his brother bounded to a new level after that harrowing experience. There was a new passion and intensity to it. From then on, there was nothing that Martin would not give to Brandon. There was no transgression that Martin would not forgive. He was driven with a unquenchable need to repay his older brother for that selfless act.

A few days later, Brandon was back to normal. There was no permanent damage. He went back to doing the things that he used to do. He was amused by his younger brother's attentions. He'd push Martin to see how far his brother would go. He'd ask him to mow the lawn for him, then clean up his room, then make him something to eat. Martin never questioned the orders. He just performed the tasks and waited to see if there was anything else. Brandon's near-death experience drew Martin closer to his older brother, but Brandon didn't reciprocate; if anything he got meaner.

Years later, Martin asked Brandon why he had done it. Why he'd jumped back into that river and risked his life to save Martin's?

Brandon shrugged. "I didn't want Mom to be upset."

Martin accepted that, but he knew that despite his older brother's outward disinterest, Brandon loved him enough to risk his own life.

BRANDON MANAGED TO GRADUATE from high school despite several threats by the district to deny him his diploma if his conduct didn't improve. He never seriously thought about going to college; he didn't see the point in sitting through four more years of boring classes. His first priority was moving out of his father's house, but he couldn't afford his own place, and his parents wouldn't give him the money. They told him to get a job. He resisted for a while, but he finally started selling clothes at a store in the Galleria Mall. During his off time, he'd hang out on campus at the University of Houston, pretending to be a student, trying to pick up women. He knew his handsome face, and carefully groomed appearance were his main assets in life. He looked like a movie star with his clear brown eyes, soft lashes and high cheek bones. His face was pretty in a way that would have seemed effeminate if not for his powerful jawbone and the chiseled square shape of his head. And although he rarely exercised, Brandon was blessed with a statuesque build, standing 6-foot-1 and a solid 190. He always dressed with care, in perfectly pressed clothes at the height of the current fashion.

Girls first started to swoon over Brandon in junior high school, and they never really stopped. While his younger brother, Martin impressed people with his athletic ability, Brandon did the same with his face. For most of his life, Brandon was able to bed any girl he desired. It wasn't just his good looks that seduced the women. He also possessed true romantic charm; a knack for telling women exactly what they wanted to hear at the precise moment they needed to hear it.

He'd never been in love, and didn't expect that he ever would be. Brandon was far too self-interested to expend energy loving someone else. He pursued women mostly for sex. But occasionally he used his talent against his younger brother.

Maisha was the first.

She was Martin's first real girlfriend in high school. She came to the McNeil house on a warm October afternoon looking for her beau.

"Martin's not here," Brandon said through the screen door, his light eyes staring through the girl making her feel hot inside.

"Oh," Maisha said blushing. "He said he was supposed to get out of practice early today."

Brandon stepped back, inviting her in to wait.

For 45 minutes they sat a discreet distance apart on the couch, watching television and carrying a quiet conversation. Maisha was comfortable, but with each passing moment, she could feel something happening to her. The air seemed charged with a strange intimacy. She was on a hormonal slide, gliding slowly downward, not really fighting the pull, but knowing that even if she wanted to, she couldn't resist it. She had never spoken to Brandon except to say hello. Now she was talking to him like she had known him her entire life. When he spoke, the soft timbre of his voice vibrated all the way through her, stirring her, making her feel. . . special. . . and sexy. . and. . .

*and horny. . .*

Horny? Maisha pressed her legs tightly together, trying to push the thought from her head. This was her boyfriend's *brother*. She shouldn't be having these thoughts. It wasn't like her.

*Maybe I should leave?*

But then she was looking into his eyes, and she knew she wouldn't leave. She wanted nothing more than to just stay there on the couch with him forever.

He leaned over and kissed her gently on the lips.

She didn't pull away.

"It doesn't look like Martin's coming home early."

She nodded, her eyes closed, her mouth hovering near his, her breath a soft whisper. She didn't have the least bit of concern about Martin as Brandon peeled away her clothing. Soon they were completely naked, making love in the gentle afternoon heat.

They didn't hear the car that dropped Martin off. They didn't notice him standing at the open door watching this act of betrayal. Martin didn't say a word. He turned and walked away from the house. He went to a nearby park, and sat on the ground near a swing set, watching a group of children play.

WHEN HE RETURNED TO the house an hour later, Maisha was gone, but Brandon was still sitting on the couch—the scene of the crime.

"Your girl came by looking for you," Brandon said not looking away from the television screen. "Wants you to call her."

"Thanks," Martin said quietly. He stood still, staring. Finally, Brandon met his gaze.

"You gonna call her?"

"I saw you." Saying the words Brandon wanted to hear.

"Saw me what?"

Martin walked to his bedroom. He broke up with Maisha the next day.

He and Brandon never talked about it.


CHRISTINA WAS THE SECOND.

Martin was a sophomore at Florida State University. He brought his girlfriend home for Christmas break. Christina was the sweetest and most intelligent woman he'd ever known. They'd been dating for about a year. Bringing her home to meet his parents was a major step in their relationship. They'd scheduled a week in Houston and then a week in Arizona with her parents. He couldn't believe how lucky he was to have found someone like her.

They had been in Houston three days when Martin woke one night with a start. The clock next to him read just past two. He'd been in the throes of a nightmare he couldn't remember. He rubbed his eyes, and turned on the bedside lamp. Then he stood, shrugged on a robe, and walked down the hall to the bathroom. On the way back, he smiled, thinking about how cute Christina must look tucked under the covers in the guest room with her pretty brown hair fanned out around her head. He decided to check on her. Give her a loving kiss on her forehead while she slept. If he accidentally woke her with his gentle kiss, then he'd keep kissing her and wouldn't stop until their passion was spent. He opened her door slowly, an arrow of light from the hallway piercing the darkness, illuminating the bottom corner of the bed; it's glare sweeping wider as he pushed the door inward.

Her bed was empty.

Martin stood still, staring at the rumpled sheets, not immediately registering what this meant; thinking that she might have sneaked into his bed while he was in the bathroom. He backtracked, hoping that she was lying on top of the covers with a smile and not much more, her arms spread wide to welcome him.

His bedroom was empty.

He looked at Brandon's door, knowing that's where she was, wondering if he should barge in on them. Catch them in the act. He pressed his ear against the door. He could hear the muted creak of Brandon's bed springs, then a soft female sigh so full of pleasure it stung his heart. Then he turned and went back to Christina's room, pushing the door toward the frame, but leaving it open just a crack so he could stare out from the darkness.

Fifteen minutes later, his older brother's door opened slowly, and Brandon peered out. There was whispering, a soft kiss and Christina tiptoed out in her robe. She looked toward Martin's door, and he thought he saw a dark shadow of guilt flash across her face. She turned back toward Brandon, smiling, her fingers tickling the air in a delicate wave. Martin opened the door then, startling her. She gasped and clutched the neck of her robe with one hand. A sudden rush of emotion brought tears to her eyes, an apology to her lips.

"Martin," she managed plaintively. The pleasure she'd experienced a few minutes earlier felt hollow in the jagged light that spilled into the hall-way. Martin walked past her, deftly avoiding her outstretched hand. Past Brandon who looked embarrassed, but not contrite. Martin went into his room, closed the door and crawled into bed.

Christina knocked a few minutes later. "Please talk to me, Martin," she pleaded quietly. "I'm so sorry."

Martin cracked the door and stared at her with cold eyes. He didn't trust his voice.

"Honey, I'm sorry," she said. Her face was awash with tears. She'd never before cheated on a boyfriend—especially not with her boyfriend's brother. She didn't know what had come over her. She wanted to explain how it happened. She wanted to beg his forgiveness. She loved him. She'd do whatever he wanted to make it up to him.

"We'll call about flights in the morning," Martin said. Christina flew out of Houston the next day. Martin never spoke to her again.

RICHARD MOBLEY LISTENED INTENTLY as Martin talked about his rela-tionship with his brother.

"I don't know if I could have handled things as you did, Martin. If Brandon had been my brother, I would have wanted to kill him." Mobley immediately regretted his choice of words. "I'm sorry, I didn't mean—"

"It's okay," Martin said. "When I look back at all the things Brandon did, sometimes I have a hard time believing that I didn't say or do anything, but I knew what it was about. Brandon needed to beat me. The only time he'd ever been better than me in his whole life was the day he saved my life at the river. After that you should have seen him. He was cold and vicious to me, but there was joy inside him. He loved the idea that my athletic abil-ity had failed me and I'd had to be rescued by him. It was the same with Maisha and Christina. Brandon could have had anyone that he wanted, but he wanted them, because he wanted to beat me. I let him have the victory."

"So why did you break up with the girls?"

Martin sighed. "My pride, I guess. I could handle my brother beating me this way if that's what he needed. But I loved Brandon in a way that I never loved Maisha or Christina. I couldn't forgive them. They'd embar-rassed me, and I couldn't get over that."

Mobley was uncomfortable asking his next question, but he got it out because he had to know: "Did Brandon ever make advances toward your wife?"

Martin chuckled wearily. "Yeah, but Jessica always seemed to be immune to his charms. She disliked him from the start, and she grew to hate him over time."

The two men sat quietly in their tiny cell. Finally, Richard said, "Given the history of your relationship with Brandon, I guess I shouldn't be surprised at the role he played in the events that led to your arrest. But I really don't understand how you and David Costanzo came to hate each other so."

That brought a long sigh from Martin. "Just ego, I guess. Mine and his. Two big egos that didn't know when to quit."

# THREE

## MARTIN'S JUNIOR YEAR
## AT FLORIDA STATE UNIVERSITY

MATTHEW FIELDS WAS 10 years old when his parents divorced. It was a sudden, shocking event. Janet taught second grade at Horizon Elementary School, where her son was a fourth grader. After school, they'd drive home comparing notes about the day, laughing about the funny things kids said and did, talking about the homework Matthew needed to complete. Most days, Matthew wasn't in the house five minutes before he was out the door again skateboard in hand one his way down to the terrain park the Marianna City Council had approved the year before. He dreamed of one day competing in the X-games, and Matthew was getting pretty good at making turns on the small vert ramp. Janet enjoyed the silence of the house during these late afternoons. She'd take a long shower, check the mail and start dinner. Her husband Richard was a civilian contractor working at a naval base in Panama City. Most days he'd get home from work about 6:30 p.m.

It was a typical late March afternoon when Janet and Matthew reached home and dropped into their normal routine; the boy raced out the door, Janet picked up the mail and strolled back to the bedroom. She was alternately shuffling through the letters and unbuttoning her blouse when she discovered the envelope that would change her life.

Her name was across the front in block letters. It was her first and last name as though a stranger had written the note, but Janet recognized her husband's handwriting. She tore open the envelope and unfolded the single sheet of paper enclosed.

*Janet—*
*There's no easy way to say this, so I'll just say it. I want a divorce.*
*I'm in love with someone else, and she's being transferred to*
*California. I'm going with her. You can have everything in the*
*house. I'm taking my car and $3,000 out of the bank. Please tell*
*Matthew that I'm sorry.*

*—Richard*

Initially, Janet didn't react. She'd had no idea her husband was unhappy or that he'd been having an affair. They had an easy, happy marriage. No major fights, no petty abuses. Just a comfortable stable home where they focused on raising their son as well as they could. But there it was, on paper, in Richard's own words. *I want a divorce.* That evening, she invented a business trip when Matthew asked about his father, kissed her son good night and went to bed.

For three days, they continued their lives as if nothing was wrong. But the facade was beginning to crack. He hadn't called. He hadn't sent another note. She had no idea how to contact her husband. Reality was seeping in: Their marriage was over.

Richard and Janet had been high school sweethearts. They were 15-year-old sophomores when they met, married at 20 and had Matthew at 22. Then after 12 years of marriage, it was over? *How could he do this to Matthew? How am I supposed to explain this?*

After a week, Janet collapsed. It was a Wednesday morning and she didn't ease into Matthew's room to shake him awake as she normally did. She didn't shower or start breakfast. She was curled in a ball on Richard's side of the bed, her body racked with confusion and pain..

Matthew woke just after eight when the phone rang; he listened for a moment, wondering why his mother wasn't answering, and finally got up and raced into the kitchen to snatch the phone from the wall. It was Mr. Mancuso calling to check on Janet. She was a no-show in her classroom, and she hadn't called in sick. The boy carried the cordless phone into his mother's bedroom and told her the principal was on the phone.

Janet took the receiver and mumbled, "I can't come in," and hung up.

Matthew crawled into bed with his mother that morning, finally understanding that his father wasn't coming back. They stayed in bed all day, hugging and crying. Mr. Mancuso came by in the middle of the day, ringing the bell for 15 minutes, but Janet didn't answer the door.

The next few weeks were a blur. The house fell into disarray; Matthew's grades suffered. His attention span was nonexistent; he didn't have energy for sports; he didn't eat; he didn't play video games. He and his mother were adrift, cut loose from their anchor and floating with no direction.

Eventually Janet realized that she had to take care of her son. Her grief was profound, but her son needed her to be strong. She resumed her normal routine. Rousting him out of bed, driving to school, asking about his homework. Finding time to play. It was tough, but she would pull them through it. They'd survive this.

When Janet saw an ad in the Sunday paper reporting that Florida State receiver Martin McNeil would be in a neighboring town for a golf tournament, she showed it to Matthew thinking he might like to meet the football star. The boy seemed disinterested, but Janet knew he loved football and was determined to do something to cheer her son. She decided that they'd drive over to Chattahoochee to meet McNeil.

THERE WERE 12 PEOPLE standing outside the Bass Creek Country Club when Martin McNeil arrived just after 7 a.m. He waved to the crowd as he got out of the club owner's Lincoln Towncar, and stopped to sign a few autographs.

By mid-morning more than 150 people had streamed onto the golf course, following McNeil's foursome as though he was Tiger Woods. They cheered every drive, jockeyed for position on every shot, and encouraged every putt. At 11 a.m. the crowd was still growing, and James Anderson, the gray-haired director of the club, dabbed a handkerchief across his forehead. He picked up the phone and dialed County Sheriff Buddy Lipson.

"Things are getting a little crazy over here," Anderson said when the sheriff came on the line. After listening for a couple of minutes, Lipson slammed down the phone and rushed over to the country club with six officers—the entire police force except the dispatcher. Lipson had seen this type of situation before, and he knew a group of excited people could be unpredictable and dangerous.

By the time McNeil reached the 18th green, the crowd had swollen to more than 500 people with lawn chairs and cold drinks—mostly beer—all hoping to get an autograph when the player completed his round.

Matthew and Janet arrived at about 1 p.m. and the boy's initial ambivalence about meeting McNeil turned into excitement when he saw the number of people at the country club. He realized that he was part of something very big. He was soon clapping and cheering along with everyone else.

The crowd had the exact opposite effect on Janet. She'd thought that getting McNeil's autograph would be a fairly simple matter of walking into the country club and asking for it. She hadn't considered that hundreds of other people would have the same idea. As she watched Matthew's growing enthusiasm, she worried that the disappointment of not getting McNeil's autograph would compound her son's depression.

McNeil finished his round and hustled into the clubhouse. The chant "We Want Martin! We Want Martin!" reverberated though the dining area. McNeil walked toward the window and said, "maybe I should just go out and sign for a couple of minutes, just to keep them happy, then jump in a car and go."

"Sit your stupid ass down," Sheriff Lipson said.

McNeil was stunned. Nobody talked to him that way. He was a star at Florida State. People catered to him, asked for his opinion, deferred to his authority.

"What did you say to me?"

"Son, it ever occur to you that you go out there things might get out of hand?" Lipson hated celebrities. Twenty-seven years in the Los Angeles Police Department had taught him that movie stars, musicians and athletes were nothing but spoiled brats who were a headache for anyone trying to protect them from their own stupidity. "You go out there, someone might take your head off."

McNeil rolled his eyes. "Sheriff, I've been surrounded by fans in worse situations than this. I don't think anyone's gonna—"

"Boy, I ain't just talking about someone that might hate you," Lipson said angrily. He knew his job and resented the condescension in McNeil's voice. "That ain't just a group of people out there—that's a mob. You got four or five hundred people standing out in the heat, drinking beer and chanting like it's a Baptist revival. That's a mob. You ever dealt with a mob before?"

"No," McNeil said quietly. He was still shocked to have been called a "boy."

"It ain't nothing nice. You take five steps out that door and a mob'll rip the clothes off your body and beat you within an inch of your life without ever meaning to. They'll be fighting to get close to you, grabbing on to you for balance when the rest of the mob pushes against them, pulling your jacket, your shirt, your pants. Someone might try to take your hat as a souvenir and once one person snatches something, the rest will too, because that's a mob out there. All they need is a direction and they start moving. You'll get pushed and pulled, punched and trampled. You're ass'll be in a hospital buck naked talking about, 'oh I was just gonna sign a couple of signatures,' and I'll be the one that looks like a jackass for letting you walk out there. So sit your butt down, "til we can figure out what we're going to do here."

The sheriff and the player stared at each other for a long minute. They were 15 feet apart like old west gun fighters. McNeil took a step toward the door; Lipson's hand moved to the butt of his gun.

Martin stopped, looking at the holstered weapon then at the determined set of the sheriff's jaw. "So now you're gonna shoot me?"

The sheriff didn't respond, but his hand didn't move.

Finally, McNeil shook his head and returned to his stool at the bar. The other golfers exhaled at once, awestruck by this display of bravado. They'd tell their friends later that they didn't know whether the sheriff intended to shoot the player, but he sure sounded serious.

James Anderson decided that he wouldn't invite McNeil back to the tournament next year—*maybe a less famous player*. He didn't need a shooting or a riot at his club, and while it appeared that they might avoid gun play, the riot was still a brewing outside.

The sheriff stepped away from the window when the limousine arrived. He'd called Mitchell Blevins an hour ago and asked him to bring the stretch. Lipson turned to the assembled deputies in the room and said, "All right, let's go." Earlier, he'd sent four officers out the door to get the three cruisers and Anderson's Lincoln Towncar, instructing them to drive all the vehicles around to the back of the clubhouse where the pavement turned left leading to a big bay garage where trucks delivered supplies for the kitchen.

Down in the garage, the sheriff put a police jacket and hat on Martin's head an ordered him into the driver's seat of one of the police cruisers. Lipson got in the back of the limo. The sheriff placed two police cars in front of the limo and one behind for the trip to the airport. The crowd went crazy when the convoy eased around the building. There were people everywhere. They rushed to the limo, knocking on the glass, screaming for autographs, pressing their bodies against the vehicle. Martin in the second police cruiser was driving slowly, hoping that he wouldn't kill anyone as he inched through the crowd. He was surprised that the sheriff's gambit was working. Everyone was so focused on the limo that no one even glanced at him behind the wheel of the police car. He made it through the crowd easily, but the limo was pinned in, slowing and eventually stopping. Suddenly, Anderson's Towncar burst from behind the building, cutting across the driving range en route to the road. In the back of the limo, Sheriff Lipson rolled down the windows and waved to the crowd. There was a groan of frustration at being fooled. The crowd's attention shifted to the Towncar, as the limo eased forward. The sheriff was proud of his misdirection. It appeared that all the vehicles would make it out with no problems. They'd stop a few miles away, and one of the deputies would drive McNeil to the tiny airport for the quick flight back to Tallahassee.

MATTHEW AND JANET WERE among those screaming for Martin's attention. As she feared, her son would not be leaving with the autograph he wanted. She worried about him being disappointed during the drive home. She ruffled his hair as they stared at the Towncar cutting across the grass. Suddenly, the long blare of a car horn overrode the screams. Janet and Matthew turned toward the police car 30 yards away near the end of the driveway. The driver stepped out of the vehicle, taking off the hat and jacket, waving to the crowd.

"That's Martin McNeil," someone screamed, as everyone, including Matthew, raced toward him.

Martin was surprised at how swiftly the crowd approached. He took the baseball cap he'd worn that day and launched it into the air. He was around the car and back into the driver's seat before the first person reached the vehicle. Then he was off, onto the road, out of sight.

Sheriff Lipson watched all this from the back seat of the limo. When he first heard the blare of the horn he worried that McNeil was in trouble. When he saw the player get out of the police cruiser, he got scared. *The hell is he doing?* His anger boiled over when the saw the hat arch into the air.

"Well, I'll be goddamned shit!!" Lipson spat. After everything he'd told McNeil about mobs, he couldn't believe the player was throwing a souvenir into the crowd. It was as though he'd poured blood into shark-infested water.

Lipson was out of the limo in a heartbeat, and the two officers in the trailing police car were a step behind. They all worried that someone might get trampled in the fight for the hat.

TWO MEN LEAPED FOR the cap like basketball players stretching for a rebound. They grabbed the hat simultaneously, holding firm as they fell to the earth and were swept under as a tumbling melee erupted.

There was screaming and panic, people were trampled and clawed. The hat was nearly torn in two in the battle for possession. At the heart of the battle was 10-year-old Matthew Fields lying on his stomach at the bottom of the pile with the hat inches from his face. He'd been knocked to the ground when the two men leaped and soon there was a pile of bodies. Matthew was surprised to discover that he could breathe on the bottom. There were other bodies right next to him, adults who were bigger than Matthew creating a nice pocket for the boy. He had room to wiggle, and he was in perfect position to fight for the cap.

Both of his hands were locked firmly on the cap, and he quickly set to working it free. He chose the closest hand and dug his teeth in deep, not letting up until he heard the owner of that hand, scream and release the cap. He moved to the next hand, gaining control of the souvenir by inches. It took only two bites, then he had enough leverage to pull the cap away from the remaining hands. Very quickly, he tucked the baseball cap safely under his chest then waited patiently for the pile to unravel. He could hear his mother's panicked voice screaming his name. He smiled happily. When the deputies finally pulled the last of the bodies off him, Matthew stood warily, clutching the trophy as he searched for his mother's face. She hugged him tightly, performing a motherly inventory of his body, making sure he was okay. He showed her the hat, smiling with so much pride that it brought tears to her eyes. The right side of the bill had been ripped away from the body of the cap and the rest was a twisted, grass-stained mess. But Matthew guarded the hat as though it was a rare diamond. And in that crowd, on that day, in that riotous mood, that battered cap was exactly that—a prized jewel.

Matthew prudently asked for police protection as he and his mother left the country club.

SHERIFF LIPSON ORDERED HIS deputies to "get all these people the hell out of here." He marched to the nearest squad car and barked into the radio: "Deputy Mitchell this is Sheriff Lipson, you got your ears on?"

After a moment, Mitchell responded: "Roger Sheriff."

"Deputy, have you got McNeil in the car with you now?"

"Yes sir, we made the switch about five minutes ago, got him in here, now we're gonna swing by my boy's school and say hello. Couple of years ago me and Jimmy Jr. were watchin' the Rose Bowl when McNeil made that catch to—"

"Is this gonna take long?"

An embarrassed pause. "Sorry Sheriff. What can I do for you?"

"Deputy, let me talk to McNeil."

"He's right here."

"What were you thinking?" Sheriff Lipson said the moment Martin said hello. He was standing outside the police car surveying the crowd that was beginning to disperse.

"I just wanted to—"

"You just wanted to get somebody killed is what you wanted to do."

"Come on sheriff. I was just—"

"Son, you are one ignorant, stupid, cocky son of a bitch. I ought to charge you with reckless endangerment, inciting a riot, littering, interfering with a police officer—"

"You can't charge me just for throwing a hat into the air."

"Okay super star, you just try me. We got people down here fighting. Kids getting' trampled. Old people knocked down and piled on, all because you wanted to throw a damned hat in the air. After everything I told you about what a mob'll do you go and throw a damned souvenir into the crowd. If anybody got hurt out here today and wants to sue your stupid ass, they got my blessing."

"I'm sorry. I didn't mean —"

"You dodged a bullet today, son. But don't come back to my county again. I can't guarantee that I won't shoot you on sight." The sheriff threw the microphone back into the car, and stormed away.

MATTHEW RECOUNTED THE DAY'S activities for hours, vowing to some-day get McNeil to autograph the hat. His mother didn't need to offer much encouragement. She just smiled and nodded, happy to see her son in such good spirits. She listened contentedly as Matthew recounted again and again how he'd first been afraid at the bottom of the pile, but fear quickly turned into determination when he saw the hat in front of him. When they got home, Matthew called every friend he could think of to share the story.

"Mom, can I take the hat to school tomorrow?"

"Of course, honey."

From that day forward Matthew Fields was a confirmed Martin

McNeil fan. He watched every Florida State Seminoles game on television, and he religiously collected every piece of McNeil memorabilia he could find. His room was decorated with articles about McNeil, action photos of the receiver and Florida State pennants and a jersey. The battered baseball cap that had come off McNeil's head held a place of honor on a table in the corner of the room.

For the next two years, Matthew had one dream: To get McNeil's autograph on the baseball cap. He talked his mother into driving down to Tallahassee on four occasions to see Florida State games hoping to get McNeil's autograph. But no matter how early he arrived or how late he stayed, Matthew could never get close enough to get a signature from the football star.

That would change when McNeil was drafted into the NFL.

# FOUR

## MARTIN'S ROOKIE YEAR

DAVID COSTANZO HAD FINALLY carved a niche for himself. His caustic, bombastic style had earned him a following in San Antonio, but his success hadn't come easy. He'd had a dozen jobs since college. Bouncing around the country chasing work; every transfer taking his career a little further in the wrong direction. He started at the *New York Daily News* when he was 23 years. He was a talented writer full of bravado and confidence, a shining star in the journalism industry. Although he was talented, he still had much to learn, but none of his editors could convince him of that fact. David thought he had all the answers. He was fired after nine months at the *Daily News* and began a painful spiral that took him from city to city, newspaper to newspaper never lasting long until he hit San Antonio. He was 40 years old then. He'd landed a gig as a sports columnist for the *San Antonio Light*, and he had a radio talk show on 840 KWED.

It was an on-air debate with *Sports Illustrated* reporter Bob Faust that sparked Costanzo's celebrity in San Antonio. It launched what would become known as "The Walk," and it would drive listeners to Costanzo's radio show and readers to his column for years to come.

"Listen up people," Costanzo said into his microphone. "As always here at KWED, I've got the straight scoop for you. I've been reading *Sports Illustrated*, *Pro Football Weekly* and the local rags, and all the so-called experts are predicting that our San Antonio Stallions will use their first-round pick to take Martin McNeil. I've got news for you. It ain't gonna happen. Martin McNeil will not be coming to San Antonio, so you can put that thought right out of your stupid little heads. The Stallions have an incredibly strong position in the draft, holding the number three overall pick, they shouldn't waste that on McNeil."

"I don't think you can say the words "waste" and "McNeil" in the same sentence," Faust argued.

"You can if you're talking about number three overall. Look, Cleveland has the first pick, and they've got no choice. They desperately need Don Tubble out of Notre Dame. He's the quarterback who will give their offense the power it lacks. San Diego's gotta take Ricardo Mercia out of UW. He is the pass rusher of all pass rushers, and he's the impact player the Chargers' defense has needed for two years."

"I agree with you on both counts," Faust said.

"So then come the Stallions who need an offensive lineman like William Randolph out of Iowa, but using the number three pick of the draft to take Randolph is like trading a brand new Mercedes head up for a brand new Volkswagen. You'd be smarter to sell the Mercedes, then buy the Volkswagen and put the difference in your pocket. The Stallions can get way more value out of that number three pick by trading it than they can by using it. They could trade down for Oakland's 19th pick or for Baltimore's 22nd still get Randolph and have four or five additional draft picks to use to improve their offensive line."

"Everything you're saying is true if they were merely in the market for an offensive lineman, but they've got an opportunity to draft Martin McNeil, and they'd be fools to pass on him. McNeil is a gold-plated stud. An impact player of the sort the NFL hasn't seen in a while. He's a lock to go in the top 10, and if the Stallions have the good sense to select him, this kid by himself will create four or five victories a year. And the good news is that the Stallions can have their cake and eat it too. They get a franchise player, and if for some reason he's a bust, they can always trade him."

"I think you've been eating too much cake, Bob. If he's a bust then McNeil will be like a new car. The minute you drive him off the lot his value drops. Why draft him and give up some of that value?"

"Not at all," Post countered. "You're forgetting how much confidence coaches have in their own ability. No matter what McNeil does his first couple of years—assuming that he stays healthy—his value will stay high. If he's a bust in San Antonio other coaches will look at game tape and say, 'well the Stallions weren't using him right. If we had him here in this system, we could really tap his potential.' The bottom line is that every team in the league is desperate for the type of talent McNeil has, and the Stallions are the one team that can get him."

"Bob, I love you but you're crazy. McNeil's value is highest right now. Sure, they can trade him later, but there's no way in hell they'll get four or five draft picks for him. If they trade him later, it might be a two- or three-player deal. The truth is that the offensive line in San Antonio sucks, so until they get that problem fixed it doesn't matter how good a receiver McNeil is. Nobody is going to have to double cover the guy, all they need to do is blitz. The line will probably give up 60 sacks this year, and then the Stallions will have to trade McNeil to try to get some offensive linemen, but they'll be dealing from a weak position, whereas right now, they can deal from a strong position and get some real value for that draft pick."

"Everything you're saying makes sense, David, but I still believe you're giving too steep a discount to the value of McNeil. He's a franchise player—"

"Yeah, but what good is a franchise wideout if the quarterback doesn't have time to throw the ball?"

"You give him time by getting a receiver like McNeil. The first time a defense blitzes, the Stallions hit McNeil on a hot route and he beats everyone for a touchdown. I guarantee you that on the next series the defense is going to be afraid to blitz. That's what they'll get with McNeil. He's a legitimate threat to score every time he touches the ball. I've watched this guy play at Florida State and he's a true phenomenon. Defenses actually get lopsided when he's on the field. He'll have a cornerback over him in bump-man, a safety cheated over 10 yards off the ball and a linebacker splitting the difference, halfway out to the flat, basically inviting the offense to run in that direction because they're afraid of the pass. But even with triple coverage, Martin would find a way to get open."

"That's college," Costanzo said. "This is the pros. He won't do that in the—"

"Man among boys. That's what the scouts say about him; 'Man among boys'."

In the parlance of the NFL "man among boys" is a phrase that is scribbled onto scouting reports, when a player's dominance of the game is beyond dispute. A player bearing that description is akin to a father playing ball with his kids on the front lawn. The kids can only win if dad doesn't use his full strength. In the view of NFL scouts, McNeil was a man among boys.

IN THE DEBATE ABOUT McNeil, Costanzo had found an issue on which he could build his fame. Everyone in Texas seemed to want the wide receiver in San Antonio, and by opposing what everyone else wanted, David had found a wave he could ride. He hit it hard every day and taking a stronger stance against McNeil every day.

"We don't need this guy," Costanzo said on the air. "Sure, he's a great player, but we don't need him here. We need offensive linemen to open holes for our running backs and to provide protection for our quarterback. Without offensive linemen, what good is a receiver going to do us?"

Callers jammed Costanzo's lines. "He's going to take us to the Super Bowl!" they screamed.

"You people are idiots who have no clue about the big picture. You're so wrapped up in this fantasy about McNeil, that you're ignoring the greater value of trading away the draft pick. I'm glad none of you is the player personnel director. You'd drive the team into the ground. If the Stallions truly are committed to getting to the Super Bowl, they'll find a way to trade their third pick of the draft for a combination of draft picks and veteran players.

"The Stallions taking Martin McNeil with their first round pick would make them the laughing stock of the league," Costanzo said. "They already have Ernie Rogers and Jamie Vaughn, both of whom are potential Pro Bowl receivers. They'd be wasting the pick, their money and our hopes of a championship if they pick McNeil."

"So now you're saying McNeil won't make a difference?" a caller demanded.

"Yes, I'm saying that. We don't need him."

"So McNeil's no good, huh?"

"I'm not saying he's no good, but he's not what the Stallions need. If you need a new heart, then it doesn't matter how many good artificial knees your doctor shows you. If it doesn't address your need, then it doesn't matter."

"You don't know what you're talking about," the caller said. "The Stallions *need* Martin McNeil."

"You're an idiot," David said, hanging up.

"McNeil is the man who will turn this team around," insisted a caller named Mike from Alamo Heights. "They'll take him in the first round, and he'll take them to the Super Bowl, mark my words."

Costanzo laughed. "What the hell are you smoking?"

"If you're so confident, let's put some money on it," Mike urged. "I'll bet you a hundred dollars that the Stallions take McNeil in the first round."

David was still laughing.

"And I'll bet you another hundred that he turns this team around," Mike continued.

"A two hundred dollar wager ladies and gentlemen, from a man who would be better served spending the money on a good drug rehab program. I can't decide whether you're this stupid all the time, or if you're just high right now."

"Sounds like you're afraid to take the bet."

"Nonsense. I'd be happy to take your money, but since gambling on the radio might get us in trouble with the FCC, but I've got another idea. Are you married?"

"Yes," Mike said, a little confused.

"Is your wife cute?"

"Of course."

"What's her name?"

"Melissa."

"All right, when we finish this conversation, I'll put you on hold so my producer can get your phone number and address so you can't welsh on this bet.. When I'm proved right—the Stallions are going to trade away their first draft pick and they will not be adding Martin McNeil to the roster—I'm going to want to get into Melissa's panties."

"You're a jerk!" Mike knew Costanzo was probably joking, but he was offended nonetheless. "Look, just put your money up or shut the hell up, cause you don't know what you're talking about."

"Now, hold on Mike. It's not like I want to have sex with your wife. I just want to possess a pair of her panties. A nice little lacy thong that I can carry around and say, 'yeah, they belong to Mike's wife'. He's too stupid to understand the nuances of football, and too ugly to keep his wife from test-driving a stud like me."

"Fine! But what are you gonna put up? I'm pretty sure I don't want to have any panties from your fat-ass wife."

"As luck would have it Mike, I'm not married. You can have a pair of my briefs if you're into that sort of thing."

"No," Mike said. "You know what I want? When the Stallions take McNeil in the first round, I want you to walk your stupid ass from the radio station all the way to the capitol building in your underwear."

The request caught David off-guard. His producer shrugged behind the glass. "All right, Costanzo said after a moment. "From here to capitol in my underwear if I'm wrong, but if I've got to do something public, then so do you. When I'm proved right, we're going to stage a little rally right here in front of the building. You bring your wife down in a skirt, and she's going to have to take off those panties and hand them to me still warm from her body."

"Deal," Mike said, so angry that he wasn't considering how his wife would react to this wager. Later, he decided against telling Melissa, choosing instead to wait and see what happened with the draft. Praying that the Stallions would select Martin McNeil.


ESPN CARRIED LIVE COVERAGE of the draft from a five-star hotel in New York City. David was at home watching nervously. He shouldn't have gone so far out on a journalistic limb in saying that the Stallions *absolutely* would not select McNeil. So far there had been no word of a trade, and although there was still time, the Stallions statements during the past couple of days gave the impression that a trade was unlikely.

Sitting in front of the television, in a pair of running shorts and a T-shirt David wished he hadn't painted himself into such a tight corner.

"Is there any way I can get out of this," he said quietly.

"No," said Nettie Richardson with characteristic directness. She was sitting beside him on the couch, proper skirt hanging down to mid-shin even while seated. Glasses on a thin black string around her neck. Theirs' was an odd friendship. Dramatically different in demeanor and lifestyle, but connected emotionally from the moment they first met.

When the draft officially began it didn't take long to reach the third pick. NFL Commissioner Paul Tagliabue walked to the podium with a white card in his hand. ESPN announcers spoke in hushed tones, issuing their final predictions that the name on the card would indeed be Martin McNeil.

David's mouth was a desert; his stomach a knot of apprehension.

"With the third pick of the first round, the San Antonio Stallions select. . . wide receiver. . . Martin McNeil of Florida State University."

Applause drowned out the sound as the camera cut to McNeil smiling in a navy suit, pulling a Stallions baseball cap onto his head. Player personnel director Eddie Goodman was pumping his hand, holding up a jersey with Martin's name and number—82—on the back. Then the camera turned to McNeil's family, hugging, smiling and crying. His mother was wiping her eyes. His father slapping everyone on the back.

David watched the scene with a painful sense of dread. He had to figure out how to handle this situation. *Should I just shrug it off and say, "Hey, so I was wrong. . . for once." Should I apologize? Maybe I should be the first to have Martin on the air. Invite him to my show.*

"The team is wrong," said Nettie. "You can argue that point for years."

Of course. Count on Nettie to deliver the simplest solution. David smiled, and kissed her on the cheek.

The next day on the radio Costanzo did exactly as Nettie suggested; he defended his position. "I guarantee you this kid will not be the savior. The Stallions should not have drafted him. They'll be trading his sorry ass in a year, and they won't get nearly the value for him that they could have gotten if they had traded the draft pick," Costanzo said.

His listeners were livid. "Why can't you just admit you were wrong?" they demanded. "Why can't you admit that you don't know that you're talking about? Why are you so bullheaded and negative? Why can't you ever find anything good to say about anyone?"

It was great for the station. David's ratings were strong. Instead of reporting the news, David *became* the news. Mike called back to demand that Costanzo make good on his promise to walk to the State Capitol in his underwear. He even offered up a pair of his wife's panties for David to wear.

"Come on," David said, "that was a damned joke."

But other callers agreed with Mike. They were insistent. He needed to hit the road in his skivvies. Soon the issue was being covered by other members of the media. "LISTENERS TELL REPORTER: WALK WITHOUT PANTS," read a headline in the *San Antonio Light*. Television stations sent their cameras to interview Costanzo. In terms of his name recognition, it was a dream come true, David was finally succeeding as a journalist.

Eventually, the program director and the general manager told David he had to make the walk. David initially refused, then argued, then threatened to quit. He liked the attention he was getting, but he'd be damned if he was going to walk anywhere in his underwear and let people laugh at him. But his bosses were firm. He had to make good on the bet. The station's promotions department began to organize an event they called simply "THE WALK."

`POLICE BARRICADES LINED THE edge of Broadway Boulevard in downtown San Antonio. Costanzo initially thought that perhaps a few dozen people would show up to watch him walk in his underwear, but the fearing the same—had managed to secure a spot in the Fiesta Texas parade. There were marching bands, floats, balloons, and David Costanzo walking in his underwear. Thousands of spectators crowded onto sidewalks and watched from office buildings as preparations were made.

Television crews from all the local stations were on hand. Newspaper reporters were weaving through the crowd interviewing spectators, and several radio stations had set up live broadcasts. It was a Friday morning nearly a month after the NFL Draft.

David, was wearing a pair of Adidas jogging shoes with white athletic socks and his legs were bare all the way up to his navy boxer shorts. He had on a KWED T-shirt and a KWED baseball cap.

He felt like an idiot.

Someone in the crowd started a chant that he couldn't make out at first, but soon it caught on, gaining steam and volume.

"Un-Der Wear! Un-der Wear!"

David kept his head down, appearing to study rare rock formations in the asphalt. A pair of police officers approached him, both burly athletic types with friendly smiles. David tried to read those grins. *Are they laughing at me?*

"We're ready when you are Mr. Costanzo," said the bigger of the two, a dark-haired man with a thick black mustache.

"I guess I'm ready," he said.

David wasn't actually going to walk the 75 miles between San Antonio and the capitol building in Austin. He was scheduled to walk the two-mile route of the parade, where he'd get the most exposure. Then he would get into the KWED van and ride to the outskirts of the city, where another group of spectators was waiting, providing another photo opportunity. Then there were brief walking stops planned in the cities of Selma, New Braunfels, San Marcos and Kyle on the way to Austin, where he would walk a full mile down Congress Avenue to the capitol building. The station's promotions department had worked hard to make sure there would be spectators on hand in each of the towns. Boy Scout troops had been recruited to the cause with promises of donations from the station for every step Costanzo took toward the Capitol. Altogether, KWED and its sponsors would donate $15,000 to different troops.

The fact that The Walk was good publicity for David and that it was raising money for charities did nothing to assuage his embarrassment. He tried to smile and pretend to have a sense of humor about all of this, but he was seething inside. It was the most humiliating experience of his life.

Immediately in front of him were two women from the promotions department carrying a KWED banner that had been imprinted with an explanation of the walk. It read: *KWED's David Costanzo made a bet with a caller that the Stallions would not draft Martin McNeil. If Costanzo lost the bet, he promised to walk to the capitol building in his underwear. See him today in his boxer shorts. Hear him weekdays from 7 to 10 p.m. on 840 KWED."*

Costanzo walked quickly, with his head held high, waving occasionally, projecting the image of a man who was always right, and who still felt "right" even walking down a public street in his underwear. When the parade route was completed, he hopped into the van, refusing to speak to or even look at the station's promotions director who was babbling about how great everything was going. He sipped from a bottle of Gatorade, and looked out the window as the van lumbered through the city. It was the same at each stop on his journey. There was always a crowd, always a chant of some sort—in Selma it was, "You were wrong! You were wrong!"

His march started at 10 a.m. and it was mid-afternoon by the time he reached Austin. He hopped out of the van and started walking toward the capitol. Congress Avenue was a long road that cut a straight swath through the city with nary a bend or a bobble for more than four miles. It dead ended at the capitol, and resumed its unwavering course on the other side of the legislative building.

David walked alone, staying on the sidewalk most of the way down Congress. A few hundred yards from the capitol, the road was blocked off and thousands of people were crowded onto the manicured lawn. *I can't believe so many people turned out for this.* When the walk started in San Antonio, David was simply embarrassed. All the people were there for the Fiesta Texas parade and he was a random idiot walking in his underwear. But now that he was in Austin, he was flattered that so many people had turned out to see him. He walked a little taller. As he made his way through the crowd, David saw a cluster of people and microphones set up on the steps of the capitol. There were at least two dozen people there, a couple he recognized as big wigs from KWED but he couldn't make out the others. He was at the bottom step before he realized that at least six were front office administrators from the Stallions, probably there to take umbrage with being called idiots. He climbed the steps slowly, not sure exactly how this was supposed to play out. The promotions department told him he would walk up the stairs and then disappear into the building. They didn't say anything about a hundred damned people on the stairs including Eddie Goodman the Stallions player personnel director with a goofy-ass grin on his chubby face, his hand extended as David approached.

The reporter reached out and shook the man's hand—what else could he do?—and felt himself being pulled toward the microphone.

"David, on behalf of all of us at the Stallions' office, we want to thank you for helping to raise money for the San Antonio community. In life, none of us can be right all the time, and we're all impressed that you were willing to follow through with your promise to walk to the capitol in your underwear. Let's here it for David Costanzo!" He raised the reporter's arm, exhorting the crowd.

A brief cheer skittered into the air.

"And to show our appreciation," the player personnel director reached under the podium, "we would like to present you with these." He held a pair of white boxer shorts with the words, "I'm Martin McNeil's biggest fan!" stenciled on the butt. The crowd roared with laughter as Goodman read the inscription. David, feeling his face flush red, clenched his jaw as he accepted the boxers. He muttered, "Thanks" into the microphone and was ready to walk the hell out of there when the personnel director grabbed his arm and stepped back to the microphone.

"Wait. Don't leave yet, David, because we have one other special surprise for you." He turned toward the capitol building, where a door was opening; Martin McNeil stepped out wearing a white Stallions jersey— number 82—waving to a crowd that roared with delight. Someone started chanting and soon the rest of the crowd picked up the rhythm, cheering "Mar-tin! Mar-tin! Mar-tin!" They didn't stop for a full three minutes. McNeil had been a member of the Stallions for less than a month and already he had achieved cult hero status.

David couldn't believe it. No one told him McNeil would be there. *No wonder there's such a crowd.* No one told him the team officials would be there throwing it in his face like that. The player personnel director was talking again, but David wasn't listening. He was watching McNeil stride toward him, seeing the arrogant grin on the kid's face, his arms raised in the air exhorting the crowd. A wave of anger washed over David, and suddenly he hated McNeil.

"—and so, we thought you might like to have your new boxer shorts autographed by the man himself," the personnel director continued, screaming to be heard over the crowd. "The newest San Antonio Stallion: Martin McNeil!" The crowd roared again, jumping up and down, clapping and whistling. Somehow all these people knew McNeil was going to be there. *Why didn't I know?* David wondered.

The player approached the podium extending his hand to David who took it only because he had to. Martin smiled toward the audience, handling the moment with surprising charisma and aplomb. Then holding up his palms he quieted the crowd. He picked up a marker, speaking slowly into the microphone as he wrote an inscription on the boxer shorts: "To my good friend, David. How could you be so stupid? Best wishes. Martin McNeil, #82."

The crowd roared with delight.


"JUST TOO MUCH EGO," Martin said wistfully in his jail cell. "I knew Costanzo was embarrassed, but at the moment, I didn't care. It was his own fault that he was standing at the state capitol in his underwear getting his ass handed to him on a platter. The crowd wanted me to rub it in his face a little bit, so I did.

"When I handed him the boxers, I leaned down and whispered this quote that I'd heard one time," Martin chuckled at the memory. "I said, "you don't tug on Super Man's cape; you don't spit in the wind; you don't look under the Lone Ranger's mask and you don't fuck with Martin McNeil." Oh man, you should have seen his face. He was red as a beat and pissed. I knew I was under his skin."

Richard shook his head. "Weren't you at all concerned that your bravado would come back to haunt you?"

Martin thought about that for a while. "Yeah, I guess it crossed my mind, but I wasn't too worried. In sports, people challenge you, and when they do, you take them down. Costanzo challenged me, the Stallions and the entire city of San Antonio and for his troubles he had to walk around in his drawers and take ribbing. I was just having fun with it, but I should have known better."

THE PICTURE ON THE front page of the next day's paper defined the exchange: Martin in full grin, laughing, staring down at Costanzo; the reporter scowling, looking up at the player, their right hands joined in a handshake, their left hands clutching the boxer shorts.

Standing on the capitol steps, David felt the swell of rage building inside him. Embarrassment, humiliation and anger all boiled together as a single bead of sweat raced down his nose. He would take care of this smart-aleck rookie when the time came. One day Martin would screw up, and David would pounce. *You want to hit a guy when he's down? Well you just wait. My time will come.*

He accepted the boxer shorts from Martin, waved them briefly in the air and then marched up the stairs into the capitol and out of sight.

THAT NIGHT, DAVID RECOUNTED the situation to Nettie. She listened to the story from start to finish, occasionally shaking her head at the odd detail.

"I've never felt so humiliated in my life," David concluded, pacing back and forth in the living room.

No one at the station knew of their secret relationship. No one in the newsroom would ever have guessed that David Costanzo would be the least bit attracted to Nettie Richardson. Costanzo wasn't handsome in the movie star sense, but he had an earthy manliness about him that was appealing to women. He'd never married, but he always had a girlfriend. Mostly ex-cheerleader types, divorced from their high school or college sweethearts. Women who had a kid or two running around and were starting to fray around the edges, but still holding it together. But since his arrival in San Antonio, it was Nettie who captured his attention. Nettie was a 39-year-old spinster. She was as simple, plain, dowdy woman. But there was something about her that was beautiful in its own way. David had once said the adjectives that describe a statue in the park applied to her: Magnificent, powerful and majestic but mostly unnoticed by the people who shuffled past. Nettie had a nice body under her demure clothing—thick farmer's breasts jutting from an otherwise trim frame—but no one but David knew that. Under a couple of layers of clothing, her substantial bosom just made her look fat.

On the surface, Nettie had the personality of a rock. She seemed impervious to life, never showing much of a reaction to anything. But David knew her looks were deceiving. Nettie was a woman of considerable depth.

It was pain that connected the two.

Nettie hadn't always had such an emotionless personality. She was never an outgoing, gregarious type, but she used to be much more friendly and engaging than she was now. She got along with people, she had a few boyfriends in high school and college, and she was married for three years to her college steady, Jack Richardson. That was years ago, before the weight of clear vision, quick comprehension and startling clarity of memory became an unwieldy burden in her life.

The expression "time heals all wounds" simply did not apply to Nettie. Healing was a function of forgetting. In the crowded confines of memory, loved ones fade into indistinct shapes, details of special experiences get lost over time, treasured possessions lose their luster. Time carried memories into the distance, creating space for peace to grow, but not for Nettie. She never forgot anything. Every slight, every bruised feeling, every unrealized dream haunted her. Life became a nightmare that never diminished in intensity. Nettie was 23 when her mother discovered a lump in her breast. It wasn't a big deal at the time. Just tiny hard spot—probably nothing. Her mother ignored it for months before finally going in to see the doctor just to be sure.

It was malignant. And it was the tip of the iceberg.

Nettie watched her mother struggle, suffer and die and every moment, every tear, every grimace, every anguished moan was still fresh in her memory. Watching her mother fade away dampened Nettie's spirit. She buried her mother on a Thursday. Nettie's husband left her six months later because he said he simply didn't recognize his wife any more.


WHEN COSTANZO MOVED TO San Antonio, he was immediately drawn to this dark pool of sadness that seeped out of Nettie. He was intoxicated by her pain, by her sadness. At the core of David, fueling the angry diatribes he spilled across the paper's pages, was a tight ball of pain that demanded attention. It pushed him forever forward, postponing his happiness until he reached some elusive destination. It was a maddening, fruitless labor. The effect of this journey made David more than just a cynic; David was frightened of life.

The only happiness he knew was his love for Nettie. She was physically and emotionally complicated; a woman whose imperfections were the root of her beauty. No one at the *Light* could imagine Costanzo being attracted to Nettie, because no one else could see her the way that he saw her.

"It's the old saw, David," she said of the situation with McNeil. Costanzo stopped pacing and faced her. When Nettie spoke, David listened.

"The pen is mightier than the sword," she said. "Especially from a distance."

THERE WAS A LOT of writing on the walls of the cell. It covered virtually every square inch of the space. Some words were written in ink, some in pencil, some in what looked like crayon. Others were carved into the concrete. Remnants of the bored inmates who had preceded them.

"Were you aware," said Richard from the corner, "that Johnny's mother swam the English Channel—under water?"

"Really?" Martin smiled. "Must have missed that in the news."

"Says it right here under the report that Rick's mother was on a street corner with a sign that said, 'will work for rap CDs.'"

The doctor, sighed, sliding down to the floor, stretching his legs out in front of him. "I was thinking about what you said yesterday about how the events that preceded your arrest were a three-legged stool. You've got your brother who has never shown you much allegiance as one leg, and the reporter, who became your arch enemy the moment you got drafted —"

"No, not right then. It wasn't until I busted his chops during the underwear walk that we became enemies."

"Ah yes, pride cometh before the fall."

"You got that right."

"So Costanzo is the second leg of the stool. That would make the man with the moniker 'Fixer' the third leg?

"The Fixer."

"Yes, Fixer."

"No, it's actually 'The Fixer' two words, like he's the only one."

PHILIP RAMEY WAS A product of inner-city Chicago; the second of four children—three boys and a girl—born to a woman addicted to any drug she could get into her body. The kids spent their early years huddled together in a bedroom listening to their mother moan loudly as she traded sex for heroine. As they got older, the children escaped their mother's addictions by spending more time on the streets. They never joined any of the gangs that proliferated the neighborhood, but by themselves they were a formidable force. They were tough kids; unfortunately the streets of Chicago were tougher. Philip was the only member of the family who survived. His mother died gracelessly in a dirty, see-through nightgown when he was 13; he didn't cry at her funeral. The Ramey children had no known relatives so they were remanded to separate foster homes and juvenile facilities in the city. They didn't last long in the state's care. Philip's sister was stabbed through the heart by a neighborhood rival when she was 17, and his two brothers were murdered in a drive-by shooting. In fact, it was only by miracle that Philip escaped Chicago alive. A pale scar down the right side of his face and neck was a jagged reminder of the day he nearly died.

Ramey had blind-sided a 16-year-old kid who called himself Crunch. The guy owed $130 to a neighborhood bookie, and Ramey was there to send a message. He rammed the boy violently against a brick wall, then drove a knee into his lower back. Crunch crumbled to the ground as if he'd been shot. Ramey reached down to grab the kid and turn him over. Suddenly, Crunch struck out with the remains of a beer bottle. He caught Ramey in the side of the neck, the jagged edge of the bottle sinking in with a sickening pop. Crunch was on his feet sprinting on pure adrenaline as Ramey collapsed to the ground. Blood spilled from his body with traitorous speed.

It was blind luck that the fight occurred less than two blocks from a hospital. Ramey stumbled into the emergency room and was rushed into surgery. At the rate he was losing blood, one block farther from the hospital, he'd have been dead.

After the surgery, the police asked for information about his assailant. Ramey answered their questions vaguely. Said he didn't really get a good look at the guy. Couldn't offer any description. The officers left in frustration. They couldn't help the victim if he didn't want to be helped. Ramey rested comfortably as a quiet assurance settled over him. Justice would be served.

Two weeks later, Crunch was dead in an alley.

That was when Ramey decided upon the name, "The Fixer." He'd been fixing situations for himself and for others most of his life. He was aggressive, ruthless and remorseless with a true talent for negotiating. At age 20, he started to move away from the drug dealers and pimps and pursued wealthier, more legitimate clients. Pro athletes were good fit for Ramey because they had money, they needed help negotiating and they liked Ramey. Most agents and attorneys count professional athletes on their client lists as badges of honor. They have framed pictures of the athletes in their offices. They brag about the relationships. They invite the athletes to golf with them, have dinner with their families, visit their kids' schools because the players are trophies to be collected and displayed. With The Fixer the situation was reversed. He had a ruthlessness and effec-

tiveness that drew athletes to him. The players took more pleasure in brag-
ging about him than he took in claiming them as clients. Ramey became a
bodyguard for Chicago Bears cornerback Jackson Baylor, moving into the
player's house and traveling with him. Baylor didn't have much need of a
bodyguard, but he liked having Ramey around. When Jackson was traded
to the San Antonio Stallions, The Fixer moved with him. It didn't take long
to set up shop in the new city. Within a couple of weeks The Fixer was
working deals for four or five guys on the team.

There were minor jobs. Picking up relatives from the airport, kids
from daycare or delivering urgent packages across town. There were jobs
of medium complexity like negotiating the price on a house or car, con-
tracting an attorney or a CPA, or finding beautiful women for his clients
who were looking for an evening of fun. Then there were the more complicated deals like negotiating terms with banks and leasing companies for
clients who were starting up businesses, collecting unpaid debts both professional and personal and serving as a private investigator for players who
needed information about a spouse, business partner or competitor. Ramey
was never intimidated by a lack of knowledge. He believed that people
were all the same, therefore all negotiations were the same.

None of his clients knew the full range of Ramey's services, but no
client could say that The Fixer had ever refused a job for any reason other
than money. There was never anything too small, too large, too serious or
too dangerous for Ramey to handle. His prices were steep, but his success
rate was unblemished. Ramey got results.

## MARTIN'S ROOKIE YEAR

WHEN MARTIN MCNEIL MET Ramey, The Fixer was angling for a job.

It was a scorching afternoon, heat pushing the mercury into triple
digits for the first time that summer. Clouds drifted on a whisper of a
breeze. Martin was standing the backyard of a house that belonged to San
Antonio Stallions free safety Steve Garnett. It was the safety's annual
Farewell-to-the-Off-Season Bash. With training camp scheduled to begin in
less than a month, more that 100 people were spread out in the backyard
eating and drinking. A third of them were children. It was a nice family
party.

"My mouth tastes like the underside of a circus elephant's tongue,"
Martin said, hoping for a laugh.

Brandon made a face. "Your breath *is* a little tart."

The smile slipped off Martin's face as quickly as it had come. In this
way they defined themselves. Martin was given to humorous self-depreca-
tion; Brandon was given to quick agreement.

"Nice house," Brandon said. An understatement. It was a 35-room Tudor mansion.

"Like something on that show *Lifestyles of the Rich and Famous*," Martin said.

Brandon nodded: "You'd probably never own a house like this." Turning even this into a failing.

Martin looked over at Brandon and wondered why things always got like this. His older brother criticizing and Martin taking it so personally. "I could own a house like this if I wanted," Martin said, trying not to sound defensive. He'd just signed a five-year, $33.2 million contract with the Stallions. He could buy anything he wanted.

"But you won't," Brandon insisted.

"I just don't see the need," Martin snapped. Calm down, he told himself. Don't let Brandon get under your skin..

Brandon laughed. "Man, you've got a lot to learn about being rich. Women like big houses and fast cars. You want to catch the ladies, you've got to put bait on your hook."

"Jessica doesn't care about all that stuff," Martin said.

"Yeah right," Brandon laughed. The mere mention of Martin's wife made Brandon salivate. He hadn't given up on Jessica, but so far his attempts to seduce her had failed. She hated him. Which was too bad, because nothing would have given Brandon more satisfaction than fucking his brother's wife. "Come on, little bro. There's someone I want you to meet."

They walked across Garnett's expansive lawn. Brandon smiling, waving and shaking hands like a politician running for office.

"How do you know all these people?" Martin said. Brandon seemed to be on a first name basis with the entire city.

Brandon shrugged. "I just mingle. Introduce myself."

They walked to the pool. There were kids in the water, their mothers hovering nearby. Brandon shook hands with Garnett and another guy built like a linebacker.

Brandon said: "Martin, this is Philip Ramey. He can help you."

Martin had his game face on, already anticipating that something was going down. "Who says I need help?"

"I hear you're planning to get a Ferrari," Ramey said quietly. Serious tone of voice. Eyes that didn't seem to blink.

Martin looked at Brandon who shrugged and said, "Sorry, I didn't think it was a secret."

"Yeah," Martin said. "I'm heading over to the dealership tomorrow."

"Listen fellas, I see a girl who desperately needs my attention," Brandon said. "Excuse me."

"Martin listen," Ramey said. "They call me The Fixer, cause —"

"The what?"

"The Fixer, cause what I do is fix things for people, make their lives easier. You ever need someone to do something, I'm the guy you can call. You talk to anyone on this team, and they'll tell you that I take care of business."

"I'll vouch for him," Garnett said nodding a little too earnestly.

Martin smiled looking the two men over, thinking this was a funny scene. "So we got The Fixer and The Voucher here, huh?" He could already tell Ramey was going try to try to sell him something. Probably something he didn't need.

"What type of Ferrari you want?" Ramey said.

What the hell, Martin thought. He'd play along. "F355 Spider."

"Nice car," Ramey said. "You sure they got one over there?"

"They've got two on the lot—red and silver. Martin smiled then rattled off the facts: "The one I want is silver, convertible, black interior, six-speed manual transmission, 375-horsepower V8 with a performance chip, chromed rims with super low profile Pirelli P Zero directional tires, tinted windows, phone, 12-disk CD cartridge and I'd like that to go please."

Ramey's tough pose broke as all three men erupted with laughter.

After a moment, Ramey said, "I guess you know exactly what you want. I'm almost afraid to ask if you have a price for all that."

Martin nodded. "I talked to a salesman on the phone last week. Told him what I wanted, and he said it would run in the neighborhood of a hundred and forty grand."

"You've never been to this dealership?"

"Nope."

"So they don't know what you look like?"

That stopped Martin. He could see where this was headed.

"Listen, Mr. Fix-it—"

"The Fixer," Garnett corrected.

"Thanks The Voucher," Martin said, making quotation marks with his fingers as he said it, with a condescending grin that infuriated the strong safety. "What are you his PR agent?"

"You better show me some respect, fucking rookie," Garnett said.

Martin kept smiling. "Way I understand it, you gotta ask for respect means you don't deserve it."

"I can't wait to catch you coming over the middle during training camp. I'm gonna put your little ass in the hospital."

"I'll look forward to it," Martin said, turning back to Ramey. "I appreciate what you're trying to do, but I think I can negotiate my own deal."

"You got an appointment tomorrow?" Ramey said.

"Yeah, at nine." Martin said, distracted, tired of this conversation with the self-proclaimed Fixer. Flies were buzzing around the table of food. Kids were screaming and splashing in the pool. Ramey had recovered his intensity, staring at Martin, calculating. Garnett was hovering as if he wanted to throw down right there in front of everybody.

Ramey laid his palms out. "Here's what we'll do. Tomorrow at nine, I'll go to the dealership, and pretend to be you. I'll negotiate the price of this car for you."

"Pretend to be me, huh?" Martin said with dead eyes. He knew how to handle a guy like The Fixer. He'd seen them all his life. If humor didn't work, you had to let them know they couldn't back you down. "Sounds like you're just pretending not to hear me. I don't need your help." He looked back at Garnett and said, "Hey 'The Voucher', you want to tell 'The Fixer' here that I don't need his help, or do I need to find 'The Explainer' for that?"

"You know who I am?" Garnett said.

"Sure, you're Steve Garnett, strong safety for the San Antonio Stallions, host of this party and 'The Voucher' for 'The Fixer'. But you ain't what I'm looking for. I want to know if you invited 'The Explainer' to this party because you and the plumber here seem dumber than a box of rocks."

"I'm a Pro Bowl strong safety," Garnett said, getting hot. "I've been in the league seven years, been voted into the Pro Bowl seven times. I've broken the jaws of four wide receivers, separated or dislocated eleven shoulders and have ended the careers of two players. I've earned my bones. You better show me some respect."

Martin looked at Ramey, hooking a thumb at Garnett, "You believe this guy? Giving me his resume. Got it all memorized like he makes that speech a lot." Turning back to Garnett he said, "You want to impress me, go get me a beer. We know you can break necks, let's see what kind of bottle opening skills you've got." Martin laughed. Garnett fumed. Ramey just stared, trying to intimidate.

Finally, The Fixer said, "You think you can negotiate this yourself, huh?"

"No doubt."

"Okay. Sticker price is a hundred and forty, what do you think you can get the car for."

Martin grinned. He was having a good time. "So this is a test of my negotiating skills, huh?"

Ramey smiled back. "Yeah, I like that. A little test just like in school."

Martin nodded. He had The Fixer pegged. "I'll bet you're a few credits shy of graduating from college aren't you? Got a little chip on your shoulder trying to prove how smart you are to everyone, huh?"

Ramey shrugged. "Quit school in tenth grade."

Martin nodded. "So this is a contest. See who's smarter, the college grad or the high school drop out."

"You could say that."

"Okay. So why don't we settle this with a different test. I choose the category. Winner wins, loser gets the fuck outta my face."

Ramey looked at Garnett and shook his head. "Is this guy for real?" Garnett shrugged and sipped his beer, still pissed, seriously thinking about taking Martin down right then. Ramey turned back to Martin and said, "Hey, I'm down for whatever."

"Your honest opinion, Ramey. Who do you think was a tougher

strong safety," Martin said, "Ronnie Lott or Steve Garnett?"

Ramey looked over at Steve, shrugged and said, "Sorry man, I gotta go with Ronnie Lott." Garnett looked hurt.

"Yeah, that's what I think too," Martin said. "Now there's a guy never had to ask anybody for respect." He took a long look at Garnett. "I'm still waiting for that beer."

"You can go fuck yourself!"

"All right!" Martin said clapping his hands. "Now that's the Steve Garnett on my wall. Big tough guy doesn't take nothing off nobody. I like that tone of voice. Keep it up man. I think I'm starting to respect you." Looking back at Ramey he said, "Tell you what. You're probably an expert on cars and girls and all sorts of manly stuff, but let's keep this academic. How well you know your state capitals?"

"I know a lot of things," Ramey said with a lopsided grin. "State capitals happens to be one of them."

Martin was beginning to like this guy. Tough, confident, sense of humor. "Alright then. Five states, my choice. You get them all right, we'll talk about my car. You miss one, I walk and you don't bother me with this "fixing" shit ever again."

Ramey laughed. "You college boys are all the same. Think you know everything and nobody else knows jack."

"We got a deal?"

"Deal."

"Capital of Washington?" Martin said.

"Olympia," Ramey said without hesitation. "What else you got college boy?"

"I'm impressed." Martin said. "Thought I might get you right off the top."

"I'm not that easy," Ramey said.

"How about Missouri?"

"Jefferson City."

"Vermont?"

"Montpelier."

"You're good," Martin said, meaning it. "Michigan?"

"Lansing."

"Oregon?"

"Salem." Ramey made a quick bow. Garnett clapped one hand against his beer.

"Very nice," Martin said, surprised.

"So you gonna answer my question now?" Ramey said.

"Did you ask a question?"

"Yeah, I said, "How low a price do you think you can get on this car?"

Martin sighed. "Well, I found out the dealer's cost on the car plus all the extras I want is about a hundred and twenty grand. I plan to negotiate up from that number rather than down from the sticker price. I can probably get the car for one-twenty-eight or so."

"Humph," Ramey said. His head down like he was calculating. "I'll go for you tomorrow and you'll pay me five grand to represent you."

The two men stared at each other. Finally Martin spoke: "Listen Ramey, I'm real impressed by your performance on the state capitals, but your math skills are looking a little suspect. There's only eight grand between one-twenty and one-twenty-eight, so if I've gotta pay you five grand, I don't see how I'm going to save much money."

"See that's a mistake college graduates make," Ramey said to Garnett who laughed too loudly. "They read Consumer Reports and think that's the price they have to work with. Me? I didn't even graduate from high school, so I'm not smart enough to figure out how much the dealer paid for the car. I just walk in and try to negotiate based on what I think the car is worth. In this case I think a hundred ought to be enough."

Martin shook his head. "That's less than they paid for the car."

Ramey stared at him for a moment. "You figure that out all by yourself?"

Martin had to smile. "Okay, you got me." He thought about it for a couple of seconds. "So you go negotiate for me then. Is your five grand included in the hundred thousand?"

"On top, but it's still a sweet deal. If I can't get the dealership down to an even hundred, then you don't owe me a penny, and you still get the car for no worse than what you're planning to pay already."

"Fair enough," Martin said. The two men shook hands.

"I'll call you when it's all done," Ramey said.

Martin nodded and took one last look at Garnett. "I guess I'll see you somewhere over the middle during training camp."

"Count on it."

#  SIX

JOHN CARRINGTON LED RAMEY back to his office after the test drive. The salesman was thirtyish with a college frat boy air about him. Carrington was wearing khaki slacks and a polo shirt with the Moulahan Mercedes logo on the right breast. His trademark smile was stretched a little bit wider than normal as they weaved through the showroom. He was going to sell a Ferrari. Life was good.

"You want something to drink?" Carrington asked Ramey.

"No thanks."

"So, was I lying to you?" Carrington said falling into his chair.

Ramey had introduced himself at Martin McNeil when he arrived at the dealership. Despite the fact that McNeil's face had been on TV and in all the newspapers, the people at the dealership really didn't know what he looked like. The Fixer was a big, black man with an athletic build. He called himself Martin McNeil and no one challenged it.

Carrington continued, still believing that he was talking to the Stallions' newest millionaire: "That car was made for a stud like you. You see the way people stared as you cruised down the street?" He shook his head. "Here's what I'm going to do." Carrington leaned forward across the desk and dropped his voice to a conspiratorial whisper. "My boss is a jerk who doesn't know much about sports but I know that having someone with your profile driving one of our cars is gonna be good for business. So I'm going to take three percent off the sticker price for you." He punched a few numbers into his calculator. "Instead of paying $142,800, you can drive out of here for only $139,000. How does that sound?"

Ramey was wearing an Armani suit. It hung loosely on him. He decided that silence was the cure for a talker like Carrington. Just drag it out see how much the guy could take.

"Hello? Earth to Martin," Carrington said, laughing a little bit, hoping to lighten things up. *How could it have gotten so tense in here all of a sudden? He's a football player for Pete's sake. Just throw some numbers at him and take his money.* "Listen, I'm gonna say we can go all the way down to $138,000, and if that's agreeable to you, I'll go ahead and start the paper work."

Still Ramey didn't speak. He was having fun sitting in the small office listening to the air conditioner hum, watching Carrington's gears turn as confusion mounted. After a while, Carrington figured it out. He shut his trap for a change. Decided he could play the silence game, too.

A full minute passed. Carrington ran out of patience. "Listen this is—"

Ramey cut him off. "I'll give you $120,000 for the car."

Carrington laughed, dragging it out for a few seconds, relieved to be talking again. "Come on, Martin, that's not even realistic. I mean, I wish we could sell you the car for one-twenty. Hell, if we could sell them that cheap, we'd have people lined up every day trying to buy this car," he laughed again, shaking his head.

"Martin, this is an expensive car. It's a *very* expensive car. You could buy a medium-sized house with the money you're spending on this car." He winked. "The truth is that if you're worried about how much you're spending, this car isn't for you. The Ferrari F355 is the for the ultra rich. It's for the strata of society that doesn't care about price tags. It's for people who can afford to buy a car that most people can only dream about. This car makes a statement about you, Martin. It tells the world—especially women, let's not forget the women you're going to pick up with this car (another wink)—that you're rich, successful and powerful. This car says there's something different about you."

Carrington paused for a breath, expecting his customer to speak. Ramey sat mutely, staring with dead eyes.

"Hey, if you're looking for a $120,000 car, I have some other models on the lot that we can talk about. They're nice cars. But based on what I know about you, I don't think you're looking for something else. I think you're looking for a Ferrari F355 Spider, and I'm prepared to give it to you for only $138,000. I'm giving you a damned good deal."

"Let me talk to your manager," Ramey said.

The salesman straightened a stack of papers in front of him. "Martin, you can talk to the manager if you want, but I promise you I'm giving you a great deal. Nothing is going to change by talking to the manager. There is just simply no way that we can sell you the car for less than $138,000. I mean, it's just simple economics. We'd lose money if we sold it for less than that."

"You gonna go get him or should I?"

Carrington's mouth formed a tight line. "I'll be right back."

He walked out of his cubicle and into a corner office. Frank Stinetti, was on the phone when Carrington entered. He was a heavyset man with an enormous belly and bushy eyebrows that danced comically with every expression. When Stinetti concluded the call, Carrington laid out the situation with Ramey. "The damned guy wants us to give the car to him as a gift.

I told him we couldn't go any lower than $138,000, but he just sat there, then he goes, 'I want it for $120,000. I said, 'No way," and then he said he wants to talk to you."

Stinetti's pinched eyebrows were thick caterpillars set to crawl down his nose. "Tell him I'm tied up at the moment, but I authorized you to go down to $136,000," he said. "If he still wants to talk to me, come back in a—"

The door opened and Ramey walked into the room.

"Martin, hey, I was just about to come get you," the salesman said about to stand up.

"Don't get up," Ramey said as he closed the door quietly. Carrington dropped back into his chair, smiling at this interruption. *An impatient customer is a good customer*. Ramey strode quickly across the room. He grabbed Carrington's left wrist and pressed the guy's hand against the desk. Ramey quickly snatched up a stapler, flipped it to the extended position and drove two staples into the back of the salesman's hand. When Carrington cried out in alarm, feeling the sudden rush of pain, Ramey dropped the weapon and clamped a hand over his mouth.

"Do not make a sound. If you're loud, I'll hit you over the head until you pass out." Tears were forming in Carrington's eyes. "Now, I'm gonna move my hand. You gonna be quiet?" Carrington nodded slowly, eyes wide. Ramey pulled his hand away from the man's mouth. Carrington held his bloody hand close to his body. Angry red holes marked the points at which the staples entered his hand. It was already swelling.

Stinetti sat behind his desk with his mouth open, eyebrows raised to his hairline.

Ramey leaned across the desk.

"I guess, he told you that you're going to sell me this car for $120,000."

"Yeah, he mentioned it," Stinetti said slowly.

"You were trying to take advantage of me, weren't you." It came out as a statement. Stinetti shaking his head, wide eyed, denying it. Ramey nodding knowingly saying: "The price just went down to $110,000."

The sales manager took a long look at Ramey looming over him, trying to figure out where to go with this. Finally he said, "have a seat, let's work this out."

Ramey's fist flew out sharply, his fingers unfurling just below the sales manager's chin striking him in the Adam's apple.

Stinetti lurched forward with a gasp, the blow catching completely by surprise stealing his breath.

"Don't tell me what to do," Ramey said, easing into a leather arm chair. He waited patiently while Stinetti hacked and coughed. Finally, the sales manager looked up and said, "You're not Martin McNeil are you?"

Very good. Stinetti was a thinker. Putting things together. Ramey liked that. He could deal with a guy like that. "I'm his representative."

Stinetti nodded. "You walk into my office and put holes in my salesman's hand. Hit me in the throat. You think that was necessary?"

Ramey shrugged, "I needed to get your attention."

"You've got it."

"So what can we do on this car?"

"John tells me you wanted the car for $120,000, now you're saying you want it for $110,000," Stinetti said, picked up his cigarette and pulled on it, regaining his composure. He watched Ramey carefully.

"Actually, the number I'm looking for is an even hundred thousand."

"Wait a second," Stinetti said carefully. "This number just keeps drifting down."

"Yeah, well now it's a hundred, what are you gonna do?"

Stinetti considered this, trying to figure a way to deal with this guy. Ramey waited him out.

"How much you getting paid to negotiate for Mr. McNeil?"

Ramey shrugged. It didn't matter. "Five grand."

"That's a lot of money for beating up a couple of lowly car guys."

"It ain't bad work if you can get it."

"You negotiate for a lot of people?"

"A few," Ramey said.

Stinetti looked over at Carrington still holding his injured hand. "Listen John, why don't you take the rest of the day off, go over to the hospital and get those staples pulled out before you swell up too much."

Carrington rose slowly, carving a wide path around Ramey as he walked toward the door. "And don't say anything to anyone about how that happened," Stinetti said. "Make something up. I don't think you want to do anything that would get this gentleman in trouble. It might come back to haunt you."

Carrington nodded numbly and crept out of the office.

"You really didn't need to get physical," Stinetti said. "All you needed to do was come talk to me. I can see by looking at you that you're a serious player." He paused to exhale a plume of smoke, feeling back on top of things. "If I give you a deal on this car, can you bring me more customers in the $75,000-plus price range?"

Ramey smiled. Now they were getting to it. "I can probably get you five, six guys looking for high-end Mercedes, Porsches and Ferraris this year."

"They all football players?"

"Basketball and baseball, too."

Stinetti thought for a moment. "Here's what I'll do. I'll give you the car for Martin for $100,000 provided he signs a contract to do a radio commercial, a television commercial and a two-hour autographing appearance for us on a Saturday. Next time you come in here negotiating for another player, I'll expect the same arrangement. He gets a break on the price as long as he endorses the dealership."

"Sounds very reasonable," Ramey said. "Except Martin's not doing any autograph sessions or commercials. We can hook that up for the other guys, but it ain't part of this deal."

"You're not giving me much to work with here," Stinetti said. "You come marching in here telling me I've gotta take a big hit on an F355 but you're not going to do anything for me in return. What's in it for me?"

"You're health." Ramey laid it out there to see how the guy would take it.

Stinetti's heart skittered. "Wait a second. I thought—"

Ramey eased him off the hook. "Don't worry about it, you'll make up the money on future deals. I negotiate about 10 cars a year, and usually I take my business to Randolph's across town, but from here on out, you're my man. It's steady, strong business."

Stinetti thought about it for a moment. "These other guys will all do commercials?"

"No problem at all."

"How much are you cutting me in for?"

"What do you need?"

"I need five grand just like you. We're taking enough off the car for you to keep five, I can keep five and your client still gets a hell of a deal. On all future sales, I'll expect the same. Of course, no one else gets this deal. Next time I can go two percent below wholesale, but you've gotta bring me fifty $100-bills for each deal."

"Stinetti's Italian isn't it?" Ramey said.

"Sure is."

"Yeah, I've always liked Italians. I respect 'em, 'cause they're ruthless. All those Mafia Dons ordering people killed and shit. You in the Mafia?"

Stinetti shook his head.

"Mr. Stinetti, you ever been hit square in the mouth with a crescent wrench?"

"Whoa, wait a second. I thought we were just talking here."

"See I don't go for all this sitting around while some Italian muthafucka tells me what the deal's gonna be," Ramey stood up. "You gonna sit there blowing smoke in my face, telling me that I gotta pay you five grand every time I want to buy a car? I think I feel like knocking a couple of teeth out of your mouth." Ramey reached into his coat pocket and pulled out a crescent wrench.

Stinetti couldn't believe it. "You carry a wrench with you?"

"Wherever I go," Ramey said, hefting it a couple of times. "It promotes tooth decay."

Stinetti tried to slide backward in his chair, but it was already against the credenza. There was nowhere to move. He raised his hands up to guard his mouth. "I'd settle for twenty-five hundred," he said.

"Come on, put your hands down. Tough Italian guy like you, I can't believe you're even worried about one little shot in the chops."

Stinetti didn't move his hands.

"Count of three," Ramey said. "You lower you hands or I just start swinging hard, break a few fingers and maybe crack your skull before I get to those teeth. And once I get there, I ain't stopping until they're all out. Or you can put your hands down, and I'll do my best to just take one tooth. You're choice; the easy way or the hard way." He paused for a moment, then started to count: "One muthafuckin. . .two muthafuckin—"

Stinetti said weakly, "how about a grand?"

Ramey stopped counting. "Did you say a thousand dollars?"

"Yeah. Thousand dollars a car. I can live with that."

Ramey slowly tucked the wrench back into his coat pocket and sat down. "I knew the minute I walked in here you were a reasonable man."

WHEN BRANDON AND MARTIN arrived at the dealership that afternoon, the younger McNeil was stunned. The price on the contract was exactly $100,000. The car had been washed, a phone had been installed, and Martin had an appointment the next week to get the windows tinted and the performance chip added.

"This is incredible," he said to Brandon. "I can't believe Ramey actually got them down to a hundred grand."

Brandon shrugged. "I told you the guy was good."

Stinetti kept looking at the brothers, sitting in his office, drinking sodas while the documents were processed. The sales manager was trying to get a feel for the player. Figure out who was running whom. Did Ramey follow direct orders from the player, or did the negotiator operate on his own? Looking at Martin, sitting there without a worry on his face, just happy with the deal, Stinetti couldn't decide. But the sales manager was pissed about the thousand dollars he'd accepted. *Why should I get stuck with just a grand, when I'm giving these guys thirty-five, forty grand off the sticker price?*

Finally, he said, "I lost an employee today because of that maniac of yours."

Martin was surprised by the sudden edge in the man's voice. "Excuse me?"

"You tell all your friends, if they ever need a deal on a car, just walk in here and talk to me, we can work something out. But don't send that guy in here, cause I can't afford the loss. I got a salesman with a punctured hand and a busted mind who's not going to be able to sell cars for me because he's not going to have the confidence he used to have. I can't afford to lose a salesman every time someone wants a car."

"A punctured hand and a busted mind?"

"That's right! Damned guy walked in here, bam bam, two staples in the back of the hand. Had to send the salesman to the hospital. Talked to him about an hour ago, he's traumatized. He's never seen anything like it. I doubt he'll be able to negotiate tough on cars again. Always be afraid that the guy sitting across from him just came from an office supply store."

Martin noticed the bruise on the sales manager's neck and knew Stinetti didn't have it when he left the house that morning.

"Look, Mr. Stinetti, I can appreciate your concerns, and I apologize if Ramey came in here and got rough with somebody, but you'd probably better talk to him about that. This was a one-time deal between him and me. I don't even know the guy that well."

"Well, it cost me a salesman," Stinetti said angrily. "You're driving out of here with a car for a hundred grand, and I'm down a salesman."

Martin shrugged. "What do you want me to do about it?"

Stinetti gave him a hard stare, thinking this might work out. "Four grand would help."

"Four grand for what?"

"You're putting me in the hole here. I'm losing money on this car, and I'm losing out on a salesman. You pay me four grand cash on top of the hundred and at least I can break even on the car."

"Cash, huh?"

"Yeah cash."

"Sort of a little servicing fee. You lose some of the owner's money on the car, but put some in your pocket."

"Something like that. Hey, you're still get a good deal, but it helps me out. Cuts me in on it."

Martin nodded. "Mr. Stinetti?"

"Yeah?"

"You can go fuck yourself."

MARTIN AND BRANDON LEFT the dealership in separate cars; the younger brother driving to a small park near his apartment complex. Ramey was waiting, sitting on a bench wearing shades and a baseball cap.

"What happened to the salesman's hand?" Martin said.

"Is it missing?" Ramey said.

"And Stinetti's throat? I didn't expect you to rough anyone up."

"Oh yeah? Just what were you expecting?" Ramey said.

Martin shrugged. He hadn't really thought about how the deal would go down. "I should have had you figured from the start. I should have known you'd walk in there and do something like that. Staples in a guy's hand? What were you thinking? This was a simple car deal for Pete's sake."

"You happy with the deal?" Ramey said.

"The deal, yes, the means no." Martin pulled a roll of hundred dollar bills out of his pocket. "Next time you do some work for me, I'll expect you to show some restraint.

Ramey smiled. "Tell you what, super star. You need me again, you tell me what you want, I'll tell you the fee, then you'll get your stupid little ass out of the way and let me handle it any way I want to. How's that sound?"

They stared at each other for a long moment, before Martin returned to his car.

He had no intention of hiring The Fixer ever again.

# SEVEN

## MARTIN'S ROOKIE YEAR

JANET AND MATTHEW FIELDS were among those cheering for Martin McNeil at training camp his rookie year. It was the date of the Stallions first intra-squad scrimmage, and it was the day Matthew hoped that his dream would come true. He had a black marker in one hand and the torn, battered Florida State baseball cap in the other hand. He'd heard from kids at school that NFL training camp was the best place to seek autographs. The players were stuck on a university campus with a predictable schedule. Practices twice a day, and meals, meetings and treatment in locations that forced the players to walk through the crowd. An ambitious kid could get an autograph from nearly every player in less than a week if he worked hard.

Matthew had pleaded with his mother for more than a month about driving out to the Stallions training camp. It was summer, he argued. They both were free from school, the weather would be nice, and they'd have fun. Eventually, Janet gave in because they hadn't done anything truly fun since Richard left two years ago. Janet still found it hard to believe her husband had just picked up and disappeared. It was two months before he even called to say hello, and he'd seen Matthew only once in the past two years. Janet was still trying to figure out how a man could disconnect himself from his wife and child so effortlessly.

Mother and son left Florida early Saturday, traveling through blistering heat across the south, spending a couple of nights in small motels, reaching Austin, Texas at about 7 p.m. Monday They had dinner at a Kentucky Fried Chicken restaurant before settling into a Best Western motel just off Interstate 35.

In the morning they reached the University of Texas at 6:30, hoping to catch McNeil on his way to the cafeteria for breakfast. Matthew had found the Stallions training camp schedule on the Internet.

| | |
|---|---|
| *6:45 - 8 a.m.* | *Breakfast* |
| *7 - 9 a.m.* | *Treatment for injuries, taping.* |
| *9 - 11 a.m.* | *Morning practice* |
| *11:15 - 1 p.m.* | *Lunch* |
| *1 - 2:30 p.m.* | *Treatment and taping* |
| *2:30 - 4:30 p.m.* | *Practice* |
| *5 - 6:45 p.m.* | *Dinner* |
| *7 - 9:30 p.m.* | *Meetings* |
| *11 p.m.* | *Curfew* |

Kids with training camp experience had told him to arrive early, pick a good location, and be aggressive. When Matthew and his mother reached the dormitory early that morning, they were both shocked to discover the number of fans already camped outside the main entrance. Matthew was dejected by the competition.

His mother said, "remember how many people were at that golf tournament? You still got his hat. This is nothing compared to that."

Matthew sighed in agreement. He'd gotten lucky once. Could he get lucky again?

At precisely 7:26 a.m.—Matthew looked at his watch to remember the moment—Martin walked out the front door and offered a cheerful wave to the people who were waiting.

Immediately, the screaming began.

"Mr. McNeil, can I get your autograph?"

"Martin will you sign?"

"Martin, over here."

"Please Mr. McNeil."

The requests came from every direction. McNeil started signing autographs, never really slowing down as he made his way to the cafeteria. Each time he finished signing his name, the crowd erupted again trying to catch his attention. It reminded Janet of a presidential press conference, when reporters all scream, "Mr. President!" whenever the chief finishes a question.

Matthew fought to get close to Martin, but couldn't muscle his way through the crowd. Martin signed his final autograph and walked into the cafeteria.

The crowd groaned and several pleas for "one more" were ignored.

Matthew found himself similarly stymied every time he tried to get McNeil's autograph that day—the crowd was simply too large, the competition too fierce. His mother had tried everything she could think of to give her son a chance. She had bullied their way through the throng. She'd discreetly nudged small children out of the way. Late in the day, she'd even faked a sprained ankle in McNeil's path, hoping that he'd be forced to slow down. But the crowd simply parted around her and Martin never wavered.

Embarrassed to admit to her son that she had faked the injury, Janet spent the remainder of the day hanging back from the crush, pretending to nurse the ankle. But it was during this false convalescence that she saw the solution.

When Matthew and his mother returned to their motel room, the boy sat the hat atop the dark brown dresser then plopped face down on the bed. For 10 seconds, he kicked his feet, pounded his fists and screamed into the comforter.

"Feel better?" his mother asked.

"No," Matthew said, sitting up. "I've got to get his autograph tomorrow."

"You will," she said, the confidence in her voice startling Matthew. He looked at his mother and smiled. "You will," she repeated.

THE NEXT MORNING MATTHEW and his mother reached the campus at six, but still there was a crowd of about 30 people already camped on the sidewalk outside the dormitory.

"Don't these people ever go home?" Janet said, exasperated her optimism dissipating. She was determined to help her son get an autograph and she resented all the competition she faced to accomplish something that should have been fairly simple. *At least I've got a plan.*

She whispered her idea to Matthew. "Yesterday when I was watching everything, I noticed that everyone jumps on Martin right when he comes through the door, and then they sort of escort him all the way to the cafeteria. But they stop before they actually get to the cafeteria door. So if you were standing right in front of that door to begin with, I don't see how Martin could avoid you."

Matthew thought it was a great idea.

Players began to straggle out of the dorm at 6:30 a.m., and as each man departed, a few fans broke away from the main group to accompany him to the cafeteria. But most of the crowd stayed put waiting for the big-name players to depart. Matthew had no interest in anyone except Martin McNeil, so he and his mother simply sat to one side of the cafeteria door and waited. Finally, they heard the mob erupt into a cacophony of requests. Everyone seemed to be moving toward them. Matthew jumped into position, uncapped his pen, got the hat ready and waited in front of the door. As the crowd grew nearer, Matthew could see McNeil moving toward him and silently thanked his mother for putting him in perfect position.

"Move it kid," a security guard poked his head out of the cafeteria door.

Matthew whirled around to face the voice.

"Get out of the way. You can't block this door."

"Please sir, I just want to get Martin McNeil's autograph, then I'll move."

"No, you'll move right now. You can't block this door. The players have to be able to get in and out right here, so move," the guard had come outside and had Matthew by the arm. He moved the boy easily off to the side.

Janet intervened: "Sir, we've come all the way from Florida"

"Lady, I don't care if you're from Timbuktu. Everybody's from somewhere, and nobody can stand in front of this door."

Moments later, Martin reached the door, signed his last autograph, and walked into the cafeteria never noticing Matthew and his mother.

THAT AFTERNOON THE STALLIONS first intra-squad scrimmage was scheduled. Martin gazed up at the sun, pulling in a deep breath of humid Texas air. On the other side of the field, sitting along a gently sloping hill were more than 4,000 Stallions fans waiting to see the progress the team was making during training camp. In a few minutes the full-contact scrimmage would begin, pitting the starting offense against the starting defense. This was the moment of Martin's dreams. His first chance to perform in the NFL; his first chance to test himself against the highest level of competition; his first opportunity to shine.

He was nervous.

Although he'd always proven himself capable when confronted with new challenges, Martin had never been in a situation where expectations were quite this high. Everyone was watching him. Everyone expected greatness. He was hailed as the savior of the Stallions, the man who would lead them to the Super Bowl, but he had yet to run a single play in an NFL game. He'd been through two-a-day practices for the past couple of weeks, and was getting a grip on the offense, but he wasn't there yet.

Martin sighed, surveying the crowd sitting on lawn chairs and blankets on the other side of the field. Before practice the fans had been lined up on either side of a path that led from the locker room to the field. They were mostly clad in Stallions black and purple, brandishing pens, markers, paper, pennants, jerseys and footballs with their hands outstretched calling to the players like barkers at a roadside carnival. Martin had dealt with autograph seekers ever since high school, but he was still surprised by the passion of NFL fans. They arrived early in the morning, and stayed late into night. Just hanging out for hours hoping to get a signature from their favorite players. There were no guarantees and no possibility that the players could keep pace with all the requests, but it didn't stop the fans from coming out. Martin smiled for a moment thinking about the kid he'd seen on his way out to the field.

Somehow in all the voices screaming to him as he walked through the corridor of fans, Martin heard a young voice. He looked right at a sandy-headed boy and said, "That's my hat?"

The screaming stopped abruptly as the crowd strained to hear what Martin was saying.

"Yes," Matthew said in a rush. "This is the hat you threw in the air when you were in Chattahoochee two years ago. Me and my mom came all the way here from Florida just to get your autograph. Will you sign it please?"

Martin, who'd never really stopped moving, smiled and said, "You know I almost went to jail over that hat. That danged sheriff wanted to get me."

"Could you sign it please?" Matthew pleaded.

"Listen, I've got to go to work right now, but I'll sign it for you after practice."

"Promise?"

"I promise."

"Okay, I'll be right here."

And Martin figured the kid would be right there when practice ended. Probably wouldn't move over to watch the scrimmage with the rest of the fans for fear of losing his spot. Martin decided that he'd invite the kid into the locker room, sign his hat, give him some stuff, let him meet some of the other guys. If the kid had come all the way from Florida, then he deserved to get the full treatment.

Martin's stomach grumbling nervously as his thoughts about the boy with the hat were replaced by concerns about the scrimmage. He closed his eyes and focused. *You can do this. Just concentrate and play football.* He'd felt this way in high school the day of his first game on varsity. He lied to his high school coach saying "it's probably just something I ate," when the coach asked him what was wrong. But it wasn't food poisoning, it was just his nerves acting up. There was no doubt that Martin had great ability. He knew it, and everyone who had ever seen him play knew it. But deep inside, Martin harbored a nugget of doubt. A fear that he might step up to the next level and find that his skills were not adequate for the task. He was the first freshman in this history of Stonegate High School to start on the varsity team. The older boys looked at him quietly in the locker room just before his first game, some envious of the opportunity he was getting, others angry that such a young kid had been promoted to their elite status. But no one taunted him that first week. No one teased him or challenged him. They were waiting to see how he'd do—trying to decide if he was the real deal. That Friday night with the lights on and his parents watching, Martin caught 12 passes for 186 yards and scored three touchdowns. He was a super star even then. Faster than anyone on the field, with great vision and the ability to adjust to every ball thrown his way.

Early in the first quarter, Martin chased down a pass that at first blush seemed to be grossly overthrown. But Martin delivered a burst of acceleration, pulled away from the cornerback running next to him, hauled in the ball and raced across the goal line for his first varsity touchdown. In the second quarter, Martin made a big-league adjustment to an underthrown pass, decelerating on the sideline, fighting off the hands of the cornerback, his back arching steeply as his eyes tracked the ball straight over his head and into his outstretched hands, carrying him out of bounds. It was a ball that most pro receivers would have had a tough time bringing in, but Martin made the catch look easy. On another play, Martin got mauled by a linebacker as he came across the middle; the defender grabbed McNeil by the face mask and twisted him so his back to the line of scrimmage. Two officials immediately reached for their flags, but before the penalty markers hit the ground, Martin had snatched the ball with one hand, actually pressing it against the linebacker's back before dragging it into his own body and collapsing to the ground.

That game Martin ran into double coverage, but still got open. He was hit by safeties but still caught the ball. He was pounded by linebackers, but still got up. He carried a reverse 63 yards for a touchdown. Martin made so many tacklers miss that night, he looked like a father dodging his kids on the front lawn. When the clock finally expired, his coach was awestruck; McNeil was the type of player the coach would talk about for decades. Martin's teammates couldn't get enough of him; the other students and parents loved him, and his own parents were beaming with pride. Word quickly traveled to college scouts who showed up for games that year getting a taste of the man this 14-year-old boy would become.

His first season at Florida State University was the same way. He'd had a phenomenal high school career. A consensus all-American for four seasons, he was offered full scholarships at 73 Division I schools and was heralded as the Texas High School Athlete of the Decade. But despite all that, Martin still was nervous about how he'd do at Florida State. It didn't take him long to prove himself. By mid-season of his freshman year in college, there was no one left to argue the point:  Martin McNeil was the real deal.

But now, in the NFL, Martin was unsure once again. He had confidence in his ability, but he didn't know how he'd do on this level. The players were bigger, faster, stronger and better than he'd ever faced. And the game was more complex; there were more plays, more formations, more defenses, more adjustments, and all of this would happen faster than ever before.

Plus there was Steve Garnett, the free safety who'd been waiting for an opportunity to get back at Martin for insulting him at a barbecue weeks earlier. Garnett walked over leading a group of defensive backs. Martin saw Garnett approaching and decided to strike first.

"Hey it's The Voucher," he said loudly, trying to sound more confident than he felt. "How's the vouchin" business going for you?"

Garnett stared hard. "I told you I'd be coming for your ass, so time's up muthafucka. You come over the middle today it's open season on smart-ass rookies."

Martin smiled, "you know it's been a while since you recited your resume to me. All the guys you've hurt. What was it, six broken bones, seven concussions, three people bored into the hospital by your constant yapping."

Garnett shook his head. "Go ahead young rook. Get the talking part done. Once this scrimmage starts, ain't gonna be no more talking. Everything 10 yards off the ball and between the numbers is mine. I own that land. You come into my territory, I'll run through your monkey ass, then we'll see if you got any more jokes."

"I guess I'll see you then."

Garnett laughed. "If you're lucky you'll see me. But chances are you ain't gonna see shit "til they wake your ass up in the hospital."

MARTIN WAS BENT OVER in the huddle, hands on his knees, purple practice jersey cut off at mid-abdomen and chin-strap dangling from his helmet. Directly across from him was quarterback Jeff Burdett. Like most receivers and defensive backs in the NFL, Martin wasn't wearing thigh, knee or hip pads because they restricted his movement and slowed him down. Speed was his friend; anything that slowed him down was his enemy.

Burdett called the play: "Gray right slot three jet quick double cross. On one. Ready?"

"Break!" 11 voices said.

Martin jogged into position on the outside edge of the numbers on the right side of the field. He was thinking about his assignment. *Quick double cross; I run a corner versus three deep coverage, a post versus two deep and a comeback versus man.*

He got into his stance and looked across the line at Dante Thompson, a cornerback in bump coverage.

"You ain't gonna catch shit today, Martin," Dante said. "But don't get mad about it 'cause it ain't personal. It's never personal, homeboy. Always business." He was squatting in front of Martin, hands in front of his chest, palms out, ready to strike the receiver as he came off the line. "Shit, I don't even know why you're out here. I'm gonna cover you like a Salvation Army picnic blanket on every Jack-ass route you run. You ain't even gonna get off the line. Once I get my hands on you, it's all over, ladies and gentlemen. Might as well call your mom, tell her you gonna be late for dinner, cause after I put that fork lift on you, you're through."

Thompson was a ninth-year corner who never shut up. He talked his way through every play of every practice and every game. It didn't matter that most of his opponents never spoke back. In fact, Dante preferred quiet receivers because he didn't have to talk over their voices. He had the stage to himself.

Martin pushed Thompson's chatter out of his head and concentrated on his assignment. *If Dante jams me at the line with inside-out leverage then he's probably in press man coverage. Outside-in leverage is two-deep zone. He's definitely protecting against an inside release, so this has to be man, versus man, I run a 20-yard comeback. Beat him off the line, accelerate, turn to look over my inside shoulder at 15 yards, make it look like a go route and let Dante catch up. Then plant at 20 and burst hard for the sideline. He'll never know what hit him.*

Martin was in his zone. While one part of his mind was listening to the quarterback's cadence, another was visualizing the technique he would use to beat his opponent. Once the play began, his route would be a combination of the technique he visualized and his reactions to the defender.

At the snap, Dante lunged forward with straight arms. He was a strong defensive back who had a knack for getting his hands on receivers and knocking them off balance or completely off their feet at the line of scrimmage. Martin knew Dante's strength, and he knew how to use it against him. The receiver took a hard step to the left, then moved quickly back to the right. Just as Dante's hands connected with Martin's torso, McNeil swung his right hand across his body as hard as he could, hitting Dante's elbow, pushing the cornerback's arm away like a karate student deflecting a blow. Martin pinwheeled his left arm up and over Dante's body and then escaped from the line of scrimmage having executed a textbook swat-and-swim move. As he raced down the field, Martin could feel Dante behind him, hustling to catch up after being beaten off the line.

At 15 yards Martin looked over his inside shoulder but didn't see Dante. He figured the defender was either trailing directly behind or running slightly outside. Martin sold the route for as long as he could. At 20 yards exactly, he planted hard, turned and was prepared to beat Dante again to get to the sideline, but the cornerback wasn't there. Confused, Martin finished his route as Burdett dumped the ball off to a running back.

"McNeil! What the hell are you doing?" Coach Starnes voice boomed across the field. "I mean, Jesus H. Christ, we've only run this play a thousand times."

Martin jogged back to the huddle, "I thought I was supposed to run a comeback against man coverage," he said.

"Well, I'm glad you know your assignment," the coach said. "Now if you could read a defense we'd be getting somewhere. You know the difference between *man* and *zone* ?"

"That was *zone*?" Martin turned to look back over his shoulder as if the defensive players were chess pieces still sitting in their final positions.

"Yes, *that was zone*," Coach Starnes said mimicking Martin's voice. "Cover two. What are you supposed to run against cover two?"

"A post."

"And what did you run?"

"A comeback."

"A comeback. So while Burdett's sitting back here reading two deep and waiting for you to break to the post, you're running down the field all by your lonesome trying to shake the shit out of man coverage that ain't there."

"My bad."

"You're damned right it's your bad. Get your head out of your ass, Martin."

Coach Starnes knew Martin was just a rookie struggling under the weight of the playbook and the speed of the defenses, but he couldn't go easy on the kid. Starnes was impressed by Martin's release off the ball. Dante Thompson was a formidable corner, and Martin had beaten him off the line with ease. Watching that release, a spectator might guess that McNeil was the veteran and Thompson the rookie. But while Martin had won that battle, Dante had won the war; he'd tricked the rookie into running the wrong route, which was as good as covering the guy. If the quarterback and the receiver were getting different reads, they weren't likely to connect on a pass. McNeil had to be ready for the first game of the season, so Starnes had to push him to make the right read no matter how hard the defense tried to fool him.

Embarrassed, Martin jogged back to the huddle.

"My bad," Martin said to Burdett.

"No sweat," the quarterback said, calling the next play.

Martin jogged out to his position and Dante moved up to cover him.

"Yeah, kid!" Dante laughed. "Got you with that old okie-doke move. Played you like it was bump man, ran with you then fell off into two-deep. Gotta watch out for me, Marty. I got more moves than a hundred-dollar hooker."

As he talked, Dante made note of Martin's alignment on the inside edge of the numbers, thinking this was a rookie mistake. Dante figured Martin was probably running an out route. Lined up a little tighter than usual to give himself some room outside after he made the break.

Dante smiled and said, "Candy from a baby Martin. Remember that phrase when you see me dancing down the sideline with an interception. Getting a pick on you is like taking candy from a baby. And believe me, I ain't never liked babies."

Thompson decided he'd hit Martin with his Rambo jam. Ordinarily Thompson played his bump technique like a basketball defender, just getting in the way of the receiver as he tried to leave the line of scrimmage. Shuffle to the right or the left as the guy departed and simply stop his momentum. But every now and then, Thompson liked to launch himself across the line of scrimmage at the snap, catch the receiver off guard and take the guy off his feet. He called it Rambo. It was a dangerous move, but Dante had been doing it for years, and he knew how to play it. Aggressive, but under control.

He'd attack Martin's inside number. If the receiver happened to be trying to make an inside release, Dante would end up in the middle of his chest and would drive Martin five yards back. If the receiver was trying to make an outside release, Dante would grab his shoulder pad and use the receiver's momentum to pull his body around into stride. Either way, he had nothing to lose, everything to gain.

At the snap, Dante was across the ball, driving his right hand into Martin's inside number. Martin knew it was coming. He'd seen the rigidity in Thompson's body. He knew the defender was tensed to lunge across the line. Knew exactly what he'd do if the defensive back came hard. As Dante's hand connected with Martin's inside number, the receiver started to spin. Letting his left shoulder fall backward, his head whipping around taking his body with it, turning 360 degrees in a split second. Dante never made solid contact, and Martin was around him racing up the field.

Thompson couldn't believe it. He'd gambled and the rookie had beaten him with the only thing that could beat the Rambo jam—a spin move. Dante was racing to catch up. He was a step behind McNeil still considering Martin's tight alignment and guessing that the receiver would break outside.

But Dante was wrong. Martin wasn't running an out-route. He was running a crossing route at 15 yards. If the coverage was zone, he'd sit in the hole between the linebackers, if it was man, he'd outrun Thompson across the field. This time it really *was* man coverage, so Martin slowed a step to let Thompson catch up.

Dante was on Martin's inside shoulder waiting for that tell-tale body movement that would tell him the receiver was about to make a break. Dante was a master at reading body language. The moment a receiver's posture, stride or head movement changed, he'd start to make his break. He'd had nine interceptions the previous year, mostly because receivers always gave away their routes.

Martin could feel the cornerback on his inside keeping pace with him. At 12 yards, Martin dropped his hips and leaned slightly to the outside. Dante was ready, he stuttered his feet and leaned, too. He could feel the out route coming. He was going to break under it, pick it off and then dance down the sideline with a flamboyant high step.

With a grunt, Martin planted his inside foot, driving to the outside, took two steps then planted his outside foot stopping himself at 15 yards, swiveling hard to the inside.

Dante reacted to that first plant, making his move to the outside. When Martin turned back inside, the cornerback was off-balance and couldn't adjust. He tried to grab McNeil—better to get a holding call than get beaten—but Martin dipped and pulled away from him. Dante slipped to the ground, dismayed, but smiled when he saw the cavalry.

Steve Garnett was closing.

Martin came out of his break and found the ball in the air. It was a perfect strike; a tight brown spiral that zipped on a line to a point just off his right shoulder. He stretched out, snatched the ball, and braced for Garnett's arrival. The safety was coming full speed, launching himself just as McNeil reached up for the ball. The safety had to make a decision as he approached. He could go for the big hit or he could make a "sure" tackle. Garnett was a Pro Bowl safety, so even his sure tackles hurt, but this time, he was coming to deliver a message. He wanted to launch Martin McNeil's body five yards in the air and then stand over the rookie while the kid tried to catch his breath. *Here we go smart-ass muthafucka!* Garnett was airborne just as Martin pulled the ball down. Martin felt the safety coming.

After all the trash talking he'd done, he knew the hit was coming to come high and hard. In fact, he was counting on it. As soon as Martin's feet touched the ground, he planted them firmly and let his upper body go limp. When Garnett hit him, Martin bent at the waist, moving with the blow. The safety was expecting more resistance, and he couldn't react quickly enough as he flew over Martin. At the last moment, he tried to grab the receiver's shoulder pads, but it was too late. Martin was racing down the field, out-running Dante and the rest of the defense enroute to a 70-yard touchdown on just his second play in an NFL scrimmage. The crowd was on its feet cheering wildly.

Even Coach Starnes couldn't help smiling for a moment before he leveled a tirade at Thompson and Garnett for letting a rookie beat them.

That day Martin McNeil confirmed it once and for all: He was the real deal.

# EIGHT

NETTIE RICHARDSON WAS SO surprised by the phone call she actually smiled. Her mouth hadn't broken into a genuine, sustained smile in years. She listened intently to the voice on the phone; a mother telling the story, a boy's voice adding detail in the background. This was it. This was just the tale David needed to hear.

She jotted down a phone number and fired off a message to Costanzo through the newspaper's computer system.

It read: *Meil's comeuppance has arrived.*

The note was sent in the simple code David and Nettie had created to keep his leads secret. Celebrity names were condensed to the first letter of the first name and the last three letters of the last name. Thus Martin McNeil became "Meil". It wasn't an unbreakable code, but the effort was necessary in the competitive news industry.

When Costanzo read the note he smiled too. And when Nettie told him the story, he laughed for five minutes. David immediately called to set up interviews with the boy and his mother; then the reporter told his sports editor about the column he'd deliver for Sunday's paper. The timing couldn't be better—Sunday was the date of the Stallions season opener. Everyone in the state was sickeningly excited about Martin McNeil, gushing about how great he was going to be, raving about his training camp performances, but Costanzo knew this story would settle that enthusiasm. The reporter was about to deliver a much-deserved blow to the reputation of Martin McNeil.

Costanzo kept a tight focus on his rage. His time had come. It was time for the rookie to pay the piper, to be humiliated just the way that Costanzo had been humiliated. David had thought he'd feel joy when this day arrived, but as always, true happiness resisted him. Instead, piping hot anger was coursing through his veins. David hammered on his computer. Digging his fingers into the keyboard. Attacking the device as if it were his enemy. Of course it wasn't. The computer was his friend. It was the means through which he would serve up a thick broth of hard justice to the arro-

gant football player who thought he was so damned smart.
The pen is mightier than the sword.

# NINE

Martin McNeil rocked from foot-to-foot barely hearing his teammate Lester McCallen as the running back talked about his girlfriend. They were in the ornate elevator number seven at the Windsor Palace in downtown San Antonio. The team checked into the hotel for every home game, eating dinner from 6 to 7 p.m. on Saturdays, followed by meetings from 7 to 9:30 p.m., and curfew at 11p.m. Years ago, NFL coaches realized they had more control over their players during road trips than they did for home games. On the road, there were organized meals, meetings, bus schedules and curfews that a coach could use to keep tabs on his players. At home, an athlete might be out all night partying or at a girlfriend's house, or catching a late-night flight into town from another city without the coach ever being aware of his actions. A movement started in the early 1990s with a handful of teams checking their players into luxurious accommodations the night before home games. Initially, most owners resisted but eventually they accepted the added expense as a necessary evil if they wanted to win football games.

McNeil watched the elevator numbers light up as they descended to the lower level. He was just about four hours away from his first NFL start, and his stomach was rumbling with characteristic nervousness. The doors opened to reveal an easel emblazoned with the words, "Welcome Stallions: Pregame Meal in the Cascade Room. Good Luck!!"

McNeil eased into the room. It was already half-full with players eating breakfast, reading the newspaper, studying their playbooks or just talking quietly. There was a buffet along one side of the room. Martin grabbed a plate and surveyed the dietary selection. It was only 10 in the morning; he had plenty of breakfast choices including scrambled eggs, potatoes, toast, bacon, sausage, grits, biscuits, gravy, pancakes and French toast. Or he could have lunch foods such as pasta, chicken, steak, green beans, corn, mashed potatoes and ham. It was the normal pregame spread.

He decided on breakfast, scooping some eggs, potatoes and bacon onto his plate, grabbing a newspaper and settling in at a table. Flipping to the sports section, McNeil emotions went straight from nervousness to *Oh Shit!* when he read David Costanzo's column.

*MCNEIL SHATTERS BOYS DREAM.*
*BY DAVID COSTANZO.*

*Pro athletes are jerks.*

*They're egotistical, self-centered babies who don't care about anything except making lots of cash off the backs of their fans. And players in the NFL—the Narcissists' Football League—seem to be the worst of the lot.*

*Take Martin McNeil for example. He's the newest jerk in the Stallions' stable, and already he's trying to earn a roster spot on the All-Self-Centered Team. There's a simple rule athletes need to learn: "Do what you say you're going to do, and if you have no intention of doing it, then don't say that you're going to do it."*

*Is that so hard?*

*A few months ago I heard from an elementary teacher who said Stallions defensive end Michael Pape was supposed to come speak at an assembly for the kids. The students posted "welcome" signs all over the school; they bragged to their neighbors about the impending visit; agonized over which Stallions paraphernalia they should wear; and prepared endless lists of questions to ask the star player.*

*On the appointed day, 537 children marched into the school gym and waited impatiently for Pape's arrival.*

*Yep, you guessed it: Pape was a no show.*

*Why? He wanted to play golf.*

*It's typical of athletes to simply not understand that when they make promises people count on them to deliver. They're so used to living in a vacuum where no one holds them accountable that they've lost the ability to be committed.*

*So now we have Martin McNeil, the rumored savior of the Stallions, who comes into town and immediately starts making a name for himself on the field as a super star wide receiver. But off the field, he's as miserable as the rest of them. The next time you hear a fan scream the word "Jerk!" in McNeil's direction, it's not an insult: It's an observation.*

*Let me tell you about a cute 12-year-old kid named Matthew Fields.*

*He's a boy who talked his mother into driving 15 hours from Florida in a Ford Escort that overheated twice enroute, just so that he could get Martin McNeil's autograph. Matthew is a kid who, for two years, treasured a battered and bruised baseball cap simply because it came off the head of Martin McNeil. This is a boy who stood in the heat of training camp for three consecutive days and did not get a single autograph from a single player, because all he cared about was getting McNeil* to sign his baseball cap.

See, the story starts out as a warm-fuzzy about McNeil. Two years ago, when he was in college, McNeil was still part of the old school of athletics. You know, back before money corrupted the game, when athletes really cared about the sport and their fans.

So a couple of years ago, McNeil was invited to play in a charity golf tournament in Florida and he actually showed up—so did several hundred fans. And at the end of the day, McNeil unexpectedly took the cap off his head and launched it into the crowd as a grand gesture to the fans.

It's nice to see an athlete showing that he cares.

Unfortunately, the next gesture young Matthew would see was McNeil giving the kid the finger at training camp this year.

The kid spent 15 hours in the car, three nights in a hotel, and three days hanging out at training camp just to get something that would take less than 10 seconds for McNeil to produce: An autograph.

"We knew it was a long shot," said Janet Fields, biting back the angry words that were eager to spill from her lips. Her son has been hurt and her instinct was to fight back. "But when Martin said he'd come back and sign the hat, we believed him."

Well, that was their mistake.

Matthew and Janet were among the horde at training camp screaming for autographs as the players marched out of the locker room. Somehow McNeil heard Matthew's voice and paused to talk to the boy, asking about the hat and laughing when he remembered throwing it into the crowd at the golf tournament years earlier.

Imagine how big a hero McNeil would have been if he had walked over and signed the cap right then. It was just another 10 feet. Just a few seconds in McNeil's life, but it would have been the memory of a lifetime for Matthew.

But McNeil didn't do that. That would have been too simple. Too easy. Too common. Instead, he pulled out a standard jerk technique, looking the boy in the eye and saying, "I'll sign it for you after practice."

"You promise?" Matthew insisted, the entire crowd as his witness.

"I promise," McNeil said.

You probably don't need any more hints from me to see where this story is going. No, McNeil did not go back after practice to sign the baseball cap. No, he didn't remember this little boy with his beat up hat that meant so much. He didn't remember because he didn't care.

He's a jerk.

Athletes don't live in the real world. They live in a bubble in which they're never held accountable for their actions. The whole idea of commitment is foreign to them.

They're not committed to their teams, to their teammates, to their fans, to their wives, or to their children. They break NFL rules and are not punished; they break the law and are patted on the back. They jump from team to team, cheat on their wives, abandon their children, all *because they have no concept of commitment.*

*After the scrimmage when the world was chanting McNeil's name and everyone in the state loved him, do you think he was going to take the time to remember a little boy to whom he made a promise?*

*Of course not.*

*Do you think he ever intended to fulfill that promise in the first place?*

*Of course not.*

*Think about it. He was on his way out to his first NFL scrimmage. He was either going to do very well, very poorly or very average. But no matter what happened, he had to know he was going to be besieged by reporters after the scrimmage. So was he planning to break away from all that ego-stroking attention to go sign Matthew's cap? Not likely.*

*What's more likely is that he's a typical professional jerk who doesn't think about anyone but himself. What's more likely is that after making the promise, McNeil never gave another thought to this little boy who wanted nothing more than one autograph from his hero.*

*Martin McNeil embarks upon his NFL career today, and I hope he heeds my simple advice: If you're not going to do it, then don't say you're going to do it.*

*Don't be a jerk.*

MARTIN SAT BACK IN his chair, his head spinning. How could he have forgotten the kid? He'd planned to sign the hat, take the kid into the locker room, give him the royal treatment. But instead, he'd been wrapped up in the moment, and had completely forgotten. For the first time, Martin found himself agreeing with Costanzo: *I am a jerk.*

On his way to the stadium, McNeil's phone rang. It was Ed Manusky, the Stallions community relations man.

"Martin, we gotta do something about this situation with this boy," Ed said without preamble.

"Tell me about it, man. Swear to god, I was planning to go back and sign the kid's hat. I just forgot."

"Uh huh," Manusky had been working in the league for nearly 15 years. He's seen it all and heard it all. He didn't spend any time with the reasons or the excuses players offered up. He just tried to put out the fires. "I've already tracked down the mother and the kid. They're back in Florida, but we're flying them in for next week's game. I'm going to bring them onto the field during pregame warm-ups. They'll be on our bench on the 20-yard-line closest to the locker room. Make sure you stop by to say hello."

"Of course. Listen man, I'm —"

"I'll remind you of it right before the game next week, since it's tough for you to remember things."

"Come on, I just —"

"I'm giving the kid a Martin McNeil jersey, a full compliment of pennants. We'll have TV there to cover it. It's not perfect, but it's better than leaving the kid hanging in the wind."

"Seriously, Ed, I was really planning to take care of this kid. I was gonna —"

"Martin, I just don't have time for it. Have a good game."

It didn't get any better at the stadium. McNeil got booed getting out of his car. He must have heard the word jerk 500 times between his car and the gate leading to the locker room. Out on the field warming up, the fans were full of venom and rage. *They hate me.* It was a novel experience for McNeil. He'd certainly been in hostile stadiums, where the opposing team fans who disliked him because he was a good player. But this was the first time he'd ever experienced the anger of a large group of people who felt he had a character flaw. Their comments were vicious and personal, and the words stung in a way that a hit on the field never hurt. He wanted to say something, or do something to show them he was sorry, that it was an accident. That he really did have the best of intentions. But the boo birds rained down, at one point erupting into the chant: "McNeil is a Jerk! McNeil is a Jerk!"

He blocked it out as much as he could for most of the game. Focusing on his job. Running routes, catching passes. But even when he made a big play the applause seemed muted. The boos persisted throughout the game, the negativity was getting to him. Late in the fourth quarter it finally became too much. He was standing on the 25-yard-line looking down field waiting for the ball to be punted.

He watched it arc into the air, moving to his right following the trajectory of the ball. It spiraled through a gusting wind, but Martin's mind was a computer, calculating millions of variables every second, making corrections in his body position, noticing that the ball was tapering off to the right a bit, floating opposite the direction the rotation of the laces suggested it should move. The Detroit Lions coverage men were converging on him, but he shut them out. He'd signaled for a fair catch. *Just concentrate and catch the ball.* It was nearly on him now. His arms bent at the elbow, hands extended palms up. The wind was making the ball dance; gusting, pushing, then stopping, then pushing again. He was calculating and adjusting. Eventually, there just wasn't enough time to react. The wind gave the ball another nudge just before it fell into his arms. The ball hit his right forearm, ricocheting into a crowd of players.

Martin dived after the ball, but it was no use. There was a pile and he wasn't in it. The Stallions were down by two points with three minutes remaining. They needed the ball. If the Lions recovered, the game was essentially over. They'd have first-and-10 at the Stallions' 25 yard line. They'd eat up the clock and lead by nine at best or five at worst. Either way, it would be bad news for the Stallions. McNeil sat on his knees watching helplessly as the officials peeled the bodies off the pile.

Detroit recovered.

Sixty-eight thousand spectators booed Martin all the way off the field. Television cameras and newspaper photographers all were focused on him. He'd never felt so exposed in his life. He'd made mistakes in high school and college, but this was different. This was the pros. This was where he was supposed to shine. Not only was he a jerk for not remembering young Matthew Fields, but now he was the jerk who lost the game for the Stallions. Martin sat down on the bench, his head held high, but his eyes blank. A few players walked by and patted him on the shoulders, but there was little sincerity in the gestures.

The Lions' offense took the field and ate up two minutes before putting the ball into the end zone. The touchdown gave them a 30-21 lead. The Stallions were left with just over a minute to score a touchdown and a field goal.

They got neither.

After the game, the reporters converged on Martin's locker with questions about the muffed punt, but more questions about the little boy he'd ignored. He tried to explain it. Tried to offer reasons that would make sense, but there was no fixing it. He'd screwed up. He was a jerk, plain and simple. There was nothing he could say to make up for the pain he'd caused that little boy.


COSTANZO WATCHED THE GAME with glee. He couldn't have asked for anything better in McNeil's first outing. He logged onto his computer and started writing.

*Not only is he a jerk. Martin McNeil is also a dud.*

*It was bad enough when he was just a jerk. Bad enough when he was lying to children, breaking their hearts, ignoring their dreams like the jerk he is. That was bad enough, but now he's a flop and that's even worse.*

*When Martin McNeil was just a jerk, we could shrug and say, "Oh well, that's the price you pay for a super star." But now that he's incapable of catching punts when his team most needs him, he has little or no redeeming value.*

*What's the return policy on a guy like McNeil? Can the Stallions undraft him? Did they keep their receipt? Can they get their money back? Can they trade him? Didn't I tell them to do that months ago? to another team for some players who can actually play?*

*I warned from the start that drafting Martin McNeil was a mistake. That the Stallions should never have wasted their valuable number three pick on a player they didn't really need. That the Stallions should have traded that pick for a slew of veteran players and other draft picks who would help the team win games.*

*I knew this would happen. I knew he would flop. I knew that when push came to shove, Martin McNeil would not make the plays we needed him to make.*

And on and on it went. Costanzo launched a campaign against McNeil that knew no bounds. Vicious columns that were mercilessly critical of the player. During his radio shows, Costanzo held court over every mistake McNeil had ever made in his life. He made it his personal mission to turn all of San Antonio against McNeil. He wanted the drive the player out of the town. He figured the day the Stallions decided to trade McNeil, was the day he could claim his victory. *See, I told you, they never should have drafted him in the first place.*

For McNeil, the process was humiliating. He'd never experienced a personal assault like this. It was unrelenting and went on for weeks. He made some good plays during those first few games, but Costanzo never made mention of those. It was his mistakes that were discussed in excruciating detail. The reporter used Martin's errors to eclipse anything good the player may have done.

McNeil eventually didn't want to go out and face the world. He was afraid fans might recognize him and ridicule him at gas stations, restaurants, or movie theaters. He was nervous about going to watch game tape with his teammates. What did they think of him? Did they hate him? Did they think he was an over-hyped rookie who still hadn't proved himself? In the locker room the only players who were unfriendly toward him were Garnett and his cohorts in the defensive backfield, but Martin wondered about his other teammates. Were they secretly upset with him?

Before leaving the house each day, he'd put on dark shades and pull a baseball cap down to his eyebrows. He didn't want anyone to know who he was.

Every now and then he'd see Costanzo in the locker room, and the columnist would walk up and mutter seven words. It was always he same seven words, and Martin was getting sick of hearing them.

Costanzo would quietly say: "The pen is mightier than the sword."

# TEN

"WELL, I'LL BE DAMNED," said George Cowers running a rough hand through what he called his "majestic white hair." His coffee stood untouched but still steaming on the round oak table. George leaned forward in his chair with his elbows on the edge of the table and with his half-shell glasses perched on the bridge of his nose. The Monday morning edition of the *San Antonio Light* was spread out before him. The *San Antonio Express-News*, still bound by a red rubber band, rested on the floor next to his chair.

George, a retired newspaper editor, read both papers from cover to cover every day. Next to his coffee cup was a pair of scissors and a size 22 shoe box. The box—and the Reebok basketball shoes that came with it—was a retirement present from his co-workers in the *Light's* sports department. George had been a delivery boy, a runner, a reporter and finally the city editor during his 52-year career with the *Light*. The sports staff delivered the super-sized shoes during his farewell party eight years earlier. A note scotch-taped to one of the shoes read:

> *Dear George—Your days of slicing and dicing on the keyboard may be over, but fortunately you prepared yourself for life after newspapers. You won't be like so many other editors out there who didn't think ahead. So many bank on their ability to spot a run-on sentence or a dangling participle, and they don't realize that they could get injured tomorrow. It could all be over in a flash.*
>
> *You're one of the smart ones. You prepared. You put in the hours in the driveway working on your lay-up. You put in the study time attending games and learning the ins-and-outs of basketball. You've traded elbows with some of the best fat guys this paper ever put on the court, and now you're ready for a second career. It is with great admiration and envy that we present you*

*with these size 22 basketball shoes. Best of luck in your second career. We look forward to watching you play in the NBA. Sincerely: The boys and the girls in Sports.*

George thought the shoes were a hoot. He pulled them out of the box, put them on over his loafers and laced them up. He wore them for the remainder of the retirement party, stumbling once despite all the beers he had that evening. When he returned to his house, the shoes found a home on the floor of his bedroom closet, and they hadn't been moved since.

The box was the more practical half of the gift. It was immediately put to use holding the sum of what George called his "most important project."

"I'm monitoring the newspapers," he told anyone who asked and a whole lot of people who didn't. "The media is a powerful entity, and I like to keep an eye on the people who are abusing their power or being irresponsible with it."

George had long held the belief that Americans had lost the ability to think for themselves. Advances in technology and the availability of information made people lazy not only in action, but in thought. *Why think for yourself when you can pick up the newspaper or turn on the television and get someone else to do it for you?* Every word spoken or written by a member of the media was gobbled up by the hungry masses who didn't care what they were fed as long as it tasted interesting.

George grimaced whenever he saw the type of reporting that was the focus of most of the media. He believed the press had a responsibility to keep people informed about things that affect their lives not to entertain them with frivolous reports about the lives of celebrities. He often preached this doctrine to high school and college students.

"*News* is stuff that affects people's lives. A big snow storm that's going to cause accidents is news. A major delay at the airport is news. Highway construction that affects the commute to work is news. Information from the legislature about laws that are going be passed is news. Advances in medicine or important steps in technology are news. But most of the stuff that ends up in the newspaper is entertainment and should be treated as such. Everyone's turning on their TVs to get the latest piece of gossip so they can talk about how terrible the whole thing is. It's sick, and I don't think it's a service that reporters should be providing."

Of course, it was this view that had forced his retirement in the first place. He didn't agree with the direction the *Light* was taking, and he often cuffed reporters who were too eager to go after the dirt.

But speculation and dirt were easy to sell. And in the end the *San Antonio Light* and every other news outlet was in business to make a profit. George Cowers was called into the executive editor's office one morning and was given the option of retiring early with a nice severance package or getting fired. It wasn't much of a choice.

That was six years ago, and at times, he was still stung by the cavalier manner in which he was dismissed. He had dedicated his entire adult life to the *San Antonio Light,* but in the end, it didn't matter.

Sitting in the kitchen with the paper spread before him, George read the latest column David Costanzo had written about Martin McNeil, and shook his head wearily. He had a special dislike for columnists. They weren't reporters, and they typically were not experts in any particular field. They were just talented writers given tremendous latitude in expressing their opinions. George thought they performed a tremendous disservice to the community, because they generally always painted grim pictures of their subjects. A good columnist could arouse the anger of the masses, but what was the point? Columnists got people worked up without ever really doing anything. And it has always struck George as odd that columnists weren't elected to their positions, because they wield the power to forcefully shift the opinions of hundreds of thousands of people, but they're not accountable to anyone. If George owned the newspaper, he would have fired every columnist without a second thought.

After reading the latest entry in Costanzo's campaign against McNeil, the retired editor decided it was time to teach the columnist a lesson. He grabbed a sheet of paper and wrote a brief note to the McNeil.

A COUPLE OF DAYS later, the Stallions media relations director delivered a cryptic note to Martin. It read: *"David Costanzo's an asshole, but I'm his former boss. I know just how to fix the kit in his caboodle."*

Martin called George that day and smiled for the first time in weeks as the former editor told him how to flip-flop the situation with David.

ABOUT A WEEK LATER, David Costanzo was laughing with friends at Monty's Grill. It was a family restaurant, but Monty's had become a popular after-work watering hole for young professionals. David was there with six other men from local media outlets; the boy who approached the table looked to be about 8 years old.

"Mr. Costanzo," said the kid, brandishing a pen and a Monty's Grill napkin, "can I have your autograph?"

David set his beer down on the table and grinned widely. "Sure, son." He didn't get many requests for his autograph, so he was especially glad this one was happening in front of his peers. "What's your name?"

"Michael," the boy replied. He was wearing a San Antonio Dodgers baseball cap. "I read your column every day."

"You do?" David said, raising his eyebrows, surprised. "Well, I'm very flattered."

"Yeah, my dad and I always go through it and find all the spelling mistakes and bad grammar that are always in it."

David stopped writing. *What did he say?*

"My dad says it's good practice for me in school," the boy continued.

David's face flushed. He laughed tightly, looking around at his friends. "So you think there are mistakes in my column, huh?"

"Yeah, but it's no big deal cause I sometimes have trouble with my spelling, too," The boy picked up the signed napkin, looking at it as if it was a treasure. "Anyway, thanks for the autograph," he said, walking away.

"Kids," David said shaking his head.

LESS THAN 15 MINUTES later a young woman approached the table.

"Excuse me, aren't you David Costanzo?" She had a soft voice that was pretty without being dainty. She had short, sandy brown hair hung down to her chin and curled under itself. Green eyes, and a long, lean athletic body. Tight jeans. Small perky breasts.

"I sure am," David replied with a knowing wink to one of his buddies.

"I thought so. I just wanted to tell you that I'm a journalism major at San Antonio College, and we always review your column during class."

"So do you want to be a columnist?" David would love to be her tutor.

"Well, if you're the competition, I might just give it a shot," she said, eliciting abrupt laughter from David's peers. "No offense, but your columns aren't very good. And there are always mistakes in them. You should tell your editors to do a better job of proofing your work."

For the first time in years, David was speechless.

THAT NIGHT DAVID STAYED up for hours going through clippings of his work, trying to find evidence of mistakes. He couldn't believe two random people had criticized him for having grammar and spelling mistakes in his columns. A little kid and a college student for Pete's sake. And right in front of his peers!

His buddies had tried to console him saying, "They don't know what they're talking about. Don't worry about it." But he couldn't stop thinking about it. He was a professional. He took pride in doing a good job. He'd be damned if he was going to forget two people who walked up and insulted him about his work.

Incredibly, the same sort of criticism came the next night and the night after that. Random people continued to approach him with barbs in virtually every public place he went. It was as if the entire city had launched an attack against him. Going to work every day became more and more of a challenge. He began to re-read his columns seven or eight times before filing them. But no matter how punctilious he was, he could not escape the criticism. Even Nettie was mystified. It had to be a plot against David, but given the diversity of people and locations from which the criticism sprung, she couldn't decipher the source.

GEORGE AND MARTIN LISTENED delightfully to the stories of Costanzo's reaction. It was George, who knew virtually every concierge and restaurant and store manager in the city, who had organized the harassment. Costanzo was a bachelor who ate most of his meals at restaurants. George had called everyone he knew in the city with the same message: If you see David Costanzo please call me immediately.

Whenever an update on Costanzo's location came in, George would ask the manager to pick a likely candidate and offer $5 or $10 to play a joke on a friend. The person solicited would then walk up to Costanzo and deliver the criticism. Martin financed the harassment and it cost him about $650 including the tips to the manager and maitre d's.

It was worth every penny.

AFTER TWO WEEKS OF continuous criticism, David confidence was beginning to slip. His one true talent was being hammered relentlessly. He was a good writer, at times even a great writer, and he knew it. Yet every day there was some new person in his face telling him that he wasn't worth a damn. It was maddening and humiliating.

The penultimate moment came on a Thursday evening while eating dinner with two NBC reporters. A young woman in an Old West costume delivered a "You Screwed Up" telegram to the tune of the Fantasy Island theme song.

Costanzo was out of his chair before the first measure was completed. His face was an angry shade of red. He was aiming for her *fucking mouth!* head, but his first punch hit her in the side of the neck. She was screaming, trying to back away from him when he punched her in the chest. She tripped over a chair, falling and David was on top of her.

"Yeah, pretty fucking funny isn't it? Pretty fucking funny!" David yelled as he continued to pummel her. A horde of people swept over him, dragging him away from the girl. He was kicking his feet, trying to hit her even as he was pulled off. She was collapsed on the floor in a heap, crying.

"Pretty fucking funny, isn't it?" David continued, oblivious to everyone except the young girl on the floor who'd had the nerve to smile at him while delivering her stupid message.

THE NEXT DAY THE singing telegram girl called him at the newspaper to say that her neck hurt and she was thinking about suing him. He tried to talk her out of it. Apologizing. Telling her how stressed out he'd been, but she didn't care. She wanted money.

"How much?" David asked, thinking he should probably let his attorney handle this.

"I want a hundred thousand," she said confidently.

David laughed, but there was no mirth in it. It was an angry sound, like a bull snorting before it charges. "Bitch, I'm not giving you a hundred grand. You just go ahead and sue me. Take this to court. I've got a good lawyer. What have you got?" *Besides herpes?*

"Well, that's what my friend said I should ask—"

"Well, your friend is wrong. I'll give you five hundred dollars, just as my way of saying I'm sorry I lost my head. If you want it, it's yours. If not, I'll see your ass in court."

She sat on the phone for a minute. Five hundred dollars didn't seem like much money after what he'd done, but her rent was due in a few days and —

"Look lady, do you want it or not."

"Okay," she said. "I'll come by the paper tomorrow to get the money."

WHEN THE TELEPHONE RANG early in the afternoon David answered with a gruff, "hello."

"You enjoying it?"

"Enjoying what?" *Who is this?*

"Being embarrassed in front of your friends and in front of complete strangers by someone who thinks he knows more about your job than you do?"

David sat up straight, his anger spilling over. "You stupid son of a bitch."

"I just wanted you to know how it feels to have someone constantly criticize you."

"Grow up, Martin," David said. "I write a column for a living. I offer an opinion about things that happen in sports, and if my opinion happens to be that you suck, then so be it. It's not personal. It's my job."

"Well, as you've learned lately, it doesn't take any special talent or ability to criticize someone," Martin said. "There must be millions of people out there qualified to do *your* job. And you always hide behind that 'I'm-just-doing-my-job' bullshit. When you write that I 'suck,' everybody reads it including my family, my friends, my neighbors and little kids who walk up to me in grocery stores and say, 'how come you can't catch the ball?' It's humiliating, and I'm glad that you have had a little taste of it."

"You're messing with the wrong guy, Martin. You hear me?" David said. There was venom in his voice. "If you *ever* step out of line, I promise it'll be over. I will run your little ass out of town with your tail between your legs."

"Why don't we call a truce," Martin suggested.

Costanzo laughed. "Why would I need a truce. I've got the power of the press on my side you no-talent fuck. Remember Martin, the pen is mightier than the sword!"

McNeil quietly hung up the phone.

# ELEVEN

MARTIN AND THE PROFESSOR were playing dominoes. They'd borrowed the bones from an inmate named Fred Delusia two cells down. It was something to kill the time, sitting in the cell, on the floor, their legs stretched out in front of them, the dominoes clicking against the concrete. Neither man was an experienced dominoes player, but Martin knew the basic rules and had explained them to the professor.

"Why do you suppose they call dominoes 'bones'?" Richard said.

Martin shrugged. "Maybe because of the clacking sound they make when you move them around. They sound like a bunch of bones clattering together."

The professor accepted that answer. It made as much sense as anything else. They played slowly with none of the flamboyance the other inmates displayed. In the break room, you'd sometimes see four guys perched at a table, slamming the dominoes onto the table, screaming out their scores, talking trash to their opponents. The inmates in the break room turned the game into an athletic event, but Martin and Richard played a quiet game, not even keeping score. Just passing the time.

"Martin, I keep thinking about your story and all the things that happened, and I've been trying to work out the timeline. In all of this acrimony with David Costanzo, when do you think that murder became a foregone conclusion."

The player thought about that for a moment. "I don't think I understand the question. Murder became a foregone conclusion when it happened I guess."

"No," Richard said, wagging a finger. "The thing about murder is that it rarely happens out of the blue. Sometimes you hear stories about random acts of violence, but few of them are as arbitrary as they seem. There's usually a progression of events leading up to the killing. If you start from the moment the body is discovered and work backward, you reach the time of death, preceded by the convergence of participants, typically preceded by an argument or scuffle, preceded by a few seconds, minutes, days, weeks or months of tension, preceded by any number of other things. It's not an exact science, but working backward, you usually find a point in time at which you say, 'X marks the spot.' That's the moment at which death became the unavoidable conclusion. It might be the moment the guy decided to carry his gun out of the house. Or it could be the moment that a worker learned he was going to be laid off. Or the moment a wife first suspects that her husband is cheating. It's a snapshot. One moment in the vast continuum of time that defines everything that follows. Do you understand what I'm saying?"

"Sort of," Martin said. "But I still don't get it. Even if a guy leaves his house with a gun, he could still change his mind, so I don't see how there can ever be a moment when you can say X marks the spot."

"Well, let me explain this a different way. Take baseball. A pitcher starts his windup. In the early stages of that windup he could stop if he wanted to, but he reaches a point at which he literally cannot stop himself from throwing the ball. The movement has started, the momentum is going, and that ball is going to leave his hand no matter how much he might like to stop it. On the other end is a batter. He's standing at the plate watching the ball fly toward him. His brain is calculating the trajectory of the ball and sending the message to his muscles to fire in a particular sequence to put his bat on course to intercept the ball. When he starts to swing, he still has the power to stop—so sometimes you see players who check swing, but don't come all the way through. But when a batter swings, there's a point along the way that he literally cannot stop what happens next. If the bat gets to point A it's a mathematical certainty that it's going to go through point B, no matter how much the batter might like to stop it. Homicide is like that. You reach a point of no return long before the actual murder."

For Martin, 6:41 A.M. on a Friday morning six weeks earlier was the spot.

Sitting in his jail cell backtracking, trying to make sense out of the progression of events, Martin sees that time—6:41 a.m.—those glowing red numbers, and knows that at that moment, murder was a forgone conclusion. *No*, he chides himself. *That's not true. I still had a few minutes beyond that. If I'd acted differently during those few minutes, this whole script might have changed.* The time was stuck in his head because he looked at the clock when the phone rang.

It rang three times in his darkened bedroom. Jessica, his wife of five years, hardly stirred. Martin's eyes were open on the first ring. He looked at the clock on the second ring, and by the third, he was awake enough to pull the receiver to his ear. Even before he heard the voice of his attorney, he knew for certain that it was bad news. Good news never came early.

"Sorry to wake you," Joseph Steadman said.

Martin groaned. He knew his attorney was lying. If he was really sorry, he wouldn't have called. Surely, whatever it was would hold for another couple of hours.

"No problem," Martin said. "What's up?"

"Well, we've got a little bit of a situation on our hands and I wanted to catch you before some reporter blind-sided you with a question about it."

"A question about what?" Was there a hint of glee in the attorney's voice? Martin often wondered about Steadman. It was as though the guy had no empathetic ability. His excitement about a new project always overwhelmed any pretense of compassion about his client's situation.

"It's a lawsuit, Martin. Filed two days ago, and delivered to me by certified mail late yesterday. Now, it would have been preferable if they had approached us to pursue a settlement before filing, but doing things this way puts a lot more pressure on us to make them a quick offer. I've been working all night trying to investigate the claimant to see if there is anything we can use against her to mitigate the suit. What I think we—"

"Her?" Martin said, surprised and fully awake now. He'd expected it to be a man. Someone claiming that Martin had beaten him up in a bar. Perhaps a guy saying he was the victim of a hit-and-run accident and Martin was the perpetrator.

"Yeah, a woman. Her name's Lisa Benson."

Martin thought about that for a long moment trying to put a face with the name. "Don't know her."

"She says you do. It's a paternity suit, Martin. She has a 2-year-old boy, and she's asking for $150,000 in back pay and $10,000 a month until the kid's 18."

Martin ran a hand across his face. It was always like this. This was America after all, land of the litigious. He'd been sued three times in four years, successfully defending himself each time. The judge threw out two of them as frivolous.

But since the beginning, Steadman had warned that there would come a time when it was better to just settle a suit than deal with the negative publicity of fighting it. A charge so inflammatory and so indefensible that even if it were a lie, Martin should just write a check and walk away from it.

The suit Steadman called about that morning six weeks ago didn't sound dangerous at first blush. Martin had never heard of Lisa Benson and was certain that he had never had sex with her. He'd get a blood test, exonerate himself and that would be that.

"What?" Martin said into the phone. It was getting worse.

"I said she's 18 years old," Steadman sighed. Again Martin was sure he detected a note of excitement in the attorney's voice. "She was 15 when she got pregnant," Steadman continued. "I don't think you want this kind of thing to hit the 10 o'clock news."

"Joseph, I never slept with this girl," Martin said urgently, but even as the words left his mouth, he felt their inadequacy. No one would believe him.

"I know, Martin, but that's beside the point. We have to deal with the suit now."

Martin thought for a moment. "How do we make it disappear?"

"Well, about all we can do is settle it quickly and then hope for the best. Once filed, the suit is a matter of public record. The terms of the settlement will not be included in the filed documents, but your name will be listed, and since reporters periodically go through the dockets looking for the names of public figures, there's a risk that this could hit the newspapers. Fortunately, the suit was filed in Guadalupe County rather than in San Antonio. And her attorney did us the favor of not sending out a press release. It's fairly unlikely that a reporter will ever find it. We just need to settle it quickly and then pray it disappears."

They talked for a few more minutes about the details and then hung up. Martin left Jessica, still sleeping soundly and walked downstairs. Lying in his jail cell thinking about that morning, Martin realized that walking away from Jessica was his first mistake. Not the fatal mistake, but the first of a series of errors. He should have awakened her. He should have talked to her about the situation, gotten her advice, taken a few minutes to settle himself before he made any decisions. Instead, he walked away.

Even then there was still time to stop the events that would follow.

His mind was racing, trying to sort through all the details, trying to figure out where to go with this. When he reached the kitchen, he snatched the phone off the wall and made mistake number two; he dialed his brother's number. It wasn't the point of no return, but it was a firm step in that direction. Brandon answered on the first ring, sounding wide awake, as though he'd been waiting for the call.

Martin gave his older brother a quick rundown on the situation. It looked bad, but Martin was optimistic about the possibility of keeping his name out of the news.

Brandon listened closely, cursing the girl, her bastard child, her lawyer and the legal system in general. Martin appreciated his brother's concern, but knew that he had to keep his own emotions under control.

"Brandon, why don't you swing by later today and we'll talk about it," Martin said calmly, making yet another mistake. He should never have involved his brother. Not at that stage of the game. Brandon was too self-centered, too unpredictable. He would do nothing but muck things up. Martin should have hung up the phone and just let his lawyer settle the issue.

"Jesus, Martin," his brother muttered. "You sure you didn't accidentally knock this chick up?"

"I'm not a slut like you," Martin said sharply.

"Yeah, all right," Brandon said, flattered. "Hey, why don't you call Ramey. See if he'll kill this bitch for you."

X marks the spot.

# TWELVE

DAVID COSTANZO NEEDED TO break something big.

People were weary of his style. A recent survey revealed that 43 percent of the *San Antonio Light's* readers were sick of David's negative outlook on life. They said his columns were tough to take seriously when he was calling for someone's head every other week. That he'd have more credibility if he was more balanced. Of course, the irony, and the saving grace for David at the moment, was that the bulk of the survey group still made a point to read his columns, even though they didn't like him. But the paper's editorial administrators were concerned. They wanted their columnists to be thought-provoking and/or controversial in the positions that they took. However, if it was a columnist's style or his general outlook that people objected to, then the paper made changes. Managing Editor Bruce Johnson had explained it this way in a recent meeting with his staff of columnists: "Say you take on an issue like abortion. You can defend either side of the argument, explaining why it's a good idea or a bad idea, and we'll stand behind you. But there has to be some intelligence in the debate. If you wrote a column basically attacking one side or the other saying that the doctors who perform abortions are murderers or the people who object to abortions are irrational idiots, then that's obviously not appealing to the intelligence of our audience, and we might not stand behind you. It's okay to enrage the readers with your positions on the issues, and its periodically okay to enrage them with your method, but if they consistently object to your style, then it creates a problem for the entire paper."

Sports editor Tom Michelson was a bear of a man at 6-foot-three, 320 pounds. He delivered the results of this survey to Costanzo over dinner.

"All I'm saying is that we have to take these surveys seriously," Michelson explained between sips of Diet Coke. "We can't be at the kitchen table with the 65-year-old grandmother when she reads the paper in the morning or on the bus with the 34-year-old business man as he flips through the sports section. So we don't have any way of knowing exactly how people react to what we write. Our only barometers are letters to the editor and surveys."

"But this is stupid," David shot back, idly twirling his spaghetti. "My columns are good. I write the truth, but the damned readers are afraid of the truth."

"I know, I know," Michelson said, a small drop of marinara sauce dancing on his chin as he shoveled another forkful of ravioli into his mouth. "I agree with you. Unfortunately, the new AME doesn't like you and he's been buzzing Johnson's ear. In the staff meeting today they said they wanted you to tone things down a little bit." Michelson was referring to Armand La Dora, the assistant managing editor.

"Tone *what* down?" David said angrily. "I'm doing my *job*. I'm getting people riled up, and I'm selling newspapers. That's a lot more than anyone can say about that jerk Marks."

"I can't argue with you, David. If it were up to me, you'd just keep doing what you've been doing. But it's not up to me, and it's not up to you. The guys upstairs think you're taking things too far, so the best thing you can do is just tone it down for a couple of weeks. Pretty soon everybody will forget about this stupid survey, which is nothing more than a piece of paper La Dora is using to bully you anyway; and then you can go back to doing what you do so well."

David stared out the window.

"They also asked me when your last serious investigative piece ran," Michelson said quietly, not looking up from his plate..

David's gaze came back. Now they were getting to it. "The hell does that mean?"

"I don't know what it means," Michelson said evasively.

The reporter continued to stare, refusing to give his editor an easy out.

Ravioli was still passing Michelson's lips at an alarming rate. With a full mouth he said: "I think they want you to do some of the hard-hitting stuff that you were writing a couple of years ago."

"You're telling me my columns aren't hard hitting?" David said, his voice rising with every word. "I'm the only guy in that whole newsroom who has the balls to write the truth about all the crap that goes on in this city, and you're saying *I'm* not hard hitting enough."

Michelson's eyes darted around the room to see who might be overhearing their conversation. Fortunately, the restaurant was mostly empty, and their table was in the back, a fair distance away from the nearest customers.

"Wait a second," he said defensively. "*I'm* not saying anything. I'm just telling you what they told me. They think that people are starting to get tired of your columns—"

"Who the hell is getting tired of them? Some idiots who live under bridges with all their belongings in shopping carts?"

"Just hear me out, David. Regardless of who's right or wrong, they have the power to cut you off, and what they want to see is an occasional investigative piece from you. And, the truth is, if you're cranking out good investigative work, you get all the power back. Then the readers will demand you, and La Dora won't be able to do anything to you."

Silence fell over the table, and Michelson took advantage of the lull to finish off his ravioli and drain his glass.

"What about Duman?" David said finally.

Robert Duman was a 32-year-old veteran who had been the beat reporter for the Stallions since the team's inception. He was a diligent reporter who covered the team well, and who also wrote an NFL column on Sundays. His columns were always well-researched and well-written, and he was developing a significant following. When David took his annual two weeks of vacation from his column—spread out over the year in three-day blocks to preserve his continuity—it was Duman who generally wrote guest columns to fill the space. Duman also produced an average of six investigative stories each year. In recent years, he'd written two-award winning pieces. The first uncovered an embezzlement scandal in the University of Houston Athletic Department. The other series unearthed a host of recruiting violations at the University of Texas that led to a three-year probation for the school's football team. Duman was talented and hard-working. There had been considerable talk around the newsroom that he was destined to be the featured columnist in the sports department; a move that would bounce David out onto the street.

Michelson paused for a moment before answering quietly. "His name came up."

David shook his head angrily. "I gotta go," he said, reaching for his wallet.

"Don't worry about it. I'll bill it to the paper," Michelson said, waving off the money. He released a weary breath as David left the restaurant.

The sports editor waited a respectable three minutes before reaching across the table to grab the reporter's plate of spaghetti.

"Waste not, want not."

# THIRTEEN

NETTIE RICHARDSON SAT BEHIND a cluttered desk at the front of the newsroom. She had been the receptionist on the city desk at the *San Antonio Light* for nearly 15 years. She had pale white skin dusted with a light sprinkle of freckles and her nose was nearly too small to support her oversized brown glasses. Although no one outside the newsroom would have guessed it, Nettie was arguably the most powerful person at the newspaper.

Her power was derived from her two main gifts in life. The first being her natural tone of voice, which through no effort of her own, conveyed reserved deference to the politicians and business types who called, while projecting cold indifference to the creeps and cranks. No caller had ever bullied or ruffled Nettie Richardson, and no situation had ever escalated out of her control.

Nettie's second gift was an inordinately analytical brain and a memory that was nearly photographic. Everything that Nettie saw during a given day was systematically recorded and evaluated. The end product was a ticker tape of logical assumptions that continually spooled in the front of her mind. Reporters often referred to her as Sherlockette Holmes and frequently consulted her regarding controversial issues in the community.

It was Nettie who five years ago suggested that political reporter Richard Harvey look into possible nepotism in the construction of a new concourse at the San Antonio International Airport. Nettie was a voracious reader who each month thumbed through all 34 magazines that the paper subscribed to, covering a wide range of subjects. Nettie's suggestion was sparked by a name that she'd seen in an Architectural Digest article nearly six months earlier. As with virtually everything else in that issue of Architectural Digest, the name Janet Keeney, an electrical engineer for the Peterson Company, had been captured by Nettie's mind and stored away until it was useful. Half a year later, Nettie read in the *San Antonio Light* that the Kohen Electrical Corporation had been contracted by the city on the airport project, and a woman named Janet Keeney, a recent hire, would be the lead engineer. Another crucial fact that had not passed unnoticed by Nettie was a listing two years earlier in the society pages of the *San Antonio Express-News* announcing the marriage of lawyer Mark Keeney and engineer Janet Stone. Nettie's mind, which was cluttered with facts like this, quickly calculated that Janet Stone and Janet Keeney were the same person, and that there were Stones in the family tree of San Antonio Mayor Earl Parvin.

Acting on this tip, Harvey discovered that Janet Keeney was in fact a first cousin of the mayor, which, by itself, did not make the hiring of her firm a crime. But further investigation revealed that of the 41 companies that had been contracted to perform various segments of the airport project, 12 of them employed either members of the mayor's family or his close friends and business associates. The clincher in this story was that the Kohen Electrical Corporation had actually hired Janet Keeney *away* from the Peterson Company as a prerequisite to acquiring the airport contract.

The citizens of San Antonio were so enraged by this breach of trust and abuse of power that Mayor Parvin was promptly run out of office.

All the while Nettie sat at her desk, reading her magazines, answering the phone and watching over the operation of the paper. She would have made a terrific investigative reporter herself, but she had no interest in leaving her current post.

Nettie took her job very seriously. Sitting at her desk each day, her brown eyes darted back and forth tracking the shuffling bodies of reporters, photographers and editors as the business of the newspaper was conducted. Her mind was constantly clicking pictures of the action, and she generally knew exactly where each of her co-workers was at every moment of every day.

Midway through Monday morning, the phone at the edge of her desk jangled softly. She looked at it maliciously, already angry at the caller for interrupting.

"City desk," she said by rote when she picked up the phone.

"I need to speak to David Costanzo," a male voice said. "I have a news tip for him."

Nettie put the caller on hold before he even finished the sentence. The moment he said "news tip" she knew he was *one of those*. The caller would have to wait. She knew that David was not in the office. It would have been fairer to the caller to take a message immediately, but that approach ran contrary to her battle plan. She smoothed the material of her skirt—Nettie always wore dresses or skirts, never pants, even at home and even on the weekends—and resumed her vigil over the newsroom.

When she first started working at the *Light*, Nettie occasionally got uptight about people who called in with tips.

"Um. . . he's on another line, can you hold on for just a moment," she'd say biting her lip nervously, praying that the reporter's line would be free soon, thinking that this "tip" could be important breaking news for the next day's paper. After 30 seconds or so, she'd get back on the phone, take a detailed message and sprint across the newsroom to drop the slip on the reporter's desk.

Time had taught her that most people who called in with tips were idiots who had nothing better to do with their time. Their information was generally important to them, but completely irrelevant to the masses. Now, she took it upon herself to screen calls for her reporters. If someone called with a tip, her first tactic was to put the caller on a lengthy hold; if the tip was important, he would wait. If it wasn't, he'd hang up and save everyone the agony of having to listen to him. If the caller did not hang up, Nettie would query him about the nature of his information to determine whether it had any news value.

When she finally picked up the line again, she said, "Mr. Costanzo is still busy, do wish to continue holding?"

"Listen lady. I've got something important to pass on to David Costanzo, and you better—" Nettie punched the hold button again, and drummed her fingernails against the hardwood surface of her desk. She had no patience for people who yelled or made demands. She left the caller on hold for another five minutes before picking up again.

"Mr. Costanzo is still busy, would you like to continue holding?" she said curtly.

Silence answered her. Then an angry but resigned voice said, "No, I do not wish to continue holding. Does Mr. Costanzo by chance have voice mail?"

"No," Nettie lied. "May I take a message for him?"

"Yeah. . . tell him that Martin McNeil. . . you know the guy?" The question hung in the air, and Nettie let the silence grow. She refused to offer encouragement. "Anyway," the man continued, "he's a wide receiver for the Stallions, and, well, he had a paternity suit filed against him that was settled out of court." The man paused expecting a reaction. He got nothing. "I thought Mr. Costanzo might want to check it out," he finished, losing steam.

Nettie tightened the grip on her frown. If she had a nickel for every paternity suit "tip" the paper received. Most of the claims were nothing more than attempts to extort money from people.

"And whom should I say called?" she said knowing the answer even as she posed the question.

"Oh . . . no name. This is an anonymous tip."

# FOURTEEN

DAVID COSTANZO WALKED INTO the newsroom a few minutes before 11.a.m. His desk was tucked into the farthest corner of the third floor space, bordered on two sides by light gray, partitions and on two sides by windows that overlooked an $8-a-day parking lot. Between the partition on his left and the window behind him was a space about two feet wide, which was just enough room for him to get into and out of his work area. He had no interest in conversation with any of his mealy-mouthed co-workers. Most days he worked from his home. When he chose to come into the office, he'd march back to his desk and wouldn't emerge again until his column was done and he was ready to leave.

David wrote four columns a week, and was a strong local personality, but somehow he could never break into the syndication market. He'd hosted a radio show for a couple of years, and he'd had tried his hand at television, but that didn't work out.

The words "message pending" flashed at the top of his screen when he logged onto his computer. He typed RMS—for Retrieve Message—into the command field and a short note from Nettie appeared.

*rock boy, meil, d claim, settle. anon.*

David's face formed a wicked grin. This was the message he'd been waiting for. Again, the note had been written in a simple code he had devised with Nettie to keep his story ideas and news tips safe from prying, competitive reporters. In football vernacular, players often refer to the ball as the "rock"; thus "rock boy" in David's simple formula was a football player. Reading Nettie's note, he knew she was talking about one of the San Antonio Stallions. Meil stood for Martin McNeil. A paternity suit, of which he had investigated many, was called a daddy claim or a "d claim."

David's outlook on the day improved dramatically. He hated Martin McNeil the way a scrawny kid hates an elementary school bully, and since the verbal blows they had traded during the receiver's rookie year, there really hadn't been many negative things to say about McNeil. During his four-year career with the Stallions, Martin had turned into a Pro Bowl wide receiver who conducted himself as well off the field as he did on the field. His reputation had grown and he was respected all over the country as one of the bright spots in professional athletics. All the gushing about McNeil made Costanzo gag. He'd been dying for an opportunity to discredit the overrated, so-called football star. He was weary of seeing Martin's smiling face on television commercials and billboards all over the city. People were always clamoring for his autograph, catering to his whims and generally treating him like a demigod who should not be offended. David didn't have an ounce of respect for Martin as an athlete, a man or even a human being. David rubbed his hands together. *Please just let this tip be at least halfway true.*

Just a hint of truth would warm the reporter's heart. Seeing the words in print would put a smile on his face that would last a lifetime. Costanzo was finally going to catch up with Martin McNeil.

As a bonus to dishing out a well-deserved public humiliation to Martin, an in-depth piece would satisfy his professional need for a big story. He hadn't had a major story in the paper for nearly two years. He needed something big and something that was all his own. McNeil with an illegitimate child was perfect.

As far as David knew, no one had ever uncovered anything bad about McNeil's personal life. He was supposedly one of the good guys, but David knew there was no such thing as a good guy in pro sports. There were only two types of athletes: those who had been caught and those who had not yet been caught.

If the tip was true, David would write the story and then tell assistant managing editor Armand La Dora to bend over and kiss the dark crack of his own ass. David knew that people were inherently predatory and deep down the masses never truly believed anyone was as nice or as good as he seemed. *When the people of San Antonio read the story about McNeil's illegitimate child they will gasp in surprise and stop treating this punk like he was the savior.* Probably, they'll regard McNeil as a typical, egotistical, pro athlete jerk, and David imagined that he would be applauded for delivering this important information.

He stood up and shoved a reporter's notebook into the back pocket of his jeans. Flipping a sports coat over one arm, he walked quickly to the elevator leading to the garage. He'd run over to the Bexar County Records Office to check for details about the suit—assuming the tip was accurate. It would have been easier to use the phone, but David was leery of being overheard by one of the other reporters in the office. Although the *San Antonio Light's* main rival was the cross-town *Express-News*, David believed his most dangerous competition was in his own newsroom. Michelson, the sports editor, and Nettie, the receptionist, were the only people David trusted with his ideas.

No one at the *Light* had ever stolen a story from him, David's tenure at the now defunct *New York Daily News* had taught him the ruthlessness of reporters. At the *Daily News* he would often log onto his computer in the morning to discover that certain notes or stories were missing from his files. He'd scan through everything in his queue and eventually call a computer technician who would search the system but find nothing. Often David would work on a story for days, and just before his deadline he'd discover that several crucial paragraphs had been deleted. And on one occasion, he researched a story for several days about baseball star David Winfield, and he never told anyone about his lead. In his youth and naivete, he'd wanted to wait until the story was verified and written before telling his editor, wanting to impress his boss by delivering the finished product. The day before he completed the piece, a sports reporter named Marty Washburn turned in a story about Winfield that was copied nearly verbatim from David's queue. David had argued his case with the sports editor to no avail.

"Look," the editor said. "Marty told me three days ago that he was working on this story. I never heard a word from you. As far as I'm concerned you must have stolen the story from him."

Enraged, David launched himself at Washburn and had a choke hold on the reporter as they tumbled over a desk. It took six people to separate the two men.

David lost his job that day. It was bad enough that he attacked a fellow employee, but thanks to Washburn's repeated sabotage, David had been consistently late on his deadlines during the past month. His attack on Washburn was as good an excuse as any for the sports editor to get rid of him.

That was when David was young and upwardly mobile. The New York Daily News was a plumb job for a 26-year-old kid not long out of college. He was part of their investigative team. Just a research assistant really, but with the freedom to work on his own ideas on the side. That was then. Now, he was not so young, and after the tumultuous changes of the past 18 years, he wasn't sure he was so mobile any more. After being fired by the Daily News, things fell apart for David and it took a long time to put his career back together. It was a long spiral that sent him from New York to Miami, then to Detroit, Houston, Sacramento, Nashville and Des Moines before he finally started to climb back up. He got a job in Cleveland, then San Diego, Atlanta and finally San Antonio. He'd been at the *San Antonio Light* for six years, which was considerably longer than he'd ever worked anywhere else. He'd found a small measure of success in San Antonio, but he'd never forgotten the experience in New York.

At home, David had more than $20,000 in computer equipment that was linked via a series of passwords to the ATEX system at the *Light*. He had software that automatically duplicated every file in his queue at the end of each day and stored them on his home computer. Never again would he lose a story due to the finagling of another reporter.

As he tipped out of the newsroom's back door, only Nettie noticed his departure. Her quick mind already calculating that he was on his way to the courthouse to investigate the claim against Martin McNeil.

# FIFTEEN

THE BEXAR COUNTY COURTHOUSE had the downtrodden look of that which is dedicated to public service. It was an ugly, brown four-story edifice that had been surrounded over the years by the beautiful glass buildings of corporate America. Inside, the hallways were dimly lit and the elevator worked no more than three days a week. The linoleum floor was a maze of cracks, and the air conditioning had recently given up its will to work. The building was alive with the buzz of portable fans that had been set up to provide the illusion of cool.

David leaned back in his chair and ran a sweaty hand through his hair. He'd been sitting in place and dripping with sweat while doing nothing more strenuous than flipping pages in the thick notebooks that held the records of every suit filed in the county. After an hour and a half of reading names, and listening to the constant babble of the people around him, he was ready to get out of the building just to breathe again. Children were crying constantly, and the whole damned building smelled like piss. He'd gone through every record of every suit filed in Bexar county during the past two months and nothing had Martin McNeil's name on it. Disappointed, David returned the notebooks to the pretty, but overweight blonde clerk. She smiled wearily, fanning herself with a sheet of typing paper.

AS HE WALKED BACK to his car—a white Porsche 911 turbo with tinted windows and vanity plates that read: IWRITE—David considered his next step. The fact that Martin's name was not listed in the Bexar County office did not mean the suit was a phantom. Bexar County covered only the city of San Antonio. The metropolitan area was a sprawling mass of suburbs and incorporated towns. The girl who filed the paternity suit could live in any of the seven other counties that were contiguous to Bexar County.

Going through the records of all of those counties would be a daunting task, but it would be necessary if David was going to track down the story.

He eased his Porsche into traffic, and raced toward his home in the affluent northeast part of the city. David owned a sprawling 3,100-square-foot penthouse apartment that actually used to be two units. He'd purchased both apartments four years earlier—just after his first book was released—and had walls knocked down, a kitchen removed, and extra windows installed. Being on the 12th floor gave David a commanding view of downtown. In his building there were six small apartments apiece on floors two through eight. The 9th and 10th floors had four condos each. The 11th level housed two 1,500 square-foot apartments and the 12th, of course, had been converted into David's penthouse. All of the apartments were independently owned, and David had seen a notice last week indicating that one of the apartments on the 11th floor was for sale. He was thinking about buying it, and converting it into an extensive game room with pool and Ping-Pong tables, a pop-a-shot basketball machine, dart boards, a shuffle board deck and card tables to host regular poker sessions. He'd also include a movie room with a 75-inch projection screen, black walls and ceiling, black carpeting and 15 to 20 black recliners for comfortable viewing. It would be perfect for inviting friends over to watch playoff games, and it would lend itself to a first-rate Super Bowl party. He'd have a staircase installed leading to his current apartment, and the new game center would become an ideal sports haven.

When he'd mentioned the idea to Michelson, the sports editor had laughed and said, "Why don't you quit messing around and just buy the whole building."

The irony of David's sports den dream was that he would never trust his peers enough to invite them to his home. His apartment was where he stored his secrets. A vault that he protected religiously.

David marched into his condo and called Jordan Adams, a senior at The University of Texas at San Antonio who occasionally did grunt work for him. The reporter paid the 22-year-old journalism major $15 an hour for his labor, and his only requirement was that Adams keep his investigative subjects a secret. The two men had been working together in this way for nearly three years; and David had learned over time that Adams was extremely reliable and possessed the ability to keep his mouth shut.

Adams, who dreamed of someday being a big city reporter, felt privileged to work under the tutelage of David Costanzo, and he loved the conspiratorial nature of their relationship.

"Jordan, I've got a job for you, but I need you immediately, and you'll need three reliable friends. I'm paying the usual $15 an hour, but if you find what I'm looking for before 5 o'clock tomorrow, I've got a $100 bonus for each of you."

Adams looked at his watch. It was just past noon. "I'll be there by one."

David took a quick shower, then moved into the kitchen to get a bite to eat. Chasing bad guys was hard work. He needed to keep his energy up if he was going to bring down Martin McNeil.

The four students stood before Mr. Jackson's desk in the lobby. Jackson was the inert security guard who'd been parked on the ground floor for about 12 years. No one knew exactly how old he was, though he had to be closing in on 80, and no one remembered his first name. He was just Mr. Jackson, the retired policeman who had little or no responsibilities, but who could be counted on to show up every day and be courteous to all the people who passed through the lobby. The building was in a relatively safe part of town, and each condo was wired with an electronic security system that would summon the police when breached. So Mr. Jackson was mostly just an ornament in the lobby who had no real security function. Every year one or two residents suggested that the man be fired and his $1,200 a month salary trimmed from the association's budget. But he was a widower with no children who needed the job more than the job needed him; and everyone liked the old guy. So if the association did vote to fire him, probably half a dozen residents, including David, would commit to personally paying his salary.

"So, what can I do for you youngsters?" Mr. Jackson said to the students. He wore a blue uniform that looked like a policeman's, except that it had a patch on the right breast with the words "building security" stitched in red. The day's *Express-News* was spread out before him, and a small black-and-white television flickered quietly on the corner of the desk. Although Jordan Adams had met the security guard on numerous occasions, the old man did not recognize him.

"We're here to see David Costanzo," Adams said.

"He expecting you?" Mr. Jackson said doubtfully, enjoying the role of the cop, knowing the students in shorts and backpacks were a little intimidated by him.

"Yes sir," Adams said.

Mr. Jackson picked up the phone and called David's apartment. "You got some students down here. Said you were expecting them."

"Hey, Mr. J. You harassing my guests?" David said.

"Just a little bit," Mr. Jackson said with a grin, knowing the drill.

"Good. Cause that's what we're paying you for. No one gets through unless they've been okayed by Mr. J. But please, Mr. Jackson, tell me you're not down there reading that rag the *Express-News*. Please tell me that's not true."

Mr. Jackson laughed the deep rumbling chuckle of a lifetime smoker. His eyes danced beneath the blue hat that sat slightly cockeyed on his head. "You know I only read it for the funny pages," he said laughing some more.

"Well, all right," David said sternly. "I ever catch you reading their sports section—"

"I know," Mr. Jackson finished for him. "There'll be hell to pay."

"Go ahead and send those kids up."

DAVID LED THE STUDENTS into his living room. He knew Jordan Adams and he had worked with two of the others before. The fourth, a tall, skinny guy with a hickey on his neck and disheveled hair, was a newcomer. Something about his mouth bothered the reporter.

"The only thing I require of you is complete secrecy," David said. The four heads in front of him bobbed in unison. "I've worked with you three before," he said pointing to Adams and the man and woman sitting on either side of him. "But you," indicating the fourth student, "could be working for the *Express-News* for all I know, trying to find out what I'm working on so you can go back and do the story yourself."

The young man shook his head violently, starting to defend himself.

"Shut up," David said harshly. It was the kid's teeth that bugged him. They were all just a little too far apart. "Nothing you can say is going to convince me. You have to prove yourself. If Jordan thinks you can be trusted then I'll trust you. But I promise you that if you give me any reason to doubt you, your ass is gone. I'll bad mouth you to every media person I know. You'll never get a job in this town."

He stared the man down.

"Okay, here's the drill," David said. "One of my contacts told me that someone filed a suit against Martin McNeil, the Stallions receiver. The suit was settled out of court. Unfortunately, my contact didn't know where the suit was filed. I've already checked Bexar County, so you need to go through all the records in all the surrounding counties. I need names, addresses and phone numbers for the plaintiff and the lawyers and anyone else involved."

"Do we know the nature of the suit?" Adams asked intelligently.

"No," David said. His natural sense of distrust made him reluctant to reveal too much. "You tell me that when you find it."

# SIXTEEN

SIX WEEKS AGO, WHEN Martin McNeil was still a free man living in his own home rather than a county jail cell, enlisting the help of Philip Ramey didn't seem so crazy. Keeping the story out of the paper was the only part that Martin couldn't handle himself. He had settled the lawsuit, paying the money and relocating the girl, but he knew Costanzo was on the trail, and he needed to find a way to keep the reporter from writing the story. Martin wasn't sure how exactly how The Fixer might do that. Maybe he had a friend at the Guadalupe County Courthouse who could make the records from the suit disappear. With no records, the media would have no story. Maybe he could intimidate Costanzo (*without hurting him!*) into giving up on the story.

McNeil and Ramey negotiated in the player's back yard. An army of slate gray clouds marched somberly across the sky, eclipsing the sun, bringing premature darkness to the afternoon. Martin stood on the patio looking at the sky, humidity caressing his face, sweat dripping down his forehead. Water was pooled on the patio from thunderstorms that had ravaged the city earlier in the day. He dropped his head, squeezing the bridge of his nose. He couldn't believe it had come to this. He was out of options.

Ramey was standing a few feet away, watching him, measuring him. The Fixer had listened intently as McNeil described the problem. He stood still for a few minutes looking into the distance, sorting through solutions, deciding upon a course of action.

"I'll handle it," Ramey said.

"How much?" Martin said.

"Not much."

"How much?"

Ramey shrugged. He could smell the shroud of fear and desperation clinging to Martin. "Hundred and fifty grand."

Martin stared at The Fixer. He knew he was being extorted, but he wasn't sure what to do about it. "That's pretty steep."

Ramey nodded solemnly like a mortician negotiating the price on a casket. "Yes, but you're in a lot of trouble." Stopping there, the truth of the statement sinking in as a single, fat drop of rain slammed into the patio like a period at the end of a sentence. Martin stared at that wet spot then another magically appeared, underscoring it. Fat, angry drops fell, stinging the skin. Still, they stood unmoving, six feet apart, lost in thought.

Finally, Martin broke the silence, laying down some rules. "I want you to resolve this situation, but I don't want you to hurt Costanzo or this girl in any way. Is that clear?"

Ramey nodded smiling. "I wouldn't think of it."

"Or anyone else, either," Martin amended. "Don't break anyone's legs."

"You watch too much television, Martin," Ramey laughed. He raised his right hand with three fingers together in a boy scout's salute. "I hereby promise not to hurt this fine young girl, and I promise not to break anyone's legs."

Then the rain came, falling in angry waves, dousing them as they stood on the back porch. Finally, Ramey said, "Guess I'd better get going." He walked casually across the lawn and out the back gate. Martin moved into the house like a zombie. Even then, he knew that some measure of control over his life had slipped away. What he didn't realize was that this decision would land him in jail weeks later, facing a lifetime of imprisonment.

# SEVENTEEN

MARTIN WEARILY RESTED HIS head against the plastic wall of the fuselage as he stared through the small window of the 737. His face was a maze of concerned lines. It was pitch black outside. Rain swirled around the plane; an angry wind tossing the aircraft from side to side like a bear disciplining an errant cub. The lights of San Antonio glimmered in the distance. Martin sighed in relief. He was desperate to get home. He wanted to crawl into bed, pull the covers over his head. It was odd to feel so helpless. Martin was an overachiever. They type of guy who set goals and reached them seemingly at will. But with this lawsuit filed against him, there seemed to be nothing he could do except sit and wait. Nothing for him to do except hope The Fixer would find a way to keep the story away from the media.

Suddenly, the plane lurched violently to one side, the left wing tipping toward the earth. Its passengers gasping and grunting as it careened through another gut-wrenching pocket of turbulence.

"You know, most plane crashes occur at landing," said Jim Davis solemnly from three rows in front of Martin.

"Yeah I know," said Michael Robinson enthusiastically from the seat in front of Davis. "Wind sheer can grab the wings and pitch the plane over just as it's about to touch down. And then, Ka-Boom! It all goes up in flames."

"Will both of you shut the hell up!" said a huge man named T.D. Cox. Thick beads of sweat dripped down his forehead and off his cheeks. His fingers wrapped possessively around the arm rests as though they would save him if the plane did go down. Cox's 6-foot-6, 310-pound frame was wedged into a seat that he had begun to view as his deathbed.

The flight was the Stallions' chartered return from a 27-17 Monday night loss to the Seattle Seahawks. It had been bumpy for the last half-hour, and Cox, an offensive lineman who was terrified of flying, was alternately praying to God for salvation and cursing the pilots for their ineptitude.

"T.D., relax, man," Davis said with an unfriendly grin. "We're just talking about plane crashes in general. This specific plane *probably* won't crash." Davis winked at Robinson.

"It will if you keep talking about it," T.D. shot back. "Planes crash all the time; and if you don't shut up you're gonna jinx us and then we're all gonna die." He was suddenly an expert on plane crashes, prepared to cite cases and list the locations of the last 100 downed flights.

"Nah, we won't all die," Robinson said confidently. The jacket of his navy Brooks Brothers suit was draped over the empty seat next to him. "Some of us will just be maimed for life. Or we may catch fire and smolder for hours." He considered this for a moment as though the prospect of roasting flesh appealed to him in some odd way. He adjusted the Windsor knot in his tie as he continued. "We'll be in terrible, agonizing pain. We'll pray for death, but we won't actually die. So don't worry about it, T.D. You probably won't get killed. With all the layers of fat you've got, none of your major organs could possibly get damaged."

"Screw you," T.D. said, staring intently at Robinson.

"Don't get mad at me!" Robinson replied raising his hands in the air, palms out in a gesture of helplessness. "What do I look like, Mother-fuck-ing-single-parent-Nature? I didn't create these flying conditions. I'm just a poor innocent crash victim like you."

Another patch of turbulence. The plane was muscled upward then dropped straight down. There were more groans and complaints and a few screams.

"AAAAHHHHH, we're going down!" Robinson mockingly screamed. "We're all gonna die except for T.D. who's gonna roast like a pig!"

T.D.'s eyes were clinched shut as he quietly and hysterically muttered, "ohmigod ohmigod ohmigod ohmigod."

"Ha Ha Ha. . . look at T.D., man he's gonna bust a gasket," Robinson said.

Martin paid no attention. It was always the same conversation; he was in no mood for games. He had to figure out the next step. There was no instruction manual for a situation like his. He wasn't sure how to react or what measures to take. His livelihood was as stranded as a shipwreck survivor on a sliver of land out in the middle of the ocean, safe for the moment, but in dire need of recovery. The message Save Our Soles had been etched into the sandy shore of his mind, a subtle reminder that Nike would be just one of the many companies who would leave him if they learned of his current crisis.

After Joseph Steadman's call, everything had been handled in a mad rush. Steadman hammered out a quick agreement with the girl's lawyer. Ramey picked up Lisa at her dilapidated trailer and drove the girl and her child to a plush new townhouse. A bank account was established in her name with a $25,000 balance. She had everything she needed. Everything seemed under control. But still, something lingered. Martin couldn't shake the feeling that something was forgotten. That there was some nugget of evidence Costanzo could snatch up and turn into a big Sunday spread in the paper.

Martin knew that his image was in serious jeopardy. He was a spokesman for Nike, Coca-Cola, McDonald's and a host of smaller, local companies. All that would go down the toilet; flushed away like a pet gold-fish gone buoyant. He wouldn't be able to fight it. Wouldn't persuade any-one to give him another chance.

There were only two variables companies considered when select-ing an athlete as a spokesperson: He had to be a great performer on the field, which Martin was, and the player must have a consistently good or consistently bad reputation in the community—Martin was a model citizen. A company will sign a bad boy like Charles Barkley or Dennis Rodman because it understands the player's infamous reputation and believe his flamboyant style will help sell a product. However, no company wants its spokesman to flip-flop. The pillar of the community they signed can't become embroiled in controversy six months down the road. Similarly the bad boy can't suddenly decide to clean up his act. Those companies are buying into a very specific aspect of a player's personality; and they're extremely possessive about that particular quality.

Martin thought of the rap group, The Fat Boys. They were grossly obese young men who sang songs about getting kicked out of all-you-can-eat establishments and other humorous fat-related incidents. Rumor was that their contract with the recording studio required them to stay fat. One of them went on a diet once and lost 10 pounds. The studio went crazy—started forcing food down the poor guy's throat until he gained the weight back. "You guys are The *Fat* Boys. Don't go getting skinny on us."

Martin wasn't certain how his endorsement companies would react if they heard the news, but he feared they would dump him. It would cost him nearly $10 million over the next five years.

It wasn't just the money Martin worried about it. He'd been famous long enough to know that fame is a proverbial double-edged sword. It's nice to be recognized in public. The pats on the back. The autograph requests. It's all very flattering. Fame is wonderful when everyone loves you. But what if they hate you? Martin wasn't sure he could handle intense public hatred. Celebrities like Dennis Rodman and Charles Barkley seemed to thrive on widespread scorn. They seemed impervious to the anger they gen-erated in others. Martin knew he wouldn't be able to handle it. The hard stares at the grocery store, angry comments at the gas station. Martin was basically a nice person who enjoyed pleasant interaction with people in the community.

As things were, if just one person in a thousand walked up to Martin and said, "I think you're a jerk," he would smile and try to let the hateful barb slip out of his mind, but it would stay with him for weeks, prodding him, hurting him. He'd rack his brain trying to figure out what he might have done to that person. *"Am I a jerk?"* Martin possessed a somewhat unhealthy need to be liked by everyone. He always signed autographs,

# Power Shift

attended charity events and was friendly to people on the street.

Martin's image was everything to him. It was how he defined himself, how he related to the world. If some disaster disfigured or destroyed that image, it would change his life in ways that he wasn't sure he could handle.

The whole fiasco with 12-year-old Matthew Fields during Martin's rookie year had taught the player to be meticulous in his private life. Always do what you say you're going to do, and don't do anything stupid or unnecessary. Martin drank alcohol in moderation, he rarely visited nightclubs, he didn't drive his Mercedes too fast and he'd never cheated on his wife.

Despite his aversion to the wild lifestyle of the professional athlete Martin still felt the pressure of constant media attention. His enormous fame made people hungry for any morsel of gossip. Therefore the media was inclined to report everything known about him. With reporters watching his every move, maintaining his image became a chore for Martin. Even the most innocuous events could be misconstrued.

He spent more and more time in his home, and in quiet places far removed from the social mainstream. On the rare occasions when he did venture into a popular bar or club, the next day's newspaper would invariably include a line in the society section reading:  Celebrity sighting—Stallions wide receiver Martin McNeil at The Stampede Bar and Grill or whatever the name of the place might be. Martin read those listings with a growing sense of dread. It was a noose tightening around his neck. He might not see them. He may not realize that anyone recognized him, but the sentries were out there, dutifully reporting his whereabouts. Silent eyes were watching his every move, waiting for him to slip up.

Once,  while at dinner, Martin and Jessica got into a quiet but heated argument with about some dumb thing—he can't even remember what it was. They were hashing it out over their hamburgers, keeping their voices low the way couples do when they're fighting in public. The next day at the Stallions' facility, beat reporter Robert Duman said, "I hear you got into a fist fight with your wife at a restaurant last night. Is that true?"

Martin's mind flashed to a button he'd seen once that read: ANYTHING YOU SAY CAN AND WILL BE DISTORTED, RE-MIXED AND USED AGAINST YOU. He walked away without saying a word. He felt surrounded.

Two years ago, he and Jessica were sitting on the living room floor in tattered sweats playing Monopoly. Martin was losing terribly, as usual. Jessica swept a strand of dark brown hair away from her face as she watched him advance around the board. Her green eyes smiling brightly when he landed on her Boardwalk property.

"That'll be fifteen hundred dollars," she said gaily knowing that Martin was nearly out of Monopoly money and would soon have to make his payments via back rubs, foot massages and the like.

He snatched up the dice and hid them behind his back, accusing Jessica of cheating. "I refuse to continue this game amid such corruption," he said.

Jessica, reacting in mock anger, jumped into his lap and tried to pry the dice out of his hands. They were wrestling playfully on the floor for a few minutes before Martin finally pinned her down. Then the doorbell rang.

Martin got up to open the door. A Pizza Hut delivery man stood there with his mouth open.

"Dude! You're Martin McNeil!" he said, his eyes dancing widely with delight.

"Yeah, how are you doing?" Martin said smiling perfunctorily, pulling $20 from his wallet.

The man ignoring the money, looking straight at Jessica, suddenly very serious, saying. "Is everything okay here?"

"What?" she said straightening the pieces on the game board that had been knocked out of place.

"I saw him attacking you through the window, and I just wanted to make sure you're okay."

Martin listened in disbelief.

"He wasn't *attacking* me," she said. "We were playing."

"Uh huh," the delivery man said, giving Martin a knowing look. "Well, you don't have to be afraid of him. If you want to leave, I'll stay right here until you're safely out of the house."

"Man, get the hell out of my life!" Martin said slamming the door. His eyes misting with fear and rage. He stormed into the kitchen for a glass of water, wrenching a cabinet door open so hard he nearly tore it off its hinges. Jessica tried to soothe him, but the pressure was getting to him. The need to always be good was cutting deep crevices into his psyche. He, like everyone else, needed privacy. He needed occasional anonymity, but it evaded him, shimmering in the distance like an oasis that was never reached. He could never relax. Not even at home. Someone was always watching.

The doorbell rang again.

Jessica answered.

"Do you guys want this pizza or not?" the delivery man said belligerently.

It was her turn to slam the door.

It was the casual misunderstandings that scared Martin. Through no fault of his own, anyone could misinterpret something he did, report it to media and his life would be ruined.

That's why the events of the past few days tore at him so badly. If reporters found out about the paternity suit, they'd crucify him. He was deep in thought as the plane continued to descend into the San Antonio area.

"Hey, Martin, how come we haven't heard anything from Williams this flight?" Davis said looking over his shoulder. Tim Williams, a running back who sat in the same row as Martin, was among the more vocal scared flyers on the team. He often required a sedative from the team's physicians just before takeoff just so that he could sit still through a flight. But even on drugs, the man turned into a banshee at the first hint of turbulence.

It was odd that no one had heard a word from him during this particularly bumpy flight.

Martin didn't answer the question.

Robinson turned around, put his knees in his seat and looked a few rows back. There he saw Williams reclined with his eyes closed and a serene look on his face.

"Yo yo, check out Tim," Robinson said to Davis. "I can't believe he's sleeping. In three years I've never seen him sleep on a flight. In fact, I've never even seen anyone near him sleep because he makes so much cry-baby-ass noise all the time."

"Well, in honor of his first in-flight nap, I think we should do something very special for Mr. Williams," Davis said. He got out of his seat and walked back to his teammate. Since the flight was an NFL charter, the flight attendants were purposely blind to and mute about the many seat-back-and-tray-table infractions as the plane approached the runway at San Antonio International Airport.

Davis clad in a white shirt and charcoal suit pants flipped his red and black tie over one shoulder. He reached up and carefully peeled the adhesive name tag off the top of Williams' seat and pressed it gently against his teammate's forehead. An audience of more than a dozen players stood to watch Davis in action. Many clamped hands over their mouths to muffle their laughter.

Williams did not wake up.

Davis peeled off another name tag and placed it on his right cheek.

More laughter.

Amazingly, Williams did not wake up.

Players began passing name tags to Davis, who stuck them carefully all over Williams' face and head. Next, airplane-issue packets of cheese were passed forward, and Davis placed three of them in Williams' breast pocket, balanced two on each shoulder and one on his head.

Everyone held their breath when the plane encountered more turbulence and the stacks of cheese tumbled into Williams' lap. When it was clear the running back was not going to wake up, Davis put the cheese back onto his shoulders and head.

A click and a flash as someone took a picture of the dozing player. Williams was still soundly asleep and his teammates were still laughing as the plane reached the runway.

Just as the wheels touched the ground, someone screamed, "FIREBALL!"

T.D. Cox cried out as the plane bounced into the air and then came back into contact with the earth. The flaps came up and the tires screeched as the place decelerated. "Ohmigod ohmigod ohmigod ohmigod. . . "

"Welcome back to San Antonio," the pilot's voice boomed over the intercom. "The local time is 2:45 a.m. and I and the rest of the flight crew want to say that we really enjoyed the game, and even though you guys lost, you looked great. We're still rooting for you and hopefully we'll get a chance to be the crew on another charter flight this year. If not, we certainly wish you the very best with the rest of the season, and we look forward to seeing you in the playoffs."

The pilot's pep talk was mostly drowned out by yelling and screaming from the players urging him to "shut the hell up," "stay off the microphone" and "quit trying to be a cub scout den mother."

"You know, T.D." Robinson said, "now that we've landed safely on another flight, we have increased the statistical likelihood that we will crash on our next flight. The god of statistics insists that there be a crash at some point, and every successful landing pushes us a little bit closer to that crash. If you really want to be safe—"

A pillow whizzed through the air striking Robinson in the back of the head. It was followed immediately by two more pillows that hit and a blanket that missed the mark as Robinson ducked down.

"Okay, you damned punks!" he screamed. Then, doing his best imitation of Al Pacino in *Scarface*, he said, "Say hello to my little friend!" He jumped up and threw four pillows in rapid succession toward the back of the plane.

Once again, the war was on.

At the end of nearly every Stallions charter flight a pillow and blanket fight erupted. There were no organized sides. Every player fought for himself. Players looked and sounded like a group of oversized fifth-graders in fancy suits and ties. Long arms stretched into the aisle to retrieve projectiles and heads darted over and under the protective height of the seats waiting for an opportunity to loose a round without being hit by return fire.

Finally, the aircraft taxied into the hanger where the players disembarked and walked to their cars.

Martin was on remote control, hardly conscious of what was happening around him. He just wanted to go home.

As Davis stood to retrieve his bag from the overhead compartment, he noticed Williams again. He was still asleep. Davis couldn't believe it. In a loud stage whisper—one that would have seemed ridiculous if he had taken a moment to consider the volume of the pillow fight that had just concluded—he told everyone to be quiet. "Let's leave Tim sleeping on the plane."

Low laughter floated to the cabin as players nodded their agreement. Slowly they filed off the plane, each stealing a last glance at their sleeping teammate.

Although their stealth didn't hurt, it wasn't necessary.

Williams was dead.

# EIGHTEEN

DAVID COSTANZO'S YOUNG INVESTIGATORS found it.

It was a paternity suit filed a few days earlier by 18-year-old Lisa Benson of Marcott, Texas. The suit claimed that Martin McNeil was the father of Lisa's 13-month-old son, Michael Alexander Benson. It was filed in Guadalupe County and settled two days later. Her lawyer was a guy named R. Winston Mickler, an associate at James Brickly Boston, an old firm in Marcott. Martin's lawyer was Joseph Steadman a partner at Barclay, Steadman, Smith & Goldberg.

"You're sure she's 18?" David said with skeptical glee. He was a good reporter, who verified his facts. But he was so desperate for her age to be correct that he almost didn't ask the question for fear that it was a mistake. He didn't want her to be older. At 18, she was perfect. But he had to confirm. He had to be positive.

"I'm sure."

"What's her birth date?"

"Um. . ." Adams shuffled through some papers read the date.

David did the math on a piece of scrap paper. He got 18. "And you're absolutely positive about the age of the kid?" If the kid was already 2 years old, then the mother was only 15 years old when she got pregnant. *It gets better and better.*

"Put my life on it," Adams confirmed.

"Good. Bring the copies by ASAP and leave them with Mr. Jackson. There'll be an envelope with cash waiting for you. Good work." He put down the phone and clasped his hands behind his head. This was huge. *A 15 year old? Martin, Martin, Martin. What were you thinking when you slid between those velvety young legs? Was she a virgin? Statutory rape rolls off the tongue nicely. Maybe superstar good boy Martin McNeil has been hanging out at the local high schools banging young cheerleaders. Only this time, he messed up. He got one of them pregnant and thought she would just disappear. But she didn't go away. She filed a lawsuit like a good little girl. Did he promise her that she couldn't get pregnant the first time? Did he tell her that he loved her?*

David decided he'd try to track down some other teenagers who had slept with Martin. Hell, after the story hit the paper on Sunday, Costanzo might be flooded with calls from young girls claiming that Martin had stolen their virginity, too. Maybe there were a couple more who've quietly given birth to his children. David smiled.

# NINETEEN

MARTIN WAS NAKED IN his king-sized waterbed, covers pulled up to his chin. He looked like a marsupial infant tucked snugly into its mother's pouch. He felt safe in his heated aquatic haven. It was a black lacquered bed with a waveless mattress and bright white sheets. Everything in the house was either black or white except for the fresh red roses in a vase on the living room table. Martin and Jessica were into modern simplicity. Above the bed was a picture of a black cat stretching languidly atop a white picket fence. In one corner of the bedroom a black television was suspended from the ceiling.

Next to him was the lithe, naked form of his wife. He was black; she was white. Together, they conformed to the decorative theme of the house. The clock on the bedside table showed a few minutes before eight on Tuesday morning. He didn't plan to get out of bed until noon. The problems of the world did not exist as long as he was wrapped in the cocoon of his down comforter, and as long as the water temperature in the bed was a perfect 82 degrees Fahrenheit. And as long as the flesh of Jessica's warm body was pressed neatly against his. He could lie there all day. Content. Unworried. Oblivious.

The phone rang.

Martin considered not answering. For starters, he didn't feel like reaching to the bedside table. It would interrupt his relaxation, spoil the lethargic mood that was maturing nicely in his mind. Tuesday was his day off. With just another half-hour of lazy meditation in bed, he would be prepared to waste away an entire day. To not climb out of bed at all unless he had to pee. Even if he had to make a trip to the bathroom, he'd squint his eyes the whole way so they couldn't fully adjust to being awake, and he'd move as slowly as possible so as not to raise his heart rate. Then he'd march slowly back into bed, and plop back down next to his wife and think about nothing for the rest of the day. It would be perfect.

The phone rang again.

Still he didn't move to answer it. There was no telling who it might be. He rarely gave his phone number to anyone outside his family and closest friends, but somehow, other people always discovered his unlisted number and called incessantly. They had a Caller ID box in the kitchen, and he kept meaning to get one for the bedroom, but he never got around to it.

He snatched up the receiver in the middle of the third ring mostly because Jessica was still sleeping, and he didn't want to wake her.

Martin recognized the voice immediately. "Hey, what's up Ramey?"

"Check out channel four. There's about to be a press conference," Ramey said.

Martin sat up in bed, suddenly sweating, nearly pressing the phone through the side of his head. "Is this about *me*?" he hissed quietly.

"Naw. Chill. They don't know shit about you. Just tune in."

"Okay," Martin breathed, relieved. "But what about . . .my situation."

"Don't sweat it. I'm takin' care of business." The line clicked dead.

Martin returned the phone to its cradle, suddenly wide awake. Adrenaline coursing through his veins. Was it just a minute ago that he was thinking about sleeping the entire day away? He reached for the remote and tuned to channel four. He turned the volume down as low as he could, and waited impatiently for the press conference to begin.


ABOUT 30 MEDIA MEMBERS and eight Stallions employees gathered in the team's main meeting room. The walls were covered with boards listing statistical goals for each facet of the game. There were offensive objectives for time of possession, points scored, turnovers, first downs, third-down conversion ratios, passing completion percentages and average yards per carry. On defense there were boards to track tackles, sacks, interceptions, third-down ratios, yards per carry allowed and average number of plays per drive. There were three boards dedicated to special teams.

To the uninitiated, the room gave substance to the idea of football as science. Everything that could be measured was measured. The significance of each event on the field was weighed and balanced, and its potential for reoccurrence evaluated. In this room, opponent's game films were reviewed with the same scrutiny the military lends to satellite photos. If a linebacker has a false step on pass plays, that fact is recorded and scenarios are developed to take advantage of it.

The room was buzzing softly with quiet conversations when Starnes entered. The reporters had received vague messages about Tim Williams and a health problem, but they didn't know the nature of it. They weren't sure if he had suffered an injury, had an accident or gotten food poisoning. The only thing the Stallions public relations department would tell them was that it was an extremely serious situation.

Starnes, a pale stocky man whose face turned bright red when he was upset, marched to the front of the room and stood behind a podium bearing the Stallions green and white logo.

He stood still looking over the group of men—there were no women.

"Tim Williams is dead," he said without preamble.

The room plunged into stunned silence.

Starnes looked down at a statement that had been prepared by the team's public relations department and started reading. He talked about how important Williams was to the team, and about what a remarkable person he was. Tim was always going out of his way to help others. Tim was very involved in the community. Tim was just a tremendous young man. As he read, Starnes occasionally wiped moisture from his eyes. The room was quiet except for the distant hum of the air conditioner and the isolated crinkle of turning pages as the newspaper reporters tried to keep pace. Starnes voice broke a little toward the end.

Then the questions began.

"How did he die?" a reporter asked.

"It looks like he could have had a heart attack or a stroke or something during the flight, but there's no telling at this point," the coach said. "There's supposed to be an autopsy tomorrow, and we should have more information then."

From the back of the room: "Do you think being at high altitude may have contributed to his death?"

"Well, again, I'm not a doctor, and they should be able to figure all that out during the autopsy. I do know that Tim was terribly afraid of flying. He suffered panic attacks every time we took a trip. The team doctor usually gave him a sleeping pill to settle his nerves, but even then he still was fidgety."

"Is it normal for the team doctor to give pills to the players?"

"The team doctor has the discretion to do whatever he thinks is right for the overall health of the players. There are two or three guys on the team who are so afraid of flying that they sometimes start hyperventilating or their blood pressure goes way up. For a guy like that, it's just better if the doc gives him a sleeping pill to knock him out for the flight."

"What other types of pills does the doctor issue?" a radio reporter asked cynically.

Starnes face and neck shifted from pale to pink as he turned his glare on the reporter. "This is a very sad day for the Stallions. I know that *you guys* aren't sad. You are all very excited that someone died. It gives you something to write about and talk about. And I know it would thrill you beyond measure if someone in this organization or on this staff did something wrong. But no one broke the rules. There is nothing wrong with giving a player a sleeping pill. Tim's death is devastating to us not only as a team, but also as human beings. If you can't appreciate that, then this press conference is over."

Starnes looked over the audience, and the reporters stared back somewhat sobered by his remarks.

"Did anyone notice signs that he might be suicidal?"

"Not that I'm aware of," Starnes said. "But we still need to talk to all the players to see if they noticed anything strange."

"We're all very sorry that Williams is dead," said one reporter, who did not sound at all sorry, "but he was a known drug user. Less than six months ago he was involved in an accident in which police believe alcohol was involved. If it hadn't taken them so long to clean up the scene and get him down to the station for a breathalyzer test, they're certain he would have been over the limit. As it was, two and a half hours after the accident, he was still at .08. He's been a general trouble-maker since the day he walked into this town. How can you say he was a tremendous person?"

Starnes nodded sadly. "We all know that Tim had his problems, but at the core, he was a good kid. He worked hard. He wanted to be good. He wanted to stay out of trouble; but trouble seemed to follow him around like an old dog with no home. I've worked with him for the past three years, and I know he's a tremendous individual. I am deeply saddened by his death."

The questions went on this way for nearly 45 minutes. The reporters were digging, but not coming up with much. It almost sounded like the guy died of natural causes, but there was no way in hell a healthy, 26-year-old professional athlete could just keel over. There *had* to be drugs involved. That was the only way. Williams was a guy who had gone to jail for a year during college after he got caught snorting cocaine. Since entering the pros he'd had his share of problems. He even failed an NFL drug test his rookie year, and voluntarily entered the league's drug rehabilitation program. But as far as anyone could tell, it didn't do him any good. Within a month of his return to San Antonio, he was running with the same people, hanging out in the same places. His attitude was *why the hell not?* He was a grown man and no one was going to tell him whom he could choose as associates. If he wanted to get drunk every now and again, then he'd get drunk; the NFL could kiss his drug-tested ass.

THE AUTOPSY RESULTS WOULD set the tone for the media coverage in the coming weeks. If drugs *were* involved in his death, it would become a huge national event that would capture the attention of millions. Tim Williams would become a poster child for every drug awareness program that ever lived. Mothers and fathers would sit their children in front of the television and say, "See what happens when you do drugs." He would be more famous dead than he ever was alive.

There would be in-depth features about his life beginning at age nine when he was recruited to sell drugs on his school playground, continuing through his high school gang fights, including the bullet he took during a drive-by shooting, leading up to his arrest and conviction for possession of cocaine, his failure of the NFL drug test, and finally his death. Interviews with his former classmates, teammates and cellmates. Scalding editorials would strike against the school districts in California that did nothing to help him when he was young, the college coaches who turned a blind eye to his many drug infractions, and the NFL for allowing a scumbag like Williams to continue to play in a league in which every player should be a role model for kids. Inevitably the San Antonio Stallions would feel the media's wrath for drafting the guy and keeping him on the roster for three years.

That's how the stories would shake out if drugs were discovered to be the cause of death.

There was a cold logic to it. A formula or sorts. Every story carried with it a sidebar story that could be prepared for the next day's paper or newscast. When the sidebars and the sidebars to the sidebars were exhausted, the media would return to the original story and look for new angles to pursue.

Even if there were no drugs involved, his death would be big news for a week or two. There would be a memorial service, a funeral and a lot of candlelight vigils to report. From a news standpoint, Williams' death was significant because professional athletes rarely died during their careers. Sad features would be written about his stunned parents. Pictures of his mother weeping at the funeral would play dramatically on the covers of newspapers and as the lead story on evening newscasts. Of course, there would still be articles about his drug problems. That would be too juicy a morsel to pass up. No one had ever done the comprehensive story on Tim Williams, and now would be the perfect time to turn the spotlight on all the skeletons in his closet.

The press conference dragged on, but there really was nothing to jump on until the reports came back from the medical examiner. That was when the direction of the story would reveal itself. But already, during live broadcasts from the press conference, radio talk show hosts were speculating about whether or not Tim Williams overdosed on cocaine or some other illegal substance. Now that the guy was dead, no one had to worry about being sued for slander. *You can't defame the dead.* So the speculation started during the press conference and would continue until the medical examiner released his findings.

When Coach Starnes finally walked out of the room, he let out a sigh of relief, grateful no one had asked about the name tags and cheese that were stuck all over the dead player's body.

MARTIN WATCHED THE PRESS conference in shock. He couldn't believe he'd been sitting next to a dead man. That he'd actually climbed over Williams' dead body to get off the plane. *How the hell Tim be dead?*

The moment the press conference ended the phone rang. Martin reached for it automatically.

It was Ramey.

"Tim Williams is dead," Martin said, numbly repeating what he had just heard. He was still staring at the television, but now there was just a commercial about a truck that could climb over mountainous piles of rock.

"Meet me in your backyard," Ramey said. The phone was dead before Martin could respond.

He quickly got out of bed, threw on a pair of shorts and weaved through his house into the backyard. The thunderstorms that hovered over the city the previous week had exhausted themselves, giving way to humid sunshine. Ramey was sitting in a lounge chair on the porch under a warm sun with his shirt off. He was a large man at 6-foot-2, 230 pounds, with the rippling muscles of a professional body builder. His light brown skin glistened under a sheen of lotion. A half-empty 16-ounce bottle of 7-up and a mobile phone sat on the table next to him. He looked comfortable like he'd been there for a while.

"Sit down." Ramey said as soon as Martin closed the sliding glass door. He pointed toward another lounge chair, and Martin dutifully moved into it.

"So what's up, Ramey?" Martin couldn't hide the nervousness in his voice. "Thought we needed a little diversion."

"A diversion for what?"

"Only way to keep reporters away from you is give them something better to chew on," Ramey said casually, fully reclined in the chair, round shades covering his eyes.

Martin, sitting bolt upright, said: "Something better to chew on? What are you talking about?" His words carefully measured. Martin got that way when he was nervous. He repeated things.

"Just saying that I'm taking care of business for you," Ramey said coolly. "See, after we talked Friday, I started thinking about everything involved here. You know, trying to figure what I needed to do to cover your ass. I realized that a reporter is always looking for a good story, right?"

Martin mumbled his agreement, still not sure where Ramey was going with this. The Fixer continued.

"But sometimes you see the stupidest damn stories on TV or in the paper. You look at it and say, how the hell did something like that make the news? You know what I'm sayin?"

"Yeah. . . I guess. . . but what—"

"Why do you think those dumb stories get on the news?"

"I have no idea," Martin said.

"Well, I do," Ramey said, sitting up. "It's a Slow News Day. That means there ain't shit happening that's worth reporting, but the TV guys still have to fill up the 10 o'clock news. So they do a story about two rare, yellow-breasted penguins at the zoo or something stupid like that. Course, the flip-side is sometimes there are Fast News Days, and a story that would usually make the news gets bumped because there's a better story. So then I asked myself, 'Is Martin McNeil's situation something the media would cover?' Of course. You're a national celebrity who screwed up. So—"

"I didn't screw up," Martin said defensively.

"Whatever. So then the next question is, 'Do we *want* the media to cover this?' Hell no. That's why you called me. So then I asked myself, 'What can we do to keep the media from finding out about Martin McNeil's situation?' The answer that kept coming back to me was, 'Create a Fast News Day.' I had to give 'em something better to cover.' Something that would last for weeks. By the time they finished chewing on the new story, your problem will be buried under so much other shit, no one will ever find it." While he was talking Ramey had slipped his shirt back over his head.

"What did you do?" Martin said, knowing the answer but not willing to believe it.

"You mean what did *we* do?" Ramey corrected.

"No. I mean what did *you* do, mother fucker!"

"Keep your voice down. Be professional."

"I told you not to hurt anybody," Martin said.

"No, you didn't," Ramey said with an admonishing finger in the air. "You said 'don't break anyone's legs,' and honestly, I was a little insulted by that. Talking to me like I'm a TV loan shark or something."

Martin was out of his chair, and on top of Ramey in a flash. He struck with his fists, delivering a flurry of blows to The Fixer's face and body. He was crying and grunting with rage as they tumbled to the ground. Martin wasn't sure whether he was more angry at The Fixer or at himself. He should never have gotten involved with Philip Ramey. He should never have thought that he could control the guy. They were grappling back and forth in the grass when Ramey's hand latched onto Martin's testicles and squeezed fiercely.

Martin gasped and stopped moving abruptly. It felt as though his testicles were being torn away from his body. Bolts of pain shot up his spine and down his legs. He couldn't move. He could barely breathe.

"Get your punk ass off me," Ramey said, squeezing even harder. Martin tried to obey this command, but his muscles wouldn't respond. Finally, Ramey rolled him over, and straddled him, keeping a firm grip on his groin. "You're lucky I'm in a good mood, otherwise, I'd rip your nuts right off your body." He gave them another squeeze for emphasis.

Martin, lay in contorted silence.

"Here's something for you to think about," Ramey said touching a finger to his bloody lip and shaking his head. "I got you by the balls even when my hand ain't down here." Another firm squeeze that brought an anguished moan from Martin. "You paid me fifty thousand down, and you got two more fifty grand installments due the next two Fridays. You decide to go to the cops, what you gonna tell 'em I was doing for a hundred and fifty thousand bones? Sending out a press release?" Ramey laughed loudly at this; a hearty guffaw that shook his whole body, but unfortunately for Martin, did not loosen his grip.

The player was mute. He was concentrating on breathing. Sucking air in deeply, letting it leak out slowly.

"See if this shit ever comes out, it'll look to the cops like you hired me specifically to knock off Tim Williams," Ramey continued. "Maybe you owed him a lot of money or maybe he was banging your wife or maybe he was blackmailing you with pictures of you and some guy named Hans. Who knows? If it ever comes up with the cops—like if you start having regrets and decide you need to talk to somebody about this—I'll tell 'em straight up that I didn't know why you wanted the guy dead; you just told me it was urgent. You told me, to 'kill him as fast as I could.' See, I don't care about going to prison. I've been there, and I ain't afraid to go back. Prison's a way of life that's chilled for a guy like me. I do my time, make some contacts and eventually get out again. No big deal for me. But for you?" Ramey laughed darkly, looking down at Martin, shaking his head in distaste. "Weak-ass muthafucka like you? Shit, you'd lose your virginity the first night and spend the rest of your time being somebody's bitch."

Ramey slowly released his grip on Martin's testicles and moved back onto the lawn chair, leaving the football player sprawled on the grass. Martin summoned all of his effort, and said hoarsely, "Can't you see that we're both going to jail whether I call the cops or not." Even though he was consumed by pain, his anger had not diminished.

Ramey shook his head. "Naw. Not unless you do something stupid."

Martin released an exasperated breath. "You've already taken care of that. The cops *always* investigate a murder?"

"Ain't gonna be no police investigation," Ramey said quickly. "When they do the autopsy, all they're gonna see is a dude that had a heart attack."

"You don't know that." Martin argued. He was cupping his testicles in both hands. They felt swollen, like two overripe peaches.

"Yeah I do," Ramey explained, the scuffle between them completely forgotten. Martin had attacked him, he'd put the guy down, and that was that. No harm done, just a quick lesson in superiority. "Few years ago, a doctor friend of mine told me how to kill a guy nice and quiet. No fuss, no muss. Drug called Digoxin. Fairly common heart medication that old people use. Sprinkle it into the guy's Coke and viola, his heart does a little stutter step like Barry Sanders juking a linebacker in the open field. Then it stops kicking. Forever."

Martin stared for a moment, something just occurring to him. "You were on the plane?" he said incredulously.

"Yeah." Ramey smiled. "You never saw me cause you were zoned out the whole flight. Off in La-La land dreaming about the Wicked Bitch of the West."

"But how did you manage that?"

"Shit it ain't hard to get on the flight. There's always about 40 businessmen who go with the team on every road trip. I made a call to a friend who made sure my name was on the guest list. No big deal."

"They're gonna do an autopsy;" Martin was more scared than ever. Tim Williams was his seat mate. If there was evidence of foul play, the police would probably talk to him first. There was no way he could outsmart the cops. He had no talent for deception. They'd see the lies forming in his head. They'd bully a confession out of him, and he'd spend the rest of his life in prison. "They're gonna test his blood and if this Digoxin stuff is in there, they'll find it. They'll know someone killed him."

"Naw, man. They ain't gonna find it. That's the beauty of this drug, the reason the doc told me to use it," Ramey said. "When they check his blood, they're looking for shit like cocaine and heroin and other stuff a young guy might have been popping that could have caused a heart attack. But in someone his age, who's never had a heart problem, ain't no way in hell they'd think to check for Digoxin. And the only way they could find it is if they were looking for it specifically."

"But still," Martin said, not convinced. "If they can't find a reasonable cause of death, then they're gonna start investigating stuff like that. They'll keep looking until they find something. I mean, a guy's heart just doesn't stop. It'll show up somewhere. There'll be damage or something."

"I doubt it. Not with a guy like Tim. Known drug user who was also afraid of flying. They'll just figure his heart was weak from all those years of drugs. Then he got so scared in the turbulence last night that his heart just quit on him."

Martin was shaking his head doubtfully.

"You worry too much," Ramey said, picking up his phone and his soda and starting across the lawn. "I'll be in touch."

Martin lay on the ground for 15 minutes after Ramey left, waiting for the pain in his groin to subside. He didn't move or make a sound. Finally, he stood and walked gingerly toward the sliding glass door.

*What the hell have I gotten myself into?*

# TWENTY

DAVID'S PORSCHE CUT A slick course through the air as he cruised down Interstate 10 at 90 mph. Empty farm land rolled right up to the highway on both sides; small groups of cows stood in fields watching him pass. Marcott was a town of about 20,000 residents about 35 miles northeast of San Antonio. The people were mostly poor, uneducated Blacks and Hispanics who couldn't find work in the small town, and who couldn't afford the daily commute into the city. According to the records, Lisa Benson lived in a run-down trailer park on the west side of the city. There were a lot of run-down trailer parks in Marcott.

His Porsche seemed misplaced on the small streets. Old men and old women puttered through the meager downtown area in rusted Chevrolets and Fords that rattled noisily with droopy bumpers and busted turn signals.

He passed a closed down family grocery, and an old video store that had dropped out of business. Just outside the eastern city limits, the franchises of corporate America had overtaken the sedate town. There was a mammoth HEB grocery store, Hastings Books and Records and a Super K-mart. Marcott had become the central shopping district for towns in a dozen surrounding counties. There was also a McDonald's that had opened five years earlier to uproarious welcome. The citizens of Marcott had lined up for miles to go through the drive through window on that first day. The arrival of a McDonald's franchise was taken as a badge of honor.

David pulled into the gravel parking lot in front of a convenience store with a big sign out front that read, "GET-AND-GO". A wave of heat and the pungent odor of ammonia slapped him when he walked through the door. He nearly gagged. He rushed to the back cooler and grabbed a 16-ounce bottle of Dr. Pepper. A mottled gray cat sat atop the front counter eyeing him suspiciously as he approached the register. It looked ferocious.

"Lupus, get the hell out the way," said the woman behind the counter, prodding the cat with one hand. It leaped down gracefully and scooted around the corner. The woman was about 40 and appeared to have lived a hard life. Her hair was gray and black. Red splotches dotted her face and arms. One of her eyes was milky and wandered lazily in its socket. Her smile was supported by only four or five teeth. A light blue Mexican sun dress hung loosely down past her knees.

David was holding his breath.

"Anything else," she asked looking at the soda disapprovingly.

"Yeah," David said trying not to breathe in. "A map of Marcott."

The woman snatched a map off a rack behind her and slapped it onto the counter.

"Anything else."

David suddenly thought they should add another word and some punctuation to the name of the store. It should read: GET-AND-GO, DAMMIT!

BACK IN THE CAR, David slumped in his seat. His head was light from holding his breath for so long. He unfolded the map and started searching for the address Adams had given him. He found it quickly, using a yellow highlighter to trace a path to Lisa's trailer park.

THE FIRST THING DAVID noticed when he reached Lisa's home was the washing machine that stood less than five feet from the front door. Apparently someone had wrestled it out of the house, and then abandoned it, too weary to move it any farther. It was old and rusted with weeds growing halfway up its sides, and a huge spider web clinging to the back. The trailer was pale gray with an aging roof and a hitch on the front as though a truck was about to back up to it and haul it down the road. Three cinder blocks were stacked by the front door as steps. There were dainty little curtains hanging from the windows, and one potted plant in the kitchen window. It was a small trailer, with only a kitchen, living room, a single bedroom and a bathroom inside. As he walked to the door, David thought he could almost hear cockroaches racing through the walls.

He knocked firmly on the door.

After a moment, he knocked again, this time leaning over to peer through a window. The place looked empty. He waited, and knocked a third time before giving up.

David got back into his Porsche and cruised slowly down the street stopping at a quiet spot under a tree where he could watch Lisa's trailer and wait for her return. He pulled out a reporter's notebook, and started making a list of questions for the girl.

*Why did she file suit? Had Martin abandoned her to this pit of a trailer park? Was a lawsuit the only way to get the jerk to help her? How did she meet Martin? How old was she when they met? Did Martin know how old she was? Did she graduate from high school? Where were her parents? Why did Martin settle so fast? How much did he pay her? Was there a blood test to confirm that the kid was his?*

David waited in his car for nearly an hour. Lisa did not come home. Finally, he decided to try the neighbors.

He banged on the door of a dingy brown trailer that was twice as long as Lisa's but not any nicer. He could hear a television playing inside, and two or three kids talking. A big woman in a yellow dress opened the door and stood behind the screen.

"Good evening, ma'am. My name is David Costanzo, I'm a reporter from the San Antonio Light newspaper." He always threw the word "newspaper" out there because occasionally people thought he was from the electric company. "I was wondering if I could ask you a couple of questions about your neighbor, Lisa Benson."

The woman eyed him suspiciously and looked past him at the Porsche parked in her gravel driveway. "I don't know no Lisa Benson."

"Oh, really," acting as if this was the most interesting thing he had heard all day. "She lives right there," he said turning and pointing to the small trailer 30 feet away.

The woman closed her eyes, a look of familiar fatigue. "Oh, *that* youngun. I never knew her last name. She's not here no more. Moved away 'bout three or four days ago. Her and her baby." The kids inside continued to argue and cry, but the woman appeared not to notice.

"How long did Lisa live here?"

She shrugged. "Year. Year and a half, I guess."

"Did she ever have visitors?"

The woman didn't answer right away. "Why you wanna know?" she said suddenly protective of her young neighbor.

"Well, it's kind of a secret," David said leaning toward the door and looking nervously over one shoulder, "but Lisa is one of the winners in the lottery."

The woman's eyes lit up. She had four lottery tickets sitting on her kitchen table. When the evening news came on she'd be sitting in front of the TV dreaming about winning her way out of that damp trailer and into a real house. "How much did she get?"

"I really can't reveal any more than that," David said apologetically. "It hasn't been officially announced yet. What I need is just a little more background information on her for the story. So. . . do you recall if she had many visitors?"

"Never saw no one," the woman said weary again. Her kids were still hollering inside the trailer. "She was all alone with her baby. Worked at that diner on the highway up by PICK & SAVE."

"Do you know where she lives now?"

"Unh uh. Got an apartment somewhere is all I know. Fancy car came and picked her up and took her away."

"What kind of car?" David said eagerly.

"Big black one." She turned back toward her living room, and yelled at the kids to shut the hell up. Remarkably, silence followed, punctuated only by voices on the television.

"What's her baby's name?" He asked to confirm what he already knew.

"Michael. . . he's a real cutie.

THAT EVENING DAVID talked to three other neighbors and learned that Lisa was a quiet, independent girl who never really talked to anyone. Nobody knew anything about her, except that she was gone.

He drove back out to the highway and looked for a restaurant near a PICK & SAVE store. He found the HITCHIN' POST DINER shortly before 10. It was a dirty little place with a dozen 18-wheelers parked off to one side, and fuel pumps under a high pavilion out front. The restaurant had the slow moving feel of all small town joints. Some of the truckers were in their rigs trying to sleep before late-night runs. Others were sitting inside finishing dinner and nursing cups of coffee, enjoying the company of other people for a while. David sat outside and watched the activity for 10 minutes before walking in.

He slipped into a booth in the back of the room, and ordered a Hitchin' Burger with cheese, a basket of fries and a root beer shake when the pretty young waitress came by to check on him.

When she brought his food, he said: "You know, I think this is the place where my niece works." He put it out there casually, taking a risk because he was white and he hadn't thought to ask the neighbors about Lisa Benson's race.

"Really? What's her name?" the girl asked, already interested in the clean-cut guy who'd arrived in a Porsche.

"Lisa," he said, snatching a fry from the red basket in front of him.

"Well, my name's Lisa," she said with a sexy smile, flipping her blonde hair over one shoulder. "But I don't remember *ever* meeting an uncle who looked like you."

For a moment, David was unsettled. Her name tag read: Monica. Was she lying on the tag or was she lying now? Was this Lisa Benson? Was it another Lisa? If this was Lisa Benson he'd have to be careful. There was no way his uncle charade would fool the real girl.

"You're not Lisa," he said shaking his head. "I haven't seen her since she was a baby, but I'm sure I'd know her if I saw her."

"Did you see me naked when I was a baby?" Three buttons were undone on the shirt revealing her robust cleavage.

David licked his lips, off. *Where the hell is this going?* He ate another fry to buy some time. "Are you Lisa Benson?"

"Did you see me naked when I was a baby?" she said insistently, leaning forward palms flat on the table. Her hair hanging down. Her breasts threatening the spill out of her shirt.

The silence grew.

*Is she wearing a bra?*

His pants were suddenly tight. He wasn't sure how to respond. Was she going to ask him to prove his identity by describing an obscure birth mark?

"No," he said quietly.

She didn't say anything for a moment. Then: "You wanna see me naked now?" Smiling, standing tall and turning a pirouette. "I'm in real good shape." She giggled lightly.

David let out a breath. "Are you Lisa Benson?"

She looked at him for a long moment, and leaned forward again. David's gaze kept slipping down to her chest. Her blue eyes were fixed on his. "No, I'm not Lisa Benson. . . and you ain't her uncle, either, so we're even."

"I really *am* her uncle," feeling in control of the conversation again.

"No, you ain't because her mom was an only child and Lisa's dad split before she was even born, so you can talk that yip-yap about seein' her when she was a baby, but it ain't floatin' with me, cause I know it ain't true."

Bingo. David was in the right place. She knew Lisa, and probably knew where he could find her.

"Sit down; talk to me for a minute," David said lightly touching her hand.

"Can't. I got work to do." She looked over her shoulder at the manager, sitting behind the register. "But I get off at 11." With a flip of her long pink skirt she turned and walked away.


THE GIRL WITH THE "Monica" name tag who called herself Lisa jumped into the passenger side of David's Porsche just after 11 o'clock, and sang part of a top 40 rap song:

*Drive fast. Speed turns me on.*
*I put my hand on his knee,*
*he put his foot on the gas.*
*We almost got whiplash we took off so fast.*
*The sunroof was open,*
*the music was high*
*and my hand was slowly moving up his thigh. . .*

She laughed deeply pulling her hand away from the reporter's leg, leaning against the door as laughter continued to erupt from her mouth. "You. . . . should. . . . see. . . . your. . . . face," she said between gasps.

David smiled, and tried to casually adjust the front of his pants. "What's your name?"

She kept laughing, ignoring his question. "Drive the car, mister. Just drive." Then in a whisper right next to his ear, "but don't go too fast cause speed really does turn me on."

David eased out of the parking lot and started cruising down the highway. A local station was playing on the radio, and her window was down catching the night air as it slipped past. He resisted the urge to punch the accelerator—just to see what would happen.

"My name is Kim," she said after a while. She ran a finger across her name tag. "I just wear this because I like to be somebody else sometimes." She was looking at David's profile in the low light from the dashboard. "You ever feel that way?"

"Sure. Sometimes it's fun to be another person."

"Like you trying to be Lisa's uncle? "

"Yeah. I guess."

"Who are you, really?"

"My name is David Costanzo. I write for the *San Antonio Light* newspaper."

"A reporter?"

"Yes, ma'am."

Kim looked out the window at the stillness surrounding them.

"So, I guess you're here about Lisa's baby, huh"?

# TWENTY-ONE

"MAYBE I SHOULD PULL over somewhere," David said, thinking that he wanted to turn on his tape recorder and get out his reporter's notebook.

"Hmm. . ." Kim said turning toward him. Smiling. "So you wanna go parking with me, is that it?"

"Not like that," David said sounding guilty.

"You're a naughty, naughty boy." She was smiling wickedly.

The swelling in David's pants started again. He could see that smile climbing up into rigs with horny truckers who were not too fat and not too old. Just nice young guys on the road who needed a little pick-me-up. Just a little value-added service from the best damned waitress at the HITCHIN' POST DINER. It was no big deal to her. She used her sexuality like a weapon. Flaunting it. Enjoying the attention. Knowing that her smile, and the swell of her breasts and the sweet spot between her legs would get her what she wanted from most men.

"Yeah," David chuckled, trying to sound more relaxed than he felt. "Let's go parking."

"Take the next exit. I know the perfect spot."

She led him through three miles of back roads to a cluster of trees that stood around a small pond. When he shut off the engine, only the chirping of crickets and the occasional call of a bird parted the air. The pond seems so far away from everything. So peaceful. A full moon reflected gently off the water. They sat silently taking it in.

"Maybe we should get started," David said, leaning into the back for his tape recorder.

"Maybe we should," Kim said, placing her hand on his crotch.

He stopped, half turned, his arms in the back seat. They stared hungrily at each other. She was unbuckling his belt and unzipping his pants.

"Wait a second. . . " he muttered half-hearted. Kim ignored him, and soon her head was in his lap and he was grunting quietly.

She moved back up his body and kissed him on the lips. He kissed her back and began to play with her breasts. "Let's get out of the car," she moaned into his ear.

They tumbled onto the ground, kissing and grinding their bodies together. David couldn't believe how horny he was. He hadn't had a woman this hot for him, since. . . *well never. And especially not a hot piece of ass like Kim.* Her skin was so young. So pliant. So soft. He ran his hands along her arms, down her back, felt her waist. He wanted to touch all of her. His fingers were committing her body to memory. Then she was pulling down her panties. She was on her hands and knees, skirt hiked up over her waist. Her small young ass staring at him.

"I want you inside me," she said, looking back at him with pleading eyes.

David stumbled forward, his pants pulled down around his knees and plunged into her urgently, instinctively and violently. She was hot and slick and soft inside. They rocked and moaned in the warm night air. A light sheen playing across his face.

"Pull my hair," she urged in a gasp.

David wrapped a hand in her beautiful blonde tresses and pulled back gently.

"Harder," she said throatily. "Pull it harder. Treat me like a slut." The reporter fell into the role easily. Slamming into her. His face contorted with violent pleasure as he pushed and pulled on her young body. She screamed loudly urging him on. He pulled harder, fucked her stronger. Out in the woods with the crickets chirping and the moon looking on, David was a savage man raping a young maiden. If felt wrong. It felt wild. It felt good.

Suddenly, reality burst through his fantasy. He didn't know this girl. He wasn't wearing a condom. He didn't know anything about her. *What the hell am I doing?* He fell away from her. "How old are you?"

"What?" She was angry. "*Now* you want to know how old I am?"

"How old are you dammit?" *This is how they get you. You start thinking with your little head, and the next thing you know, you're plunged hip deep into some shit you never should have touched.*

"I'm old enough for you not to worry about it," she said. "Now, will you *please* finish what you started?" She was wiggling her ass back and forth. It was beautifully shaped. Two perfect globes separated by a delicate cleft.

"I just need to—"

"I'm 19. Okay," she said softly. Suddenly understanding his need to know. "I'm 19, and I'm horny as hell, and if you don't get back over here, I'm going to scream my lungs out."

Relief. She could be lying. But he believed her. She didn't look underage. She looked 19. He'd check her ID later. He didn't have a condom, but that sweet ass was still rocking back and forth. It was calling to him.

"Well, we can't have you doing any damage to those beautiful lungs now can we?" David said, getting behind her, reaching around to take a breast in each hand.

Then he wrapped a hand in her hair, pulling back firmly, and they picked up where they left off.

WHEN THEY FINISHED, THEY got dressed and climbed back into the car. David turned on his tape recorder, and with very little prompting, Kim told him everything she knew about Lisa Benson.

"Lisa had always been a very pretty girl, easily the best looking girl in our school, but she never had dates. Guys were intimidated by her. She was so beautiful that all the boys in school thought she would say, 'No' if they asked her out. So no one ever did. And since she never went out on dates, everyone assumed she was stuck up. But she wasn't. She was a nice girl who wanted to go out and have fun, but her beauty was working against her.

"She was one of the first girls to get boobs, and when she got them, boy did she get them. They started coming in sixth grade, and by eighth grade she was wearing a C-cup. And they weren't just big, they were shapely. Nice and round and perfect like the rest of her. She had a small waist and long athletic legs—even though she really didn't work out much. As a seventh grader she had the maturity and the look of someone who was a junior or senior in high school. When she was a freshman in high school, she could have passed for a freshman in college.

"You ever read the little descriptions of those women on the cover of magazines like Cosmo or Elle?" Kim asked David from her side of the car.

"No, can't say that I have," he said.

"Well, sometimes you wouldn't believe how young those women are. They look like they're 28 or 29, but then you see their birth dates in that little section about the cover model, and you figure out that they're only 17 or 18. That's what Lisa's got. I don't know what you call it, but there's something about her looks and her. . . um. . ."

"Demeanor?" David offered.

"Yeah. Something about her demeanor that makes her seem older than she is.

"Her freshman year in high school, Lisa started dating a guy named Sam who was a student at Southern Christian University, a small private school on the west side of Marcott. He was 20 years old and he had a fake ID. He helped Lisa make a good ID so they could go to clubs in San Antonio together. She was 14 years old and getting into nightclubs. They used to drive into the city nearly every weekend to go out. At the clubs lots of guys would hit on Lisa, but she was totally loyal to Sam. She wouldn't give them the time of day. But all those guys still made Sam jealous as hell, and he always accused her of doing something to make them interested in her. But that wasn't true. She was just a beautiful, young girl, and men were naturally attracted to her.

After a couple of months, Sam couldn't take it any more, so he broke up with Lisa, halfway thinking that she would chase after him and beg him to take her back. But she didn't. She let him go like he was never there in the first place. Turned off her feelings for Sam just like that. After a few days, he started calling, saying he was sorry and he wanted her back, but she wouldn't say two words to him. She never thought about Sam again.

"She started bringing 'going out' clothes in a bag when she came to work at the Hitching Post. After work she'd get one of the truckers who was going through San Antonio to drop her off in the city. She never worried about getting back home, because she knew she would meet some guy who would beg for the chance to drive her back to Marcott.

"So that was her routine," Kim said. "She'd go into the city by herself every weekend. I always wanted to go with her, but I didn't have a fake ID and even if I did, there was no way I could pass for 21 years old. The first time I tried to use the ID the bouncer probably would have laughed in my face, taken the card away, and sent me back into the street.

"So usually Lisa went out by herself. Which is really strange when you think about it, because mostly girls only feel safe when they're surrounded by their friends. When a group of girls goes out, sometimes we'll just walk onto the dance floor and start dancing together in a little circle with our purses slung down in the middle for safety. If we're just standing around and a guy asks one of us to dance she'll either say 'No' or she'll grab the wrist of one of her friends and drag her out onto the dance floor, too. Girls can't even go to the bathroom by themselves. We go in pairs and sometimes in threes. We'll go into the LADIES, and all cram into the same stall talking about this boy or that boy while they take turns squatting over the toilet, holding up our skirts, not letting our butts touch the seat.

"But Lisa wasn't afraid. She'd march into a club by herself and enjoy the way everyone's eyes shifted toward her. She was completely comfortable with it. Content to wait for someone to buy her a drink, knowing the guys would practically line up to talk to her.

"She wasn't a slut or anything," Kim said as if David had suggested it. "At the time, her old boyfriend Sam was the only guy she'd ever slept with. So she wasn't trying to get laid. She just loved the attention. After going for so long without even being asked on a date by the boys at her school, she had begun to feel a little insecure about her looks. Maybe she wasn't as pretty as everyone said she was. If she really was beautiful, then the boys at school should be killing themselves to get close to her. Right? That wasn't happening.

"So it felt really good to have the men of San Antonio lusting after her. Asking her to dance. Buying her drinks. Vying for her attention.

"LISA DIDN'T HAVE MUCH money. The chump change she made at the Hitching Post went to pay for her makeup—although she really didn't need any—a new outfit every now and then, and gifts for her brothers. She lived with her mother and her two little brothers in a small house that was nice except that it had mice. She didn't know who her father was, and she and her mother never did get along very well.

"I always thought her mother was jealous of her beauty," Kim said. "Like she was mad at Lisa for being prettier than she was.

"They fought all the time about this and that, and it got to the point where Lisa was hardly ever staying at home. Sometimes she'd go into San Antonio on a Friday after work. Get some guy to drive her back out to Marcott Saturday morning so she could go to work. Catch a ride with a trucker back into the city after work Saturday night, and get a guy to drive her back to Marcott Sunday.

"Most of the time during the week, she'd come stay at my house, because we were best friends and my parents didn't mind," Kim said. "I think my dad even had a little crush on Lisa. He was always coming to check on us when we were in my room talking. I think he just wanted to see her in her panties or something, then fantasize about her when he was humpin' Mom." Kim shuddered at the thought.

"Anyway," she continued, "toward the end of my junior year, Lisa's sophomore year, we weren't hanging out too much any more. We were still best friends, but things were changing because she was going out by herself all the time and then, well, I got a boyfriend.

"Girls always believe their friendships with each other will last forever, but then a boy comes along, and he's all you can think about. You forget all your friends. They're not important anymore. You want to spend every waking moment with your boyfriend, kissing and hugging and talking. Thinking about the future. Dreaming about a big wedding and kids. It's stupid really, but you become totally infatuated with a person, and you can't think about anything else.

"His name was Devan Porter. He was a junior, too, and he was a stud on the basketball team. He was tall and coordinated and he had the coolest haircut. It was trimmed close on the sides and around the back, but the top was longer, and it hung down in his face. He was a decent student, but not so smart that the other kids would think he was a dork. He was just *cool*. He used to date Heather Perham, who was a cheerleader and who was the homecoming queen last year."

"She's such a little bitch," Kim said.

"After Devan and Heather broke up, all the girls started dreaming about him. He was the most eligible bachelor at Marcott High School, Home of the Fighting Eagles. But he didn't really seem interested in anyone.

"Then one day at lunch, he brought his tray over and just sat down next to me. Just plopped down there with his lunch like it was the most natural thing in the world. I was so excited I thought I was going to have to run home and change my panties. And you know what he said? You know that the first words out of his mouth were?"

"Uh. . . Hi, I'm Devan?" David ventured.

"No. Oh God, you won't believe it when I tell you. It was *so* cute. I mean, when I think about it, it just blows my mind. The first thing he said was, 'Are you going to eat your Jell-O?' Isn't that cute? I mean, to just sit down next to a total stranger and say, 'Are you going to eat your Jell-O?' It kind of shocked me because I wasn't expecting something like that, so I looked at my Jell-O—it was orange—and I realized that in his own way, he was asking me to 'go' with him. So I said, 'It's all yours.' And that's how our relationship started. Isn't that funny?"

David laughed dutifully. "What happened with Lisa?" he said trying to get back to the subject.

"Well, like I said we weren't hanging out too much any more, so I don't know all the details. I just know she met a guy she really liked, and she rocked with him, and she got pregnant.

"Lisa didn't sleep with the guys who courted her. Sex was a pretty sacred thing for her. For some girls it's hard to say no. After they agree to leave a club with a guy, they feel guilty about not having sex, like they owe him something. But not Lisa. Her beauty actually made it easier for her to put guys off. Guys tended to see her as a trophy more than anything else. If she was ugly, she'd have to be putting out on a regular basis just to get dates. But Lisa would give a guy a terrible case of blue balls, and he'd be eager to see her again the next week, because being seen in public with her stroked his ego. If everybody in the club saw her leaving with a particular guy, that guy was so proud it was like he was having 10 orgasms at once. If he didn't get any actual sex out of it, he didn't really care. As far as everyone in the club was concerned he was boffing her brains out, and for a lot of guys appearances are what matter the most, anyway.

"So Lisa wasn't sleeping with anyone, but there was this one guy that she really liked," Kim said. It was creeping up on 1 a.m. but neither Kim nor David seemed to notice. Even in the middle of the night, the air was warm and the breeze was still. "She always saw him at these different clubs, but he had never spoken to her. He was always standing talking to different people, laughing with really perfect, friendly teeth, and looking like a nice guy. Lisa was always watching him out of the corner of her eye. He was handsome, and he seemed confident, outgoing and smart. And he was famous or something, too, because a lot of people knew who he was."

David's eyes lit up. "Famous? What do you mean?"

"It was just that everyone seemed to know who he was, and he looked like he was really rich. Perfect teeth, perfect clothes, perfect car. You know, the works."

"Do you know his name?" He said it a bit too eagerly.

"No. Like I said, Lisa and me weren't very close back then. I remember her mentioning his name one time. It slipped out of her mouth before she realized what she was saying. I didn't think much of it at the time. But later, when I asked her what his name was again, she wouldn't tell me. I got the feeling it was some kind of big secret or something."

David smiled at that. *A big secret is just the kind of thing a jerk like Martin would try to make of this whole affair.* Kimberly continued: "Lisa saw this guy from across the room just about every weekend for a month, and then finally one night while she was talking to some random dude, her dream man walked over and handed her a rose. He didn't have any way cool line to throw out. He just said, 'Hi. Thought you might like this.' But it really didn't matter what he said, because Lisa was already totally in love with him. She was about to ask him what his name was when he simply walked away. Just turned and disappeared into the crowd. Her eyes followed him, and a rush of emotion hit her. She felt like she was going to cry. It was the craziest feeling she'd ever had. She smelled the rose and looked around for his face in the crowd.

"Five or 10 minutes later, he came back. Lisa was smiling the moment she saw him. She wanted to ask him if he wanted to go somewhere else. Somewhere quiet. Where they could talk without screaming over the pounding music. She desperately wanted to spend time with him.

"'Hi,' she said as he approached.

"'Hey,' he said, looking embarrassed. 'Listen, I'm sorry, but I need this back.' He gently took the rose from her hand, offered a contrite smile. 'Sorry.' He turned and walked away again.

"Lisa's eyes filled with water, fat tears leaking out of the sides. She excused herself from the guy who was still babbling about the car that he and a buddy had built. She rushed into the bathroom. No man had ever affected her that way. She was a rock. A confident woman who could not be shaken. She could take anything men had to offer and throw it back in their faces. Her looks intimidated, and her attitude conquered. But this guy wasn't affected. She didn't understand it.

"There was a soft knock at the door to her stall.

"'Someone's in here,' she said impatiently.

"'I know. I want to talk to you.'

"It was him. Lisa unbolted the door, looking at him with surprised eyes as he moved casually into the stall, edging her back until she sat back down on the commode. He squatted in front of her.

"'Listen, I'm sorry about the flower thing,' he said gently. His eyelashes were gorgeous. 'I've seen you here many times, and I figured you would be back, so I bought that rose for you. But then after I gave it to you, I saw this couple fighting. It was a girl who was kind of overweight, but still trying to hold it together with a tight dress and a lot of makeup. Well, they were fighting because her date ran into his ex-girlfriend. You could tell he didn't want to have anything to do with his ex, but the girl he was with was getting pissed. So I took the flower back from you and gave it to her.'

"'She was totally flattered. I talked to her for a minute, and then her boyfriend got jealous and came storming over ready to fight. I don't think any guy has ever made a fuss about this girl, let alone two guys acting like they're going to fight over her. So it was the right thing to do, but now, I need to apologize to you. I mean, giving you a rose and then taking it away like that is pretty . . . abrupt. I guess that's the word I'm looking for. I didn't have time to explain everything to you. But I hope you understand now why I did what I did.'

"Lisa was all ears. He had beautiful brown skin, pretty hazel eyes, and a square jaw. He was handsome, with a wonderfully deep voice and a great body. And he seemed to be the kindest man who ever lived."

"Wait a second," David said crossly from the driver's seat, parked by the lake. He was staring hard at Kimberly. "Hazel eyes?" Martin McNeil was a black man with plain brown eyes. The reporter was positive of that. He'd seen his ugly mug on enough billboards and commercials to know he didn't have hazel eyes.

"That's what she said," Kimberly confirmed, nodding her head, not sure why it mattered.

The reporter chewed on that for a minute. *Maybe he has contacts. Wears them to impress the ladies.*

"Should I continue?" Kimberly asked.

David was distracted, but he needed to hear the rest. "Yeah, go ahead."

"Well, when this guy, asked her to go home with him to talk, she said 'yes' right away.

"His home turned out to be a big, beautiful townhouse on the Northeast Side right behind the Red McCombs Toyota Dealership. Inside, they attacked each other. Lisa didn't have much sexual experience—she'd only slept with Sam—but she went at it with a vengeance. They ripped their clothes off and dropped down right there in the living room and starting humping like rabbits. They did it three times that night and twice the next day, then he drove her back out to Marcott. He kissed her goodbye and said he was going to call her, but he never did.

"She missed him.

"She kept going to all the clubs where she used to see him, but he was never there. It was like he had vanished from the earth. She didn't know his phone number and every time she went by his townhouse, there was no answer at the door. She kept waiting, thinking that he would call, but he didn't. She even found herself lying in bed late at night crying softly, wishing that he was there with her, wanting to feel his soft touch again. It was the first time she had ever been hurt by a man."

As David listened to this story, his mind was already sorting through the facts, finding the interesting parts and adding necessary details. He was writing the story in his head as he heard it, thinking that it could be a great magazine piece. He closed his eyes and began to add flavor to the sketch Kimberly was making of Lisa's life.

*About a month after they slept together, Lisa started to get worried because her period hadn't come. She got really nervous, the way girls do when they're late. She was already assuming the worst. Counting backward in her head, trying to remember exactly when her last period was. Trying to be sure that she was actually late and not just imagining it.*

*Calculating the date she'd had sex with this guy trying to figure out if she could really be pregnant.*

*Her mind was playing tricks on her. It was telling her that it could feel her breasts enlarging. Just getting bigger with every pump of her heart; building up the reserve of milk they'd need when the baby arrived. They were tender, and that scared her. Every time she looked in the mirror, her face seemed fatter. Was that her imagination? No. Her cheeks were puffing up. Swelling in concert with her belly. Surely, everyone could tell. She had to pee every five minutes. Rushing into the bathroom, just getting her panties down before the stream started. It was maddening.*

*She got her paycheck on Friday. She cashed it at the bank down the street, and drove over to Luling, a small town about 30 miles east of Marcott. She had $113 dollars in her purse. She went into a drug store to buy a home pregnancy test. But she couldn't get up the nerve to just grab one off the shelf, and go pay for it. So she got a cart, and wandered the isles for a nearly 45 minutes, snatching cereal, fruit, magazines and anything else she could find and dumping it into the cart. The last thing she picked up was a generic pregnancy test, then she took care to bury it in her basket.*

*She was sweating at the register. Trying to appear interested in the tabloid newspapers in the rack nearby. Actually pulling one of them down, and flipping to a story about an Ohio woman who gave birth to aliens.* Born to an Ohio woman they're not aliens, they're U.S. citizens, *she thought idly, barely noticing that for the moment her mind was off the baby that may or may not be growing inside her.*

*The woman behind the register was chomping violently on a piece of gum. Big, curly, round, red hair surrounded her pudgy face. The gum dancing between her teeth threatening to fly of her mouth. She was mumbling under her breath. Lisa felt herself leaning closer trying to decipher what the woman was saying. She couldn't make it out.*

*The cart was getting emptier. The Cherrios came out, followed by the Ben & Jerry's Ice Cream, followed by the bananas, followed by the quart of 10w30 motor oil. The pregnancy test was getting closer to the top of the pile. Lisa's eyes danced back and forth between the cart and the Ohio woman who found out about her alien twins by using a home pregnancy test. The article read:* She knew the father had to be the alien, because he/it was the only person/thing she had slept with in the past few months. Her husband was a drunk who never made it to the bed. Spent virtually every night on the couch falling asleep as all-star wrestling raged on the television.

*Lisa could see the test. It couldn't be more than three or four items away from the woman's hand. The gum was still flapping in her mouth. The checker was still mumbling. Suddenly, Lisa could hear her. She was saying the name of each product as she pulled it out of the basket.*

Why the hell is she doing that?

*Feeling panicked. Knowing that the woman was actually going to see, the test when it came up.*

*Just a quiet murmur. Talking to herself, as her hand reached into the basket. Reading the names of the items. "Decker sliced bacon. Berol number two pencils. Carmex, for dry chaps lips. Pregnancy Test. Treetop apple juice. Sugar Cain sugar. . . ."*

*She was past it. Never noticed it. Lisa was shaking. Trying to put the tabloid back on the rack. Her eyes never leaving the pregnancy test that was sliding down the black conveyor belt into the hands of the bagger, who flipped it absently into a bag and out of sight.*

*Lisa let out an audible sigh. The woman looked up at her for a moment, then went back to her mumbling. The final bill was $93.03. It was a very expensive pregnancy test.*

*The checker took her money, and punched a few numbers into the register. When she was handing back the change, she took Lisa's hand in hers, holding it firmly with surprising compassion, saying, "I'll be praying for you and that baby inside of you."*

*The motherly concern in the voice washed over Lisa, nearly pulling an anguished cry out of her mouth. She clenched her jaw, nodding mutely, and slipped her hand out of the woman's grip. She marched out of the store.*

*When she got into her car, the tears came. Her emotions were going haywire. She didn't know what she would do if she were pregnant. She wasn't ready to deal with a pregnancy.*

*Back home, she raced into the house with a bag under each arm. The pregnancy test already secreted in her purse. Her mother and brothers were shocked by the bags, and more so when she said there were six more in the car. The boys ran outside going crazy over the bounty. They'd never seen that many groceries all at once. They were tearing through the bags, eating the ice cream out of the container. Her mother was suspicious, asking a million questions. Lisa said she simply felt like doing something nice. They needed the food.*

*Then she disappeared into the bathroom. She stared at the box for a long time. Half reading the directions and half dreaming that this wasn't happening to her.*

*She was only 15 years old.*

*There was a small plastic stick inside the box. It was a fairly simple process. Hold the absorbent strip in her urine stream for five seconds, then wait for the result. She pulled off her pants and underwear, and sat down on the toilet, scared and nervous.*

*She couldn't go. She could feel her bladder ready to explode, but nothing would come out. Okay, relax. Just relax. She was bent over the sink, trying to drink water, trying to make her body aware that it needed to get rid of some of the old to make room for the new.*

*She was back over the toilet, waiting. Finally, a trickle began. She held the plastic stick under her, then cut off the stream in a way that boys* can never duplicate. With boys, once that river starts to flow, there's no stopping it until the reservoir is empty. But girls can start and stop. She didn't want to waste all of her urine. She might need to do the test again if she didn't like the first result.

She waited three minutes. It took that long for the chemical reaction that would read the future for her. There was a circle and a rectangle on the testing stick. A blue line through just the rectangle meant that she was not pregnant. A blue line through the rectangle and a pink line through the circle would indicate that she was pregnant. Her mother was knocking on the door asking if she was okay. Lisa said she was fine, she'd be out in a couple of minutes. There was a blue line through the rectangle. Then a faint pink line through the circle. After another minute, there was nothing faint about it. Two solid lines.

She snatched the box off the counter reading the instructions. She could replace the absorbent tip and test again. Back on the toilet. Peeing again. Testing again. Please God, let it be negative.

She didn't know what she would do if this one was negative. What does one plus and one negative give you? She didn't know. And she didn't have another 90 bucks to spend on another test. In the end, she didn't have to worry about it. The second test produced another positive.

She sat on the toilet and cried.

She knew it had to be him. He was the only guy she'd slept with in a long time. She didn't know what to do. She was panicked. She wasn't ready for this. She couldn't afford to have a kid. She was too young to be a mother. She was a 15-year-old sophomore in high school, for Christ's sake. She looked for the father again. This time not motivated by a desire to be with him again, but by a need to share this secret with someone. But it was a half-hearted attempt. She went to his house once, ringing the bell and waiting half a minute. She didn't go to any of the clubs she'd seen him at before, where a bouncer or a bartender might have known his last name. Although she wanted to tell someone about the baby, not knowing the guy made everything easier. She ended up doing what a lot of young girls do when this type of crisis comes barreling into their lives; she put a Do Not Disturb sign on the issue and hoped that it would go away. She quit going to the clubs on the weekends. She kept going to school. She didn't tell anyone that she was pregnant. She was scared, and she couldn't think straight.

KIMBERLY BRUSHED HER HAIR back with flat hands, leaned back in the passenger seat of the Porsche. "About the third month she started to show. But she hid it pretty easily. She wore loose clothes, and nobody noticed.

"Then one day during the fifth month, her mom accidentally walked in on her while she was getting out of the shower, and saw her swollen stomach. She went on a flying-off-the-handle, fit-to-be-tied rampage. She was ranting and raving. Throwing stuff around. Hitting the walls. Slamming doors. The two boys were so scared they were curled up together on one bed screaming their lungs out. Lisa was crying. She already had all those pregnancy hormones racing through her body, so she was an emotional wreck. With her mom yelling like that, and with the boys wailing she just about lost her mind. Her mother slapped her a couple of times, and then shoved her out the front door with just a towel on. Lisa tried to get back into the house, but she couldn't. She was banging on the door. Begging. She was embarrassed. Some of the neighbors were standing on their porches watching Lisa, the men secretly hoping that the towel would fall away from her body. Upstairs, Lisa's bedroom window opened and her mother started dumping all of her clothes onto the lawn. "I'm not going to have a *whore* sleeping under my roof!" she screamed.

"There was nothing more Lisa could do. She cinched that towel tightly around her, and then started to gather up her belongings with as much dignity as she could muster. She even smiled at the Mirtles and told them that her mother was drunk. The neighbors felt sorry for her. A couple of them invited her into their homes, but Lisa wouldn't go. She was humiliated. "At least come in and put some clothes on," Mrs. Mirtle said. But Lisa just walked away in a peach towel with about three days worth of clothes in her hands. She could take care of herself.

"So she came marching over to my house in her towel," Kim said, able to laugh at the memory now. "I thought my dad's eyes were going to pop out of his head when he saw her. We went up to my room and she lay on the bed and started crying like you wouldn't believe. I've never seen anybody cry as hard as she did. It was so sad. She was trying to tell me what had happened, but every time she started the tears would come again, and I wouldn't be able to understand what she was saying. She lived with us for about a month, and I think my parents would have let her stay forever, but Lisa was determined to take care of herself. The only thing she would take from my dad was the $250 he offered to help her buy a car, but then she paid that back two months later.

*It was a beat up 1973 Chrysler Newport with a thunderous, unhealthy engine. When she turned the car off, the engine would sometimes rattle and shake for another five or six seconds. Black smoke billowed out of the exhaust pipe. She took the rest of her meager savings and rented a tiny trailer house for $150 a month. She kept working at the Hitching Post, and she surprised a lot of people by staying in school for the last month of the year. Most girls just drop out the minute they find out they're pregnant, but Lisa kept going to class. Her seventh and eighth months were during summer break, and she worked full time then to make some extra money to take care of her baby. She worked right through the ninth month, and she didn't enroll for school in September. Her due date was at the end of the month, but the baby didn't come. When* *she was a couple days late, she started to get worried.*

David's eyes were closed in the car as he imagined what Lisa must have been going through. *Finally, lying alone on her kitchen floor, Lisa gave birth to her son, Michael Alexander (McNeil?) on a stormy October night when her grunts of pain, fear and loneliness were drowned out by thick drops of water that pelted the tin roof and dripped onto the soggy living room carpet.*

*Three days later she was back at work moving on weary legs. The manager let her keep Michael in the back corner when there wasn't a rush, but she had to take him into the break room when the restaurant was full of customers. Lisa seemed so exhausted all the time, but she kept pushing. She was determined to make it on her own.*

"Okay," David said. "So this was more than a year ago, why did she wait so long to file a paternity suit?"

"Well, she didn't know who the guy was," Kim said. "She met him, slept with him and then never saw him again. Plus, Lisa's just not that kind of girl. She would never try to sue someone for money. She doesn't want any handouts. She wants to make her own way."

"Well, you can't say she would *never* file suit, because she did file against Martin McNeil."

"Yeah, but that was the lawyer's idea."

# TWENTY-TWO

THE DARKEST HOURS OF the night were surprisingly light, a full moon reflecting off the pond casting shadows in the brief stand of trees. David and Kimberly were still in the car talking. Fog was drifting down from the sky; a cloud that had lost its wings. The moon danced in and out of view behind whispers of vapor, and the crickets, who must do all their sleeping during the day, continued to chirp in the grass.

"If Lisa wasn't the type of girl who would sue, then why the hell did she get a lawyer?" David said.

"She didn't go out and get a lawyer. He found *her*.

"Even though Lisa quit going to nightclubs when she got pregnant, there were still plenty of men who were interested in her. Most nights of the week there were dozens of cars and trucks parked in the lot at the Hitching Post. Those drivers could have gone to the Judd's place down the road about two miles. It's a real modern, well-lit store with digital gas pumps, a nice restaurant and a small, clean motel. But the Hitching Post gets more traffic mostly because of Lisa.

"And because of me, too," Kim added with a toothy grin. Leaning over to give David a kiss. Dragging her chest across his arm in the process. "I mean, she's *way* prettier than me, but I catch the boys' eyes, too."

"No doubt about that," David said, returning the kiss quietly, acutely aware that the tape recorder was running. Not wanting there to be a record of their kiss. He still hadn't checked her ID. "So what about this lawyer?"

"I'm getting to that part, Mr. Impatient." Kim pouted a moment before resuming.

"We were the two beautiful waitresses who drew the men into the Hitching Post. I was the outgoing, flirty one who could be coaxed into a truck for a little snuggling. Lisa was the quiet, mysterious one, who really couldn't be coaxed into anything, but who was good to look at. Eye candy was the way men described her; worth the drive from any part of the state just to see her.

"About a year after Michael was born, a young lawyer started coming into the Hitching Post. He was new to Marcott. Fresh out of law school working at a place with a lot of people's names I don't remember, but he said it was the oldest firm in the county. His name was R. Winston Mickler, and his friends called him R. Winston. He wouldn't tell anyone what the R stood for. He drove a blue BMW 325 convertible, and he never seemed to wear the same suit twice.

"But he couldn't have *that* many suits," Kim said, crinkling her nose. "He just always seemed to be wearing something new. Maybe it was cause his ties were so cool. They were like, really wild designs and everything. Sometimes, the right accessory can make an outfit look entirely different, so maybe that's why we never noticed whether his suits were the same or not. I read in *Cosmo* once, that you can use a scarf like six different ways to—"

"Kimberly. . . " David said. "We're talking about Lisa here, right?"

"I know. I was just going to tell you. . . " sighing, frustrated ". . .never mind." She stuck her tongue out at David.

*R. Winston found the Hitching Post by accident one weekend. He came in and sat down, and you could practically hear his jaw hit the table when Lisa came around the corner. He could barely speak when she took his order. After that, he went into the restaurant a few times on his lunch break, but Lisa was at school. He started coming in for dinner about three nights a week, and would usually squeeze in at least two meals on the weekends. He wore a wedding ring, but no one in the restaurant ever saw his wife.*

*It was a Saturday when he met little Michael Alexander. Lisa had the day off, but she came in to pick up her check. Michael was a beautiful olive-skinned boy of 12 months. He had hazel eyes and thick, curly golden hair. When he smiled large dimples formed in his chubby cheeks. He smiled a lot as he walked through the restaurant. A few truckers tried to get his attention, but Michael just kept moving. Finally, he stopped in front of R. Winston, who was holding out a French fry.*

*"Here you go, little man," the lawyer said with a smile. He was wearing heavily starched blue jeans and a long-sleeve, white polo button-up shirt with the cuffs rolled up.*

*"Michael, leave the nice man alone," Lisa said, rushing over to get her child. She was wearing tight jeans-shorts and a snug white T-shirt. Her hair was pulled back into a pony tail. There was no makeup on her face. She looked fabulous.*

*"Hey, we're twins," R. Winston said, pointing from his blue jeans and white shirt to hers.*

*Lisa smiled politely, grabbed Michael's hands and started to turn away. The restaurant was not very busy. It was about 10:30 a.m. A little late for the breakfast crowd, and a little early for lunch.*

*"Well, not exactly twins," he corrected, sounding almost shy. "Your*

*son is very cute."*

*"Thanks," Lisa said, trying not to encourage a conversation. "He's a handful." It came out like a closing statement.*

*"You said his name is Michael?" R. Winston said desperate to continue the conversation.*

*"Yeah. . . Michael Alexander," Lisa said moving away.*

*"Where's the father?" R. Winston said.*

*She stopped and looked at him. He was a handsome man, but she was definitely not interested. She could see the mark on his finger where his wedding band should be. He'd taken it off. Pretending to be single. Hoping that would help him get her in the sack. Hey look at me baby, I'm available! Now he was trying to figure out if she was married, or spoken for. She was neither. At that moment it stuck her as odd that she used to adore the attention of men just like him, but their interest felt like a curse the moment she discovered she was pregnant.*

*"There is no father," she said after a while. "It's just me and Michael."*

*"Oh really," the lawyer said, concerned. "You want to sit down for a minute?"*

*"You want to call your wife first?"*

*"Hey," R. Winston chuckled easily. "It's nothing like that. I want to talk to you on a professional level."*

*"About what?"*

*"About you needing a lawyer."*

*"I don't need a lawyer."*

*"I think you might." He extended a hand toward the other side of his booth, but Lisa made no move to sit down. Michael was walking in circles around her legs, still sucking on the French fry the lawyer had given him. Enjoying it. "Well. . . I just. . . you said there is no father, but there has to be a father."*

*"I don't know who the father is," Lisa said.*

*"Oh." R. Winston said, suddenly uncomfortable. Did she sleep with so many men that she had no clue who the father could be? "You could have a blood test," he said feebly.*

*"Listen. I know you look at me and you see a pretty girl, and I've got a child, and you want to rescue the damsel in distress. Well, I don't need to be rescued. I'm doing just fine."*

*"I'm not trying to rescue you, I'm just thinking of your son," R. Winston said, disarming her a bit. "I became a lawyer because I wanted to help people. And I think I can help Michael. I know you want the best for him. What mother wouldn't? You want him to be well-fed, clothed, go to a safe day care, maybe someday go to college, right? You want him to have all the opportunities he deserves. Isn't that right?"*

*"Of course I do," Lisa said defensively, standing a little taller. "I just don't think I need—"*

*"I'm sure you don't need anything, Lisa. You're a self-assured,*

very capable young woman. It's just that your son deserves to have a father. The guy who walked out on you, also walked out of Michael's life, and that's not fair. He needs a dad, and if he can't have a father, then he's lucky to have a mother like you who is willing fight for him to make sure he's financially taken care of in life."

They stared at each other for a moment. Lisa biting her bottom lip. She was alone. She had not talked to her family since the day her mother kicked her out. She had ostracized herself from the few friends she had at school. She'd quit going out to nightclubs. Even she and Kimberly were not the close friends they used to be. All she did was work, go to school, go home and take care of Michael. She struggled every month to pay the rent in her leaking, roach-infested trailer. Groceries and diapers were always in short supply. A little extra money would really help, but she had always looked down upon women who got themselves pregnant in order to trap men. She didn't want to be that kind of girl.

"I know you probably feel weird about having to ask the father for money," R. Winston said as though reading her mind. "But you're not asking for a handout. You didn't get pregnant by yourself, so you should-n't have to raise the child by yourself. If the father can't physically be there, then he should at least provide some financial assistance to make sure his son has clothing, food and a decent place to live."

Lisa stood by the table considering all of that.

"Sit down with me for a minute," R. Winston said gently. "Lisa, it would be very easy to straighten this situation out."

She moved slowly into the seat opposite the lawyer.

"It's in Michael's best interest for you to do this," R. Winston said. Then started the line of questions that would eventually lead to a paternity suit against Martin McNeil.

In the darkened Porsche by the pond, David said: "So the lawyer says 'who's the father?' and Lisa says, 'Martin McNeil, right?'" He wanted clarity on that point.

"I guess so. I really don't remember the guy's name."

"Kimberly, Martin McNeil is the most famous person in San Antonio, surely if you heard his name, you would have recognized it and remembered it." Costanzo was letting his frustration show.

"Well, maybe it wasn't that name then, because I don't remember," Kimberly said defensively. "I guess Lisa got some money because she came in and quit work on Friday. She moved away, and she didn't even tell me where she was going."

IT WAS FOUR IN the morning when David returned Kimberly to her car in the diner's parking lot. During the drive back, David was trying to decide how to get rid of her. He didn't want to see her again. She was far too young for him (he had finally checked her driver's license to confirm that she was

19). But he had never been good at extricating himself from women. As they were pulling into the parking lot he decided he would feign interest in her, take her phone number and then never call. It was the easiest way.

As the car rolled to a stop, Kimberly said goodbye with one last lingering kiss, not asking when she would see him again, apparently not caring. After thinking that he would have to fend her off, David was a little insulted by her casual departure. *Does she think I'm too old?*

"Bye bye my sweet prince," she said climbing out of the car. She looked back smiling lasciviously, lifting her skirt, showing him her bare ass. "Thanks for the good lovin'." And then she walked away.

"Hey, wait a second," David said.

Kim stuck her head back through the window.

"How'd you know I was interested in Lisa's baby?"

"What do you mean?"

"Earlier. When I told you I was a reporter you said 'I guess you're here about Lisa's baby."

Kimberly smiled. "Silly. The lawyer told me reporters would be coming."

David drove away slowly, shaking his head. Putting Kimberly out of his mind. Thinking about the story that was developing. He needed to talk to Lisa, but he didn't know her address or her phone number. The reporter decided to get a few hours of sleep and then track down the lawyer.


AFTER DAVID LEFT THE parking lot at the Hitchin' Post Diner, a sleek black BMW 540i eased into the slot next to Kimberly's car. She looked up expectantly, smiling.

"Hi there sexy man," she said as Philip Ramey stepped out. "Did I do good?"

"You were perfect." He extended an envelope through her window. Kimberly reached up with a delicate hand and grabbed it. Ramey didn't let go of his end. "So whadya tell him?" he said.

"The truth. I did just like you said. I just told the truth and nothing but the truth so help me God. It was easy."

Ramey nodded, pleased. He had instructed her to be honest, because the reporter would have seen through her feeble attempts at deception. Better for her to be up front with him, and let The Fixer deal with the cover-up. Plus, Ramey wanted the reporter to get excited about the story. It would make it that much more enjoyable when he met the writer and told him that there wasn't going to be a story.

"How'd you enjoy the other part?" The Fixer said.

"It was kind of fun," Kimberly smiled, her eyes drifting upward dreamily. Then with youthful confidence: "He was like all the rest of the guys. Once I showed him what I had, he couldn't resist me."

Ramey erupted with laughter, shaking his head. "You're something else girl."

"I know," Kimberly said proudly.

"Here's the other half of the two grand. Don't spend it all in one place." He turned back toward his car.

"Wait. When will I see you again?" Kimberly said, pouting.

"I'll call."

AT 9:15 A.M. WEDNESDAY, after only four hours of sleep at the Comfort Inn in Marcott, David parked on the street in front of James Brickly Boston. It took only a quick call to Nettie to ferret out the name of the oldest law firm in Guadalupe County. It was a law firm with four partners and 12 associates operating in an historic house just outside downtown Marcott. Two stately columns rose on either side of the stairs supporting porches on all three levels of the white house. Inside, mahogany floors, walls and furniture were polished to a deep shine. With so much dark wood, the house would have felt damp and dreary if not for the enormous windows along the front generously admitting sunlight to every room.

David waited 10 minutes for the lawyer.

"Mr. Costanzo?" A man in his mid-twenties approached. His blond hair was slicked back, and he was wearing a light gray suit with the most colorful tie David had ever seen; reds and blues swirling with magentas and fuchsias. It was hypnotic. "I'm R. Winston Mickler," he said, extending his hand. "Why don't we step into the conference room."

The reporter followed the young lawyer through a door just off the foyer. It was a large room overlooking a small parking lot on the side of the house that was probably a tennis court at one time. They sat down across from each other at a table designed to seat 12.

"What can I do for you?" Mickler said.

"Well, I need some information about a lawsuit filed by a client of yours against Martin McNeil."

"What client would that be?"

"Lisa Benson."

"Lisa. . . Lisa. . . Lisa?" Mickler said, making a big show of thinking aloud.

David stared for a moment, realizing this wasn't going to be as easy as he'd hoped. How many lawsuits could the guy have filed against Martin McNeil? How many suits could this kid have filed, period? He was just a young lawyer trying to play it tough.

"Come on, Mickler. You know who the hell she is. The suit was filed 11 days ago, and settled out of court. And you sure as hell haven't been out of law school long enough to have forgotten a client." Slapping him with it. Letting the lawyer know he was still a rookie.

Mickler smiled indulgently. "There's a trick to negotiating that you apparently haven't mastered in all your years of reporting. The key here is that you shouldn't start off by insulting the person from whom you hope to extract information."

"Look, I've been on this story a couple of days now," David said. "I know all about Lisa and her son. I know about the one night stand she had with Martin McNeil, and how her mom kicked her out of the house when she was pregnant. I know how you used to go over to the Hitching Post Diner, twisting your wedding ring off in the car, hoping you'd get lucky with the pretty young waitress who didn't even know your sorry ass was alive. I know you talked her into filing suit, and I know that Martin settled out of court just a few days ago. I'll find out the rest because the suit is a matter of public record, but as Lisa's attorney, I thought you might like to pass on the information. Give you a chance to spin it in terms that are most favorable to your client. You don't want her to come off looking like a money grubbing little bitch who got herself pregnant just to entrap an athlete and score a bundle of cash."

"I see you've been talking to that little minx Kimberly," R. Winston said, smiling. Then in a whisper: "Women just can't keep secrets." Winking. A little bonding between two men with enough experience with the fairer sex to know this was true. David returned the look. He was in his element now. Working a source. Telling the man what he needed to hear in order to spill the story that was screaming for release. David knew that most people had an inherent distaste for secrets. Secrets were no fun unless you could share them with someone. He could tell that this arrogant lawyer was desperate to tell someone about Lisa and Martin.

He's probably already told other lawyers in the firm about how he had found the beautiful girl in a diner and coaxed her into filing suit against a pro athlete. It was a home run. Filed and settled within a matter of days, with R. Winston scoring one-third of the bundle. Costanzo could hear him talking to his lawyer friends now: *"Shit I made so much money in that case, I paid off my Beemer, bought a Lexus for the wife and made a down payment on a house."*

"I said, 'did you sleep with her?'"

David was startled. "Excuse me?"

"Young, delicious, sexy, Kimberly. Did you have sex with her?" Mickler stared intently at David. "Yep, I bet you did. Did I mention that she was young?" The lawyer being smug. A funny guy.

"Fuck you."

"I'm sorry. Didn't mean to pry. Just curious."

The two men sat in silence for a moment. Mickler tapping his fingers lightly on the table. "Hey, she didn't show you that fake ID did she?"

David's mouth went dry.

"I mean, it's a pretty good ID. Says she's 19. See, she likes to pretend that she's a year older than Lisa—like she's the older and wiser of the two—but she's really a year and a half *younger*. Plenty of experience with men though. Started working at the Hitching Post when she was 14. Fooled the manager. He thought she was 16. Almost from day one, she was working the male customers. And I've heard she's quite a performer. Course, you'd know that better than me." Another wink. "She's discreet though. Ordinarily you wouldn't have much to worry about. She's never ratted on any of the other dirty old men who've screwed her. But I'm working on that. Statutory rape is a very serious offense."

"All we did was talk," David said defensively.

"I'll probably represent her if she decides to file against you," Mickler said casually. "In fact, when I speak to her later today, I'll recommend that she does."

That hung between them for a moment. David tapped his foot nervously.

"Anything else on your mind this morning?"

David was lost in thought.

"I said 'is there anything else?'" R. Winston repeated impatiently.

"Why was there no blood test?"

The lawyer sighed and stood up.

"Listen, my pedophile friend," Mickler said. "I'd love to sit and talk with you, because really, you're a fascinating person. But I have another appointment. Thanks for stopping by."

"Where can I find Lisa?" *Come on dammit!*

"It was truly a pleasure to meet you. Maybe I'll see you again. . . . in court." Mickler chuckled dryly as he ambled down a hallway, leaving the reporter sitting alone in the conference room.


DAVID JUMPED BACK INTO his Porsche, and drummed his fingers angrily against the steering wheel. The attorney had pissed him off, but he couldn't to let his anger distract him. He had a couple more stops to make before leaving Marcott, and the first was at Lisa's mother's house.

Despite Kimberly's assertion that Lisa hadn't spoken to her mom since she was kicked out of the house, David wasn't entirely convinced. Families were weird that way. Siblings fighting violently on the front lawn or parents attacking their children, everybody swinging wildly and launching from their mouths the most spiteful barbs of truth their minds can fetch.

But 15 minutes later, when it's time for dinner the atmosphere can be completely different. As though the reenactment of a scene from *One Flew Over A Cuckoo's Nest* never happened. Everything forgotten and perhaps forgiven; the sense of family restored.

Even though Lisa's mother had humiliated her in front of the neighbors, he believed that the two women may have reconciled their differences. Mom may have regretted her actions the moment her daughter walked down the street. The girl may have left thinking that it was all her fault; if only she had told her mother that she was pregnant. In the end, they would have made an effort to see each other—maybe Christmas Day or on Lisa's birthday. Maybe they had hugged tightly, overcome with joy and regret, crying together, apologizing and promising to never be so foolish again.

David drove quickly through the narrow streets of Marcott thinking that he wouldn't be the least bit surprised to see Lisa sitting on her mother's front porch drinking lemonade with her son in her lap.

THE BENSON RESIDENCE WAS precisely as Kimberly had described it sitting in the middle of a quiet neighborhood on the east side of Marcott. The houses were spaced evenly along the street with large pecan trees stretching languidly overhead. David pulled into the driveway and surveyed the house. It was a muscular one-and-a-half story home with peeling white paint, and wooden steps that bowed slightly as they marched up to the covered porch. The yard was freshly cut, and on either edge of the sidewalk leading up to the porch were narrow strips of dirt bursting with chrysanthemums, roses and tulips. David walked quickly to the door, taking the three stairs in a single bound. He knocked hard. There was no movement inside. He turned to look at the rest of the neighborhood, trying to imagine Lisa running around in a towel collecting her clothes off the lawn. The image made him smile. He'd never seen the girl, but based on the Kimberly's description he was sure it must have been some sight.

He knocked again.

David was only mildly disappointed to find the house empty. He had expected it. He didn't really figure that Lisa had moved back into her mother's house, but he had to check. He had to be sure. Investigating all the variables was just part of good reporting.

His next stop was the Perry Dry Cleaning Shop, a small storefront in a strip mall right behind the Guadalupe County Courthouse. A bell over the door jangled sharply as he entered, and a petite woman named Sarah Perry came around the corner rubbing her hands across the front of an apron. Her eyes danced over him quickly. He didn't have any clothes to turn in, and he didn't have a yellow claim ticket in his hand.

"We can't release your dry cleaning unless you have your ticket," she said firmly.

David smiled.

"It's for your own protection, you know," Perry said before he could launch into his story about how he lost his ticket. She was the owner of the small shop and she had heard all the stories. It didn't matter what they said; no ticket, no clothes. Perry didn't care if the customer could give a detailed description of every article of clothing that was being held. She'd take a name and number, and if the clothes were not claimed by someone else in 30 days then, and only then, would she release them.

David was still smiling. She eyed him suspiciously.

"Actually I didn't have anything to pick up today. I'm a newspaper reporter. I need to talk to one of your employees for a moment."

"Oh," she said, surprised. Then smiling for the first time, fussing with a light brown tangle of hair: "May I ask what this is about?"

"Actually, it's a personal matter," David said apologetically. "I need to talk to Mrs. Benson."

"Of course, of course," Perry said, eager to accommodate. "Please come on through."

Behind the brief partition, the shop was crowded with a convoluted conveyor system for storing clothes, and work stations where women mended holes and treated stains. Mrs. Perry led him to a far corner, where an attractive woman in her early forties was sewing quietly.

"Missy, there's a reporter her to see you," Perry said. She stepped a little to the side to let David through, and them moved away from them, but no so far away that she couldn't hear every word they said.

Melissa Benson stood up, looking at him disinterestedly.

"Hi, Mrs. Benson, my name is David Costanzo. I'm a reporter from the *San Antonio Light* newspaper." He extended his hand, but she made no move to take it. She crossed her arms slowly, frowning suspiciously. David continued: "I was wondering if I could talk to you for a minute."

"It's *Ms.*, and you're talkin' to me now," she said. An angry line formed between her eyebrows.

"I mean, *privately.*" The other employees were staring at them through racks of shirts and suits. Mrs. Perry was pretending to sort through a pile of clothing nearby.

"Ain't got nothin' to talk about."

David cleared his throat uncomfortably. "I want to ask you a few questions about Lisa."

"Don't know no Lisa," Ms. Benson said quickly, adjusting her frown.

"Your daughter, Lisa."

"I just told you I don't know no Lisa."

They stood looking at each other for a moment, machinery hissing and clicking in the background. David realized this was not one of the families that saw the happy ending. They weren't coming back together with smiles and apologies.

"Listen," he said gently, trying another track. "I know about the argument you and Lisa had the night you kicked her out of your house. I understand how angry you were with her, but now Lisa's in a lot of trouble. She's in a tough situation, and she desperately needs your help."

Ms. Benson's eyes twitched involuntarily. She was still angry with Lisa. Flaunting herself around like she did, letting men have their way with her. Ms. Benson tilted her chin up slightly at the thought of it. She was resolved. Willing to live with her decision.

*But what if Lisa is in trouble?* Ms. Benson tried to steel herself against sympathy. *She took a bad road and now she had to travel that evil path alone. If she's in a jam, then she'll just have to handle it.*

David leaned toward her and said quietly: "Have the police contacted you?"

The woman shook her head slowly, her mouth a thin line, her eyes wide.

"Anyone from the hospital?"

Shaking her head harder, her vision blurring with tears. "What happened?" she croaked.

David looked at her sadly, the empathetic face of one charged with delivering bad news. "Apparently Lisa has some type of medical condition. She went to the emergency room a few days ago complaining of severe headaches."

Ms. Benson gasped softly and put a hand over her mouth. *Headaches?* She was already assuming the worst. Her brow was screwed up in pain, and tears leaked down her face. The reporter continued: "They ran some tests and told her she had to have surgery immediately. I guess she was scared because she ran right out of the hospital. The police have been looking for her since yesterday. It's a matter of life and death."

"Oh my God," Ms. Benson said. She collapsed into her chair, her face in her hands. Her severed relationship with her daughter stabbing her heart like a rusty sword. "Is it a tumor?" she said fearfully looking into David's eyes.

The reporter stared back solemnly, not speaking a word; his eyes telling her that her worst fears were true. He handed her a handkerchief from his back pocket. "Ma'am, it's a matter of life or death. We have to find Lisa and get her into a hospital."

Ms. Benson nodded, wiping her eyes, trying to think of where her daughter might have gone.

"Has she contacted you during the past three or four days?" David said.

"No," she said in a small voice. "I haven't spoken to her in nearly two years." The shame of it tore at her.

"I spoke with her friend Kim at the diner this morning, but she hadn't seen Lisa, either," David said. He handed Ms. Benson a business card. "If you hear from Lisa, find out where she is and call me immediately. I'll make sure an ambulance rushes over to take care of her."

"Okay," the woman said, gripping his hand tightly as she took the card from him. "Thank you." It came out in a whisper.

David nodded and walked slowly out of the shop, brushing past Mrs. Perry who was pulling lint off a sports coat.

Back in his car, he slammed the door hard. Another dead end.

*That's what's wrong with America today. Families don't stay together.*

# TWENTY-THREE

MARTIN SAT IN THE Stallions' meeting room in a blue lycra Nike sweat suit that was zipped all the way to his chin. A white NBC Sports hat was pulled down tight over his eyes. He wanted to disappear. Hide somewhere so no one could get a good look at him and see the guilt that enveloped him.

Coach Starnes was up at the front of the room telling the team about Williams' death. Everyone had already heard the news, but it was still a shock. No one made a sound. Tim's teammates were thinking about the cheese and stickers they had stuck to Williams' head during the return flight. It made them queasy to think that they had been messing with a dead man.

"Just go home and be with your families," Starnes said. "We'll come back tomorrow to start getting ready for the Oilers game. The funeral will be held in a couple of days." He paused for a long moment. Then with a sigh: "See you guys later."

The players filed out of the room in silence; an unspoken respect afforded Tim Williams.

Martin sat down at his locker and put his head in his hands.

"You okay?" It was Dexter Smith, a 293-pound defensive lineman.

Martin looked up startled. "Yeah. I'm just shocked, I guess."

"It's freaky man," Smith said shaking his head. "I ain't never heard of nothin' like this. I mean, brothas don't just *die*, you know what I'm sayin'?"

"Yeah," Martin said hesitantly. *Does Dexter know something?*

"Somebody capped that nigga," Smith said, his thick head nodding slowly, his nostrils flaring.

"Come on man, that's crazy." Martin hoped there was adequate conviction in his words. Smith suspected someone had killed Tim.

"Shit, *you* crazy." Smith looked around suspiciously. He sat next to Martin. "What I'm thinkin' is the white-bread management here decided they didn't like that nigga, so they offed his ass, you know what I'm sayin'?"

"Why the hell would they do that?" Martin said, relieved that Smith's suspicions were so far off the mark.

"Look around yo monkey ass. How many niggas is on the team?"

"I don't know," Martin said wearily. "Twenty-five? Thirty?"

"I'll tell ya how many. Sixty-five percent, that's how many. Sixty-five percent of the workers is niggas; but dig this, you know how many brothas is in the front office?"

"Two?"

"One. They fired that lazy-ass muthafucka James the other day. You see what I'm saying, man? This is just slavery all over again. You think I'm bullshittin, but them muthafuckas killed my boy Williams just like they used to do back in the slave days."

THE MOMENT HE GOT home, Martin threw off his clothes and crawled back into bed. Jessica was in the den watching TV, and without a word, she undressed and crawled into bed with him. She had become something of a professional student, working on a second master's degree at Trinity University. She had two bachelor's degrees, one in English literature and another in philosophy, plus a Masters in English lit. Then a year and a half ago, she decided her education was too weighted in liberal arts, so she was working on an MBA. Despite her husband's millions, Jessica worked retail at Northwest Plaza Mall from 2 to 10 p.m. six days a week; her classes met on Tuesdays and Thursdays. She didn't need to work. Martin could have paid all of her college expenses without a thought, but she insisted on it.

"Martin," Jessica had explained years earlier, "you've provided this wonderful house for me and a car to drive. I want to pay for my own education. I don't want to be the athlete's wife who sits at home and obsessing about how to spend her husband's money or which fabric will look best on the couch. I don't want to be part of some social club meeting other wives for lunch. I like working at the mall. I like selling clothing. I like making my own money. I like writing my own checks to pay for my tuition. I need that."

There were hundreds of things Martin loved about Jessica; her fierce independence was one of them. He knew so many players used their fame and wealth to get women. But Martin had never craved that life. He and Jessica got married during their senior year in college, but even if he'd been single, he guessed that he'd be a major disappointment to most of the women he would date. He didn't spend money lavishly. He had a 3,500-square-foot house. It was comfortable without being lavish. He'd dropped some cash on the Mercedes Ramey had negotiated and a Jeep Grand Cherokee. But his suits were off the rack, his watch was a Timex, and his spending habits were pretty modest. He and Jessica mostly ate at home, but when they went out it was to normal family type restaurants. They enjoyed movies, bowling alleys and bookstores. He couldn't imagine being with anyone but her. She was his friend and his lover.

GIVEN THE GENERAL AMBIVALENCE both Martin and Jessica had toward the $19 million dollars in his investment account, it was odd that money was the only real source of disagreement in their relationship. Well, money and Brandon.

Jessica hated Martin's older brother. She thought he was a conniving, manipulative, freeloading, womanizing, egotistical jerk.

"It's painful to watch you when you're with him," Jessica said to Martin during a recent argument. "He doesn't care about you at all, and he's not the least bit considerate to you. All he ever wants from you is money, but you don't seem to notice that. Whenever he calls or comes by, you just smile and say 'no problem' as you write him another check. Can't you see that he's totally taking advantage of you?"

Martin shook his head slowly. "Don't be so quick to judge our relationship. You just don't understand him. You don't know everything that we've been through together. He's family."

"Family members love each other," Jessica said pointedly. "If he loves you he sure does a great job of hiding it."

"Not everyone shows their love in the same ways."

"Okay, that's fine. I'm sure he does love you in his own way. But I'm also sure he is a total leech. He doesn't work. He spends half his time just throwing away the money you give him, and the other half trying to screw anything that walks."

"Anything female that walks," Martin corrected.

Jessica considered him for a moment, then sighing as if unloading a burden she said:  "You know what he said to me a long time ago when I barely knew him?"

"I can only imagine."

"I never told you, because I didn't really know anything about your relationship with him and I didn't want to be the cause of any conflict between the two of you." She paused to give Martin a chance to speak, but he didn't appear to have anything to say. He watched her impassively, waiting for her to continue.

"He came over one day and let himself in with the key he used to have to your house. I was in the backyard lying out, working on my tan. None the neighbors can see me when I'm back there, so I was naked. I'd been out there about 45 minutes when I heard the sliding glass door open real quietly behind me. I was lying on my stomach, and I thought it must be you planning to sneak up on me. I just kept reading my book and pretended that I hadn't heard a thing. I was waiting for you, but four of five minutes passed and nothing happened. I didn't want to spoil your surprise, but I was getting impatient, so I turned around to look for you. Brandon was standing there on the porch staring straight at me. I screamed and rolled over to cover myself with a towel. I said, 'Brandon what the hell are you doing here?' He didn't say anything at first. He just stood there smiling. Then you know what he said?"

"What?"

Jessica was shaking her head like she still couldn't believe it. Her face was a mixture of rage and humiliation. "He said, 'mmmm, mmmm girl. You've got legs like I like 'em; feet at the bottom, pussy at the top.'"

She waited for Martin to react, but he didn't say a word. "This is your brother Martin. The one who you think loves you so much. I couldn't believe he would talk to any woman like that, but especially your wife."

"What did you say after that?"

Jessica let out an exasperated hiss of breath. "What difference does it make what I said after that, you obviously don't care."

"I do care."

She stared hard at Martin for a long moment. "I said, 'Brandon you're a jerk and a fucking pervert. Why don't you just leave." He just smiled, winked at me and walked back into the house. When I went inside about 15 minutes later, he was gone. That was the day I called the locksmith and had all the locks changed. Remember I told you I changed them because I lost my purse and I was afraid of someone breaking in because they had my keys and my address?"

"Yeah, I remember."

"Martin, I know you love Brandon, but he doesn't care about anyone but himself. He doesn't return your love. All he's interested in is your money."

"That's not true," Martin said quietly.

"It is true," Jessica pleaded. "Look at his life. He hasn't worked a day since you signed your first contract. Your rookie year he asked you for three hundred thousand dollars and you gave it to him. Then you bought him a townhouse. So far you've purchased four cars for him. You pay all of his bills, and you get him season tickets for the Stallions and Spurs games. And even that's not enough. Every time you turn around, he's asking you for something else. I mean, he's not calling to ask you to go see a movie with him, or to go hang out and shoot pool. He calls when he needs money, and that's it."

Martin was sitting on the couch looking down at his feet, his hands clasped in his lap. "Jessica, all my life I wanted Brandon to be proud of me. When I was growing up, everyone thought I was so great. My teachers complimented me on my grades, my coaches raved about my athletic ability, my parent beamed whenever they talked about me. But with Brandon there was nothing. It was like I didn't even exist. I did everything I could think of to get his attention, but nothing worked. Nothing I did ever impressed Brandon.

"Then I got drafted into the NFL, and suddenly he wanted to be a part of my life. I'm not stupid. I know that what he really wanted was the money, but it was my performance that created that money; so indirectly, Brandon was interested in me for the first time in my life. When he asked me to give him three hundred grand, I didn't even think about it. I had more money than I could ever spend, and my brother wanted some of it. I figured, 'what do I care if he's using me?' He's my *only* brother. And if giving him money is what it takes to keep him in my life, then I'm going to keep giving him money."

"But do you have to give him *everything* he ever asks for? Do you have to let him rob you blind?" Jessica said.

"I say 'no' sometimes."

"No, you don't."

"I do."

"Martin, when have you ever said 'no' to one of your brother's requests?"

"I said 'no' to him a couple of weeks ago, when he asked for some money to invest in a night club. He got pretty upset about it, and that's why we haven't been talking lately. Now, I wish I'd just given him the money."

"No, honey. You did the right thing. You shouldn't let Brandon take advantage of you. I think it's wonderful that you finally said 'no' to him."

BUT THE TRUTH WAS that Martin would have been smarter to give Brandon the money. His refusal to deliver the gift spawned Brandon's desire to ruin his younger brother's life.

Brandon had spent weeks talking to other nightclub owners, learning operational procedures and looking over cash flow and income projections. He was confident that he could run a successful nightclub, but to get started he would need several investors, or one big investor. He turned to Martin.

And for the first time ever, Martin said "no."

"Brandon, I'm not going to throw $500,000 into a nightclub. It's too risky."

"It'll be a great investment for you because I'll be running it," Brandon argued, trying to recover from the shock of this Martin's first refusal. "I live in nightclubs. I go to a different club almost every night. I know what's good and what's bad about them. I know what people like in a club, and I know I can create the perfect party place."

"I don't doubt your ability Brandon, I just think it's a tough business and it's way too risky for me to invest $500,000. I'd be willing to give you $100,000, but you'd have to work out the rest of the financing yourself."

"Martin, a hundred grand isn't going to do shit for me. With finding a site and remodeling and purchasing and installing all the electronic equipment and lights, this is going to cost about $1.2 million to get off the ground. I've talked to a guy at a bank who said he can probably arrange $700,000 in financing, but I've got to come up with the five hundred in cash first."

Martin shrugged. He was standing firm. "Well, if I give you $100,000, you only need to raise another $400,000 to get the deal done."

"Man, that's bullshit."

"Brandon, what about the $300,000  I gave you my rookie year.

Don't you have any of that money left?"

"Come on Martin, that was four years ago. I had to get myself set up in town. I had to get to know people, buy furniture, take some trips. That money is gone. We're not even talking about that money. We're talking about $500,000 for a club."

"I just can't keep throwing money at you. I don't understand what you expect of me."

"I expect you to give me the money!"

"If I could afford to just throw away $500,000, then I would do it for you Brandon, but that's just too much money. I can give you a hundred, but that's all."

Brandon waved an angry hand in the air. "Man, that chick has got you so pussy whipped it's not even funny."

"Jessica doesn't have anything to do with this."

"Of course she does. She's the one who's always telling you that you shouldn't give me any more money. She's the one who's whispering in your ear right now, saying, even though this is my dream; even though this is the opportunity of a lifetime; even though your help would make me happier than I have ever been; even though you've got more money that you can ever possibly spend, don't give any to your brother. Make me walk away with nothing. Turn your back on me. Kick me out. That's what she wants you to do and that's what you're doing."

"Brandon, I'm not turning my back on you. I've offering to give you, not loan you, *give* you a hundred grand to help you open your nightclub. I think that's a very generous offer."

Brandon stepped up close to his little brother and said, "You're going to regret this Martin. You're really going to regret the day you decided to fuck me over."

X marks the spot—for Brandon.

# TWENTY-FOUR

MOST PATRONS WOULD CONSIDER it the worst table in the house. It was tucked into an alcove away from the band, away from the Latin dancers, close to the kitchen, out of view of nearly everyone. On a typical night in Giovanni's—a hot new Brazilian restaurant—no one was ever seated at table 17. Even with a long waiting list, most people would rather stand at the bar than take that table. People went to Giovanni's to be seen; not to eat in seclusion at the back of the restaurant.

But it was the perfect spot for Martin and Jessica. They'd stopped going to restaurants years ago because it was impossible to balance between the extremes of accommodating all the autograph requests or none of them. Once the first person approached the table, it was as though the entire restaurant was watching the exchange. If Martin smiled and signed the autograph without complaint, it was a signal to everyone else that he was friendly and it was safe to approach. There'd be a steady stream of people stopping by the table for autographs, pictures and "just a moment of Martin's time."

If Martin said "no" to that initial request when the rest of the patrons were watching, then he wouldn't be bombarded with requests, but he'd pay the price in other ways. Saying no to an autograph was the quickest way to earn the scorn of the general public. Everyone in the restaurant saw one person walk up to his table. They knew it would have taken only a few seconds to sign the autograph. But instead of signing the paper, Martin had sent that person away, making the football player appear to be an insensitive, egotistical jerk.

It was a battle he couldn't win, so he and Jessica had simply given up on restaurants, except on those occasions when a back room was available away from the crowds.

Giovanni's proved to be the perfect location for them. When they wanted to come in for dinner, they'd make a call to manager Federico Guttierrez who would position one of his valet drivers at the back door to take Martin's car. They'd come in through the kitchen, right to the private table in the back. No one in the main dining area would see them. They could still hear the band play and get some of the ambiance of the restaurant without enduring a gauntlet of autograph seekers. It was the perfect table.

They were nearly finished with their meals, when Jessica finally asked about Martin's mood. "You don't seem like yourself today Martin?"

"No?"

"You seem distracted, upset, uncomfortable, something. I can't put my finger on it, but you're giving off a really weird vibe."

Martin shrugged. "I guess I'm just freaking out because of Tim's death. I was sitting next do a dead man on the plane."

Jessica nodded. She could understand his discomfort, but she didn't believe that's what was bothering Martin. Something had him shaken, and she didn't know what that could be. "Martin, I love you, and I'm here to help you with anything that's going on. I'm not sure exactly what's eating at you, but you're working on some problem. Talk to me about it. Maybe I can help."

Martin wanted to tell his wife, but he was afraid that she wouldn't believe him. He knew that he should have included her from the start, that this situation probably would never have spiraled out of control if he had turned to her when he got the initial phone call from his attorney. He'd thought that he could handle this himself, but now he understood just how wrong he was.

Martin looked at his wife for a long moment, then took a deep breath and told her about Lisa Benson. He told her about the lawsuit and the call from his attorney Joseph Steadman. He told her about settling the suit to avoid negative publicity and about moving Lisa into a townhouse. And finally he told her about hiring Ramey to keep the story quiet.

"You hired Brandon's gangster friend to help contain this situation?" Jessica said. "What could he possibly do to help you?"

Martin looked at his wife, afraid to say the words. He spoke quietly. "Ramey killed Tim Williams."

Jessica was confused. "Tim died of a heart attack or something?"

Martin shook his head. "I hired Ramey and he killed Tim. That makes me a murderer."

"No, no, you're not a murderer," Jessica said, her instincts kicking in. She didn't understand what was happening. She didn't know whether her husband had cheated on her and gotten another woman pregnant; she didn't know whether her husband participated in the murder of Tim Williams, but her instincts told her that he needed her support. Her questions would come later. Right now, she needed to be strong. "You're not a murderer, Martin. You hired Ramey to protect yourself. You could never have anticipated that he would kill someone." She squeezed his hands tightly across the small table. "I just don't understand why Philip Ramey killed Tim?"

Martin wiped his face. "He said it was a diversion for the media. Something to keep them busy so they wouldn't find out about my lawsuit."

"Ahh."

They finished their dinner in silence.

MARTIN AND JESSICA STOPPED at a video store on their way home, indulging their favorite pastime. When they returned to the house, Brandon was sitting in the living room watching television.

"How did you get in here?" Jessica said, angrily.

"I've got a key," Brandon said, dangling it in front of his face.

"I changed the locks," Jessica said pointedly.

"Yes, I know. That was awfully industrious of you," Brandon said, his eyebrows raised, his eyes sparkling mischievously. "But wasted effort, because my dear brother simply gave me a new key."

Jessica turned to Martin, who smiled sheepishly and shrugged. She exhaled an angry breath and then said to Brandon, "Don't you have your own house?"

"Come on, don't start this again," Martin interrupted.

"Where do you want to watch the movie," Jessica said in a huff, "the den or the bedroom?"

"Bedroom," Martin said.

Jessica stormed away. Brandon stared pointedly at her rear end. "Damn Martin, she looks better every time I see her." He turned and smiled at his younger brother. "Is she a good fuck?"

Martin stared hard at his brother, but said nothing. "What do you want?"

"Just wanted to let you know that everything went smoothly. Me and Ramey picked up Lisa and her kid, and they're safely tucked away in her own townhouse. She's got furniture, food in the fridge and twenty-five grand in the bank. You sure you didn't bang this chick?"

"*Yes*, I'm sure," Martin said.

"I only ask, 'cause Lisa is some sweet meat."

"Brandon, don't mess with her," Martin pleaded. "We've got enough trouble without you sleeping with her and adding to our problems."

"Hey, it's cool," Brandon said. "I'm not gonna pursue her."

"Thank you."

"But if she comes after me, that's another story."

# TWENTY-FIVE

BACK AT HIS APARTMENT, David sat down at his computer and started writing. There were still a lot of details to discover, holes to be filled, but what he had so far was good. The most compelling piece of the story was the cold, basic truth that underscored everything that followed: A 15-year-old girl got pregnant and two years later filed a paternity suit against Stallions receiver Martin McNeil; the player settled the suit out of court. Those facts alone would be enough; a single headline's worth of information. Just write that, toss in a photo of the player in his uniform, maybe a picture of the girl with the baby sitting in her lap. People would fill in the gaps. They'd invent all manner of sordid details to explain their hero's fall from grace.

But Costanzo didn't want to leave anything to the imagination of the readers. He wanted the rest of the story. He wanted 5,000 damning words, spelling out the full breadth of McNeil's failings. He wanted to be sure that no one could dispute the absolute horror of the story that would change forever the way the people of San Antonio, and probably the nation, looked at Martin McNeil. He didn't want to simply skim the surface. David wanted to dig trenches into McNeil's life, showing the world the cancerous truths beneath the top soil.

His main problem was that he couldn't *prove* McNeil was the father. Sure, Martin settled the suit, but maybe he was just trying to get rid of it. A public battle over the child might have damaged his image even if he were exonerated. It wouldn't have been the first time that a celebrity paid off someone just to protect his reputation.

Also a bit unnerving was Kimberly's firm belief that the father had hazel eyes. David didn't know how to find out if Martin owned hazel contacts. He could ask other reporters or he could ask some of the player's teammates, but that was dangerous. Someone might get suspicious an odd question like that and start looking into Martin's life. Costanzo didn't want anyone else to have this story. The destruction of Martin McNeil was all his.

*Why the hell didn't he just get a blood test like any reasonable man would do?* Even if Martin was worried about his image, a simple DNA test would have proven beyond a doubt that he was not the father, and surely his reputation would have been fine. The public would have understood that he had been falsely accused. But he didn't get a blood test. He paid her off. He *must* be the father.

David slammed a flat hand down on his desk and walked away from his computer. This was important. He had to get it right. He had to prove conclusively that Martin was the father; that the guy was banging a 15-year-old girl; that he had refused to help her until she filed suit. Those were the nails in the coffin. There had to be a way to sort this out. David walked into his kitchen and pulled a carton of orange juice out of the refrigerator. He had all the other details.

*I need a blood test!* With it, he could seal the story with the line: "a DNA test revealed a 99.998 percent probability that Martin was the father of the child."

But maybe he was making too much of the lack of a test. He had a suit that was filed and settled quickly and quietly out of court. That was a fundamental truth. To the average citizen that's an open and shut case. Martin was the father.

The tragedy of Lisa's life would play well spilled onto the pages of the newspaper alongside photos of Martin. She'd be the perfect victim in yet another do-em-and-dump-em drama starring an egotistical pro athlete. A young girl who hadn't had a break in her whole life, who fell in love. Who surrendered her virginity—well almost—and for her trouble ended up pregnant. She tried to get help from the athlete, but he turned his back on her. Left her to die in the streets with their child. Eventually, she was forced to resort to a paternity suit to wrangle a little bit of assistance from her child's wealthy father.

David could write *that* story. He could write it well. By the time he finished, the entire city would hate Martin with a passion generally reserved for mass murderers.

*Screw the blood test!*

He returned to his computer and continued to write.

Five minutes later he stopped with a frustrated sigh. What if the story runs and then Martin gets a blood test proving that the kid is not his? That would be professionally embarrassing for Costanzo. There was also a potential libel suit if he was wrong. Or even worse: What if the story ran then McNeil got a blood test proving that he wasn't the father and was able to spin the story to make himself look like a hero for supporting a kid who wasn't his.

David wasn't sure what to do. So he did what he always did when he was confused. He typed a quick message to Nettie Richardson.

> *Serious Qs. Meil settle no D-test. Why not? Also, source recalls hazel peeps, Meil's are brown. Fake? How confirm?*

Nettie thought about the questions. In her mind racing through the possible reasons that Martin McNeil would settle a paternity suit without first getting a paternity test. The question of Martin possibly owning hazel contacts was tough. It's a personal item that only a handful of people may know about. If David starts asking those people, he may inadvertently arouse the interest of other reporters.

Nettie pushed her glasses up her nose and fired off a response.

> *Q-1: Probably no time. Fear of exposure so quick resolution. Q-2: No good way to find out without arousing interest from others. Best solution on both counts: Ask him. He might just tell you.*

MARTIN WAS SURFING THE Internet. Jessica had left about an hour earlier to go to class, and would not be back until late evening. Martin was paralyzed. He'd returned from Tim Williams' funeral that morning, stripped off his suit and shuffled around the house. Coach Starnes had given the team the day off to mourn. Martin was mourning more than most, wrestling with a guilt that his teammates couldn't imagine. Some of them were disturbed about the way they had desecrated Williams' body on the airplane. But none of them was responsible for the man's death. None of them had hired a killer. That was Martin's burden.

He was flipping through ESPN.com when the phone rang.

"Hello."

"Hi, is this Martin?"

"Yeah."

"Martin, it's David Costanzo over at the *San Antonio Light* newspaper. How you doin?"

Martin pulled the phone away from his head, and cursed silently. "I'm okay," he said cautiously. He didn't want to talk to Costanzo, but he was curious to discover how much the reporter knew.

"I need to interview you for a feature story I'm writing."

"What's the story?"

"Your dead teammate, Tim Williams," David said, there was a confidence in his voice that terrified Martin.

"What about him?" McNeil's heart sank. Costanzo knew. He *knew!* Ramey had promised that no one would find out about the murder, but Martin knew that was impossible. The medical examiner would find the truth. Costanzo was calling for a pre-incarceration interview.

"I was just wondering if he knew you were fucking a 15-year-old?"

The question caught Martin off-guard. He answered with silence.

"Lisa Benson," David said, mirth tickling the edge of his voice.

"Who?" Martin said. His throat was dry.

"Don't play games, Martin. She's the teenager you were banging, sued you last week, and you settled with her nice and quick."

"Never heard of her."

"There's no point lying, Martin. I know the whole story."

"You know so much, why you calling me?"

"Fairness," Costanzo said. "Give you a chance to tell your side of the story."

"Fairness?" Martin said.

"Yeah. This is an objective piece," David said. "See, I don't want to have to paint you as the mega-rich bad guy who deserted the young mother of his child and refused to give her a dime until she took him to court. I want to be fair. Let you tell your side of it."

"Sounds like extortion."

"It's just an interview."

"You call me up and say, 'Listen, Martin, I'm about to screw up your life with a few lies I've cooked up. Wondered if you'd like to comment. That's extortion."

"Is the baby yours?" David said.

"What baby?"

"Martin, let me ask you one very serious question."

"Oh, "is the baby yours" wasn't serious? What was that a warm up question?"

"One question." David insisted.

Martin sighed. "Shoot."

"Do you own hazel contacts?"

It was a non sequitur that made no sense to McNeil. He issued something between a cough and a laugh. "What are you talking about?"

"Do you?"

"No!" Martin said exasperated. "What does that have to do with anything?"

The reporter sighed. He hadn't expected the player to answer his questions, but he had to try. "Martin, I told you years ago that I would catch up with you one day. Looks like my day has come." Then in a cold whisper: "I'm about to *destroy* you."

"So there's the threat again, huh?" Martin said.

"You should never have fucked with me Martin. The pen is mightier than the sword."

# TWENTY-SIX

Philip Ramey answering the phone with a command: "Speak."

"It's Martin," McNeil said, trying to stay calm, but not succeeding. "David Costanzo just called. He knows everything. *Everything!* He's gonna—"

"Calm your monkey ass down," Ramey said harshly. "I'll meet you out back in half an hour." He hung up.

Twenty-five minutes later, sitting in lounge chairs on the back porch, Martin replayed his conversation with David.

"Did he ask you any questions?" Ramey said, sitting there with his shirt off and his shades on like a white guy working on his tan. His black skin was glistening.

"No! You're not listening to me. He knew everything! I'm paying you a lot of money to take care of this! What the hell are you doing besides killing innocent people?"

Ramey stared hard at the football player. "Keep talking to me like that. . ." A threat.

Martin tried to return the look, knowing he shouldn't back down, but too scared to act tough. He took several deep breaths. "He wanted to give me a chance to tell my side of the story."

"So he didn't ask any questions?"

Martin sighed. "Yeah. He asked if the baby was mine."

"What'd you tell him."

"Nothing. Then he asked me if I had hazel contacts, which I didn't understand at all."

"Hazel contacts, huh?" Ramey thought for a moment. "He doesn't know shit."

"Of course he knows." Martin could feel his voice rising but managed to keep it in check. "He knew about Lisa. He knew about Tim. Asking me if Tim knew I was sleeping with Lisa. How did he make that connection? He knew everything."

"Naw. He don't know nothing. I guarantee you he doesn't know about Tim, and he can't be sure about the kid because you didn't get a blood test. That's throwing him."

"We gotta do something about him. We can't let this story get into the paper," Martin said desperately.

"Oh, so *now* you wanna play rough. You're Mr. Big Time now, huh?"

"Nothing drastic!" Martin was suddenly scared. "Just, I don't know. Something to scare him off."

"I'll take care of it," Ramey said.

"Wait!" Martin said quickly. "Maybe I should talk to him."

"What's a weak ass nigga like you gonna say to him?"

Martin swallowed. "I thought you might have some suggestions. I mean, I'm paying you a hundred and fifty grand to keep this quiet, and now Costanzo knows everything. You could, you know, advise me a little. I could go negotiate with him."

"Bitch, you're not strong enough to negotiate."

"Man, fuck you."

The Fixer smiled, standing up. "Wait here," he said, walking across the grass and out the back gate. Martin waited nervously, the sun licking at his skin, sweat beading up and rolling off his forehead, wondering what Ramey was doing. He thought of a maxim he'd been taught by teammates who'd grown up in the ghetto. They said: *"If you're ever in a fight or argument with a guy and he walks toward his car, you better go tackle his ass or start running the other way 'cause he's going to get his gun."* Sitting on the back porch, Martin wondered what he should do. Ramey had said, "Wait here," and sure enough, Martin was waiting like a dumb hick about to get his ass shot off. *Maybe I should get my gun.* Martin had a permitted .38 in his bedroom closet, and some bullets in a drawer in the kitchen. He looked nervously at the back gate, then stood and moved to the sliding glass door. He was just pulling it open when Ramey came back through the gate.

Ramey had something in his hand but Martin couldn't tell what it was from that distance. *Could it be a gun?* They were looking at each other. Ramey halfway through the gate, Martin halfway through the glass doors. Both waiting to see what the other was going to do.

"Where you going?"

"Thought I heard the phone ringing." Martin closed the glass door and walked back to his seat. Ramey came across the grass, his hand mostly covering the object in his hand. Martin was nervous, but finally decided it definitely wasn't a gun.

Ramey tossed it to him. "If you're gonna talk to David, this might help you." Then he turned to walk away.

Martin sat looking down into his hands, wondering what the hell this had to do with anything.

"Yo Martin," Ramey, turned back toward the house. He was halfway across the lawn. "Piece of advice. Brotha gets up and goes to his car, he's probably getting a gun. You wanna stay alive, you don't sit and wait for his ass to shoot you."

# TWENTY-SEVEN

NETTIE WATCHED FROM HER perch as David walked into the newsroom. She was immediately aware of the excitement in his eyes, the swagger in his gait. She knew the tip on Martin McNeil had borne fruit, and the story was coming together.

"Any messages for me?" David asked quietly when he reached her desk. His eyes flitted about nervously, trying to keep track of everyone.

"Yes," she said, holding up a stack of pink slips. "Everybody's upset about your columns about Tim Williams."

During the past few days, Costanzo had written several columns in which he stated that Tim Williams was a drug addict who didn't have much to offer society anyway. So he's dead. Who gives a crap?

"Throw 'em away," David said to Nettie, waving a hand.

Nettie dropped them into the trash can. David looked at her intently.

"Let me ask you something," David said in a low voice, moving around her desk, dropping into their code. "Meil settles this D-claim with an 18-year-old girl in Marcott, and she moves out of her trailer the next day. Where do you think she'd go?"

"Was it her parents' trailer?"

"No. It was her place."

"She didn't move back home?"

"Mom won't have anything to do with her."

Nettie thought for a moment, her gears turning rapidly. "You said, her mom won't have anything to do with her, so her parents don't live together. Have you checked with her father."

David shook his head. "According to a friend, the girl never knew her father."

Nettie eyes blinked quickly the way they always did when her brain was working full tilt. She was consuming the available information and spitting out probabilities. "Well, if she moved the next day, she had money or someone helping her or both. That means Meil settled the suit with a cash payment or at least gave her cash as part of it. He was probably worried about reporters picking up the story, so he had someone pick her up and move her into a new apartment."

David nodded. "Neighbor said a big black car came to get her."

Nettie was still clicking. When she was working like this, she was almost clairvoyant. She could see things other people couldn't see. Recreate the past. Anticipate the future. But unlike a true seer, she wasn't tuned into the spirit world. It was just cold logic. "Does she have a job in Marcott?"

"She did, but she quit on Friday. The same day she moved."

Nettie thought for a moment. "Okay. If she quit the job, she has no reason to stay in Marcott. If Meil was concerned about her, wanted to keep an eye on her, he'd move her into an apartment somewhere in San Antonio, not far from his house. Then he could check on her, make sure she wasn't talking to anyone."

David was thinking, getting excited. "That makes sense. He's got a house in Alamo Heights on the North East side."

"How long did they date before the girl got pregnant?" Nettie said. It disgusted her to think that Martin was cheating on his wife, but that just made him like all the other men in the world.

"They met at a club here in town. Had a one night stand."

"Hmm," Nettie said, thinking about Martin's wife, figuring that he probably didn't take this girl to his house for their one-night stand. It was unlikely that they drove all the way to her place in Marcott. So that meant they got a hotel room, borrowed a friend's bed or Martin has another apartment for those occasions. "Where'd they go to have sex that night?"

David shook his head, then smiled and resisted the urge to kiss Nettie's cheek. "You are absolutely amazing, you know that?"

Nettie blushed; a coquettish smile.

He walked away from her desk toward the sports department, thinking about the "beautiful town house on the North East side right behind the Red McCombs Toyota Dealership" that Kimberly had described.

"I'VE GOT SOME SERIOUS shit on Martin McNeil," David said in a coarse whisper to sports editor Tom Michelson. He tucked a strand of curly brown hair under his baseball cap. His eyes swept the area diligently ensuring that no one was eavesdropping on his conversation.

He'd only come into the office to pick Nettie's brain and to let Michelson know what he was working on. Immediately after meeting with the sports editor, he would leave to continue sleuthing out the story. He could have called, but he didn't trust the phones.

"What's cookin'?" Michelson said in the same confidential tone.

"Seems our glory boy may not be as clean as he'd like everyone to think," David said. "A teenager filed a paternity suit against him."

"How old?"

"She's 18 now, but she was only 15 when she got pregnant."

"Damn!" The sports editor ran a rough hand across his jaw. "Is this confirmed?"

"Up, down and sideways. Girl was practically a virgin when he popped her. First time in the sack and she's a mommy."

"Statutory rape?" Michelson said eagerly.

"I was hoping for something like that, too, but it ain't gonna happen. Settled out of court."

"Humph," Michelson said, shaking his head disappointedly. "Blood test?"

"Nope. It settled too quick for them to have ordered a test."

"Settled reads as good as a confession, though."

"That's how I see it."

"Hmm. We can run with that, but we need something to cover us. We need a quotable statement from one of the principles or some other sort of confirmation. We don't want this to come back and bite us in the ass."

"I'm working on it," Costanzo promised. "I'll have it for you Friday."

"Great, we'll run it as the lead of our Sunday package."

# TWENTY-EIGHT

As THE SUN DRIFTED toward the horizon, David Costanzo turned off Broadway and drove one block east past an ornate sign marking the entrance to the Palm Court Townhomes. He knew he was close. Lisa Benson would talk to him tonight and he would clear up all the uncertainties in his story.

After leaving the newsroom, he'd dashed over to the Bexar County Tax Assessor's office and discovered Lisa's address. It was simple really, and he was ashamed of himself for not thinking of it sooner. At the assessor's office, David learned that the Palm Court Townhomes were located on Ironton Street, adjacent to the Red McCombs car dealership on Broadway. From there it had been a simple task to skim through the records for the 75 units to discover that the owner to units 26 and 61 was Martin McNeil. A quick call to a friend at the utility company showed Brandon McNeil as the resident at number 61, while no name was yet listed for number 26.

David pulled into an empty spot in front of unit 26 and sat there for a moment taking in the scene. There were two lights on in the downstairs area, and a single light burning upstairs. The place had a just-moved-in look about it.

He grabbed his reporter's notebook and pulled his tape recorder from the back seat and walked quickly to the door. He hummed quietly while he waited. When the door opened, his breath leaked out of him like air spilling from a punctured tire. Lisa Benson had light green eyes and young blonde hair pulled back into a haphazard ponytail; a few loose strands framed her face. Her cheekbones arched gracefully, her lips were pursed in expectation. She wore no makeup. She didn't need any. Lisa didn't speak a word as she stood with the door half open, appraising David.

The reporter couldn't speak. Just before he managed to form a word, she closed the door. She didn't slam it. She just moved it shut, her eyes never leaving his as the space between the door and the frame narrowed to a sliver and then disappeared.

David breathed again. "Wow," he said under his breath. He'd expected her to be good looking, but he hadn't expected a damned super model. She was incredible. *Perfection.* He ran a hand through his hair, licked his lips nervously and adjusted the collar on his shirt. He rang the doorbell again.

She answered after a moment, opening the door with the same dispassionate gaze. He spoke quickly, feeling himself being hypnotized by her eyes. "Good evening, Lisa. My name is David Costanzo. I'm a—"

"I know who you are," she said. Her voice was quiet but strong and surprisingly mature. He had to remind himself that she was only 18.

He cleared his throat. "Well. . . I was. . .wondering if I could talk to you for—"

"Why?"

"I'm working on a story, and it's almost done; but I have just a couple of quick questions to clear up." The air shifted between them. It felt a couple degrees hotter to David. Beads of sweat rolled from his armpits down the sides of his body. He pressed his arms in tightly, trying to stanch the flow.

"I really don't have anything to say." She took a step back, clearing space to close the door.

"If I could just ask you a couple of questions," David said urgently.

"Do you have to get permission?"

That confused David. "Permission to ask questions?"

"To write a story."

"Oh, you mean, does an editor have to approve my story ideas?" David was prepared to impress her with the level of autonomy he enjoyed at the newspaper.

"No. I mean permission from the people you're writing about."

They stood there in the evening sun looking at each other across two feet of threshold. David was thinking this one through. "No. I guess I don't have to get permission. But most of the time that's a moot point, because you can't do a story without talking to the people who are involved. They want to see it in the paper."

"And if they don't?" She stared levelly.

"Well, then it depends on the story. See, one of the basic tenets of the free press is that we're a police unit for the community. When a politician does something wrong, or a corporation dumps toxic wastes into our drinking water, the public has a right to know. So sometimes people who don't want to have anything written about them find their names in the paper anyway. The best thing for them to do in that case is cooperate with the media and make sure their side of the story is accurately told."

She nodded briefly. "But what if there are no politicians involved. No public funds. No corporations violating the environment. What if it's a private matter between two people and it's really no one else's business. Do you have to get permission then?"

David could see where she was going with this, and it wasn't going to work. Martin McNeil was a celebrity, and as such, he didn't have a right of privacy. "Lisa, I need to know if Martin McNeil is the father of your child."

She nodded again. It wasn't a confirmation. Just a slight bob of the head; she was getting herself centered. "So even though none of the people involved want to see this story in print, you're going to write it anyway? The public has a right to know." Her words were tinted with subtle sarcasm.

"It's important," David said.

They shared a moment of silence, the reporter feeling light-headed under her scrutiny. "I called the police," she said.

"What?" David unconsciously brushed off the front of his shirt. Cleaning himself up, as though she had called the cops because of his appearance.

"When you pulled up in front of the house. I called and told them a reporter named David Costanzo was here harassing me."

"Hey, I apologize. I'm not trying to harass you."

"Then go away, and don't write this story."

"Lisa, it's not as simple as that."

She nodded again. "When they get here, I'll tell them that you've harassing me for a month. Used to come by my trailer in Marcott peeking into my windows, following me when I go out, just scaring the hell out of me. I moved into the city and you followed me here. Finally, I had to call the police because I didn't know what else to do." She paused. "You think the public has a right to know about that story, too."

David was genuinely hurt. "That's a lie."

"So is the story you're writing."

A police car pulled up in front of the townhouse and two officers got out.

Lisa and David looked at each other for a moment, he could see the trace of a smile playing at her lips. He turned and walked away from the door, marching quietly toward his car.

"It's okay now officers," Lisa sang. "Thank you."

They scowled at the reporter as he sank into his Porsche. As his car backed out of the space and cruised away, they stood in place, like they were planning to stay there all night to guard against his return.

DAVID DROVE ABOUT A mile to a restaurant called Emily's tucked between a grocery store and a Radio Shack at the corner of Broadway and Alameda. It was a diner with a 1950's theme; records from the era were pasted behind the counter and posters of rock'n'roll stars presided over Formica tables with sticky black vinyl bench seats that were bolted to the floor. The wait staff bounced around with energetic smiles, and they all wore name tags bearing names like Mary Lynn, Peggy Sue and Jimmy Joe. They called their customers Big Daddy, Daddy 'O, Little Missy and Big Mama. It was as good a place as any to kill some time and give the police a chance to leave Lisa's complex.

David was led to a booth by a gum smacking woman in her early 40's who was wearing a "Wanda Jo" name tag. She called him Sugar Plum, Sweet Thang and Cool Daddy before they even reached the table. Costanzo slid into the booth, ordered a cup of coffee and starting thinking about his next step. Finding Lisa Benson had been his number one priority. He wanted to track her down, interview her, get the crucial details of the story, get a photographer over for pictures of her and the kid, and basically hammer the nails into Martin McNeil's coffin. But she didn't want to talk, and that surprised Costanzo. Experience had taught the reporter that most people who filed lawsuits against celebrities were eager to talk. They were usually very angry and welcomed any opportunity to vent their frustrations. They needed to feel vindicated and often the money they received via a lawsuit wasn't enough. They wanted their abuse to be publicly acknowledged. That's what David had been counting on with Lisa. He figured that after getting pregnant, being abandoned by Martin, ostracized by her family and forced to live in that dumpy trailer, she might feel just a *little* bit bitter. It had been nearly two years since the night Martin and Lisa slept together. Two years was a long time for a woman's anger to simmer.

But somehow, Martin had persuaded Lisa to keep quiet. Maybe his settlement offer was contingent upon her signing a confidentiality agreement. That made sense; *you can have the money, but I take it all back if you breathe one word of this to the media.* However, that didn't jibe with the woman David had encountered at the door minutes ago. She seemed happy, confident, content and not the least bit angry at McNeil. She didn't seem sorry that she couldn't talk to Costanzo. She seemed annoyed that he had knocked on her door.

Wanda Jo returned with a steaming cup of coffee and a handful of cream and sugar. "Here ya go, Sugar Pie," she said, placing the cup in front of Costanzo. "You need anything else?"

"No, I think, this will be fine," Costanzo said, trying to talk over the crackle and pop of her gum.

"All right, Sweetie." She put a motherly hand on his shoulder. "You just holler for Wanda Jo if ya need anything."

Costanzo smiled quietly as she left and wondered if he was seeing her real personality or a performance to match the decor of the restaurant. He took a sip of the coffee—it was delicious—and decided that if Wanda Jo was acting then she should be in Hollywood instead of Emily's because the lady had talent.

After another sip of the steaming coffee, Costanzo decided that Brandon McNeil was his obvious next step. He was the brother of the accused and he lived just a hundred yards from Lisa. He would know the entire story. Costanzo didn't know whether Brandon would talk to him, but he was moderately optimistic. Again calling on his vast reserve of experience, he knew that the relatives of famous people seemed to crave the spotlight more than the typical citizen. Perhaps indirectly experiencing the perks of fame made the relatives that much more hungry for notoriety in their own right. David couldn't begin to recount the number of times he'd seen a brother, a mother, a sister or a father, eager to speak out on behalf of their famous relative. He'd seen the television interviews with so-and-so's Dad as he sat in the stands watching his son play. The dad was always so proud and so flattered that the television reporter would want to interview him. He'll talk about the interview for months and even years later, forever likening himself to his famous son.

Yes, Brandon McNeil might be a little eager to be the celebrity for a little while. And Costanzo was more than willing to accommodate him.



BRANDON MCNEIL'S FRONT STOOP a testament to the man's vanity. There was a mat that proclaimed the dwelling *BRANDON'S* in large cursive letters. Costanzo smiled and wiped his feet. *This is going to be good.* He rang the doorbell. The townhouse itself was a brown, brick, two-story with a wide front door and windows extending to the ceiling of the second floor. The blinds were open and through a window beside the door, David could see hardwood floors, leather furniture and several clusters of trees and plants.

After a few moments, David watched a young woman come down the stairs and march across the living room. She was in her early twenties, though with a baseball cap and a pony tail of brown hair sticking out of the back she looked like a teenager. She stood about five-feet-four and had a gymnast's body. She looked a little angry as she approached, but she was smiling broadly when she opened the door.

"Hi," Costanzo said, returning the grin. "Is Brandon in?"

"Sure, come on in." She stepped back and closed the door behind the reporter. She seemed accustomed to opening the door to strangers at Brandon's house. "I'm Julie," she said extending her hand. "I don't think I've met you before."

"No, no we haven't met. My name is David."

"Cool," Julie said. "You know, I'm glad it was you at the door."

This was unexpected. "Really. Why is that?"

"Well, it just seems like every time I come over here, there's some other girl who's calling or knocking on the door looking for Brandon. I'm just sick of dealing with that all the time. Brandon says women pursue him, and he doesn't encourage them. But I'm not stupid. I always feel like I have to be on my guard when I'm here. You're not gay are you?"

David chuckled. "No, not me. I'm as hetero as they come."

"Good, cause I don't know if I could compete with a gay guy. Not that Brandon's gay or anything, but you know, you never know. Seems like people are always coming out of the closet, and I didn't even know there was a closet in the room."

"Since I've passed inspection as a heterosexual male, does that mean you'll go get Brandon now?"

Julie smiled and shook her head. "You're as bossy as the girls who come over here looking for Brandon." She clicked her heels together and saluted. "I'll go get him for you now, sir!"


BRANDON MCNEIL DESCENDED THE stairs with all the drama of a rock star taking the stage. It was the middle of the afternoon and he was wearing blue silk pajama bottoms and a silk robe that floated in his wake, baring his well-defined chest and abdomen as he moved down the stairs. His skin was the color of milk chocolate, his hair was wavy and perfectly coifed, and he was wearing sunglasses.

He stopped on the landing and stared down at David for a long moment. Julie was following him and stopped when he did, but quickly lost patience with his posing and moved around him and down the stairs.

"I don't know you," Brandon said, staring intently at David.

"My name is David Costanzo. I'm a reporter for the *San Antonio Light* newspaper."

Brandon thought about this for a moment. "What do you want?"

"I need to talk to you about Lisa Benson."

Brandon shook his head. "I don't know anyone named Lisa Benson."

"Sure you do. She's the girl who filed suit against your brother last week. He settled out of court with her, and now she's living in a townhouse not a hundred yards from here. I just came from visiting her. She and I had a long talk. I was just hoping to talk to you to clear up some of the details."

Brandon walked the rest of the way down the stairs. "What did she tell you?"

"Just about everything."

"And what's 'just about everything?'"

"Well, in a nutshell, she told me she met Martin at a nightclub about two years ago. They hit it off immediately and they drove over here to your townhouse and had wild sex. She got pregnant, and tried to get in touch with Martin, but he ignored her. Finally, through an attorney, she filed suit against your brother, and now he's supporting her."

"That's what she told you, huh?"

"That's what she said."

Brandon plopped down into a white leather recliner. "Julie, will you do me a big favor?"

"Sure, hon."

"Get the fuck out of here, so I can have some privacy."

Julie was stunned. "You're such a jerk!" She grabbed her car keys off a table in the foyer and stormed out, slamming the door behind her.

Costanzo sank slowly onto the couch. "I'd say she's a little pissed."

Brandon waved a hand dismissively.

They sat in silence for a minute, Brandon waiting for Costanzo to begin, the reporter trying to find the right question to start the conversation. Brandon was ready for this. He was ready to talk. He didn't care what happened between with Martin. He'd talk to the reporter on the record, give him all the quotes he needed, then wait for the story to run. Brandon couldn't wait to see the look on Martin's face when he saw his own brother quoted in the story that ruined him. *That'll teach him to fuck with me.* He didn't want to destroy Martin, because Martin was a cash cow, and Brandon didn't want to lose that. He just wanted to see Martin's spotless reputation damaged.

"So, what do you want to know, Mr. Reporter?"

"For starters," David said, pen poised over his notebook, "I guess I need to clarify your relationship with Martin. Are the two of you close?"

Brandon chuckled. "When Martin moved to San Antonio, I moved to San Antonio. Martin bought a house. He bought me a house just a couple miles away. He has a key to my place. I've got a key to his place. We go to parties together. So what do you think? Are we close?"

"I guess I'd have to say yes. And that answers my next question about whether he has a key to your townhouse."

"Yeah, he's free to come and go as he pleases."

"Does he visit your house much?"

"Not a lot. Just when he's got some chick lined up and he doesn't want to risk taking her home or being seen at a hotel. He's married and he's got this hoity-toity reputation to uphold."

David fought to contain the smile he felt inside. Brandon apparently hated his brother and wasn't going to pull any punches. "How often does he use your house for a sexual rendezvous?"

"I don't know. Maybe once every couple of weeks."

"Does he use your house only when you're gone?"

"No. A lot of the time I'm here with one of my girls. Sometimes, I can hear him and the girl going at it in the other room. Once I accidentally walked in on him and a beautiful Hispanic chick doing it in the kitchen. She was fine." Brandon smiled at the memory.

"Were you here the night he brought Lisa Benson over?"

"No. I think I must have been out that night."

"When did Martin first learn about the suit Lisa had filed against him?"

"Oh, late last week. His attorney called and told him about it."

"And what did he do?"

"What do you mean 'what did he do?' He settled."

"No. I mean, what did he physically do in terms of moving her out of the trailer and getting her into an apartment."

"I thought you said you talked to Lisa about all of this."

"I did," David said, lying easily, "but in my job I've got to try to verify everything that I can, and usually, if two people tell me the same story, then I know it's true."

Brandon sat in the recliner with his shades on and his robe open and thought for a moment. Finally, he said, "Martin asked me to go pick her up, and bring her over to my place. So that's what I did. She stayed here Friday and Saturday, then moved into her own place Sunday."

Costanzo was scribbling furiously. "And Martin paid for everything?"

"Yeah."

*Now we're getting to it.* "How'd he know it was his kid? Did he get a blood test?"

"Naw. He just knew, I guess."

"But how could he be sure?"

"What do I look like a fuckin' mind reader? I don't know how he knew. He just knew."

"Okay, that's cool. Hey, does Martin own any colored contact lenses?"

"What kind of stupid question is that?"

"Well, I was just curious. You know how some people like to change the color of their eyes. They go from blue to green or from brown to hazel or something like that."

Brandon smiled. *I see what you're getting at.* "Yeah, I think Martin has a pair of hazel contacts that he wears every now and again."

David's face lit up as he made a notation in his notebook. "Did you know that Lisa was only 15 when Martin had sex with her?"

Brandon shrugged. "I'm sure he's had sex with a lot of 15 year olds."

Costanzo stopped. "Are you saying that Martin regularly has sex with underage girls?"

"Man, fuck you if you can't hear," Brandon said, standing up. "Get out. I've got shit to do."

CostANZO PRACTICALLY FLOATED BACK to his car. Brandon had been everything he could have hoped for and more. The guy was clearly pissed off at his brother for some reason. He didn't give a damn about what he said, and he sure as heck didn't hold anything back. He confirmed everything David knew about Martin's relationship with Lisa. Although there was still no blood test, a quote from Martin's brother saying, "He just knew," was as good a confirmation as the reporter would ever need. *Regular sex with underage girls? Martin! You bad, bad boy.* This story could turn into a four-or-five part series. Costanzo would start with the paternity suit in Sunday's paper. After that, the city's entire media stable would be digging into McNeil's life uncovering all of the dirt about his sexual forays with high school cheerleaders.

BRANDON WATCHED THE REPORTER leave with perverse pleasure. He walked into the kitchen and poured himself some brandy. He hit the remote control for the stereo and soon jazz music was floating lightly in the air. He was tired of seeing his little brother get so much glory and fame. Martin didn't deserve it. He wasn't that great. Brandon was the one who had the good looks and the smooth tongue. He could talk his way out of any situation or into any girl's panties. *That* was talent, but he couldn't be famous doing that. Instead, his stupid little brother who happened to be good at playing a child's game got paid millions of dollars and was nearly as famous as God. And everybody thought he was so damned *nice*. It was sickening.

Brandon walked into the kitchen marveling at the skill he had displayed in setting up this entire affair. He'd known about Lisa and her baby for some time, but it wasn't until his brother pissed him off recently that he decided to use the girl to serve his purposes. Inquiries with friends in the area had supplied the name of R. Winston Mickler, an ambitious young lawyer who loved to party and make money, often in that order. Brandon had purposely bumped into Mickler at a nightclub and suggested that the young lawyer look up a girl named Lisa Benson who worked at the Hitchin' Post Diner. "She's the mother of Martin McNeil's illegitimate baby, but she's never filed suit," Brandon said in the lawyer's ear. After that bit of information was dispensed, Mickler could think of nothing except the hefty commission he would earn if he could talk Lisa into filing against Martin.

Mickler's only concern was Brandon. Was he going to want a cut of the action? "I'm Martin's brother," Brandon replied, "and it disgusts me to see the way my brother has treated this girl. Mostly, I just want to see justice served." Mickler had nodded fiercely saying, "Of course, of course. Serving justice is the reason I entered this profession."

"However, I assume that you do have some type of standard referral fee don't you? I mean, if someone provides information that leads to a quick and easy settlement, you would take care of that someone wouldn't you?"

"What did you have in mind?"

"Oh I was thinking conservatively. Say a 20 percent of your cut."

After the suit was filed, it was Brandon who made the anonymous phone call to the *San Antonio Light* leaving the tip for Costanzo about the paternity suit. Brandon smiled at the image of him whispering the words of destruction into the ear of his brother's worst enemy. After calling Costanzo, Brandon called The Fixer and told him to expect a desperate call from Martin. Later he talked Martin into hiring Ramey to keep the story quiet. It was really a nice set up for Brandon. In addition to the modest fee he received from R. Winston Mickler, Brandon had also negotiated a 30 percent commission on The Fixer's fee. Brandon accomplished this hefty portion by convincing The Fixer that Martin would be so scared and desperate that he could literally set his fees as high as he wished.

That was really all it took to get Martin's demise rolling. The lawyer and the reporter did their jobs and Ramey did his. Brandon had watched the events unfold with barely contained delight. He knew that Ramey killed Tim Williams and had even given thought to calling the police to leave an anonymous tip for them. But he later thought better of it. He wanted his brother to be ruined, but he didn't necessarily want him in prison. He just wanted to teach Martin a lesson. The player would still make millions on his football salary, but the paternity suit scandal would cost him a lot of his endorsements and it would make him a lose the pristine image that he had. That was really all that Brandon wanted. Ever since Martin's birth, Brandon had been annoyed at the way everyone treated the kid. In the eyes of his parents, friends, teachers, pastors, police etc. Martin could do no wrong, and Brandon could do nothing *but* wrong. Everybody loved Martin. Everybody thought Brandon was a screw up. Well, that was about to change. The world was about to find out that Mr. Perfect wasn't so perfect after all. The story would hit the paper soon, *probably Sunday*, Brandon guessed and he was going to read every word with great pleasure.

His only regret was the spontaneous decision he'd made a few minutes earlier in lying to David Costanzo about Martin sleeping with a lot of young girls. *Why push things too far?* Will people believe that Martin is regularly banging high school cheerleaders? Brandon wasn't sure. And now he wished he hadn't dropped the suggestion. The trick to selling a lie was to be subtle. If people think the grass is green and you tell them it's actually aqua, they just might believe it. Tell them it's black and they'll look at you like you're crazy. People will believe a lie, but only if it isn't too great a departure from what they already believe. They think Martin is a great guy, but they also think that a lot of pro athletes are womanizing jerks. Tell them Martin conceived a child with a teenage girl and they'll believe it. Tell them that Martin sleeps with young chicks all the time, and they'll resist belief because Martin is perceived as such a great guy.

*Oh well, what's done is done.* Costanzo probably won't use that information anyway. The reporter has libel issues to worry about. David will probably investigate a little bit to see if he can turn up some young girls who've slept with Martin. If he can't find anyone, he'll have no choice but to forget about that part of the story for the time being. If he's going to accuse Martin McNeil of committing multiple statutory rapes, he'd better be prepared to back up those charges.

Brandon looked down at his glass and decided that he wanted a double. He grabbed the bottle of brandy and poured another two fingers. *Oh Martin. All of this could have been avoided if you had just shown a little understanding for me when I needed your help. But instead, you chose to listen to your little bitch of a wife who made you turn your back on your own blood relative. That's okay, though. In the end, you'll see that it's always best to look out for family.*

Brandon walked back into the living room and sank back into his recliner. He held the drink in his lap for a long moment, then lifted the glass to eye level with one outstretched arm and said, "My dearest, darling, brother Martin. I toast the end of your reign as a perfect little soldier."

Brandon took a small sip. The liquor felt smooth and rich as it slid down his throat.

# TWENTY-NINE

COSTANZO PICKED UP ON the first ring, shoving the phone into the crook of his neck. "This is David." His fingers were flying on the computer keyboard.

"David, it's Mr. Jackson downstairs."

"Mr. J, what's happening?"

"You got a visitor."

He wasn't expecting anyone. "Who is it?"

"Says his name's Martin McNeil."


MARTIN WALKED INTO THE apartment wearing all white—white jeans, white tennis shoes, a white Polo shirt and a white baseball cap. He had a black backpack slung over one shoulder like a college student. David held the door open for him, looking at the player and wondering what the hell he was doing here. He figured Martin must be pretty nervous about the story to be making a personal appearance. *His brother must have told him I stopped by.*

They moved into the living room and stood facing each other like two gun fighters in the old west. Actually physically close to one another for the first time since that afternoon on the steps of the capitol building.

"Should I get my tape recorder?" David said.

"No," Martin said plopping down on the couch. "Just wanted to talk off the record."

The reporter perched on the arm of a chair. "Okay, so what's on your mind?" David was enjoying this, knowing he had all the power.

"I want you to drop the story you're working on."

"And exactly what story is that?"

"You know what story I'm talking about."

"Well, let me think here. I'm working on so many things." He looked up at the ceiling, pressing a finger against his chin. "You must mean the little piece I'm doing about an underage girl who was impregnated and then abandoned by a big *star* football player. The supposedly philanthropic ball player dumped her and then prayed that she and their child would die in the streets. But alas, she survived spoiling his plans. Eventually, she filed a lawsuit; and wouldn't you know it, the suit was settled quickly and quietly out of court. Now she's living in the player's town house, and the player is at my house begging me not to write the story that will destroy his life. Is that the story we're talking about? Oh, and I forgot to mention the most important part. A source close to the player said that he regularly has sex with underage girls and this was not the first time that one of them has ended up pregnant. Now, did I about cover everything?"

Martin's eyes were wide. *How could Costanzo know so much and be so wrong at the same time?* Martin could deny the charges, but he knew no one would believe him. People would read the article in the paper, and they'd believe it. "Look. I know you think you're onto something, but I am *not* the baby's father. I had never even met this girl until last week."

"Uh huh."

"It's not my kid," Martin repeated feebly.

"I'll be sure to include that line in the story." He picked up a reporter's notebook from an end table and scribbled quickly. "Anything else?"

"Why don't you drop this?" Martin said.

"I can't do that."

"Of course you can."

"Jesus, don't you understand anything? This is my *job*. I have to write this story the same way you have to catch the football when the quarterback throws it to you. You drop too many passes you lose your job. I drop too many stories like this, I lose *my* job."

"So you're saying, no?"

David made a sound like steam rushing out of a tiny vent. "I'm saying 'hell *fucking* no.' I'm gonna bury your ass so deep you'll suffocate before anyone can dig you out."

Martin reached into his bag and pulled out the VHS tape Ramey had given him in the back yard.

"The hell is this?" David said.

"Turn it on."

The reporter walked slowly to his VCR trying to figure out what could be on the tape. He popped it into the slot. The image on the screen left him slack-jawed. He was on his knees by the pond with Kimberly. He was pulling her hair back, slamming hard into her. She was screaming, "No! No! No! Please! Stop! Please! Oh. You're hurting me! Nooooo!" Blood drained out of David's face as he watched the tape.

It looked like he was raping her. Her skirt hiked up over her waist as though he'd been in a hurry. He was behind her, his hand wrapped in her hair, a look of angry concentration on his face. She was looking into the camera, her face contorted in what looked like pain. And then the audio. That was all wrong. *It didn't happen like that. She never asked me to stop. She initiated the whole thing. She got on her knees and asked me to take her from behind. She begged me to pull her hair, to fuck her hard.*

There was no doubt it was the reporter. It was a full moon and his face was clearly visible. They were next to his car. *Was the whole thing a set up? Was Kimberly in on it? She must have been in on it. She had to be in on it.* Everything made sense now. She led David to that exact spot. Suggested that they get out of the car. She told him how she wanted to do it. *The whole thing was a set up. Martin was probably working the video camera? Laughing his ass off. Thinking he could get an edge to keep me from writing the story?*

David didn't rape that girl, but from the tape it sure looked like he had. *Maybe I can get out of it. Get someone to analyze the tape. Prove it was doctored. Prove that the audio and the video came from two different sources. Prove that Martin is trying to blackmail me.*

*Who the hell would be videotaping a rape? If it was a real rape, the person behind the camera should have intervened.* He smiled at the thought, seeing it as a way out.

But he was still pulling her hair, ramming into her. It looked bad. She could argue that he set up the camera on a tripod, filming her violation so he could get off on it later. Or that he had a buddy working the camera. *Shit!*

Martin didn't say a word as the tape rolled on He was trying to read David's reaction. The longer the tape ran, the more confident Martin was about Costanzo dropping the story.

When the screen went fuzzy, David turned off the VCR and fell wearily into a chair.

"So here's the deal," Martin said. "You drop the story, and I don't do anything with this tape. But if you keep going on the story, I'll send a copy of this tape to the police and to every media outlet in the state."

David felt trapped. He was pissed at himself for succumbing to that little bitch. He couldn't believe he might actually have to dump the story. *Damn, why didn't I see this coming?*

"And you know everybody in town hates your ass," Martin said. "Remember how they lined the streets to check out your underwear when you said the Stallions wouldn't draft me? Imagine what they'll do when they find out you raped an innocent young girl."

That was precisely the wrong thing to say. Memories of that day formed the reservoir from which David's rage sprang. He'd walked through Central Texas in his shorts. There had been no place to hide. No escape. Then, just when he thought it was all over, there was that arrogant display on the steps of the Capitol. Martin McNeil. Smiling that smile. Playing to the crowd. Autographing the gift boxer shorts. Embarrassing David even more. That was the memory that had kept David going for four years. It was the day the name Martin McNeil was etched into the hard marble of hate embedded in his mind. The day he dedicated himself to spawning the public humiliation and destruction of Martin McNeil.

It was the wrong thing to say.

David steeled his mind. He would not be intimidated. He didn't care what McNeil did with that damned video tape. Most of the people in the city already hated the reporter anyway. *If they hated me more because I supposedly raped some girl, so what!*

He turned toward the player with icy eyes. "The story will run Sunday morning."

Martin was unsettled by the determined set of David's jaw. "Kim's ready to press charges against you. Send you to jail."

"So? By the time I go to jail, this story will have already destroyed your cockamamie little life. That's all I care about. They can send me to prison for life after that, and it won't matter."

Martin stood quickly, dismayed that things had unraveled so quickly. He wasn't sure what he should say.

"The whole sordid tale will be in the paper Sunday," David said, gleefully. "You might want to buy some extra copies to send to grandma and the cousins."


RAMEY LAUGHED WHEN MARTIN told him what had happened. They were in the back yard again. It was almost midnight. They were sitting under the yellow porch light. Although Ramey carried a cell phone with him everywhere he went, he didn't like talking on it. "Not a secure line," he often said. He'd always want to meet somewhere. Talk in person. It was better that way.

"So the tape didn't scare him off, huh?"

"No," Martin said morosely.

"Like I said, you don't know how to negotiate."

Martin didn't say anything.

"Tell you what. I'll go talk to him tomorrow. Get this whole thing taken care of. But it's gonna cost you another fifty grand."

The player looked up now. He stared at Ramey like he was ready to fight. Ramey stared back, ready for anything.

"You're already getting a hundred and fifty thousand for this job, and you haven't done anything. I'm not paying you another dime."

"So far, I've steered away everyone except this one guy. That service alone is worth more than a hundred fifty grand. Now to go personally deal with this one guy, I gotta charge you extra. Nothing major really. Just something to cover my expen—"

"Man, you are unbelievable!"

"Hey, you don't want me to talk to him, just say so. I'll bring muffins, you can make hot tea, and we'll read the story together Sunday morning."

Martin closed his eyes, not speaking for a few minutes. Then;

"Whatever conversation you have with him, it better work. You'd better kill the story."

"Shit nigga, I'll do better than kill the story."

# THIRTY

THOUSANDS OF PEOPLE CHASED Martin down a long, lonely street. There were mothers, and grandmothers, fathers and grandfathers, all screaming angrily at him as they ran, yelling his name over and over like a mantra. The great speed that had propelled him to the Pro Bowl so many times had somehow abandoned him, leaving him exposed and helpless. He was running as hard as he could but it wasn't fast enough.

Leading the mob, and closing on him with every step was an angry woman in her late eighties, firmly gripping a walker with both hands. She pushed the four-legged metal frame out in front of her, then used it to leverage her body forward. Unlike the other pursuers, she never said a word. But she never blinked either, and that seemed worse.

She was wearing a pale yellow dress that looked like *it* might have had grandchildren. The garment hung loosely down to the middle of her shins. White socks and white nursing shoes. A thin yellow belt was cinched around her waist, straining against her frame with every step. Tucked into the front of that belt was a section of newspaper.

Martin's stared at the woman, trying to resolve the image he was seeing. *Why would an old lady with a walker have a newspaper tucked under her belt like she'd left the house in a hurry? Was she looking for a job? A new house? Reading the personals?*

After a moment, he realized it was a sports section. He tried to imagine her waking up every morning, reaching for the sports page as though the results of the previous day's games really mattered. The more he thought about it, the more it bothered him. He wanted to stop and ask her why she had the paper.

It was then that he realized that *everyone* was carrying the same sports section. His pursuers were brandishing copies of the paper like weapons, gripping them in tight fists, making angry slashes through the air as they chanted his name.

Flashing past a small store front, Martin could see a paper through the window. It was flipped open to the cover of the sports page. The headline loomed under the banner like a gallows.

McNEIL ABANDONS UNDERAGE MOTHER: STATUTORY RAPE CHARGES INVESTIGATED.

It was the story that spelled the end of everything for him. He stared vacantly at the headline, trying to breathe. He wasn't aware that he had stopped moving until the old woman was upon him, her walker raised high overhead, the cold metal descending on a dangerous arc as the rest of the mob converged on him.

Then, blessedly, he woke up.

Shivering at the dream, Martin hopped out of bed and walked quickly through the house, pulling on a robe as he moved. He was out the front door, picking up the morning paper and back inside before he could even think. He yanked the rubber band off and tore the pages apart.

What he saw when he reached the sports page nearly stopped his heart. His hands quit moving, his eyes locked on the image in front of him. The headline that graced the front of the sports section didn't have Martin's name in it. In fact, it didn't appear to have anything to do with him. But it scared the life out of him. It read: MEDICAL EXAMINER RELEASES FINDINGS IN WILLIAMS' DEATH

Everything was about to fall apart. Surely the coroner was smarter than Ramey had believed. Surely a drug powerful enough to cause a healthy professional athlete to drop dead with a heart attack would not be overlooked during an autopsy. Soon the police would come to talk to him, and he would break under the pressure. He knew he would. First-degree murder. Martin wasn't sure how that worked. All he knew for certain was that he was going to spend the rest of his life in prison.

He looked again at the newspaper in front of him. Beneath the headline, framed by columns of news type, was a scowling mug shot of Tim Williams. The picture made him look more like a suspect than a victim.

Calm down, Martin told himself. The headline says, "death" not "murder." That means they don't know anything. Everything looked normal when they did the autopsy.

It was a rational thought and it soothed his raw nerves. He quickly scanned the article and was perversely happy to read quotes from the medical examiner indicating that Williams died of natural causes.

*But if they thought he was murdered, they wouldn't tell the media right away, would they? They'd try to lull the suspects into a false sense of security by releasing some bullshit like this, and then close the net on us.*

That made sense, too. A fresh wave of fear washed over him.

*Why did I ever get involved with Philip Ramey?*

# Power Shift

MARTIN FOLDED THE NEWSPAPER and trudged into the kitchen for a glass of orange juice. He felt that his life was slipping away from him. How did events become so tangled? Suddenly, Ramey's promise from the previous night echoed in Martin's head. *"Shit Nigga, I'll do better than kill the story."* What the hell did that mean? The guy was a lunatic. He'd already killed one person, and now he was getting ready to kill again. *That's why he wanted another fifty grand,* Martin realized in a panic. He raced into his bedroom and threw on some clothes, being careful not to wake Jessica. He had to get over to David's apartment before Ramey got there. Just as he was leaving the room, Martin remembered the gun on the closet shelf. He stood in the doorway for a long moment trying to decide whether to take it, then sighed and went back to the closet. He got bullets from a kitchen drawer near the pantry and threw the gun and the ammunition into the trunk of his car. He had no intention of using the weapon.

He was already going to prison for the murder of Tim Williams, but he rationalized that he wasn't really responsible for Tim's death, because he didn't know what Ramey was going to do. But now, he knew full well Ramey's intentions for David Costanzo. If he didn't act, the reporter's blood would be on his hands. As much as he disliked Costanzo, he couldn't sit back and let Ramey kill again. He had to try to save Costanzo's life.

As he was walking out the door, Martin stopped and grabbed the kitchen phone. He called Brandon and woke him up.

"Man, it's early, what the hell do you want?"

"I need your help. It's Ramey. He's gone crazy." Martin thought for a moment, then decided to confess to the murder already committed. "I hired him to keep things quiet, like you told me to, but he's been a total wild card. He killed Tim Williams," Martin said the last sentence quietly.

"He did what?" Brandon said with feigned alarm.

"He killed Tim to create a diversion so that the media wouldn't find out about the paternity suit against me."

"Jesus, I knew Ramey was crazy, but I didn't know he was a fucking nut."

"I know. Now I think he's gonna kill David Costanzo."

This did alarm Brandon. He didn't want Costanzo dead, he wanted him alive and alert, tapping away on his computer, getting the story ready for Sunday. "Why the hell is he going to do that?"

Martin told his brother about the conversation he'd had with Ramey the previous evening and The Fixer's ominous words at the end of that conversation. "I'm heading over to Costanzo's place now."

"Swing by and pick me up."

# THIRTY-ONE

AN AGITATED MOAN CREPT out of David's mouth as he opened his eyes to stare at the blaring alarm clock. The illuminated numbers spilled red light across the bedside table. He turned the alarm off and forced himself out of bed. In a couple of hours his story about Martin McNeil would be finished and ready to file. He couldn't wait. This was the day he had dreamed of. He was going to destroy the football player.

He stood slowly and stretched. His fingers clasped together, arms extended toward the ceiling. An exaggerated yawn. He walked to the window. A shock of burnt-orange light pushed the darkness away from the horizon as the sun peeked at the world.

"Get away from the window."

The voice was behind David. He turned quickly hands up ready to fight. Philip Ramey was sitting in a chair in the corner of the room. He was in the shadows with shades on. Relaxed.

"Who the fuck are you?" David said, trying to sound tough despite wearing nothing but his boxers. Feeling self-conscious.

"Get away from the window."

David stood his ground.

"I like it here by the window."

Ramey smiled. The reporter was showing some balls. Not really knowing what he was getting himself into. Not knowing that Ramey was about to jack his ass up. He was standing his ground, trying to be a tough guy. It impressed Ramey.

"I just want to talk to you," Ramey said, not putting any venom in it. "Sit down somewhere. Wherever you want. No big deal."

David stood there for a minute. Locking eyes with Ramey thinking about whether he would sit down or not. Not wanting to do it, just because the guy told him to.

"Why are you here?" he said.

"Didn't I just say I wanted to talk to you?" Ramey getting a little pissed off now, letting it show.

"I'll sit over here," David said moving toward a chair opposite Ramey.

They stared at each other. Ramey was a silhouette in the dark corner, jingling something in his hands that sounded like car keys. "I hear you've been asking a lot of questions lately."

"That's my job."

"Questions can be dangerous sometimes."

"Depends on who's asking." David figured this guy to be an ex-con. *Screw an ex-con. I'm an arm's reach from the gun in the top dresser drawer, and that motherfucker is loaded. So bring it on daddy-O.*

"I'd like to respectfully request that you stop asking questions about our friend." Ramey said, asking the question formally just so that later, he could say that he'd asked.

David smiled. "So Martin asked you to come have a chat with me. See if we could settle this 'out of court' so to speak?" David was feeling comfortable now, sitting on the edge of the chair buck ass naked. Having some fun with this guy, but getting a little annoyed by the jingling keys in his hand.

"Something like that."

"What's he got to offer?" *Probably thinks he can buy his way out of this. Throw some money at me. Give me a tip, like I'm a fucking bell-boy.*

"Your life."

It was tense again. David wondered if this guy was for real. He figured Ramey was carrying a gun, but in the morning gloom, David couldn't tell. The reporter thought he could probably get to his gun before Ramey could pull his out.

"So let me understand this," David said. "Martin McNeil sent you here to tell me to drop the story or I'm *dead?*"

"No. He didn't say that," Ramey admitted. "I changed the assignment on the way over."

*What the hell does that mean?*

"So what'd he tell you to do?"

Ramey thought for a moment, taking his time. "He asked me to visit you. Thought maybe you were a reasonable man, and I could talk you out of writing this story."

"But what? On the way over, you decide maybe I'm *not* a reasonable man?" *The gun in the drawer is so close. Just grab it and put it in the guy's face. Make him get rid of his gun. Make him stop jingling those stupid keys. Then call the cops. Add it to the story, that Martin McNeil was so desperate to keep the story out of the paper that he sent a hit man to kill the reporter.*

"No. You sound reasonable enough. I'm just in one of those moods where I'd rather kill you than mess around with you."

David stared back. Scared. The guy sounded for real. "What do you want me to do?"

"I want you to drop the story."

David pretended to think about it. Then: "Okay." Standing up saying, "I'll drop the story." Then he lunged toward the drawer with the gun in it. Ramey reached to the small of his back. David rushed, his hand inside, the gun came out, the reporter whipping around to face Ramey. The hit man sat still, leaning forward, his weapon half drawn; he was suddenly looking down the barrel of David's gun.

"Put your fucking hands in the air!" Costanzo said. Ramey tucked his gun back into his belt, and sat back slowly. "I said, 'put your hands up.'"

"There's no need for a gun," Ramey said.

"There's not, huh?" David breathing hard, feeling an adrenaline rush, enjoying the shift in power. "What you got back there?"

Ramey shrugged. "Military issue nine-millimeter Berretta."

"Nice gun," David said, meaning it, holding his Glock nine-millimeter in both hands. He was aiming at Ramey's chest from seven or eight feet away. "Now take it out real slow and put it on the floor."

"Or what?"

*Or what?*

"Or I'll shoot your ass dead and then call the cops. You forget you're trespassing in my house?"

"Just put the gun away and let's talk," Ramey said.

David stared. He was thinking that he should do something to show Ramey he's for real. Maybe shoot him in the leg, get his attention.

"Listen," Ramey continued. "We had a deal right. You agreed to drop the story."

"Forget the story! You've got a serious situation right now," David said. "You need to reach behind you and pull out that gun—slowly—and put it on the floor."

Ramey didn't move.

David adjusted his stance. He wished he was wearing clothes. "Okay, here's the deal. I'm going to count to five. . . Then I'm going to pull the trigger."

Ramey didn't move. He knew David wouldn't have the balls to pull the trigger.

"One."

Silence. Both men immobile.

"Two."

"Three."

David exhaling angrily through his nose, his lips clenched. Getting himself psyched. "Four"

"Five."

Ramey waited patiently. Costanzo said, "Last chance." Then, adjusting his aim, going for Ramey's right thigh, pulling the trigger.

CLICK. He pulled the trigger again. CLICK.

Ramey reached behind him and pulled out his gun. Holding it casually on his lap. "Sit down. Let's talk." He opened his fist showing David a handful of bullets.

*That's what he was jingling.*

Ramey, dropped the bullets onto a small table, and screwed a silencer onto the muzzle of the gun. "I emptied the clip while you were sleeping. A little precaution."

David sank back into the chair.

Ramey said, "You're gonna call your boss, tell him you're leaving town on an emergency and you can't finish the story."

"Why should I do that?" David said, trying to stay in control.

"Because I have a gun, and unlike you, I ain't afraid to use it."

David digested this.

Ramey continued: "He won't be in the office this early, so leave a message. Tell him you need another week to finish the story."

David shook his head. "You're just gonna have to shoot me." *If you need me to make a phone call, then you can't kill me.*

Ramey got up slowly, pulled a pair of pliers out of his back pocket and walked toward the reporter. "Stick out your right hand."

David stared at the pliers for a moment, losing confidence. He put his hands behind his back. "Hey, it's cool. I'll call him. Tell him I had to leave town."

Ramey stuck the gun in his face. David had never before looked at the business end of a silenced nine millimeter pistol. He was not prepared for the sudden fear. The dilated pupil of the silencer's muzzle stared at him with menacing arrogance.

Ramey stood still for a moment. Gun in one hand, pliers in the other. "Stick out your right hand."

"Come on, man. We had a deal, right? I'll do whatever you want."

"I'll count to three," Ramey said.

"I gave *you* a five count," David said. A joke.

Ramey was all business. "When I get to three, I'm going to shoot you in the foot. You don't want to get shot in the foot, you can put the little finger of your right hand between the teeth of these pliers before I get to three. You understand your options?"

David's face was ash white. "Wait a sec—"

"One-mutha-fuckin."

"I'll do whatever you want!"

"Two mutha-fuckin." Ramey trained the gun on David's right foot and squinted one eye dramatically.

The reporter whipped his right hand out put his little finger into the teeth of the pliers.

"Smart boy," Ramey said, closing the pliers just firmly enough to get a grip on David's finger. "Stand up." He led the reporter, by his finger, over to the bed and instructed him to sit down. "Grab that pillow over there," Ramey said.

"Please. . . I'll go call him, just please—" The pliers dug into David's finger at the middle knuckle; the pain was a bolt of lightning racing up his arm dragging out the word "please" turning it into "pleeeeeeeeeeeeeeeeeeze."

"Do what you're told," Ramey said keeping a firm grip on the pliers. "Put your face in that pillow."

David stretched for the pillow, moving slowly, unable to take his eyes off the tool that was gripping his bulging finger. He would never have believed his pinkie could translate so much pain to the rest of his body. It felt as though his entire body was trapped between the jaws of the pliers.

"What are you—" the pliers dug in again.

"Slow learnin' muthafucker. Don't talk!" Ramey stared at him for a moment. "Put your face down in that pillow and keep it there."

David obeyed.

Once the reporter was in position, Ramey squeezed the pliers violently, twisting them as they caught on bone and gristle, crushing the middle knuckle of the reporter's finger with a sickening pop. Ramey squeezed and twisted like he was trying to loosen a rusty bolt.

Face in the pillow, David screamed wildly, lurching from side to side with big heavy sobs. He had felt pain this intense once in his life. He was 15 years old and had broken the tibia in his left leg during a lacrosse match. But even that wasn't as bad as his crushed pinkie finger. His broken leg was blind luck. The wrong place at the right time. Three bodies colliding, getting tangled and falling in a heap. His left leg caught in an unfortunate position. An engineer's load-bearing nightmare. The full force of the two other bodies falling onto it. An audible snap followed by the rush of blinding pain. David had thought nothing could ever be worse than that moment. But now, with his finger being wrenched away from his body, he knew he was wrong.

It wasn't just the pain. It was the complete sense of violation and helplessness. His screaming was due partly to his fear of what his brutal assailant would do next.

He knew Ramey was for real.

AFTER HE RECOVERED, DAVID made the phone call, leaving a message for his sports editor, actually surprising himself with his acting ability. His finger was throbbing. It curved off at an odd angle from the rest of his hand, and a large bulb of fluid was collecting in the joint.

"Now go to your computer and call up the story about Martin McNeil," Ramey said.

"It's not on my computer here," David said, lying automatically. "It's on the system down at the newspaper."

Ramey responded calmly. "Let me tell you what I know about you. You don't trust the computer system at the paper. You don't trust anybody except your editor and that fat bitch Nettie Richardson who sits up front.

So get your ass up, go the computer and call up the story. From now on, every time you lie to me you'll lose another knuckle. When I run out of fingers, I'll rip your dick off before I start on your toes."

David cradled his hand, trying not to cry.

"Move!"

The reporter lurched over to his computer. He used his left hand to call up the story. The part of his brain in charge of self-preservation was screaming at him to just follow orders. Just do what the man says and pray that he'll leave quietly. Another part of him was thinking about how simple it would be to outsmart his assailant. How easy it would be to pretend that he was conceding defeat, while at the same time scoring victory so subtly that the man with the pliers would never know it. His computer was linked via modem to the newspaper's system and with the push of one button he could send the story down to the paper. Just one key. He kept looking at the button. It was a quick command programmed to copy the file and then dial up the *San Antonio Light's* mainframe and duplicate the file after Costanzo quit working for the day. The dedicated reporter in him knew that it would be so easy. So quick. This maniac in his house would never know the difference. Would never know that David was still able to destroy Martin McNeil despite this attempt to abort the story.

"Delete it," Ramey said.

Blood was pounding in David's head. He stuck his hand out, tentatively at first, then with fatal confidence, pressing the F8 key which copied the story and queued it for delivery the moment David shut down. Then he hit the keys that would delete the story. It was all done in one quick sweep of his hand. The automatic movements of a man who spent eight hours a day typing. Surely, someone like Ramey would never notice an extra key stroke.

As the story disappeared from the screen, seemingly lost forever, David was elated. He might lose the battle in his apartment, but he had just won the war. Electronic impulses would course through the phone lines, delivering his story to the safety of a new hiding place. It was saved. His in-depth piece would still grace the cover of Sunday's paper. It would still destroy the hoax of Martin McNeil's image. David allowed himself a small victorious smile.

The pliers closed on the top of his right ear.

Ramey sighed loudly. "You think I don't know you're linked to the computer downtown? I disconnected your modem while you were asleep."

Fear drove David's heart into his throat. Tears leaked down his face. The cold metal of the pliers dug into his ear. He couldn't think straight. Couldn't bear this loss of control. He was completely at this man's mercy. Then Ramey yanked down, pulling David's ear half off his head. The cartilage ripped away at the top, hanging loosely like the flap of an old dog's ear. Blood streamed down the side of David's face. Mixed with the pain was the sick feeling that this was only the beginning. There were more tortures to endure before it was over. *Before he kills me?* David felt his gorge rising.

He tried to fight it, but couldn't stave it off. His next wave of screams brought with it a mass of vomit spraying onto his computer.

# THIRTY-TWO

MR. JACKSON HAD JUST come on duty when Martin and Brandon reached Costanzo's building. The security guard was sitting at his desk reading the newspaper, not paying attention to the people who were marching through the lobby on their way to work. Martin took a breath and stopped just outside the door. Brandon looked inside, then looked hard at his brother and shook his head. "Just walk past that old fool," Brandon said. "What's he gonna do, shoot us?"

Martin shrugged and followed his brother across the lobby. He tried to walk purposefully toward the elevator, acting like he was supposed to be there. "Excuse me, gentlemen," Mr. Jackson said from his perch, suddenly vigilant. "Can I help you?"

Brandon ignored him.

"Uh..no thanks," Martin said awkwardly, still striding toward the elevators. "Just giving a friend a ride to work. We'll just go up and get her." The elevator doors opened just as they reached the wall, and the brothers boarded quickly.

"Wait a second," Mr. Jackson said, getting out of his chair. "All guests are supposed to be announ—"

As the doors shut Martin smiled. "We'll just go on up."

When he reached the twelfth floor, Martin pulled out his gun. "Let me lead the way." This was his problem and he intended to handle it himself. He wasn't going to hide behind his big brother.

Since David owned the entire floor, the elevator opened into a small vestibule leading to the reporter's front door. Martin listened for a moment, and thought he heard a man crying. He tried the knob; the door was open. Inside, he could clearly hear David's anguished pleas, though they were muffled by what Martin assumed was a gag. He moving quietly into the apartment, holding his gun in front of him in two hands the way he'd seen cops carry their weapons on television. Brandon walked at a casual pace a few feet behind him, a little amused by his brother's intensity. Martin stopped by the fireplace and grabbed a poker. He stuck the gun into his waistband and hefted the tool. He'd rather hit The Fixer over the head than shoot him. "You want one of these?"

"No thanks," Brandon said.

Martin led the way down a dark hallway following the sound of muffled screams.

At the door to David's bedroom, the two brothers stood stunned. The reporter was tied face-down and spread-eagled on the bed. The Fixer squatted over him, fully clothed with a razor blade in one hand and a towel in the other. David's back was a covered in blood, and The Fixer was alternately cutting lines into the reporters skin with the razor and blotting the blood with the towel.

"What the hell are you doing?" Martin said.

The Fixer leaped off the bed, dropping the towel and razor, pulling his gun from his waistband and turning toward the voice in a smooth, practiced sweep. His silenced gun and eyes landed on the McNeil brothers at the same moment his index finger squeezed the trigger. Just before the gun fired, he pulled back a fraction sending a bullet thudding into the wall just over Martin's head.

Martin dropped to the floor, the gun and the fireplace poker skittering away. "Jesus Christ, Ramey. It's me!"

Brandon stood his ground, a tight smirk on his face.

The Fixer smiled. "Sorry, shouldn't sneak up on a brother like that. Nearly got your ass shot." He tucked the gun away and said cheerfully, "Come check out what I've done here."

Martin and Brandon walked over to the bed, and stared down at David's bloody back. The reporter's head was turned to the side; he was staring up at Martin with pleading eyes. All of the anger that Martin had felt toward David during the past four years was suddenly gone. Looking into the Costanzo's eyes, he saw not a monster, but a man. A man who was suddenly helpless and desperate. A man whose life, Martin might be able to save.

The Fixer used the towel to soak up the blood that was pooling on the reporter's back and said, "It's not done yet, but what do you think?"

Martin grimaced. Etched into the reporter's back was the number "00" with "C-O-S-T-A-N" written above it. When it was completed, it would spell out David's last name.

"Interesting," Brandon said.

"I figured a guy like him probably always wanted to be an athlete," The Fixer explained, "but he was never big enough or good enough. So he got a job criticizing jocks instead. Now, David's got his own jersey that he can wear for the rest of his life."

The brothers considered this.

"Ramey, I want you to let him go," Martin said.

The Fixer studied Martin. He shook his head sadly and said, "I really can't do that. I have a reputation to worry about. What if word got out that I quit in the middle of a job?"

"I'll pay you another $50,000," Martin said quickly.

"Another fifty grand?" The Fixer rubbed the side of his face with a gloved hand, thinking about the offer. "Naw, I think I'd rather keep trying to persuade him to drop the story."

David squirmed on the bed, moaning in fear.

The Fixer walked across the room and picked up Martin's gun and handed it back to him. "But I'll make a deal with you. You shoot me, then I'll stop." He winked at Brandon, who smiled back. Brandon wasn't sure how far he wanted The Fixer to go with this; he wanted Costanzo to be left with enough strength to finish his story. If the guy died after that, c'est la vie, but until that story hit the paper, he wanted to keep Costanzo alive.

"Come on, Ramey," Martin said, the gun held down at his side.

"I'm telling you. You gotta lift up that gun, point it at me, and pull the trigger." The Fixer spread his arms wide offering his chest as a target.

Martin looked to Brandon for help, but his brother just shrugged and spread his hands. There was nothing he could do. Martin slowly raised the gun and aimed.

"See, everyone thinks shooting somebody is easy," The Fixer said. "They think you just point the gun and pull the trigger. But there's more to it than that. You've got to be mentally prepared to perform an act of violence on another person. Cavemen used to attack their enemies with rocks. Do you think you could do that? Pick up a big rock, sneak up behind a guy and bash his head in?"

Martin shook his head slowly.

"Most people couldn't. It's too bloody, too violent. You kill a guy like that, you hear his skull crack open and you watch his brains and his blood leak out of his body. It gives you nightmares for years. But that's how people committed murder back then. They got good at it, too. Eventually, people got good at throwing rocks, and they could damn near kill you from 10 feet away. Then some guy invented a slingshot so they could throw a rock even harder and farther. If it hit the right spot, it could even penetrate the skin. There were some other inventions along the way, but eventually we got to the gun, like the one you're holding in your hand. With one little pull on the trigger you can send a rock flying at me so fast it'll break my bones or stop my heart as it rips through my body then slams into the wall. And all you've got to do is pull the trigger."

Martin stood with the gun pointed at The Fixer, seriously thinking about killing a man for the first time in his life.

The Fixer climbed back onto the bed and resumed work on the bloody jersey he was creating. "You want to stop me, shoot me."

"Come on Ramey, this is crazy," Martin said.

"Shoot me."

"Get off of him Ramey!"

The Fixer didn't turn to look at Martin, he just kept cutting with his razor blade. Costanzo screamed through the gag in his mouth. The gun shook in the player's hand. "Ramey please don't make me do this!"

"Not only do you have to have the courage to shoot me," The Fixer continued, "but you also have to be prepared to deal with the police when it's all over. Someone will hear your shot and call the cops. Then they'll come up here and find my dead body and the bloody body of David Costanzo. They'll find out that you hired me to kill Tim Williams and David Costanzo, but midway through the second job you changed your mind."

Martin shook his head and almost smiled. He looked at Brandon as if sharing a secret, then said, "Ramey, if you're dead, they'll never find out about any of that stuff."

"Sure they will Martin. I'm sure Mr. Reporter here has heard every word I've said, and he's certainly not going to forget about the star football player who ordered a contract hit on him. And your brother is a conscientious young man who would never think or harboring a criminal." This drew abrupt laughter from Brandon. "So your choices are to let me go ahead and finish the job, or shoot me. After I'm dead, you'll have to shoot David *and* your brother. That's the only way you're going to keep all of this a secret."

The only thing that seemed certain to Martin was that no matter what decision he made he was going to spend a lot of time in prison. He sank slowly to the floor still holding the gun in his hand, but not pointing at anything. He listened to The Fixer whistle as he carved David's back. He watched the reporter writhe and moan on the bed. He watched Brandon view the scene passively from the corner. Every sound in the room seemed amplified, but still it wasn't loud enough to drown out the voice that was buzzing insistently inside his head, urging him to lift up the gun, stick it in his mouth and pull the trigger.

# THIRTY-THREE

JESSICA'S STRETCHED OUT YAWNING powerfully, mouth gaping, back arching as her body pushed out of sleep. She reached for Martin's body. She liked to touch him first thing when she woke up. He was her anchor, and she his. That first touch each morning centered her.

His side of the bed was empty.

Jessica was wide awake and suddenly afraid. She knew instantly that Martin was out with The Fixer. Out trying to fix a problem that was not his to fix. She needed to talk to him. She needed to help him. She snatched the phone and dialed Martin's cell phone.

"Martin where are you?"

"I'm on my way home." He sounded exhausted. Defeated. Then scared: "Honey, you've got to leave! Get out of the house. We're on our way there and you can't be there."

"Who's we, Martin? What's happening?"

"Ramey's gone ballistic. He's got David Costanzo. I'm following him. He's going to the house. You've got to get out of there."

"Wait, he's kidnapped Costanzo, and they're coming here?"

"Ramey wants this to happen on my property."

"He wants *what* to happen on our property?"

"Jessica, I think Ramey's going to kill him."

"I'm going to call the police, they'll —"

"If you call the cops Costanzo is dead," Martin said, matter of fact. "I've been thinking about the police all morning, but Ramey would just kill the guy before he gave up to the cops. Tim Williams is already dead because of me, and now David Costanzo is going to die because of me."

"Honey, the baby is not yours."

Silence. Then, "I know that."

"Really, Martin. I know you know that, but I didn't know that. I love you and I trust you, but I had to know this girl who filed suit against you. I had to know whether you cheated on me. I had to know if this was your baby. So I went to Lisa's house yesterday, and talked to her. The baby is not yours."

"You went over there? How did you know where—"

"We talked for a few hours yesterday. I was going to tell you about it this morning but you were gone."

"Honey, what are you saying?"

"Brandon is the father, Martin. It's Brandon."

Martin shook this off. "Jessica, we're at Promous and Mississippi. You've got to get out of there. We'll be home in 15 minutes."

"Your brother is the one who's doing this to you, Martin. Your brother is stabbing you in the back again. It's always Brandon."

"Just get out of the house Jessica. Promise me you won't be in the house when we get there. I don't want you to be anywhere near Ramey."

"I'll be gone, but I'm coming back. I'm going to get Lisa. She can tell her story to Costanzo and convince him that little Michael is not your baby."

"Costanzo is the least of our problems right now," Martin laughed miserably. "Costanzo's probably going to be dead in half an hour, so Lisa doesn't need to explain anything to him."

"No, honey, I think Lisa is the only one who can save David's life. You're probably right about The Fixer killing him if the police show up. But that's because The Fixer always gets the job done. In all the years we've been here, every player who has ever hired him always got results no matter what Ramey had to do to make it work. So here he is again. He has a goal in mind, so he killed Tim to help achieve that goal. Now he's kidnapped David to help achieve that goal. If he has to, he'll kill David to achieve that goal. So the only way to stop Ramey might be to convince him that the job is done."

"Yeah, but how? I already told him that I wanted him to stop. I even offered him more money to stop, but he wouldn't do it."

"Lisa can stop him by telling the truth. Martin, she told me that when she first met Brandon he said he was you. When he picked her up a few days ago to take her to the new house, he was still calling himself "Martin." He's been impersonating you, and all this time he knew that you were not the father of this baby, because it's his baby. If David can hear her story and he's convinced that the baby is not his, then he won't be writing that particular story, and Ramey's job would be done. I'm sure Costanzo will write a story about being kidnapped, but that's a separate issue. But this might be our only hope of saving his life."

"I don't know."

"There's nothing else we can do, Martin."

"We're 10 minutes away."

"Stall until I get back. I'm going to get Lisa."

Jessica pulled on a pair of jeans and raced out of the house.

DAVID COSTANZO SAT IN the middle of Martin's garage, still wearing his boxer shorts, bound to a kitchen chair, blindfolded with a sock stuffed in his mouth. His back was a maze of gaping cuts. The little fingers on both hands were twisted and bent at odd angles. One ear was hanging precariously. Where his body was not covered with blood, it was soaked in sweat. He was breathing through his nose in sharp panicked bursts. There was a nail sticking out of his right foot about an inch behind the point at which his third and fourth toes met.

"He wouldn't stop fidgeting, so I had to pin him down, so to speak," Ramey explained about the nail. Then with an evil smile: "But don't worry. I'll give him a tetanus shot later."

Brandon was standing off to one side, watching. The Fixer had insisted that they drive nearly 30 minutes through traffic back to Martin's house. He wanted Martin to be inextricably tied to the crime.

"This place just has a nice feel to it," Ramey said, running a hand along the concrete walls. "Rich guy's house. Four-car garage. A Ferrari parked nice and neat, a Suburban in the driveway, and a bleeding reporter in a chair. It doesn't get any better than this."

Martin felt sick. "So what are you going to do with him?"

"Well, I thought maybe I'd kill him very slowly. Very painfully," The Fixer said, sitting on an overturned crate in the corner. He had his silenced pistol, a pair of pliers, a hammer, a phillips screwdriver and a box of nails laying on the floor next to him. "The story's deleted from his computer. I got all his cassette tapes and notes. Ain't nothing left to do but get rid of him."

"You did what!" Brandon screamed marching forward.

"I got rid of everything," The Fixer said, "just like I was hired to do."

Brandon hadn't counted on The Fixer being so meticulous. He wanted The Fixer to create havoc, to push Martin further and further down a dangerous path until the demise of his brother's reputation was assured. But he didn't actually want him to kill the story. Brandon wanted the story to hit the papers. He *needed* the story to run on Sunday. If Ramey had destroyed everything Costanzo had written, then Brandon needed the reporter alive to recreate all of that.

"Costanzo, do you have a copy of the story on your computer at work?" Brandon asked.

The reporter thought for a moment behind his blindfold, trying to guess at the right answer to that question. Should he say "yes" so they'd know that they needed him alive to get rid of the story. Or should he say "no" to show that he's no threat to them. Finally, David shook his head. There was no point in lying, Ramey already knew that he didn't have another copy of the story ferreted away.

"You did all that work, and didn't make a back up copy anywhere?" Brandon said. Costanzo shook his head again.

"What do I look like? An idiot?" The Fixer said. "I took care of all that shit. I used a magnet to delete all his disks. I burned all his notes, and

I watched him delete the story from his computer. *Everything* is gone. Only thing that's left is what's in his head, and I know how to get rid of that too."

"Maybe we should slow down here," Martin said, measuring each word.

"Slow down? Slow down?" The Fixer walked toward him. "All you wanted to do from jump street was slow down. That's your muthafuckin problem. You can't pull the trigger. We don't need to slow down." He was in Martin's face now. Reaching over and grabbing David by the hair, saying, "*This* muthafucka needs to *die*."

Costanzo squirmed under the touch, and screamed against the gag. Ramey slapped his head. "Shut up before you get another nail."

Brandon said, "Hold on a minute Ramey. Maybe he's right. Let's let Martin talk."

Ramey stared hard at Brandon, then at Martin. A shrug. "Go ahead. Talk it up young buck." He retreated to a corner hefting the hammer.

Martin pushed the blindfold off David's head and pulled the sock out of his mouth. The reporter coughed for a few moments gasping for air. "Please. . . don't kill me. . . sorry. . . just doing my job. Please, don't—"

"We're not going kill you," Martin said, looking at Ramey.

"What are you gonna do?"

"Well. . . I was thinking that as long as we're both here. . . we may as well do that interview you wanted."

David barked a dry laugh. "You're kidding right?" He was looked nervously at Ramey.

"Well, it's either the interview or you deal with him."

David took a moment to think about it. Shaking his head, unable or unwilling to believe the situation. "Okay, but will you untie me? My hands and feet are killing me."

The Fixer said: "You either stay tied up, or I nail you to the chair. Your choice." David looked to Martin, desperation in his eyes, but the player just shrugged. There was nothing he could do.

"Let's just do the interview," Martin said quietly. "That's all we can do right now. That's all that's left."

David squirmed in his seat, trying to get comfortable. His body was on fire, and he was afraid of what was going to happen after the interview. But he was still curious enough to want the truth, and somehow strangely confident that Ramey wouldn't kill him if Martin and Brandon were present.

"Is the baby yours?" the reporter asked, getting straight to the point. "No."

David sighed loudly. "What's the point of talking about this if you're going to lie? I know Lisa filed suit against you. I know you settled with her. I know the baby is yours."

"I'm not lying. The baby's not mine." Then, turning to glance at his brother, "Brandon is the father."

"Your brother?" David said skeptically.

"Yeah." Martin looked at Brandon for confirmation, but his brother didn't react. "Brandon I know about you and Lisa. Jessica talked to her. I know that you pretended to be me."

"Well, is the kid yours?" David said to Brandon.

Brandon raised one fist up in front of his face then slowly extended his middle finger. He held this pose for a long moment, then tucked his finger back into his fist and recrossed his arms.

The room was silent. Ramey was angry. *Martin doesn't need to tell this punk anything.* He was tired of messing around. He wanted to kill the man. *That's what you do with a guy like Costanzo. Tell him to stop and if he doesn't listen, you whack his ass. Sends a message to the next guy who comes along and tries to act smart.*

But instead of just killing the guy, Martin was talking to him. *Confessing his life story like the guy was a damned psychologist or something.*

David said: "If the kid's not yours, then why'd she file suit against you instead of your brother?"

Martin shrugged. "When Brandon met her, he told her that his name was Martin McNeil, so she thought he was me."

"So why pay her off?"

"I didn't know it was Brandon's kid until this morning."

"But you knew it wasn't *yours*."

"Yeah, but no matter whose kid it was, I had to keep the story quiet. I didn't want someone like you to be writing a story about it in the paper."

"You could have gotten a blood test and exonerated yourself."

"There was no time. Nobody contacted me to say pay up or we're going to file suit. It was just filed, and I was afraid that if I took the time to get a blood test, everyone in the world would have known heard about it."

Costanzo thought about that for a moment. He was actually glad that Ramey had refused to untie him. His limbs had fallen asleep under the tight ropes and with their slumber came relief from the throbbing pain of his broken fingers and punctured foot. He was so wrapped up in thoughts about his numb limbs that he didn't notice how much time had passed since Martin stopped talking.

Ramey filled the void. "You magpies about finished?"

David's heart galloped. He nearly cried out in relief when Brandon said, "Don't be so impatient Ramey. Give 'em five more minutes." Brandon was still trying to figure out how he was going to get the reporter out of this jam and back in front of a computer. Ramey stared hard for a moment, then sat back down.

The reporter spoke quickly: "Hey, maybe I could write a different story. A story about how you found out that this girl was pregnant by your brother and you rushed over to take care of her. Put her up in a nice place, gave her clothing and food." David had no intention of writing such a story, but he had to say something to fill the air. Talking to Martin was the only thing he could do to keep Ramey away from him. As soon as he got out of this predicament, he was going straight to the police. He would have Ramey arrested for murder and assault, Martin for murder-for-hire and assault, and he was going to write a first-person account of the torture he endured at the hands of Martin McNeil and his henchman.

"Is that all you see when you look at the world?" Martin said.

"What do you mean?"

"Another story?"

"Well, the tale of you taking care of your brother's obligations would be a *good* story."

"See, that's the problem. When you look at the world you don't see people, you see stories. If something is a good story, you write it. The next day you forget about that story and go on to the next one. There's always another story for you and you never stop to think about the people you affect along the way."

"But this would be a great warm fuzzy kind of story." He was pleading now. "People would read it over their Cheerios and it would make them believe in human nature again. We could show them a side of you that they've never seen."

Martin shook his head. "I perform in front of hundreds of thousands of people every Sunday. And I do television, radio, magazine and newspaper interviews because it's part of the job. I have people who recognize me everywhere I go. If I'm at the grocery store buying Oreos, someone is making note of it. If I'm at the video store renting Big Breasted Bikini Babes, someone is making note of it. I don't have much privacy. So I don't look at everything in my life as a potential story the way you do."

"But don't you think it's important for people to hear this. It's a *great* story?"

"What about Lisa?"

David shrugged. "What about her?"

"Did you interview her?"

"I tried but—"

"She didn't want to be interviewed," Martin finished for him.

"No."

"But that didn't bother you did it. You had your teeth into a story and you weren't going to let it go no matter who might get hurt. Did you even care about what she wanted? That she didn't want you to do a story about her?"

"Wait, wait, wait," David said. "This was a legitimate story. I found out about it and I was investigating it. That's my job. It's not a personal thing. It's what I do for a living."

"Well, your *job* sometimes ruins people's lives."

"You're blowing this way out of proportion," David said.

"Am I?"

"Yes, you are."

"Okay. Let's look at it. You write a story about Lisa's paternity suit. First, it's going to make me look like an asshole. People are going to condemn me for sleeping with a 15-year-old girl, and then for abandoning her after she got pregnant. I'll probably lose a lot of my endorsements, and I'll lose the respect of a lot of people in the city—all over something I didn't do.

"Then there's Lisa. Your story would make her look like a gold-digging bitch, which she is not. Lisa's family, her neighbors, her co-workers and anyone else who knows her would read this story and some of them might have a bad opinion of her. And then there's her son Michael who would be the focus of all of this. He'd be labeled as the kid Martin McNeil tried to deny. Can't you see that after you wrote this story, you'd move on to the next story, but Lisa, Michael and I would have to live with the consequences of that article?"

There was silence again. Both men seemed to have run out of things to say. The Fixer moved from the corner quickly, pulling a plastic bag over David's head. The reporter thrashed about, his chair rocking back and forth, but Ramey's grasp was firm.

"Ramey, No!" Martin screamed.

The Fixer smiled malevolently and said, "Just takin' care of business for you home boy."

Every airless gasp the reporter took put him one step closer to the grave and a step further from ever writing the story that would destroy Martin's life. Brandon had no intention of letting the man die. He needed David Costanzo. He reached into his pocket for the small pistol he'd been hiding. Before he could get it out Martin spoke with surprising authority.

"Ramey, take it off," Martin said.

The Fixer looked up and saw Martin standing with a gun in his hand and his arm extended like a GI Joe action figure. Ramey smiled. *Young Martin pointing a gun at me.* "You had your chance to shoot me earlier. Now, put that shit away before I pistol whip your ass."

Costanzo was turning red.

"Ramey, I'm warning you," Martin said, taking a step forward.

"I know." Ramey said still smiling.

The report echoed loudly in the garage, the gun jerking upward in Martin's hand as a bullet leaped from the barrel. Ramey stood there for a moment, shocked, and then fell forward onto the dusty floor. He was dead before he hit the ground.

Martin moved forward quickly and pulled the plastic bag off David's head. The reporter gasped for breath, sweet air stinging his lungs.

THE FIRST THING JESSICA noticed when she returned home was The Fixer's BMW parked in the driveway. The garage door opened about two feet and stopped. Martin slid beneath it, his white Nike sweat suit picking up dirt and tar from the asphalt as he shimmied through the narrow space. His eyes had a haunted look about them, darting back and forth, surveying the neighborhood before racing to his wife.

"Where is he?" Jessica said, meaning Ramey.

"He's inside," Martin said softly. They both turned and looked toward the garage door with dread. Then Martin added: "I shot him."

MARTIN, JESSICA, AND LISA all shimmied under the cracked door of the garage. The reporter was still in the chair but his hands and feet were untied, and a car cover was spread over his lower body. Brandon was back where he started, leaning against the wall, apparently amused by everything that was happening.

Lisa looked first at David's bloody body then at Ramey's prone form. She began to cry. She started softly but gained volume with every breath. Her tears initially seemed a natural reaction to such a grisly scene, but as her sobs increased in intensity, everyone turned to look at her curiously. Jessica moved close and hugged her tightly.

Lisa's eyes went from the gun tucked into Martin's waistband up to his face. She gazed hard at him and said, "How could you shoot your own brother?"

"I didn't."

"He's dead!" she screamed.

"That's not my brother," Martin said defensively. "That's my brother." He pointed at Brandon, who was laughing. It started in his belly, working its way up, shaking his whole body with its force. Soon Brandon was laughing so hard that he couldn't breathe. He was holding his stomach and sliding down to one knee until finally his mouth was wide open, but no sound was coming out. Everyone stared at him.

Costanzo figured it out first. Earlier he'd seen Ramey simply as an enforcer; someone who hired himself out to do other people's wet work. If it was illegal or if it involved physical violence, Ramey was your man. He was a muscular man in Italian loafers, slacks and silk shirts. He was wearing discreet jewelry including a small diamond stud in his left ear. He was equal parts suburban yuppie and Mafia hit man. His appearance fit the role so perfectly that David had not noticed anything specific about him.

The reporter was reminded of a focus group that had been conducted to determine the effect of uniforms on the observer's eye. During the study, two men interrupted a focus group that had been convened to evaluate an advertising campaign. The first was a middle-aged Caucasian wearing a sports jacket and tie. He stepped fully into the room said, "oh, excuse me I didn't realize anyone was here," and then walked out again. The focus group saw him for less than three seconds. Fifteen minutes later, a middle aged Caucasian police officer in uniform walked into the room and said, "oops, sorry to interrupt," and quickly departed. He was in the room for no more than three seconds.

Minutes later a moderator asked the members of the group to stop the discussion they were having and write down detailed descriptions of the men who had interrupted their meeting. Despite the nearly 20 minute lapse since the first man's appearance, nearly everyone in the room remembered his dark hair, light skin, mustache and glasses. About the police officer whom they'd seen only minutes earlier, the group recalled virtually nothing except that he was white, tall and wearing a uniform with a gun on his hip.

Most significantly, no one in the group realized that it was the same man who interrupted both times. The uniform blinded them to the other details.

Costanzo considered himself to have a keen eye for detail, but he had never noticed that The Fixer had hazel eyes. The one thing that had bothered him ever since Kimberly mentioned it that night by the pond. Hazel eyes.

The reporter turned to Lisa. "He's the father?" He pointed down at Ramey.

The girl nodded.

"But he told you his name was Martin McNeil, when you met him?"

Again Lisa nodded, still crying.

Jessica was confused. "I thought you said Brandon was the father."

"No, he was," pointing at Ramey. A fresh burst of tears.

Martin said: "Jessica, when you talked to her what did she say?"

"She said that you came to pick her up on Friday, but I showed her a picture of you, and she said you weren't the one who picked her up. I said it was probably your brother Brandon who picked her up, and she said, 'well, I guess you should know, he's also Michael's father.'"

Martin nodded. "Brandon *and* Ramey picked her up on Friday."

"Who is he?" Lisa managed still sobbing.

Jessica squeezed her close. "Ramey was a very evil man who hurt and killed people for a living. You're lucky that you never really knew him."

Costanzo shook his head and turned to Brandon. "You lied to me?" the reporter said.

"Fuck you," Brandon said.

Martin looked in shock at his older brother. "You talked to David?" he said. Since the moment Costanzo first called, Martin had wondered how the reporter had learned of the story. He assumed that Costanzo had simply come across the notice in the Guadalupe County Records, but it had seemed the worst possible coincidence that his greatest secret would be discovered by his greatest enemy. "You told him about this?"

"Fuck you, too!" Brandon said, spittle flying from his lips.

Costanzo released a weary breath. "He told me that you were the father of Lisa's baby. He said that you used his townhouse to sleep with underage girls. And he said you owned a pair of hazel contact lenses."

Martin was stunned. He'd thought that their childhood estrangement was a thing of the past. *We're a family now.* "Why?"

Brandon leaned defiantly against the wall, his face a mask of rage.

"Because I hate you. I've always hated you. You think you're so damned perfect. You've got everybody fooled. But that shit was going to end. The world was going to find out that you aren't the goody-two-shoes little saint that everyone thinks you are."

Jessica had been right all along, Martin realized. *Brandon doesn't love me and he's never loved me.*

"But it doesn't matter," Brandon continued. "You'll get what you deserve. You'll get exactly what's coming to you!"

Brandon pulled out his gun. "I've dreamed of this day." Everyone in the room screamed at once. Martin stood his ground, too stunned to defend himself. A lifetime of rage burned in his older brother's eyes.

Suddenly, Brandon's head drooped down, and a thick stream of blood poured out of his mouth as he fell. The room went silent, except for a quiet spitting sound.

David Costanzo was standing in the corner near Ramey's collection of tools. He was holding The Fixer's silenced pistol in both hands, pulling the trigger over and over again. Brandon's body continue to twitch on the floor as the bullets ripped into his body. When the gun was empty, Costanzo stood still staring at Brandon's dead body.

Finally, Costanzo dropped the gun to the floor.

Martin collapsed in tears.

# THIRTY-FOUR

THAT'S HOW MARTIN MCNEIL ended up on trial for his life. A week-long nightmare that resulted in three deaths. No charges were filed against David Costanzo in the shooting death of Brandon McNeil. All the witnesses confirmed that it was justifiable homicide. If Costanzo hadn't opened fire, Brandon would have killed his younger brother. Unfortunately, the same argument didn't shield Martin from prosecution. Martin saved Costanzo's life, but the prosecution charged that if Martin hadn't hired the hit man in the first place, he wouldn't have had to commit murder to stop the man from fulfilling the contract.

Tim Williams' death was to be handled by Martin's conscience, rather than by the justice system. Martin had shared the entire story with his attorney, who advised him to say nothing to the police about Ramey killing Williams. A quick and discreet investigation by Martin's lawyer revealed that Digoxin is a drug that helps the elderly by creating stronger contractions of the heart, but in the body of a healthy person, it would over-stimulated his heart sending it into fatal arrhythmia. The coroner didn't screen for Digoxin, so he didn't find it in Tim's blood. As things stood, Tim died of natural causes, and no one would ever argue differently.

"ALL RISE."

Martin stood slowly looking over his shoulder at his wife and his parents as everyone in the courtroom rose to their feet. The nervousness he'd felt before every new athletic challenge in his life was gone. It was replaced by sheer, helpless terror. The entire trial had been out of his hands. He'd relied on his attorney to convince the jury that he was innocent, but he wasn't sure the argument had been compelling. *If I was on the jury, I'd probably convict me.*

Judge Mary Westmoore shuffled quickly out of her chamber, up the steps to the bench. The bailiff ordered the courtroom down, then the jury filed into the courtroom.

The charges against Martin included illegal entry—for going into

Costanzo's home—kidnapping, assault, attempted murder and felony murder.

To prove the case against Martin the prosecution focused on Ramey.

They knew a lot more about Ramey's activities than Martin expected. Ramey had been in San Antonio for about six years, and Martin had believed that he somehow operated under the police radar, working his intimidation and extortion deals without ever arousing suspicion. But the cops had a thick file on Philip Ramey. They'd been following him for years, but had been unable to arrest him for anything serious because the victims were too afraid to bring charges. Now that he was dead, people who had quietly endured his extortion were speaking up. They told the prosecution everything they knew about The Fixer. Every detail was presented to the jury during two weeks of testimony explaining the full range of The Fixer's services. Players trying to open restaurants hired The Fixer and found that their permitting problems disappeared. Fundraising for charity foundations was easier with The Fixer's help. Cars, houses, furniture and vacations were all cheaper when The Fixer was involved. Most damning for Martin was the testimony of John Carrington and Frank Stinetti from Moulahan Mercedes where The Fixer had negotiated the deal for Martin's Ferrari. They testified about the violence The Fixer employed, and the money he was paid to negotiate the deal.

Stinetti took great pleasure in telling the jury about Martin's final words to him after he complained about the Fixer's violence.

"I told McNeil that this guy he hired had come in and put staples in the back of my salesman's hand, and had whacked me in the throat, and McNeil just sat there cool as can be and said, 'Mr. Stinetti, you can go fuck yourself.'"

On cross-examination Stinetti had been exposed as an embezzler who had been working side deals through the dealership for years, but overall, his testimony was bad for Martin. The prosecution was building the case that Martin was not naïve. When he contracted The Fixer to take care of business for him, he knew exactly the type of violence the man would employ and therefore was responsible for everything The Fixer did on his behalf.

The prosecution presented bank statements showing that Martin McNeil paid all of his bills with checks of credit cards. In the four years he'd lived in San Antonio, he'd never once made a cash withdrawal for more than $10,000. But just a few days before Costanzo was kidnapped, McNeil made a cash withdrawal of $50,000. Police investigators had discovered a safe and six safety deposit boxes that belonged to The Fixer. In total they held more $750,000 in cash. The prosecutor couldn't prove that Martin's money had gone to The Fixer, but in Martin's opinion, the connection was pretty obvious. He was just glad that the $150,000 deal he'd struck with Ramey had called for three weekly payments of $50,000 instead of one lump sum. Ramey was dead before the second payment was due, so the jury thought $50,000 was the full amount of the contract. *And that's bad enough.*

"Has the jury reached a verdict?"

"We have your honor."

The bailiff took the verdict from the jury foreman and delivered it to the judge. She read it, her face giving away nothing, then handed it back to the bailiff. "The defendant will please rise."

Martin came to his feet, more scared that he had ever been in his life. Just two weeks ago, his cellmate Richard Mobley had been convicted and sentenced to three years for drunk driving. The professor had been confident throughout the trial that his argument against the constitutionality of drunken driving law would earn his freedom. His attorney tried to persuade the jury that Mobley should not be imprisoned for merely being drunk, just as a person should not be imprisoned for merely eating food behind the wheel, or using a cell phone or doing anything else that temporarily impairs his judgment. Drivers should be prosecuted for actual violations of the law. If a man can control his vehicle while having a blood alcohol level of .15, eating a hamburger and talking on the phone all at once, then he should not be prosecuted. Punishment should come only when he proves incapable of safely operating his vehicle—weaving, speeding, following too closely, etc. The prosecution had conceded that Mobley's argument was sound in many ways, but that drunken driving was different because it involved a degree of "permanent" temporary impairment. The driver who's reaching for French fries may be distracted for a moment, but once and emergency develops he's capable of reacting with 100 percent of his attention to the crisis on the road. The same of someone on a cell phone, or disciplining children in the back seat. However, a drunk driver has a degree of "permanent" temporary impairment that will not allow him to summon 100 percent attention until the effects of the alcohol wear off. Therefore, drunken driving must be treated as a greater risk to public safety. Martin recalled the hollow mask of Richard's face as the verdict was read—the media covered Mobley's trial because he was Martin McNeil's cellmate. The confidence was gone. Richard stumbled out of the courtroom in handcuffs on his way to prison—*is that what I have to look forward to?*

The jury foreman was a 43-year-old contractor and father of three boys. He'd seen all the evidence in the case, and considered the charges very carefully in leading the jury through six hours of debate. "On the charge of illegal entry we find the defendant guilty."

Martin was holding his breath; his eyes misted with fear.

"On the charge of assault we find the defendant guilty."

*Here it goes,* Martin thought. *I hired Ramey, so everything that Ramey did falls to me. If he assaulted Costanzo, then I'm guilty of assault. If he kidnapped Costanzo, then I'm guilty of kidnapping. I'm going to prison.* Martin didn't think he could stand up any longer. He needed to fall back into his chair and catch his breath.

"On the charge of kidnapping, we find the defendant guilty."

A low moan was building in Martin's throat. He'd had nightmares about his trial, about the verdict coming back guilty on all counts, and now he realized those weren't nightmares, they were premonitions.

"On the charge of attempted murder, we find the defendant not guilty.

*Not guilty?* Maybe they wouldn't convict him of felony murder either. Maybe he could avoid the charge that would require that he spend the rest of his life in prison.

Oddly, while felony murder was the most serious charge against Martin, it was also the charge that required the least amount of proof. With felony murder, the prosecution didn't need to prove murderous intent or even that Martin believed that death was a potential outcome. The prosecution argued that the felony murder statute allowed prosecution if *anyone* died during the commission of a felony—even if the victim was a co-conspirator. Martin was involved in the original felony—kidnapping—and since both Ramey and Brandon were killed during the commission of that crime Martin was responsible.

The argument seemed flawed from the outset. Given everything the jury learned about Ramey and Brandon during the trial, there was no doubt that both were bad men. The jury knew that it was Brandon who set up the false lawsuit against his brother, and it was Ramey who had a history as the violent fixer of problems. In death, neither man evoked much sympathy. Humanity was better off without them. But the prosecution hammered away, arguing that the jury should ignore the backgrounds of the men who died and focus on the statute. Jury members who follow the statute must realize that their duty is unavoidable. If a felony was committed and someone died, then anyone who participated in that felony is guilty of felony murder.

"On the charge of felony murder," Martin's mouth was agape, his eyes pleading. The next words out of the foreman's mouth would determine the rest of his life. "We find the defendant not guilty."

The courtroom erupted in brief applause, the judge brought her gavel down on the bench calling for order. Martin's attorney whispering in his ear that the penalty phase would be next. They should be able to minimize his prison time.

# THIRTY-FIVE

## SIX MONTHS LATER

It was a cloudless day in San Antonio, the sun pouring humid heat onto the city like boiling water from a cauldron. Martin McNeil was sitting on his back porch sipping iced tea. "He's really a cute," the player said.

Michael Alexander Benson raced through the backyard on stumpy little legs, giggling as he pushed and chased a beach ball.

"Yep, definitely a cute little kid," David Costanzo said from a chair a few feet away. David and Martin had become nearly inseparable friends since that day in Martin's garage.

Jessica, Lisa and Ms. Benson were in the kitchen preparing lunch. Nettie Richardson was watching basketball with Lisa's little brothers. These picnics had become a monthly affair. They were a big family, bound together by murderous ties.

Ms. Benson had been angry with David for the cruel lie he'd told her about Lisa having a brain tumor, but she decided she owed him a debt of gratitude for bringing her family back together. Every time she looked at her grandson, she couldn't believe she had nearly missed out on his childhood by being a stubborn old woman.

Sitting in the backyard, Martin thought back to that fateful day six months earlier. It was Costanzo who saved him from going to prison. Costanzo wrote the story of his abduction in a three-part series that was reprinted in newspapers all over the world and in 14 magazines. In his story, Costanzo described the tenacity with which he pursued the information. He talked about the hatred he'd felt for Martin McNeil and the joy he would have felt seeing the story in the paper that would have ruined McNeil's life.

It was an amazingly candid piece that sparked radio and television commentary among millions of people all over the world. To date, David had received half a dozen journalism awards for his series, though there was no word form the Pulitzer committee.

And Martin believed it was David's testimony that saved him during the sentencing phase of his trial. Costanzo came in as a defense witness and told the entire story from start to finish. He agreed with the jury's assessment that technically McNeil was guilty of illegal entry, assault and kidnapping, but in practical terms, McNeil was a valiant hero who first rushed to the aid of an impoverished young mother and who saved David's life when it really mattered.

"There I was the guy who was trying to destroy him, and Martin was desperately trying to save my life. I learned a lot about character and integrity during those hours I was tied up. I used to hate Martin McNeil, but now I look at him as one of the truly good people on this planet. This man doesn't deserve to go to prison."

The judge agreed, sentencing Martin to three years of probation plus time served—setting him free.

On the back porch with heat drizzling down on them Costanzo said, "I never did say thank you for saving my life."

"Yes, you did," Martin said.

"Did I?"

"Only about a hundred times."

"Well, then thank you again."

"You're welcome," Martin said, fingering a small locket that hung around his neck. Inside was a picture of Brandon. He met with a counselor three times a week, and they talked about life. Martin was slowly coming to terms with the reality that Brandon had been an evil, vindictive, narcissistic man who likely *would* have shot his younger brother if Costanzo hadn't intervened. Martin was beginning to accept the possibility that Brandon may never have loved him. It hurt, but he was getting there. "I don't believe I've thanked you for saving *my* life," Martin said to David.

"Oh, you did."

"Did I?"

"Only about a hundred times," David said.

"Well, thank you again."

"Hundred and one."

Jessica poked her head out of the door and said, "Lunch is served if anyone is interested."

"I'm interested," Martin said, standing up.

"And I'm definitely interested," David said.

"I'm infested, too," Michael said, racing over to the patio.

Everyone laughed, and Michael looked up with the cute, confused gaze that small children possess. He knew he had done something funny, but he didn't know what it was.

"Now that you mention it," Martin said. "I think we're all in*fest*ed."

# STALLIONS

## Reggie Rivers

**The following is a preview of**

**STALLIONS....**

SCA Publishing, Ltd.
10 Inverness Drive East, Suite 210
Englewood, Colorado 80112

# ONE

JIMMY AND GARY WERE standing in front of kid-sized urinals at Piney Woods Elementary School. The bathroom was empty as they took care of business, temporarily excused from their classes.

"You're crazy," Jimmy said. "I'll bet you a quarter the Raiders kick the Chargers butt on Sunday."

"A quarter?" Gary said uncertainly. His allowance was only a dollar a week. He wasn't sure he wanted to gamble away any of his money. He didn't know anything about the Raiders or the Chargers. When the argument with Jimmy started, he'd simply repeated what his father had said about the Raiders—that they were too undisciplined to win on Sundays.

"Yeah, a quarter," Jimmy said. "What are you a little scaredy-cat?"

"I ain't scared," Gary said, suddenly confident. If his dad thought the Raiders would lose then that was good enough for him. "The Chargers could beat the Raiders any old day."

"Put your money where your mouth is sucker."

"Alright."

"Loser's got to bring the money on Monday," Jimmy said walking out of the
bathroom.

"Deal," Gary said. Then quietly, "Dang. A whole quarter . . ."

EVELYN HELD THE DOOR for her good friend Ann, stopping to lock the card shop behind her. Both women were widows in their sixties. They'd been friends for forty-two years and planned to make a run at forty-two more, Lord willing.

"You think our boys can beat the Oilers this weekend?" Ann said.

"I don't know," Evelyn said, hooking her arm with Ann's as they strolled down the sidewalk. "But I bet ol' Howard ten dollars that they'd win?"

"You made a bet with that old scoundrel?"

"Yeah," Evelyn said with a wry smile. "Course that dirty old coot said if he wins he wants a roll in the hay instead of the money."

Ann looked at her friend with wide eyes. "I hope you gave him a good piece of your mind!"

"Heck no, honey. It's been a long time since I've had some good lovin'. Honestly, this is one bet I hope to lose."

"Oh my." Ann was flustered. Then she smiled. "You don't suppose he'd make the same bet with me do you?"

They giggled together, feeling just the way they had when they were in high school sharing a joke. "He's certainly a randy one," Evelyn said. "But I don't know if that ol' bastard could handle two hot mamas like us."

"We'd knock his socks off."

They laughed all the way to the corner.

WALTER AND GILBERT WERE arguing over their beers at the Green Fox Tavern. It was same type of fight they had every time they went out drinking together. Walter always acted as if he knew everything there was to know about sports, and treated Gilbert like an uniformed rube. It always pissed Gilbert off.

"Okay," Gilbert said, thumping his hand on the bar, his mind made up, "I'll take Philly and the points."

"Whoa now my good friend," Walter had a hand raised like a school crossing guard. "Nobody said anything about points. This here's a straight-up bet. Winner wins, loser loses."

"Come on Wally. You want me to bet you head-up when the Eagles are six-point underdogs going in?"

"That's what I'm saying man. Those guys in Vegas don't know what they're talking about on this one. You want to take the Eagles that's the way it's going to be. There ain't no points."

"Then I ain't bettin'." He purposely said this in a childish way. They watched Sportscenter on the television behind the bar. Finally Walter said,

"Okay, tell you what. I'll give you three points."

"Nope."

"Come on man. Whoever set the spread on this game needs to be drug-tested. Ain't no way in hell the Eagles should be underdogs to the Falcons. If anything, they should be *overdogs*.

That brought a long peel of intoxicated laughter. "Overdogs," Walter repeated, spilling his beer. "Red Rover Red Rover, send the Eagles right over." A couple in a corner booth frowned at them. They didn't get the joke, which made Walter and Gilbert laugh even harder.

Finally, Gilbert said, "screw the underdogs and overdogs. The paper says six points so that's what I should get." His voice was slurring just a hair. "You don't want to give me the points, then you can take your bet to some other sucker."

"Alright you little crybaby. You can have your stupid six points." They shook hands on their fifty-dollar bet and drank their beer in silence.

After a moment, Gilbert said, "how about a side bet?"

"On what?"

"Ten bucks says the Eagles score first."

"Touchdown or field goal?" Walter said.

There he goes again, Gilbert thought. Always trying to make the rules like he's smarter than everyone else. "Whoever scores first dipshit!"

"Well, you know, sometimes people wanna specify."

"I ain't specifyin' shit. I'm saying the Eagles are gonna score first. It might be a touchdown, a field goal or a safety. I don't care as long as they score first. You want the bet or not?"

"Yeah, that's cool," Walter said. "Even if I lose that one, I'll make it up on the fifty you pay me when the Falcons kick their ass."

AMERICANS WAGER MORE THAN five hundred billion dollars annually in traditional casinos, riverboats, Indian reservations, card rooms, pari-mutuel horse and dog racing, state lotteries, slot machines and video poker. The amount of money gambled illegally is not known, but law enforcement officials estimate that figure at more than two hundred billion dollars each year.

More money is wagered on NFL games than any other sporting events. Gambling is both a benefit and a detriment to the league. Although the NFL doesn't collect a direct share of money wagered, the league reaps other benefits. When ordinary Joes bet their hard-earned money on a football game, they have a vested interest in the game and are more likely to watch the contest. That means stadiums sell more tickets, sports bars do better business, satellite receiving systems sell better and more televisions are locked onto NFL games. This all contributes to higher advertising rates for the broadcasters which leads to higher licensing fees paid to the NFL. The most recent set of television contracts paid the league nearly eighteen billion dollars over four years for the right to broadcast the games.

Gambling is good for football.

However, it's the one thing that could destroy the league as well. The NFL will survive strikes, lockouts, court judgments, injuries and players who get convicted. But if gamblers infiltrate the league and manipulate the outcome of games, the integrity of the NFL will undermined, and the fans would slowly disappear.

"Stallions" is a story about a crime family's attempt to influence the outcome of NFL games, and the league's efforts to stop them.

AT AGE TWENTY-FIVE, Michael Gasca had a private talk with Uncle Nick. They were sitting in front of the fireplace in Uncle Nick's Philadelphia mansion, the lights turned down, their conversation accompanied by long periods of silence.

"You know that's not how we run the business, Mikey," Uncle Nick, wagging a finger. "We're like conservative bankers. We run a nice quiet organization. We make our money, and we never get greedy. Greed is a gambler's problem. We don't gamble."

"Hear me out on this one, Uncle Nick. The reason we're not gamblers is that we try to reduce our exposure by sitting right in the middle of all our bets right?"

"That's that I've been telling you since you were a kid."

"We want fifty percent of the money on one team and fifty percent on the other team."

"You're talking my language now, Mikey." Uncle Nick puffed on his cigar contentedly.

"All I'm proposing is that we develop a system to hedge our bets."

"Ah, don't use that word, Mikey. We don't bet, so we don't need to hedge anything. That's the way gamblers think. They hover around teams trying to develop relationships. They read the papers every day. They're constantly making calls to find an edge so they can make their can't-miss bets. But you know what? Eventually they all miss. Eventually, the gambler loses, but we don't lose Mikey. We're like a big casino letting our losers pay off our winners and taking a small percentage off every wager. As long as we run a smart business and stay in the middle, we'll always make money, and there's no sense in trying to do anything more than that."

Gasca thought for a moment.

"Say a guy walked up to you and said, 'I'll bet you a hundred dollars that the sun won't come up in the morning.' Would you take the bet or would you wait to see if you could get someone to bet the other side first?"

Uncle Nick contemplated this, then with a sly look said, "Depends on where I'm living."

"Come on Uncle Nick. The fuck difference does that make?"

"Say I'm living in Alaska the day before they start having that six months of darkness. Then, no, I wouldn't take that bet." He barked a hoarse dry laugh.

Gasca laughed with him; the two men sitting in the living room in front of the fire sharing a private joke like the old days.

"Okay, so what if you're living right here in Philly and a guy wants to make that bet?"

"Hell Mikey, of course I'd take it. I know damned well the sun's gonna come up tomorrow."

"That's all I'm saying Uncle Nick If we've got a bunch of people willing to bet that the sun won't come up tomorrow and we know for a fact that the sun will come up, then we're not gambling, we're just taking their money." Gasca was on the edge of his seat. Uncle Nick was not really his uncle, and no one else in the family referred to the sixty-seven-year-old patriarch as uncle. Everyone else called him "Sarc," but Gasca had always had a special relationship.

"I've been working on some things, Uncle Nick, and I think we're in a position with the San Antonio Stallions to not just predict the outcomes of their games, but we can actually influence those outcomes. We can create some situations so that we know what's going to happen."

Uncle Nick held up a weathered hand, silencing Gasca. He stared into the fire. Over the years there had been a lot of men who wanted Domenick Sarcassi to take more risks. They always had new ideas. They were always saying that Sarcassi's way was the old way, that it didn't fit the bold new face of gambling. They griped about the money they could make if they were allowed to be more aggressive. But Sarc was a cagey, strong-minded man who knew how to run his business. He'd seen many organizations fall in the face of their own greed, and he didn't intend to let that happen to his empire.

Sarc had a personal net worth of about a hundred and twenty million and everyone associated with the family lived a comfortable life. But now here was Mikey with a proposition. Mikey who was his favorite. Mikey who was so smart and talented, and who had shown a certain genius, even as a preteen, for running the business. The fire crackled and popped, warming the air. Sarc watched the flames dance and thought that he was getting old. Maybe it was time for something new. His sons wouldn't like it. Each of his three boys envisioned himself as the next leader of the family, but Sarc knew that Gasca was the man for the job. Despite being only twenty-five years old, Gasca was the only person Sarc trusted to keep the family on track.

Finally the old man said, "tell me about this plan of yours."

*"Stallions" will be released in Fall of 2001*

# About The Author

Reggie Rivers is a former NFL running back who played six seasons with the Denver Broncos (1991-1996). He is a columnist for Pro Football Weekly and The Denver Post. He hosts a daily talk show on 630 KHOW radio in Denver, he's an analyst for ABC Sports college football coverage, and he's co-host of Countdown to Kickoff, a Broncos pregame show on KCNC Channel 4 in Denver. Rivers is an in-demand speaker for corporations, organizations, schools and other groups. In 1994, Rivers wrote "The Vance: The Beginning and The End," the as-told-to autobiography of former Broncos receiver Vance Johnson. "Power Shift" is Rivers' first novel.